RING OF

TIME

Tales of a Time-Traveling Historian in the Roman Empire

ANDREW M. SEDDON

Being the reminiscences
of
Robert A. Cragg, Professor Emeritus
Department of History and Temporal Archaeology
CamOx University
October, 2655

Ring of Time
© Andrew M. Seddon 2014

ISBN: 978-1-927154-38-0

Cover Design: Grace Bridges
Street photo: Grace Bridges
Space photos courtesy of NASA

Published by Splashdown Books, New Zealand
http://www.splashdownbooks.com

For Olivia: now and forever

ACKNOWLEDGEMENTS

I am indebted to Professors Paul Davies and J. Richard Gott III for answering questions about time travel, to my father for suggesting a way out of a plot difficulty, and to Dr. Marc Jaeger for helpful comments and suggestions. Special thanks to Rachel Schaffer, Werner Lind, and Colleen Drippé for their expertise in critiquing this manuscript. And to my wife, Olivia, for reading more drafts of these stories than anyone should have been called upon to do.

Two stories have been previously published:
"The Ghosts of Kourion" in *Infinite Space Infinite God II*,
Robert and Karina Fabian, eds, Twilight Times, 2010.
"Tyndareus and Krikor" in *Hereditas*, Vol. 2.2, Summer 2006, p. 5-13.

Both have been revised for this publication.

Quotation from *Ecclesiasticus* from the *Revised English Bible*, ©1989, Oxford University Press and Cambridge University Press.

With the exception of "The Philosopher's Ring," all stories are based upon the remains of true people unearthed by genuine archaeology.

CONTENTS

"Let us now praise famous men, the fathers of our people in their generations...

Some held sway over kingdoms and gained renown by their might. Others were far-seeing counsellors who spoke out with prophetic power.

Some guided the people by their deliberations and by their knowledge of the nation's law, giving instruction from their fund of wisdom.

Some were composers of music; some were writers of poetry.

Others were endowed with wealth and strength, living at ease in their homes.

All those won glory in their own generation and were the pride of their times. Some there are who have left behind them a name to be commemorated in story.

Others are unremembered; they have perished as though they had never existed, as though they had never been born..."

Ecclesiasticus 44:1-9.

To be ignorant of what occurred before you were born
is to remain always a child, for what is the worth of human life
unless it is woven into the life of our ancestors by the records of history?

Marcus Tullius Cicero, c.50 BC

I

I have made my final trip through time.

Will anyone look for me? I think not. But if anyone is so tempted, I urge them not to. I am where I want to be; where I am meant to be; with whom I want to be.

Do not search for me.

For I do not wish to be found.

II

The bright circle of the Temporal Displacement Ring glittered like a celestial halo above the yellow orb of Gliese 876. The star itself was fairly unimpressive—no match for Huygens-7, shining over my homeworld of Heliopolis, or warm, golden Sol—but at the moment it was the most important star in my life. For that insignificant star powered the Temporal Displacement Ring—and that Ring, I fervently hoped, was about to change my life.

I couldn't tear my eyes from the Ring as the naval supply vessel that had brought me the fifteen light-years from Earth gently decelerated past the remains of the motley collection of uninhabitable planets that had provided the raw materials for the Ring's construction. I knew the Ring was large—several hundred kilometers in circumference—but the numbers hadn't prepared me for its immense reality.

The design was simple, hearkening back to the ring space-stations of centuries ago. Most of the Ring comprised the technology for warping time and space.

The habitable section was a module that—my wife would have said—disrupted its austere symmetry. It was to this module that the supply ship headed, finally easing into a landing bay.

Fifteen light-years. Not far, on a direct hyperspacial route from Earth, but far enough in case anything went wrong.

The Ring—perhaps humanity's greatest scientific project—had been under construction for some twenty years. Rigorous testing had been completed; short displacements had shown that the science was correct, the mechanism feasible, and the process survivable by humans. Now it was time for a full-fledged mission.

And I was the guinea pig, the expendable, recently bereaved junior professor, bound by no family ties, whose work made him qualified for the mission, but who wouldn't be overly missed should he fail to return…

One again, the raw, burning pain of anguish vied with the cold bitterness of desolation. I hated the present which had robbed me of so much, leaving me a shattered semblance of myself. I would have given anything to leave the present—and now the Ring offered me the way out which I so desperately desired.

Even seeing the Ring with my own eyes couldn't lessen the surprise I still felt that I had been offered the chance to become the first historian to voyage *to* the past.

I had submitted my application purely because of the slender chance of relief from hopelessness that it offered, never really believing that I would be selected in the face of competition from many more qualified and senior people.

Those rejected colleagues regarded me with envy. They assumed that I wanted the fame of being in the vanguard of the new discipline of Temporal Historico-Archaeology.

They couldn't have been further from the truth. Fame mattered nothing.

Some men in my position might have thrust out their jaws and stridden boldly into the future, shaking their fists at the Fates and daring them to do their worst. Others might have accepted their misfortune with the calm resignation of faith and trust in Divine Providence. I should have been one of the latter.

Instead, I simply wanted to escape. Pure and simple.

Two losses. My happiness vanished in the blink of an eye. The world nothing but a bleak, unendurable prison from which grim-faced suicide had beckoned me. I had resisted that beckoning, and my friends saw the stoical veneer of professional ambition that I wore—because I hadn't lost all interest in work—but not the dreadful emptiness inside.

Grief was to be expected—what man in my situation wouldn't have mourned? But I had gone beyond normal grieving. I had plunged into an abyss of self-pity from which I seemed powerless to extricate myself...as if I was drawn by inexorable forces into the ravenous maw of a black hole, only the slenderest thread of hope and prayer keeping me from absolute destruction...

"Professor?"

I started, and looked up at a pretty Naval lieutenant who regarded me with a concerned expression.

"Yes?"

"Are you all right, sir?"

I tried to gather my composure. "I'm fine. I was just thinking."

Her features relaxed. She motioned toward the exit. "If you would follow me..."

"Of course." I scrambled to my feet.

"Impressive, isn't it?" she said, allowing a smile to touch her lips as she led me into the station's wide, gleaming corridors populated by uniformed technicians and civilian scientists.

"Unbelievable," I murmured assent.

Impressive. And powerful. And my means of escape.

For soon it would hurl me some 2300 years into the past, to the island of Cyprus, lying blissfully unaware of the gradually approaching shadow of its own, impending tragedy...

III

I had been extensively briefed on what to expect, but two weeks later, as I stood facing the gray, mist-like wall that was the Ring's temporal interface, I realized the inadequacy of the descriptions I had been given. It was like nothing I had ever seen before; like nothing that existed in nature—and nature was full of strange things.

It was profoundly disconcerting to stand alone before this artificial construction where past and present met. I wore a tunic and sandals and carried a pouch of gold and silver coins—nothing that could be identified as coming from the future. I looked like a man from the fourth century bewildered by the technology of the twenty-seventh.

My eyes strained to focus on the featureless interface, and when at last they did, I saw that it wasn't completely void of detail—rather it writhed and pulsed and shimmered as if charged with energy. Or as if it were alive.

I shivered.

On the other side of this unnatural boundary lay the unknown, a vanished world full of vanished people. A mysterious world that fascinated me. I was excited—yet also hesitant—to cross the boundary, to enter past-time.

And yet, what was time but one step after another into the unknown? What matter if the steps were forward or backward?

Perhaps because one way was natural, and the other wasn't.

"We're fairly certain it's quite safe," the chief technician had attempted to reassure me.

"Only *fairly?*"

She'd shrugged. "There are no guarantees, Professor. Nothing *should* go wrong."

I looked up, down, and around. The interface seemed to extend for ever. I stretched my hand toward the flickering gray mist, and the hairs prickled.

That was where my future lay. I couldn't stand here dithering forever. Not when I was being observed by the Ring personnel, my image captured for countless news feeds, the moment being recorded for posterity.

I squared my shoulders, took a deep breath, and with a quick prayer on

5

my lips, stepped into the mist.

"You won't feel much of anything," I'd been told by one of the Ring technicians. "It'll feel like walking from one room to another."

It wasn't true.

It was as if a tiny, electrically charged needle pierced every cell of my body. My flesh crawled and my muscles twitched. It was, in fact, excruciating. But it lasted only a moment, and was gone as quickly as it had come.

I blinked in bright sunshine as a sound like distant thunder rumbled through the cloudless sky and faded away. I turned, and behind me a patch of gray mist flickered with weird, unearthly colors and gradually dissipated.

A warm, dry breeze rustled my tunic, and brought me unfamiliar scents—the scents of the past.

As my eyes adjusted to the glare, I took stock of my surroundings. I was standing on a low hill, next to a pair of shattered columns—perhaps the ruins of a forgotten temple. Gnarled, wind-whipped olive trees dotted the hillside, and in the distance blue sea sparkled. There was no sign of human life.

With the fading of the interface I was now totally cut off from my own time, with no method of contact until the pre-arranged day when Ring Control would re-establish the interface. Until then, I was dependent on my own skills and resources, my success or failure resting in my own hands.

I struggled not to be overwhelmed by it all. I was not the first man to travel through time—that honor belonged to a brave scientist on the Ring project—but I would be the first to spend significant time in the past, actually living there and being a part of it. Had I been dropped onto the surface of a totally alien planet I could not have felt any more strange or out of place.

Well, here I was and there was nothing for it but to get on with the work. I headed down the hillside, threading through the olive trees into a patchwork of rocky fields where I startled a goatherd who surely hadn't been expecting to encounter anyone in this lonely spot. I gave him a friendly wave and directed my steps toward the jumbled buildings of distant Kourion, not knowing what lay ahead, and hoping that I would discover a way to integrate myself into the society.

Otherwise, my stay in the past was likely to be unpleasant, unproductive, and potentially short.

I dared not fail.

IV: THE GHOSTS OF KOURION

She came toward me out of the darkness as she had done many times before, appearing exactly as she had done in life—the same slight tilt to her head, the half-smile as if she was amused by some private joke, the skipping walk.

Occasionally she seemed to see me, but this time her eyes looked past me, focused on something behind or beyond me.

"Emily," I called. "It's Daddy! I'm here!"

She didn't hear; she never heard. She continued walking at a deliberate pace. I stretched out a hand to smooth the wild tangles of her hair as I had done so many times before, but she remained maddeningly just out of reach.

"Emily!" I called again, but she didn't respond.

And then another figure emerged from the shadows behind her. A mule, its ears askew, its ribs prominent, ambling with heavy, weary steps. A single wilted flower adorned its bridle, and with each lurching step it took, clay amphorae restrained in a leather harness clunked dully together...

The girl turned her head in my direction, and for a moment I thought my presence would register with her, but then her face changed and it was not my Emily, but Philippa, and disappointment crushed me—

I awoke to the thudding of my heart and the scrabbling of a mouse somewhere in the room above the wine shop that I had purchased from an aged Cypriot shortly after my arrival. I had been fortunate to encounter him and acquire the perfect base for my operations. Pale moonbeams threaded through cracks in the warped shutters and created twisted ribbons across the dusty floor.

No! I couldn't have been sleeping! Not tonight, of all nights!

With mounting anxiety I realized that despite my best efforts to stay awake, sometime in the dark hours of the night I'd succumbed to the temptations of Morpheus, the Greek god of dreams.

Berating myself as a weak-willed fool, I threw off my thin sheet, dashed to the window, and flung open the shutters.

The city of Kourion, on the island of Cyprus, slept bathed in silver moonlight, its sand and time-worn walls standing as they had for hundreds of years. A shiver of mixed excitement and fear trembled over me.

Turning away from the window, I rummaged in a pile of clothes tossed on the floor and shrugged a tunic over my shoulders. I strapped on my sandals and clattered down the stairs into the shop where amphorae of choice vintages surrounded me like shapeless statues. I opened the door and raced out, leaving it swinging behind me.

From far below came the dull roar of the surf pounding the beaches. Otherwise, the pre-dawn twilight seemed preternaturally quiet—no wind in the trees, no dogs barking or cats fighting, not even a drunkard singing his slurred songs to the shuttered buildings.

It was the morning of July 21, A.D. 365, and it was to be Kourion's last morning. Were there hours left or merely minutes?

Cinching my belt tighter, I ran down the street, the slapping of my sandals on the cobblestones echoing off the tiled-roof buildings, praying that I would not be too late—and that, despite what the physicists told me, I could make a difference...

It was on this very street that I had first met Philippa several weeks ago. Dusk was falling and the blinding daytime heat was yielding grudgingly to the semi-coolness of the evening sea breeze. Even so, people still thronged the streets—slaves running errands for their masters, tradespeople desperate for one final sestertius of profit, wealthy youths loitering in search of diversion.

Soon, the shops would close and brothels and taverns open; already I spotted one or two young women taking up positions obvious enough to advertise their availability, but not so obvious that they'd attract the unwelcome attention of Bishop Makarion, who took a very dim view of such business.

Kourion's bishop never wasted an opportunity to relate a story from the apocryphal *Acts of Barnabas the Apostle* in which saints Paul and Barnabas (a native Cypriot) encountered stark naked men and women running "an abominable race." Barnabas rebuked them, and an earthquake ended the race. So it was said.

Bishop Makarion himself was too gentle to call down divine wrath. And this girl Philippa had nothing to fear from the bishop. As tired-appearing as her mule, she was simply one nearly indistinguishable person among many. She looked like every other thirteen-year-old poor freeborn girl. No more than five feet tall, she wore a shabby knee-length stola. She possessed no jewelry, not even a hairpin to restrain her ragged locks. She was so ordinary that even a pair of lusty young toughs ignored her. Such girls were common all across the decaying Roman Empire.

In my era, she was no more than a footnote in an old book, mere bones discovered during the twentieth-century excavation of Kourion. But those few recorded details had inclined me to choose doomed Kourion as my destination. The city was making the transition from paganism to Christianity in a fairly peaceful manner. Officially, my project was to study the effect of this transition on the common people.

"Are you crazy?" my department Chair had asked when—after my unexpected selection to the project—I submitted my research proposal. "Wouldn't you rather schmooze with Antony and Cleopatra? Help Constantine win the battle of the Milvian Bridge? *In hoc signo vincis* and all that? Trade literary notes with Virgil or Ovid?"

Sometimes it could be hard to tell whether or not he was joking. But the scowling brows and drumming fingers indicated that this was not one of those times.

"Great people don't make all the history," I replied, quoting something my father had told me, "they're just the ones who get remembered by it."

"So you want to go back and meet a girl with a mule?" If the Chair's eyebrows had raised higher he'd have lost them completely.

"It's better to begin modestly," I replied. "Perhaps later I may develop the skills to impersonate nobility…"

I'm not sure that I convinced the Chair. But after much grumbling he approved my proposal.

People as individual persons have always interested me more than people as representatives of broad social trends, so I hoped to enhance our knowledge of the past by meeting this girl and learning her story. So few of the people who have lived are known to history. I wanted to add one more.

Why her, in particular? She wasn't famous; no memorial stone marked her grave; we didn't even know her name. She was simply a young girl with a mule. Perhaps that was why.

I had wondered how to gain her confidence. She visited the shop infrequently to buy wine for her father. Normally the shop-boy attended to her while I dealt with the more affluent customers. But on this particular day fate took a hand. I was standing outside the shop trying to drum up business when she happened to be passing by.

Her gaze fixed firmly ahead, she didn't glance in my direction. What would she have thought, I wondered, had she known that the man in an ordinary, wine-stained tunic was actually a historian from the far future who had traveled over two thousand years back in time just to observe *her*?

Her mule stumbled over a loose paving stone, and its burden of amphorae shifted dangerously. She whirled with a shriek of alarm, but I rushed over to steady the clay jars so they didn't crash to the street.

"You're lucky not to have lost them," I said. "Your straps were too slack." I pulled them tighter. "There. They won't shift now."

I turned away from the mule to face her and gaped. For a moment, I thought I saw my Emily, but then the instant passed, and I realized that despite superficial similarities, this girl was really quite unlike my daughter. Yes, the soft brown eyes, the pert upturn of her nose, and her delicate ears were the same. But the cast of this girl's cheekbones proclaimed her different ancestry, as did the tone of her voice, and the Greek she spoke. And my daughter had been dead for three years…

My daughter—to the world in which I now walked—would not even exist for two millennia. She was yet to be born; yet to die. But to me, she had already lived, already died—as had the young girl who regarded me with wide eyes and pink cheeks.

It was unnerving. It was more than that.

She thanked me, her eyes lowered, blushing slightly. "My father would have been most displeased if I had broken them."

I pulled myself together. "Well, you won't have to worry now," I replied, as I wiped my hands on my tunic.

"Good day, sir," she said, gave a respectful nod, and began to walk away.

It was silly—quixotic—but I didn't want her to leave.

"What is your name, child?" I asked, to prolong the moment.

She paused. "I am Philippa, the daughter of Petronius and Antonia." She patted her beast's muzzle. "And this is Eirene."

"A fine animal," I said. Then, "Wait here." I hurried into the shop and returned with a small flagon that I handed to her. "Please give this to your father with the compliments of Cassius the wineseller."

It was a spur of the moment idea, and probably not a very good one. It was unlikely to bear fruit, but I needed to obtain some kind of introduction to her family, and perhaps this would provide some impetus.

"You are very kind, sir." With a shy smile she trudged off into the glare of the setting sun.

I shook my head sadly. There were many such poor folk in Kourion; indeed, not only on Cyprus but in countless other backwaters of the Empire. I suppressed the absurd desire to follow her to make sure she arrived safely. I told myself sternly that no matter how much she might remind me of my daughter, she wasn't. Emily was dead, and not all the wishful thinking or prayers in the world could bring her back.

Inside my shop I wandered among the amphorae of Chian, Falernian, Gaulish, Greek, and Syrian wines, names as familiar to me now

10

as Burgundy, Napa Valley, Rhine, and Ffinzi'an had once been…and which I could now identify by taste rather than as mere textbook names. The lengthening sunrays cast a warm, mellow glow over the buildings of Kourion, and I began to close the shutters.

I thought I'd been adapting quite well to my life here, but conversing with Philippa made me feel as out of place as the day I'd first arrived. Despite my extensive advance preparation, both on Earth and at the Ring, entering the past turned out to be an ordeal. Everything was different— from the taste of the water to the attitudes and customs of the people, from the gritty bread which seemed to contain more sand than flour to the social niceties of the bathhouses and public latrines. Sometimes I wondered if I'd ever gain my footing. Taking over the wineshop had been the easy part.

I wondered if I'd ever be able to relax in the past. Because always in the back of my mind was the lurking fear that I'd make a mistake, and be discovered. Or worse…

Now, as I ran along the dark streets, my fears returned—and not at the thought of the worried technicians who had prepared for my prearranged return yesterday. Since I had no way to contact them, they in turn had no way of knowing the reason for my non-appearance. I could imagine the Director of Ring Operations shaking with anger as he berated me—"You delayed your return to try to rescue a peasant girl? To try to change history? Don't you realize this is a scientific project, not an emotional one?" Well, I'd face that confrontation when the time came. And as for my return, the technicians would have to recalibrate and reopen the interface every day until either I showed up or they abandoned me as lost.

No, I wondered instead whether I had been wise to come here—not to the past *per se*, but to come *here, now*…

I skidded on a patch of spilled grease or oil as I passed a hot food shop and nearly fell. I forced myself to go slower. I would help nobody if I broke a leg—or my head.

Unless, of course, I was meant to.

Despite a facility with languages and an eidetic memory, I have no mind for physics.

It seemed a simple thing to live among long-gone people, study them, and take my findings and memories back to my own time for my colleagues. What harm could result if, for example, they wanted to know what a particular ruin represented, and I went and looked at it? Or if they wanted to know who lived in such and such a house, and I knocked on the door and talked to the occupants?

Yet what if I changed things?

The physicists told me it couldn't happen. I called it the Self-Consistency Principle: the concept that history was done and past and that nothing I did would change anything. I could walk and talk, eat and drink, sell wine with impunity. There were no paradoxes to worry about, no infinity of universes for the world to split into, nothing.

"Are you certain?" I'd asked Paul, one of the project physicists, unable to escape visions of altering the past, of wreaking incredible damage and turning my world—the one I wanted to leave behind—into a nightmare. I couldn't do that for the sake of the people who were happy in it.

"Positive," was the confident reply. "You can *affect* the past, but you can't *change* it because you were always a part of it."

Trust a physicist to give you an answer that leaves you more confused than you were before!

"Look, Robert," he said in response to my look of incomprehension, "if you *will* go back to ancient Rome, then you *were* there, and if you *weren't*, then you *won't*. Understand?"

"One more time?"

He began to sound exasperated. "You cannot change the past or create a paradox, Robert. Anything—and I mean *anything*—you do in the past must have been done already, or you couldn't have been there to do it in the first place. It is logically impossible to change the past. Even God can't change the past."

Personally, I've always felt a little uncomfortable placing constraints on the Deity, but I thought I was beginning to have a glimmer of insight into what Paul was saying.

"What you're trying to express, I think," I said, attempting to make him feel guilty for my lack of comprehension, "is that I can't travel to the past unless I've already been there, and when I get there I'll do what I've already done."

"Exactly!" He beamed as if I'd suddenly become his star student. "Been there, done that."

Four words. Why couldn't he have said them in the first place?

"Even though I don't remember what I've done."

"Because those events, although in the chronological past, are still in your personal future."

"So nothing I do will matter?" I added, in a last bid for reassurance.

The scowl returned. I had obviously flunked. "It's *already* mattered, Robert!" He raised a finger and shook it at me.

I hurried away with his last words ringing in my ears. "Time happens only once. There are no second chances."

No second chances...

I turned down a narrow alley, hoping it would be a short-cut and not a dead-end. I'd taken solace in the Self-Consistency Principle, but now found myself praying that it wasn't inviolable.

Emily...Emily...

I'd been unable to do anything to save Emily when she'd contracted a hitherto unknown and impossibly rapidly progressing prion disease on Grainger II where I was attending an archaeological meeting. Was there any chance that I could save Philippa? Any chance at all, no matter how slim...?

I'd seen Philippa frequently after that first encounter and studied her as I would have studied any ancient relic. Inevitably she was leading her mule along the lanes. Sometimes it carried amphorae of food or wine, sometimes sacks of grain, sometimes bundles of firewood. Always, there was a flower tucked into its bridle. She'd smile and wave discretely when she saw me, and I'd wave back. Further contact would have been inappropriate in this culture.

Now that the ice had been broken, I made it a point to serve her myself whenever she came to buy wine. She would answer my casually-posed questions, but rarely initiated conversation. And so I was surprised one day when, as she handed me a few bronze coins to conclude a transaction, she asked, "Your accent is very strange, sir. Where do you come from?"

"Britannia," I replied disingenuously; not the Britannia of her time. But coming from a distant province on the edge of the known world had its advantages. I could blame my social lapses on the different customs of Britannia and be politely excused. Similarly with language, because while learning Latin, Greek, or any other language was easy enough, we had no idea of the accents of the past. It was one of many things which made fitting into an ancient culture difficult.

The other, for me, was the lack of sunglasses. I'd have given all the wines in the shop for a pair of cheap shades. I wondered if I was developing a permanent squint.

"What brought you to Kourion?" she asked.

"Do you know what the weather's like in Britannia?" I countered lightly. "It's a wonder anyone lives there."

She laughed and seemed content with the answer.

"Were you born here?" I asked.

She nodded. "My family has always lived in Kourion."

My next breakthrough came about two weeks later, when Philippa showed up at my shop alone.

"Where is Eirene?" I asked.

"She has a sore hoof," Philippa replied. "My father asks if your boy could deliver the wine."

I'd been wanting to see their house. I nodded. "Tell him it shall be delivered."

I sent the shop-boy home at closing time, loaded two jugs of wine onto a hand cart, and set off across the city.

I had no trouble identifying Philippa's home as the artist's renditions with which I was familiar were remarkably accurate. It was a villa near the marketplace, once the home of some wealthy person, which, so the archaeologists said, had been damaged in an earthquake, lapsed into disuse, and then been subdivided into dwellings for several families. Philippa and her parents lived in a single room on the ground floor. They shared a common kitchen with a young couple who had an infant child and a laborer who kept a cat. A cistern and a storeroom comprised the remainder.

Petronius greeted me warmly as I carried the jugs through the doorway.

"I apologize for the inconvenience," he said. "I wasn't expecting you to deliver the wine personally."

"It's no inconvenience," I replied.

Petronius was, like most Cypriots of his day, barely over five feet tall, making me feel like a star basketball player. He was darker complected than Philippa, but despite a rugged face didn't appear robust. He walked stiffly and limped, and the ring which doubled as his door key was jammed onto an arthritic finger.

His wife Antonia, who hovered nearby, resembled an older version of her daughter. But she was unhealthily pale, and sagging skin-folds showed that she'd lost weight. Her only adornment was a pair of rings—one bronze and one gold.

Neither Petronius nor Antonia could have been even forty—my age—but the toll of life was evident in their careworn features. The poor freeborn endured hard, short lives. It wasn't a good time to be a Cypriot, as famine, drought, and plagues had decimated the island. Petronius and Antonia were probably lucky to be alive.

The house was dusty, not surprising in Kourion, where sand continually blew up from the beaches below. The walls of the room that I entered were covered with faded, nearly indecipherable frescoes. It might have been a charming room once, but was now only a sad remnant of vanished prosperity. Several storage jars were spaced around the walls, and Petronius directed me to put my amphorae with them. A wooden table bore a copper pitcher. A pair of pretty deep-sea conches provided the only decoration.

"I brought them up for Antonia," Petronius said. "I used to be quite a diver before the fever wrecked me."

I expressed sympathy, then turned to leave.

"It's getting late," Petronius said. "In thanks, may I offer you the hospitality of our table?"

"You're very gracious," I replied.

"Would you like to say hello to Eirene?" Philippa asked, emerging from a doorway in a jerry-built wall.

"Hush, child!" Petronius admonished. "Don't bother our guest."

"It's no bother," I said, "I'd love to see her. How's her hoof?"

Philippa's downcast face brightened, and she ushered me into the stable, where the mule was tethered to a stone trough that must have weighed seven or eight hundred pounds. I scratched her ears while Philippa looked on proudly. The professional side of my mind, though, was racing, recording details that confirmed archaeology's assessment of this house.

A glass jar containing copper coins, probably the family's entire savings, perched discreetly on a shelf. A marble table and a pair of elegant standing bronze lampstands seemed out of place, since one lamp looked to be about three hundred years old.

"They were here when we moved in," Philippa explained when I inquired about them.

Petronius showed me to my place when we reentered the main room, then he and I made small talk as Philippa prepared food under Antonia's watchful eye. I assumed the family normally ate together, but with a guest present the women became as unobtrusive as a single room allowed.

"My daughter tells me you're a newcomer to Kourion," Petronius said. "Have you no family?"

I looked down at the rough wooden table. "My daughter died of illness. My wife was killed in a…a cart accident a month later."

I would never forget the moment when two black clad police officers interrupted a class I was teaching to break the news that Erica had been killed in an aircar collision over London. A one in ten billion chance that the supposedly foolproof safety systems would fail.

"A hard blow for even the strongest of men," Petronius said sympathetically, and once again I heard the voice of the priest attempting to console me after Erica's funeral.

"You're called to bear a heavy cross," he said, at least not trying to sugar-coat my grief with platitudes. But even his honesty hadn't helped.

"I don't want to bear a cross!" I'd snapped. "I just want my wife and my daughter!"

I became aware of Petronius' steady gaze. I, from the technologically advanced future, had neither wife, nor child, nor contentment, but this poor man from a primitive era had both. It wasn't fair.

I cleared my throat. "I decided to begin a new life."

"That is wise," Petronius said. "A man cannot live in the past."

I glanced up sharply, but saw only concern in his eyes.

Philippa finished laying out the meager fare of coarse bread, cheese,

15

olives, and a few soggy fruits and vegetables that were probably the remnants from a vendor's stall. The plates were chipped, cheap redware, locally produced.

Petronius poured a small amount of wine into a clay cup, held it aloft, and murmured a brief prayer to Apollo before pouring it to the floor.

"In this house," he said to me, "we still follow the old ways. Do you?"

"No," I replied. My hand went to my throat, to the small bronze pilgrim's cross I wore beneath my tunic. Erica had given it me. She'd bought it in an antique store in Bath, pleased to have located something that dated to the early centuries of Christianity. "I was raised as a follower of Christus."

He sighed. "Since the Emperor Constantine, it seems as if the followers of Christus are taking over the world. The old gods are passing. It's hard to know what to believe."

"Very true," I agreed.

"The old gods served their purpose, men say," Petronius continued. "I heard a philosopher in the forum claiming that the old gods were men's groping toward higher things, and that now that the higher—by which he meant the new religion—has been revealed, they will fade away, like the light of the moon when the sun rises."

"A not unreasonable interpretation," I said cautiously. I didn't want to offend my host. But the old customs were indeed passing, and soon they'd be like the increasingly neglected Temple of Apollo nearby, quaint relics for the curious mind. "But how would the world be without the light of the moon?"

Petronius smiled. "I've lived too many years to change. New revelations are for the young." He pointed toward a blocked-up doorway in the far wall. "Our neighbors believe as you do."

"I met them once at a fish-seller's." The young husband had been recognizable because of a ring that he wore bearing a chi-rho symbol—the first two letters in Greek of the name of Christ.

Petronius glanced at Philippa. "I suspect my daughter is a follower of this new religion."

Philippa blushed and studied the floor. "Yes, Father," she murmured. "As I wish you and Mother were."

I hoped I wasn't about to witness a family conflict, but Petronius seemed neither excited nor upset—merely resigned. "The future cannot be fought," he said, "merely faced." He turned his tired eyes to me. "You are at least more charitable toward the old gods than many Christians."

"Charity towards neighbors was one of Christ's teachings," I said, reaching out to lay my hand briefly on his arm and hoping that I didn't sound patronizing. To lighten the conversation I smiled and said, "Besides,

I don't wish to upset a customer."

He snorted. "If you rely on our patronage, your stay in business won't be long."

"Every drop of wine sold is better than none," I said, and he chuckled.

The conversation moved on. It was late that night when I bid goodnight to my hosts.

"It is kind of you to care for a stranger," I said.

"Hospitality is the way of Kourion," he replied. "Perhaps we shall see you again?"

I caught the glance that passed between him and Antonia and that seemed to include Philippa.

I murmured something, not wishing to impose further upon these poor people.

I'd walked home slowly, deep in thought. Muted music—wind and strings—and laughter came from behind shuttered windows, from a late dinner yet in progress. A drunk snored in the shadow of the theater and a youth and a young woman embraced near a fountain, seeming as insubstantial as ghosts in the dim light...and abruptly, as I climbed the steps to my rooms above my shop, I understood the meaning of the glance that Petronius and Antonia had shared...

My sprint reduced to a slow jog, I passed the fountain where, weeks ago now, I'd seen the young couple embrace. The square was deserted. I wished I could run faster. How much time did I have? How much?

Each day, each week had brought closer the disaster that stalked Kourion like a panther stealthily approaching an unsuspecting gazelle.

The ancient city had survived the vagaries of history since being founded in the twelfth or thirteenth century B.C. by Mycenaean Greeks, from Assyrian King Sargon II's extortion of taxes and homage from King Eteandros, to King Pasikrates sending men and ships to aid Alexander the Great's siege of Tyre.

This time, destiny's hand was against the city.

And there was nothing I could do about it.

"What if I raise an alarm?" I had asked Richard, one of the other physicists, back while the mission was in the planning stage. After all, what person of conscience, knowing the exact date of a disaster, could fail to warn the people who were destined to die? Only a monster would allow people to go blindly to their doom, and I hoped that whatever else I might be, I wasn't a monster.

He'd shaken his head. "You would be like Cassandra of Troy," he said, using a concept I could understand and not some abstract, labyrinthine scientific argument.

In Greek mythology, Cassandra had been blessed with the ability to forecast the future coupled with the curse that no one would believe her prophecies. The comparison was obvious. The alarm had not been raised in Kourion; therefore, I could not raise it.

"Go ahead and try." He'd shrugged, and I'd understood him completely. I *must* fail because I *did* fail. Or *had* failed. Or something.

Knowing that I could not avert the disaster should have enhanced my objectivity, while helping me act more naturally, preventing mental and emotional damage, and averting self-condemnation. My job was to observe history, to do what I had done—whatever that was—and not to despair over how events had turned out.

There are no second chances…

Despite the pronouncement of science, I couldn't get the faces of Philippa or her parents out of my mind. How could I have foreseen that this simple girl with the mule would affect me so?

Was knowing the manner of their deaths a privilege or a curse? I'd thought the former; now I wasn't so sure. What would I have done differently if I'd known how and when my Emily would die? Would it have mattered?

If only Kourion had been destined to perish slowly. If only…

My lungs burned; would these streets never end?

It seemed much further from my shop to Petronius's house than it ever had before, almost as if I was running to Emily and Erica in a dream…

Could I return to the days when my wife and daughter were alive, I'd asked Richard?

"It won't work," he'd told me, putting his arm on my shoulder. "Think about it. You would already be there. You would observe yourself with your wife and daughter. Not only couldn't you undo what had happened, you couldn't even relive the past. You'd be merely observing what you had already done, how you had already lived. Believe me, Robert, it's best to live with your memories. Don't torture yourself needlessly."

He would have none of my protests. "Search your recollections," he'd said. "Did you ever see an older version of yourself observing you?"

"No."

"Were you ever introduced to yourself or shook hands with yourself?"

"No."

"Did Erica ever tell you that she'd met a future you?"

"No."

"Robert, if you *weren't* then, you couldn't *be* then. You *can't*—or you

18

won't—go back to them, because you *didn't.*"

The truth had numbly sunken in. Reluctantly, I acknowledged that while it was theoretically possible to return to my own past, it was impossible to relive my life. My wife and daughter were lost to me this side of eternity. And eternity seemed to lie a long ways away.

Philippa would soon be lost to me, as well.

I'd tried to put the feelings of friendship toward this Kourion family aside and perform my research with a semblance of detachment. I forced myself to concentrate. Research seemed a shallow thing. Yet I had pursued it after my dinner with the family, even accepting an invitation from Petronius to view the Temple of Apollo of the Woodlands which was Kourion's only claim to fame.

I didn't participate in the Eleusinian Mysteries or the worship of Apollo—realizing that those studies required religious scholars more knowledgeable than I—but I did attend Mass with the Christians—and noticed Philippa in the company of the young neighbor couple. I memorized liturgical nuances for the religious scholars, frescoes and mosaics for the artists, melodies for the musicians, and details of building construction for the architects.

I spoke to Bishop Makarion, who offered me spiritual solace—but I could only partially explain my wounds.

Petronius and Antonia must have taken a liking to me, because I received further invitations to share their table. Even poor free people embraced their social duty to entertain, if only on a humble level. I was hesitant to deplete their meager provisions by accepting, but risked discourtesy by refusing. Instead, I invited Petronius sometimes to dine with me. We talked of many things, although the relationship of the old gods to the new seemed to interest him the most. For a common man, he was quite conversant with the topics of his day.

One time I bought a pair of silver-plated bone hairpins from a jewelry maker in the Forum because I thought Erica and Emily might have liked them, and, with Petronius's permission, gave one each to Antonia and Philippa. Both women were delighted with the gifts. I never saw Philippa again without the hairpin proudly displayed.

From time to time I was able to offer Philippa work making wine deliveries for me, when the unreliable young chap I normally employed was unavailable. She seemed happy to help, singing songs while going about the business, and always thanking me on behalf of her family for the coins I paid her.

It became harder and harder for me to remain isolated from my emotions, no matter how many times I reminded myself that I was observing people who had already lived their lives. Philippa began to seem more like a daughter than a subject; Petronius and Antonia like a brother and sister. My objectivity began to erode like a sandstone cliff assaulted by heavy waves.

All the while, the knowledge of Kourion's certain destruction burned within me like a festering appendix.

"What do you wish for?" I asked Philippa some months later while she tended to Eirene in the stable room. She paused in thought. "A better life," she said with a sparkle in her eyes that confirmed my earlier concern.

I spoke to Petronius, and when I realized that he was so desperate to obtain a husband for dowry-less Philippa that even a widowed wineseller three times the girl's age was a possibility, told him I was in an extended period of mourning, and was not prepared to remarry. It would have been cruel to encourage his hopeless aspirations. He accepted the news with his characteristic resignation, but with disappointment in his tired eyes.

One day at the shop, when I was fastening a jug of cheap wine to her mule for her parents, Philippa said, "Thank you, master wineseller."

"For what?" I asked.

"For giving me hope." I must have looked puzzled, for she continued, "My life, here, in Kourion, will go nowhere, but now I have a better life to look forward to."

"I don't understand."

"For the longest time, my father tried to convince me to return to the old ways. He told me it was foolish to chase after a new god."

"But what did I—?"

"My father admires you," she said, as she turned to lead the docile animal away, "because you have traveled across the Empire…seen many places, many cities. If a man like you can believe in the new god, then it seems so much more reasonable. My father even wonders if perhaps you are right."

I probably looked like her mule, with my mouth hanging open.

What a strange turn of events! Had I inadvertently become a missionary to the past? Did the Self-Consistency Principle apply to eternity as well as to normal time? Could flocks of future missionaries descend upon the past? Probably not. There would be no future missionaries because there had been no past ones…unless they were already a part of the past. I felt another headache coming on.

As the days passed, the burning that gnawed within me became uncontainable. No matter what Paul said, I had to try.

"Would you ever leave Kourion?" I asked Petronius one evening. It was an oblique opening, but I didn't know quite how to broach the subject without sounding like a madman.

He laughed. "Where would I go? Kourion is a poor city, for poor people like me."

"But if something bad were to happen…a disaster…"

"Who can predict the future? It's one thing to believe the word of a god, quite another to believe the guesses of a prophet. Are you a prophet, Cassius the Wineseller?"

"Well, I—"

"If it is the will of the gods for Kourion to be punished, then how would leaving help? Can the gods not find me wherever I may go? Fate cannot be avoided, my friend."

"Petronius," I pleaded. "I beg you to leave this city. I will give you the money—"

He was shaking his head before I even finished the sentence.

"Antonia—" I began, turning toward his wife who sat quietly in a corner of the room.

"Where my husband stays, I stay," she said. And I knew Philippa would never leave her parents.

"Are *you* leaving Kourion?" Petronius asked pointedly.

What could I say? *Yes, via the awesome power of the Ring?*

There the matter ended.

The first rays of the sun began to peek over the horizon, and almost—almost—it seemed as if history had been mistaken, and that this would be yet another ordinary day. Down by the shore, the fishermen would be readying their boats and preparing to sail; soon, the people of Kourion would arise and resume their daily business. But no; surely this calm was illusory.

Gasping for breath, I realized that I had reached Petronius' house. I was in time! Perhaps history wasn't as immutable as the physicists claimed.

I paused at the door. It would be locked; Petronius was meticulous about keeping his premises secure. I raised my fist, and hammered on the wood with blows that shattered the silence of the dawn. "Philippa!" I called. "Petronius! It's Cassius!"

Silence answered me. Not only the silence of a sleeping building in a sleeping city, but something deeper. The surf! The sound of the distant surf had vanished! Cold fear clamped its hand about my heart.

Then the silence was broken by the low, restless snorting of a disturbed mule. A light flickered through chinks in the shutters. I heard Philippa's voice soothing Eirene.

She was awake! I hit the door again. If only she would answer it—if only

Petronius would listen to me now—

A low, visceral rumble that came from everywhere and nowhere growled like the warning vocalization of a giant, disturbed beast. A vibration, faint but increasing in intensity, quivered underfoot.

"Philippa!" I shouted again.

And then it was as if a supernatural being lifted Cyprus from the sea and let it drop again. I staggered, recovered, and then staggered again as a second temblor, stronger than the first, rocked the town. Buildings crumpled as if hit by the fist of Zeus. I fell to my knees as roofing tiles shattered on the cobblestones and chunks of building stone crashed around me like hail thrown by Titans.

The lamplight went out.

"Philippa!" I yelled, yanking frantically on the door handle as the building imploded before my eyes. "Philippa!"

The sound of falling masonry obliterated my cries.

Kourion awoke, only to die. The fortunate perished instantly, buried by collapsing buildings. Others made it into the streets, only to be smashed by falling bricks. A nearly palpable terror gripped Kourion. I could hardly believe the rapidity with which the city disintegrated.

A woman disheveled by sleep and wearing her night garments grabbed my shoulder.

"My husband!" she cried, pointing to the heap of rubble that had once been a building. She began scrabbling at the pile. "Help me!"

But my mind's eye presented me with the smoking pile of twisted metal that had taken Erica's life. I had to see it to convince myself that the unimaginable had really happened, and that my Erica was gone.

"There's no use," I said dully. "He didn't stand a chance." The doctors had said almost the same thing when Emily's illness outstripped their treatments.

Erica's mangled body…Emily's illness-wracked form…and now Philippa and Eirene, Petronius and Antonia—gone, all of them!—the Christian couple and their child, the woman's husband, a single man and his cat—I saw their splintered skeletons surrounded by the shattered fragments of their possessions. I saw them just as archaeologists had unearthed them. Philippa lay near her mule, the hairpin that I had given her ejected from her hair. Eirene was still tethered to her feeding trough, which had been thrown across the room and broken by the force of the earthquake.

I felt sick at the thought of Philippa's sweet spirit—like Emily's—being snuffed like a candle that had only just been lit.

Once, I could have reported the bare facts about past people with utter lack of sentiment. Julius Caesar was assassinated in 44 BC. Queen Victoria died in 1901, John F. Kennedy in 1963, the inhabitants of Kourion in 365.

They were simply names, people I had never known, to whom I was unattached.

Now it was all different.

Time happens only once.

The words burst into my consciousness like a bolt of lightning. This was *real*. It was *really* happening.

With a sickening jolt I understood—fully, not in some abstract manner—that I wasn't seeing a replay or repeat of time, like watching a movie. I was seeing what happened *as* it happened, the *only time* it happened.

Choking from dust, I fell back from the ruined building. Paul and Richard were right. I could change nothing, make no difference. Those who were fated to die would die and those who were destined to live would live…It was I who was the ghost, a piece of flotsam from the future, a useless cosmic shard, an interloper who had merely read accounts of the disaster…

Just after dawn there were frequent flashes of lightning, and the rumbling of thunder, wrote Roman historian Ammianus Marcellinus in the fourth century, not long after the disaster. *Then the firm and stable mass of the earth trembled and shook, and the sea withdrew, its waves flowing backward. The sea floor was exposed, revealing fishes and sea creatures stuck fast in the slime. Mountains and valleys that had been hidden in the unplumbed depths since the creation of the world for the first time saw the beams of the sun.*

Intimately familiar with this account, I'd tried to visualize it, but my mental images were only pale impressions of the awful reality.

Boats were left stranded in these newly created lands, and men wandered fearlessly in the little that remained of the waters, collecting fishes with their bare hands.

How many times had I seen the fishermen readying their boats as they had done this morning, heading out into the waters pinked by the morning sun? *Then the sea returned with an angry vengeance. As if resentful of its forced retreat, the sea roared and rushed through the seething shallows, dashing through every open space and leveling countless buildings in the cities and wherever else they are to be found, so that amid the mad discord of the elements the altered face of the earth revealed marvelous sights.*

Those unfortunate fishermen and coastal villagers, now scoured from the face of the earth!

For the great mass of waters, returning when it was least expected, killed many thousands of men by drowning, and by the swift recoil of the eddying tides a number of ships, after the swelling of the wet element subsided, were found to have been destroyed, and the lifeless bodies of shipwrecked persons lay floating on their backs or on their faces. Other great ships, driven by the mad blasts, landed on the tops of buildings (as happened at Alexandria) and some were driven almost two miles inland, like a Laconian ship which I myself saw in passing near the town of Motho, yawning apart through long decay.

But it wasn't the waves that killed Kourion. It was the incomprehensibly powerful earthquake that shook the ground as a woman shakes out a sheet. And as the city tumbled around me, I ran, stumbling and lurching along madly swaying streets that buckled underneath my feet, twisting and turning to avoid crashing walls and falling debris. People joined me in my madness, fleeing the devastation that was Kourion.

After what seemed a relentless series of aftershocks, the tremors ceased. Then came the fire. The sky glowed red behind me as everything that was burnable in Kourion ignited. A cooking fire, an oil lamp, an overturned brazier—whatever the cause, the fires, once begun, devoured everything they encountered.

I staggered down barely passable lanes and alleys, as the fiery breath of Hell blew past me and the air grew thick with smoke. The malevolent glow of the fires pursued me, leaping from building to building.

Where was the city gate? Which way was I going?

Was it my lot to die in Kourion? Was it even possible to die in the past? I had visions of the bizarre prospect of walking in my own century while my bones lay undisturbed and undiscovered beneath me.

I'd asked physicist Richard. "I see no reason why not," he replied. "But I wouldn't worry about it. Have you archaeologists ever unearthed somebody that you could identify as having come from the future?"

Well no, but that didn't mean it couldn't happen someday. And it was fine for him not to lose any sleep over the question; he wasn't going back in time.

"Just don't annoy the locals," he'd added.

I'd sought a second opinion from Paul, who'd disagreed. All closed causal loops must be self-consistent, he explained, so it would not be possible to die in the past. That made about as little sense to me as anything in temporal physics ever did, but it made me feel marginally better to know that one out of two physicists thought I might return alive. I had entered the past not overly concerned about my fate, but over time my will to live had strengthened.

A pile of rubble loomed out of the smoky darkness, and with a shudder, I realized I was standing in front of the ruins of my shop. Somehow, I had circled the theater and the city baths and returned to my starting point without even realizing it. This section of the city seemed free from fire. I remembered dully that only part of the city had burned.

A trickle of dark liquid from the many shattered wine vessels seeped across the threshold. I pushed open the door and ducked inside. It wasn't a safe thing to do; although the walls still stood, the roof had caved in and it wouldn't take much to bring the tottering edifice crashing down. But I needed the temporary security of a familiar location.

My eyes recoiled from the awful images I had witnessed. My ears echoed with the screams and cries and wails of grief, the crash of crumbling masonry and the crackle of flame, all dissolving into a ghostly silence where once there had been sounds of life. I had longed to experience the past in all its glorious vitality. Even though I had seen Kourion's bleached bones in my own era, I couldn't bear the stark reality of its agonizing death.

Later, some people claimed that the calamity was divine judgment inflicted because of Julian the Apostate's abandonment of the Christian faith and attempt to reassert the worship of the old gods. But the earthquake killed indiscriminately, Christian, Jew, and Pagan alike. It spared no one, nothing.

It was brute nature in action, the processes of Earth releasing her pent-up energies without concern for the humans and animals that roamed her surface.

I stared at the jumbled wreckage of my shop without really seeing it, and wondered how I had ever thought I could flee my hurts by venturing into the past. How foolish to imagine that I could hide among the long-gone ghosts of the past—shades of people whose lives had been lived long ago, phantoms that couldn't hurt me!

How pathetic my attempt at detachment! I cared for these people, these inhabitants of a long-gone era. Petronius and Antonia had offered me friendship. Philippa was like a second daughter. They weren't objects. They weren't specters. They were real people, full of all the desires, imperfections, emotions, motives, and loves common to all humanity through all time.

I rested my forehead against the rough wood of a warped doorpost.

What were my own hurts compared to those of these people in the midst of their suffering? How could I have been so small-minded and so hard-hearted? How could I have been so foolish as to think I could hide from the pain of caring and loss?

Tears came to my smoke-sore eyes, and there, in the midst of the devastation, in the ruins of my own aspirations, I wept for the ghosts of Kourion.

In the street outside, I saw Bishop Makarion stagger past, an unconscious woman cradled in his arms, a pair of crying children clinging to his soiled robes. For a moment, as he twisted beneath his burden, the streaks of dirt on his chest made the shape of a cross. I'm sure he didn't see me, but in my mind I heard again the words of the priest in my own time— "You're called to bear a heavy cross"—and heard again my own words of denial. I wore a cross, but I was unworthy of it.

Bishop Makarion turned a corner and was gone. I stepped into the street, wondering whether I should follow him.

"Help me."

The voice was no more than a croak. By all rights I shouldn't have heard it, but for some unfathomable reason it stopped me in my tracks. I searched for its source.

The man who spoke was beyond earthly aid. He lay in the shadows at the corner of a building, the lower half of his body crushed beneath a slab of stone that would have required the efforts of half a dozen men to lift. He seemed too weak even to move his arms. His mouth worked, but no further words emerged.

I don't know why, but in the movement of his lips, I thought I saw Richard's: *You will do what you have already done...*

I repeated the words to myself. *You will do what you have already done.* Of course! There were no second chances, but this wasn't a second chance. This was my *first* chance! I could yet pick up that cross...

I glanced around and spotted a public fountain a short distance away. Motioning to the man that I would return, I ran over to it. On the way, I picked up a jug lying on the street. The top had broken off, but the bottom was intact. I dipped it in the fountain, took it to the injured man, and held it to his lips.

"May God bless you," he whispered, as his eyes closed in the final sleep.

I set the broken jug on the cobblestones. Surely—*surely*—I had made a difference. Maybe not to history, because nothing had changed, but to a dying man in his last moments. It wasn't only in my own era, where the future was still to be formed, that things really mattered. Things mattered here, too.

Filled with a new purpose I roamed the convoluted cityscape. Even though my rational mind still balked at the notion that I could assist souls who had died long before my birth, I pulled people from rubble. I rescued a screaming infant and handed it to a frantic mother. I released a chained dog that licked my hand before vanishing into the dust-filled semi-gloom.

I had my God-given chance; even though history had no record of my presence here, I would *be* a part of it.

For I too was now one of the ghosts of Kourion.

V

Was it possible to erase an eidetic memory? To wipe clean the face of remembrance and start afresh? To eradicate all recollection of pain, distress, and suffering? If so, what would disappear along with it?

Personality—inextricably bonded to memory, like conjoined twins, where the removal of one would cause the death of the other.

How many memories would I have erased had I could? How much of myself would I have lost?

I toyed with, and discarded the question.

The sights and sounds and smells and taste and touch of Kourion had become an indelible part of me. Just like Erica. Just like Emily.

And so there was nothing to do but come to grips with the memories, to assimilate them, and make them part of me.

So I told myself.

VI

I left my century as a veritable nobody, known and recognized only within the limited circle of my profession; I returned as a celebrity. In retrospect, I suppose I should have anticipated it. But initially consumed by my own personal grief, and subsequently by the emotional calamity of the destruction of Kourion, I had given no thought to my return.

I knew that I could not remain as a ghost of Kourion—my place was not there, in that ruined city, among collapsed buildings and shattered lives. The events of that tragedy ran their fixed and unalterable course. The survivors picked themselves up and moved on. And so did I.

The gleaming circle of the Temporal Displacement Ring was a thing of beauty, a silver band framing a collection of far-distant, diamond-like stars. I was glad to be back among my own people, in my own time, surrounded by all the comforts and technology to which I was accustomed—even though some of that technology was used to probe my body down to the last molecule to ensure both that the trip hadn't adversely affected me and that I hadn't brought back some horrible organism from the past to which present people lacked immunity. It appeared, though, that I was safe to be returned to the general public.

"You're fine," the medic pronounced cheerfully when the final scan was complete. "Not even a worm to show as a souvenir of your trip."

I thanked him for his thoroughness with as much sincerity as I could muster.

I endured two tongue-lashings for missing my scheduled return. One from the Director of Ring Operations—"When you didn't show up, we thought we'd lost you!"—and another from the Chair chastising my tardiness for, as he put it, "personal reasons unconnected with the research project."

I returned, as I said, a celebrity, totally unprepared for the attention I received. Naively, I had thought to hole up in my study and prepare reports for respected journals. Instead, hardly had I set foot back on Mother Earth than everyone wanted to meet the time-traveling historian! I had become a subject of study in my own right, and endured countless interviews, answering the same questions with the same fixed smile until my mind was numb and my face ached. My image was viewed on every human-inhabited world (and maybe on some with other sentient beings, as well).

The noted composer Vaughn Tieffen of Tokarski IV wrote a *Time Symphony* based on melodies I brought back from Kourion.

Erica would have been proud; my heart ached, and I would have given anything to have her standing beside me. I was offered multiple honorary doctorates (which I accepted) and university positions (which I declined). My loyalty lay with CamOx, which had encouraged my career, stood by me during my tragedies, and allowed me the opportunity to visit the past. In short, I thought the agony would never end.

I had imagined, irrationally, no doubt, that, coming from the future I should have had godlike powers in the past. But I didn't—I was only one ordinary man among other ordinary men, as powerless as they in the face of disaster. But for the grace of God, the experience, coming so soon after my bereavement, could have deepened my wounds. But it didn't—it acted like a cautery. It was—although it took me a while to see it—like love.

Faith, hope, and love abide.

But not fame. All celebrity fades in time, and eventually I was no longer newsworthy. Eventually, too, I was able to write the academic papers that cemented the project's place in history. Life began to return to normal. The routines of teaching and study reasserted themselves.

Normal, at least, until I was summoned to the Department Chair's office. He wasted no time in getting to the point once I had seated myself.

"Are you ready to go back again, Robert?" he asked, staring at me from beneath bushy white brows like a bald eagle eying a particularly enticing morsel of carrion.

"I—" Words failed me. For some reason, I had always considered a single trip to the past to be enough for any man, any lifetime.

"Don't dazzle me with your enthusiasm," he continued.

"I really hadn't—"

"The science whizzes have completed their analysis of the project," he continued without waiting for me to finish my sentence, "and are quite happy with the results. So happy that they want to push back the target date by about four hundred years or so. Is there anywhere you want to visit about that time?"

"Um…35 BC, give or take…"

He nodded impatiently.

"I'm sure there's something," I fumbled, my mind still reeling. "Caesarea was being built around that time, 15 BC or so…"

"You've got a week to come up with something."

"A whole week?" I gasped.

My sarcasm was lost on him. "Sooner, if possible." He rose, circled his desk, clapped a hand on my shoulder. "CamOx is proud of you, my boy."

"But isn't there anyone else who wants a chance—?"

"Practically everyone in the historical sciences," he laughed. "You know how everyone is looking to make a name for themselves."

"But why—?"

"Because the project is still in the development and testing phase," he said, interrupting me once again. "You've made one successful trip—"

"And so I'm the official guinea pig?" I said, getting my own back in an irritated way.

"At this stage," he said, unperturbed and nodding again. "Once the program is running at full capacity and its capabilities and limitations more clearly defined, we'll have people visiting the ancient Egyptians, Incas, Indians, Assyrians…anyone you can imagine."

"Zoologists going back to the Jurassic?"

"Deep Time?" He almost smiled. "I wouldn't put it past them. But at the moment we really don't know the Ring's capabilities. For the moment, it's you. And Rome. And have your target location and date on my desk as soon as you can."

He resumed his seat on the other side of the mahogany expanse, and raised his eyebrows. "Is there anything else?"

I clambered hurriedly to my feet. "No…I think not."

"Good."

I was just about at the door when he said, "And Robert, return when scheduled this time, all right? Don't hang around for a disaster."

My ears burned, and my mind replayed the royal chewing out the Chair had given me.

I mumbled, "I'll do my best."

My students that afternoon probably saw me as yet another feeble-minded professor whose time spent reading about the past had left him incapable of coherent mental processes in the present. Perhaps they weren't far off the mark.

Another trip to the past.

I was both eager and hesitant, excited and anxious.

All too soon, I was on board a transport for Gliese 876, because the past was waiting for me.

VII: TYNDAREUS AND KRIKOR

"Get away, you flea-bitten cur!"

The exclamation, followed by an oath, a rumble of cartwheels, and a yelp cut short shattered my reverie as I ambled along the Street of the Three Bakers in Caesarea-On-The-Sea, making my way between the small, brightly-painted shops that lined both sides, wares displayed on wooden tables by their doors. Malodorous gutters ran down the center of the narrow street, which was barely wide enough for two carts to pass each other. It was a pleasant day eminently suitable for ambling. I looked toward the source of the disturbance.

A cart, heavily laden with marble paving stones destined, no doubt, for some lavish villa or public building, had almost reached the end of the street and was preparing to turn. The driver, a rough-looking tradesman, was glaring back over his shoulder at an inert, furry lump in the road.

"Serves you right!" he shouted. "Try it again and I'll run over you properly next time!"

The wagon rounded the corner and was gone, but now a second was clattering at speed along the street, and its wheels would run right over the limp form that lay sprawled across one of the wagon-ruts worn into the cobblestones.

Nobody else seemed to be paying attention. The locals were probably used to the sight of stray animals being run over. Conflicting emotions raced through me. Injured animals are prone to bite, and I had no desire to experience Roman health care first-hand. But I could almost hear Erica's voice telling me not to be a coward—*she* wouldn't have hesitated. I took a deep breath, dashed out, scooped up the injured dog—it weighed only twenty-five or thirty pounds—and was safely across the street just in the nick of time. The driver of the second wagon regarded me with a mixture of surprise and pity, obviously thinking I must be drunk, a foreigner, or a fool. Who else would risk his own hide for a stray dog?

I laid the dog down outside a pottery-shop and knelt beside it. It wasn't crushed, so maybe it had hit its head as it lunged for the cartwheels. It was already coming to, its eyes open but unfocused. I ran my hands over its legs and chest.

The dog appeared to be a hound of some kind, its fur a mixture of tan and white. Probably one of the many mongrels that scavenged the streets and alleys for a living.

"That's my dog!"

I glanced up to see a man approaching at a lumbering jog. I stood as he neared, but he ignored me, stooped, and picked up the dog in his brawny arms.

"It was injured in the street," I said, feeling miffed by the curtness of his attitude. "I-"

"I seen what you done," he replied shortly. "Poor little Krikor." He stroked the dog's head and it raised its muzzle and flicked its pink tongue toward him.

"I don't think he broke anything," I said.

"He's a tough one."

So, I gathered, was the dog's owner. He was about five feet six, average from the waist down, but impressive from there on up, barrel-chested and broad-shouldered, with biceps that a gladiator or wrestler might have envied. His poor-quality tunic was stained and holed, and his Greek was abominable. His scarred face hadn't experienced the caress of a razor in some time. He smelt of sweat, salt, and pine tar. A sailor, I judged, one of many in Caesarea.

He seemed to have forgotten me, and I turned and began to walk away, struck once again by the unchanging nature of human impoliteness.

"You!" he called, and I faced him again. His face twisted in what he might have intended as a smile, but a grim row of rotten stumps punctuated by the gaps of missing teeth ensured that it wasn't a pleasant sight. "If you ever need help down on the docks, just tell them you're a friend of Tyndareus of Samos. Everyone knows me."

"Thank you," I replied, mollified by his belated offer.

Stroking and talking to his dog, he disappeared into the streams of passersby, and I put the encounter from my mind, never imagining the ramifications to come from this seemingly trivial incident. Blissfully unaware of the surprise in store for me, I continued my researches in this spanking-new city on the coast of Palestine.

It was the year 15 BC, and King Herod had been building Caesarea for some seven years. It was named, of course in honor of the Emperor Augustus, with whom Herod wished to curry favor. He needed to; Augustus was in no doubt about Herod's vile character and propensity for killing off family members as well as rivals—"I would rather be Herod's pig than his son," the emperor had said acidly.

Herod took a decaying town named Strato's Tower and rebuilt it in gleaming marble. He fashioned a large harbor to protect ships from the crashing surf generated by the onshore winds. Opposite the harbor he built an imposing, beautiful temple with immense statues of Caesar and the goddess Roma.

What was it like, this city built by a Jewish king to honor a Roman emperor? How did Greek-speaking pagans mix with Jewish migrant workers and Samaritan tenant farmers? To attempt to understand this, I wandered the city's streets and public buildings, visited the towns and villas sprinkled across the Plain of Sharon, and attended the theater and gymnasium. I studied Herod's palace from a distance, and the Drusion lighthouse and the statues of the imperial family at the harbor entrance from closer perspectives.

I enjoyed the city immensely, and even began to feel some of the anguish of Kourion and stress of my professional life recede. And I thought no more of the incident with Tyndareus until two weeks later when I went to the harbor to look for passage to Italy. It hadn't been my original intention, but the idea of some bright spark in the Maritime Research Institute.

"Why not take a sea voyage to Pisa or Rome?" she suggested. "You could be picked up there just as easily as at Caesarea."

"Why don't you read the book of Acts?" I retorted negatively. "See how St. Paul enjoyed first century seafaring." I had absolutely no desire to experience the Roman equivalent of a Mediterranean cruise.

"Think of what you could learn…" she enthused.

"On a worm-eaten tub with no lifeboats? Forget it."

Not to be put off, she went to my Department Chair who, naturally, since his skin wouldn't be at risk for a soaking, thought it a Brilliant Idea.

"Do it, Robert," said the Chair. "Consider it as a paid cruise courtesy of the department. Probably the only one you'll ever get."

"But—"

"You're a historian, Robert! Go and live some history!"

Grinding my teeth at the Brilliant Idea I surveyed the vessels in Caesarea's bustling harbor with a mixture of trepidation, dismay, and outright fear. Several appeared to be so unseaworthy that the weight of an additional seagull would send them plunging toward the seafloor. The majority of the remainder, I learned by making inquiries, had itineraries that didn't suit my needs. When I finally found one which did, it turned out to be commanded by a singularly odious captain. Despite my misgivings, we had just about reached a deal when a familiar voice startled me.

"You don't want no part of him."

I turned to see Tyndareus standing behind me.

"This is none of your business," the captain snapped. "Be off with you!"

"You're sailing with me," Tyndareus said, clamping a meaty fist around my arm and pivoting me away.

"Now hold on!" the furious captain expostulated.

Tyndareus leaned close to whisper in my ear. "He'll leave you stranded on some gods-forsaken shore, he will, and make off with your money. Done it before, he has."

I waved a hand to serve the dual purpose of bidding goodbye to the captain and dispelling Tyndareus's rank breath.

The captain launched into a torrent of profanity.

"Where are you bound for?" Tyndareus asked, as we made our way along the crowded quay.

"Italia. Pisae, if possible."

"The captain'll be pleased to have a proper gentleman like you on board for a change, not like some of the riff-raff we 'ave to carry."

"You're really too kind—" I began to protest, but Tyndareus shrugged my comment away.

"Nonsense. You want a safe passage, I have a good ship. Fair bargain. Here she is. The *Happy Dancer*."

It might turn out to be a fair bargain, but I wondered if perhaps Tyndareus got a few extra sestercii from his captain for locating suitable passengers.

Tied up at a wharf was a fairly typical medium-sized single-masted cargo ship. She was deep-bellied, about fifty feet long, and appeared reasonably shipshape. A sizeable deckhouse graced the upper deck, and her sail was neatly furled.

The *Happy Dancer* made a good first impression, and, given that the Romans built the largest sea-going ships until the Spanish galleons of the 17th century, perhaps this voyage wouldn't be so bad.

Not that I was expecting my first voyage on a Roman ship to be especially comfortable. Comfort, in the Roman world, was for the wealthy—not for sailors or middle-class passengers on smaller cargo ships. I felt quite like St. Paul making his last voyage to Rome—an event still well in the future—and prayed that my journey, unlike his, would be uneventful.

Several sailors were slinging sacks of grain up from the wharf to other men who carried them down the stairwell situated in front of the mast. Stacks of amphorae on the dock presumably contained wine, fruits, nuts, and olives.

Abruptly, Tyndareus broke away from me.

"Not like that, you idiot!" he bawled at a sailor carrying a burden that tinkled like glass. "You trying to break them? It'll come out of your pay, it will. Carry it like this." He crossed the dock to the offending sailor.

"Can I help you?" a new voice said.

A middle-aged man approached me from behind a pile of bales of cloth. He was lean, weather-beaten, with deeply sunken eyes. His tunic, while hardly a fashion statement, was of better quality than Tyndareus' worn affair.

"I'm looking for the captain of this ship," I said.

"I am he." The man's eyes narrowed. "I've paid my taxes, if that's what you're after."

I shook my head. "I need passage to Pisae," and when he still seemed suspicious added, "Tyndareus told me you could help."

"You're a friend of his, then," he replied, relaxing.

"So to speak."

He motioned. "Come on board, and we'll discuss it over a cup of wine."

Our negotiations in his small cabin in the deckhouse were amicable and enhanced by a very pleasant Syrian vintage, and we soon settled on a price for a berth in the deckhouse. I had no desire to spend the trip under canvas on the main deck or sleeping on top of the cargo in the hold.

"Has Tyndareus been with you long?" I wondered.

"Twelve years. Never seen a man with a better eye for a piece of rope or a sail." He laughed. "Him and that dog of his."

We parted on friendly terms, and I made my way back onto shore. I couldn't see Tyndareus, but I heard his voice raised once again in disapproval. The captain certainly seemed to have a strong right arm in the rugged sailor.

The ship was due to sail in three days, which passed quickly as I tidied up my affairs in Caesarea. I presented myself at the *Happy Dancer* at the appointed time, carrying only a few possessions, and a sailor showed me to the small square of space that was to be my home for the next several weeks. I noticed that a clay cup of wine had been placed there. I smiled, picked it up and sipped. Poor stuff—the kind of wine a sailor would drink—but I appreciated the thought.

I went back on deck and watched as sailors readied the ship for departure. I spotted Tyndareus at the bow, and he greeted me with a curt wave. Perhaps fifty or sixty other passengers were aboard—a small number, considering that St. Paul's ship had carried well over two hundred. Perhaps it was off-season.

Unlike the saint, I wasn't accompanied by a centurion to guard me, but I noticed a couple of men with military bearing—probably retired legionaries making their way home. The majority of the paying passengers were lower-class individuals—since those of senatorial or equestrian rank wouldn't be caught dead on a ship like the *Happy Dancer*—tradespeople, merchants, trusted slaves on their master's business, and the like.

35

The only other passengers in the deckhouse were a sickly youth from Corinth returning to Rome after tending to his father's business affairs, who made it quite clear that he wasn't interested in talking to me, and an elderly matron accompanied by her retinue who entered her quarters and never reemerged.

A favorable wind filled the sail, and Herod's dream city faded into the sea haze, a mirage of shimmering marble slowly subsiding beneath the azure waves. Soon the *Happy Dancer* was rolling with the ocean swell. Thankfully, I have never suffered from seasickness, and I enjoyed the lift and fall of the hull; other passengers weren't so fortunate, and soon the rail was crowded with a motley collection of unhappy humanity losing their stomach contents. Seabirds followed us for miles out to sea, scavenging in our wake. The sun shone down from a cloudless sky, ropes and rigging creaked, the helmsman stood at his post, and the captain kept a vigilant eye on everything.

"A pleasant day to sail," I commented to him.

"Hopefully it will remain that way," he replied.

"Are you expecting bad weather?"

He shook his head. "No. But Neptune's a fickle god."

I heard a yapping from the hatch, and a moment later Krikor, looking much better than when I'd last seen him, emerged with the limp form of a dead rat hanging from his jaws. He ran and presented it to Tyndareus. The sailor threw the rat overboard and praised the dog.

"Don't like dogs myself," the captain said, "but we'd be overrun with rats if it weren't for him."

I knew I'd sleep better knowing that Krikor was on duty.

Our first port of call was Cyprus. It was a strange experience seeing the island some four hundred years before the earthquake leveled Kourion. The memory of Philippa was still fresh in my mind and sore in my heart.

We made landfall not at doomed Kourion but at Paphos, where, in some hundred years, the Roman proconsul, Sergius Paulus, would become one of St. Paul's converts. I spent a pleasant couple of days wandering the city's narrow streets, which frequently led to unexpected vistas over the sea. I made certain to refresh myself at the public baths, not knowing when the opportunity for cleanliness would come again.

All too soon it was time for the *Happy Dancer* to depart. We hugged the coast of Asia Minor to Lycia, then skirted Greece and made for Messana, on Sicily. The sight of the Greek islands dotting the sea would have stirred me to poetry had I been so gifted. We frequently saw other ships in the distance; the Romans regarded the Mediterranean as their own private lake. I feared that one of those sails might belong to a pirate vessel, but thankfully those fears didn't materialize.

My harsh feelings toward the Department Chair began to soften as I realized that, despite some negative aspects, I was actually coming to enjoy this primitive sea voyage.

The *Happy Dancer*, though, was an indifferent sailor, her pleasant roll giving way to a sickening lurching motion in high seas. Like most Roman ships, she performed best with a following wind; adverse winds forced her to tack inefficiently back and forth, and sometimes it was easier to go wherever the billows carried her. She lacked amenities. The latrine was located on a gallery open to public view above the stern. There was no entertainment, and the company was marginal.

On the positive side, there were no smelly animals being transported. The food was adequate, bread and cheese washed down with cheap wine. The ship's galley (larger than the ones on Columbus's ships) produced hot meals that warmed the insides on a cool evening.

The captain was pleasant but uncultured, and knew little beyond the mechanics of seafaring. Barely literate, he'd read nothing of Roman literature, philosophy, poetry, or science. He had opinions about Julius Caesar and Augustus, but a few conversations quickly eliminated his fund of knowledge. That left me listening to his absorbing tales of seafaring around the Mediterranean. Perhaps someday I shall compile my recollections of those conversations into a book—*Tales of the Roman Seas* by Quadratus Porcius, as told to yours truly.

The sailors, a polyglot crew, provided company only for themselves, telling crude jokes and off-color stories, or singing ballads, none of which fit into my fields of research. Jokes just don't travel well across eras. A collection of Roman jokes would fall flat in modern times.

Tyndareus had even less to say than the captain. He was a walking cliché—a gruff, taciturn man whose only love was his dog. I wouldn't have dared invent him for a work of fiction. I learned only that he'd been born on the isle of Samos to a poor family, the only child of five to reach adulthood. His father died when he was fourteen and his mother soon after. He'd gone to sea and spent all his life on ships.

He'd found Krikor as a stray in Massila. The dog had been mooching for scraps outside a tavern. Tyndareus had obliged him with a hunk of gristle, and the dog had followed him back to the docks and right onto the ship, and stayed there ever since. The two had become inseparable, except on occasions when they ventured ashore and became separated in city traffic as had happened in Caesarea. Usually, Krikor made his way back to the ship without difficulty.

Once I'd exhausted the conversational skills of my traveling companions I spent the days lounging on deck, reading a few scrolls I'd brought along, writing up notes, and dozing. Though I wouldn't take them back with me, I found that writing notes helped me organize my memories, concentrate on the important details, and eliminate the superfluous. My notes were couched in language that would raise no suspicion of my occupation in the unlikely event that they ever fell into the hands of a literate person. If pressed, I could claim that I was writing a natural history in the vein of Herodotus, Strabo, or Pytheas.

Occasionally the captain invited me to play a board game with him, and I learned the rules of many games which have been lost over the centuries. Perhaps I shall write them up, too.

At night I'd hear the scurrying and gnawing of rats, and the excited barking of Krikor when he caught one. His name meant "vigilant," and he lived up to it. But no matter how many rats he caught, there were always more. I suspect a fresh troop came on board at each port. He, at least, lacked nothing for pleasure.

One day, the wind began to freshen from the northeast, which sped us on our way. But through the day the sky darkened, the wind shifted further toward the north, and before long we were running due south before a gale. The waves rose until they were surging across the stern. There was no way to hold our course; we were at the wind's mercy.

I began to feel more like St. Paul, although I didn't share his faith in a successful outcome.

The *Happy Dancer* was anything but happy in the seas that frothed and surged on every side. She wallowed like a three-legged pig in a muddy sty. And she leaked.

The sickly youth retched incessantly on his side of the thin partition that separated us. The only time I couldn't hear him was when the howl of the wind or the lashing of the rain drowned him out. The wretchedly miserable deck passengers fled below to share the already cramped space in the hold. Soon the lower deck reeked of vomit.

Krikor curled up out of the way and stayed there.

Even the sailors began to worry. I saw the anxious glances that passed between them. They worked furiously, bailing, plugging leaks, lashing down anything moveable.

"The *Dancer's* weathered heavier storms than this," Tyndareus said once, shouting to make himself heard. I had ventured on deck for some fresh air and to escape the horrible noises of the retching youth. The sky was black in all directions, and squalls pelted the ship with raindrops that hit with the force of slingshot projectiles.

Tyndareus gripped one of the mast stays with a strong fist. With his hair streaming back and rain dripping down his face he seemed to be enjoying himself, as if there were no greater delight to be had in life than defying nature.

"The sailors seem anxious," I shouted back.

"They're a lot of cowards! We'll make land all right, you'll see!"

I only hoped that we didn't run into it.

Soon, the wind-driven artillery fire of rain drove me inside again. Eventually, though, the wind shifted, lost some of its fury, and the helmsman was able to steer us in a westerly direction. Finally, the storm began to abate, and on the third day, the clouds broke. The dull purple of land was visible far off the port side.

"Do you know where we are?" I asked.

The captain peered into the distance. "That's Africa, I expect. We're probably not far from Carthage. We'll put in there."

How he could possibly have guessed our position was beyond me. But he was right. It wasn't long before a keen-eyed sailor spotted Carthage.

I was glad to set foot in that fabled city while the *Happy Dancer* underwent repairs to her hull and her tattered rigging. Some of the passengers deserted the ship, preferring not to travel on.

Carthage (under the patronage of Juno) and Rome (favored by Jupiter) had been rivals for centuries and fought three bitter wars before Rome put an end to Carthage's dreams of empire. The legions had done their work well, and I spent my time trying to visualize what the city had looked like before Roman troops ploughed it into the dust.

They'd razed ancient Carthage so well that I might have walked unknowingly over the entrance to a tophet, an underground shrine where priests of Astarte sacrificed noble children in times of dire distress. The unfortunate little ones met their fate in front of a statue of the goddess and then were burned in a brazier and their pitiful remains placed in an urn. But though I looked, and though I felt the occasional cold shiver, I saw nothing to indicate the site of a tophet's entrance. They would have to remain hidden, awaiting discovery by the archaeologist's spade.

Still, thinking about these gruesome reminders dampened my enthusiasm for Carthage, and made me as eager to leave as I had been to arrive. Fortunately, the *Happy Dancer's* cargo had remained largely intact, with only the loss of several amphorae and some glassware. The captain had grumbled, but said it could have been worse.

I remained on board the day prior to departure. I noticed several disreputable men board and speak to both Tyndareus and the captain. I didn't ask their business, but suspected that both men were engaged in some illicit trade that wouldn't come to the attention of Augustus' tax collectors. Tyndareus saw me watching and gave a covert wink, and I pretended I had witnessed nothing.

We departed in the morning, and it wasn't long before the *Happy Dancer* was drifting northwards beneath sunny skies. We coasted past Corsica and made landfall at the port of Ostia, where the sickly young man, looking more ill than ever, bolted for shore as quickly as possible, glad, no doubt, to be free of the ship and its low-class riffraff. The elderly matron and her retinue departed as well.

From there it was a short sail up the Italian coast to Pisae. We arrived in late afternoon, maneuvering up the inland waterways while shafts of golden sunbeams streaked from behind a dark mass of cloud that blotted out the western horizon.

"Another storm coming," I commented.

Tyndareus nodded. "Early, this year."

"Going to be a bad season?"

"I expect so."

Krikor romped about the deck, unconcerned by the weather. The captain anchored us in the waterway close offshore, since other ships were tied up along the wharfs and there wasn't room for the *Happy Dancer*.

But we were safely in port now, I thought, as the sun succumbed to the clouds. An inky darkness enveloped the lowlands upon which the city sat and the mountains and hills which contained it in a valley. I studied the twinkling lights that sprang up in the city.

Pisae had already been a port for some 800 years; its backwater and pier had been built by the Etruscans, and enlarged by Rome as a naval base. Now it was growing rapidly as new roads connecting Pisae to Rome increased the port's desirability as a trading port.

"Where are you staying?" Tyndareus asked, joining me at the rail as I watched the last of a series of harbor boats ferry the passengers ashore. The sailors and captain prepared to follow them in the *Happy Dancer*'s boat. It was inconvenient and risky to unload in the dark. Tonight, the men would undoubtedly enjoy the low pleasures of Pisae; tomorrow, when a berth at the quays opened up, they'd unload the ship.

I shrugged. "At an inn or a tavern."

He sniffed the air. I too could detect the scent of rain, and the breeze was picking up.

"You don't want to look for lodging at night in a strange city when there's a storm coming in," he said. "Stay on the ship with me and Krikor."

"You're not going ashore?" I asked.

"There's nothing but expensive women waiting to relieve a man of his pay," he snorted. "Besides, someone has to stay on board to watch the ship."

"Harbor pirates?"

He nodded. "An unwatched ship is fair game."

It was a sensible suggestion. I could endure one more night on the *Happy Dancer*. I signaled to the captain that I would stay, and watched the boat carrying the crew pull away.

Tyndareus and I went below, and the sailor lit an oil lamp. He poured out two cups of wine, and we sat down to play a game of Lentuli. Krikor seemed restless, prowling, pacing, and whining, until Tyndareus told him sharply to be quiet, at which he curled up disconsolately by our feet.

"Don't know what's gotten into him," Tyndareus said. "Storms don't normally bother him. Seen it all, he has, same as me."

"Maybe he's caught all the rats," I replied.

Soon, we heard the patter of rain on the deck and the wind gusting through the rigging. The ship creaked and tugged at her anchor.

"Going to be a wild night," Tyndareus commented, as the rain increased to a constant hammering on the deck.

"At least we don't have to worry about being blown to Carthage."

The tugging against the anchor became more violent, and the *Happy Dancer* seemed to groan in all her timbers.

"It'll hold," Tyndareus said calmly, answering my unspoken question.

As the storm intensified, I began to wish I'd gone ashore.

The rain and wind crescendoed to a wailing, screaming climax as if the gates of Tartarus had been opened, and then abruptly faded, to be replaced by an eerie silence that enveloped us like a shroud and that frightened me more than the storm's fury.

Krikor whined, breaking the awful stillness.

And then the *Happy Dancer* rolled. It must have been a tidal wave, my mind suggested in a shocked moment, boring up the waterway from some event far out at sea, spawned by a distant earthquake or by the storm that had been buffeting us. Or perhaps a freak flood rushing down from the hills.

Our game board clattered to the deck and the pieces rolled away. My gaze locked with that of Tyndareus as the *Happy Dancer* rolled further and further over until it seemed impossible that she could remain upright. Amphorae in the hold began to fall and crash.

We sprang to our feet and scrambled up the stairway just as the *Happy Dancer* completed her roll. Had we remained below, we would have been crushed by the shifting cargo. As it was, we emerged into a nightmare of raging water, thrashing ropes, and falling wood. The mast snapped with a crack of tortured fir. The lull in the storm had been a fluke; it had returned with a vengeance.

The ship's unstoppable roll catapulted us into the seething water. I went deep and came up coughing and gagging. I gasped and swallowed a mouthful of harbor water as a heavy piece of wood or other debris smacked into my ribs. I floundered to keep my head above the surface.

Something gripped my leg and began to pull me under. I reached down to find that a rope had wrapped itself around my ankle. I fumbled to free myself, but the rope only tightened as whatever its other end was attached to sank deeper into the harbor.

"Help!" I cried into the nightmare. "Help me!"

A figure emerged from the darkness. It was Tyndareus.

"My leg is caught!" I gasped.

He shoved a furry body toward me, and I gripped Krikor's collar with one hand, using the other arm and my one free leg to keep myself above water. The sailor pulled a knife from his belt and dived under. I felt his grip on my trapped leg, and then the pressure released, and my leg was free. Tyndareus surfaced again.

"Can you swim?" he asked.

"Yes."

He took Krikor back from me, tucked the little dog under one arm, and we began to stroke toward the twinkles of the city, intermittently glimpsed above the turbulent waves.

Unlike most Roman sailors, Tyndareus was a good swimmer, and he began to pull away from me. I had been a decent swimmer in my youth, but hadn't maintained the skill.

There must have been a second tidal wave or a surge from the first reflecting off the piers and breakwaters, because without warning the sea heaved like a giant beast and all became a maelstrom of air, water, and debris. I tumbled over and over, not knowing up from down. I surfaced just long enough to catch a breath before another wall of water and debris toppled over me.

Something struck my head with immense force; pain skewered me from ear to ear, and then I knew no more.

I awoke to a throbbing headache and sense of overall discomfort. My entire body ached.

I was lying in mud, but underneath the slimy veneer, I felt the cold of stone.

I pulled myself to my knees and looked around. The dense mass of clouds had vanished, and the sky was the dull gray of dusk. A few desultory raindrops still splattered to earth, but the worst of the storm appeared to have passed by. I was above the waterline, surrounded by a welter of debris—fragments of wood, a crushed wicker basket, strands of seaweed. To this day, I don't know whether the waves deposited me there, or whether some unknown benefactor pulled me from the harbor.

Carefully, I gained my feet. My sodden, filthy tunic clung to me like a wet blanket.

I wasn't far from the docks…although they were a shambles of damaged ships and drunkenly leaning masts. Willing my heavy legs to move, I trudged over to where a crowd had gathered.

A man spotted me, did a double-take, and ran over. It was the *Happy Dancer's* captain. His eyes were wide with panic.

"What happened?" he blurted, grabbing hold of my tunic.

"I hoped you could tell me," I replied, wrestling his hands free.

"Where's my ship?"

I gazed over the harbor. Several vessels had survived the tidal wave and were afloat; others had been driven up on the pier or the docks; and of others, all that remained were half-submerged hulls and drifting planks. Of the *Happy Dancer* there was no sign.

"Gone," I said dully.

"Gone?!" he shrieked. "Do you mean stolen? Pirates?"

"Not pirates, the storm—"

He didn't seem to hear me. "It couldn't have been Tyndareus! I can't believe it! The one man I would have trusted above all others with my ship…"

"Sunk," I said heavily, wondering if the man's mind had snapped.

The captain clutched his head and dropped to his knees, cursing the gods. The ship and the business it represented were probably all he owned—assuming that he owned the ship and didn't captain for a wealthy trader who'd be angered at the loss of the vessel.

Tyndareus. I studied the crowd, hoping to catch a glimpse of the gruff sailor and his little dog. When I didn't see them, I wandered along the frontage, from one end to the other, calling and looking, but in vain. Man and dog seemed to have vanished from the earth.

I berated myself—if I hadn't stayed on board, if I had gotten off the ship sooner and not been snagged by the rope—if Tyndareus hadn't taken those few precious moments to free me, perhaps he himself might have lived.

I recalled—precious little good it did now—reading about the skeleton of a man and dog discovered in the long-lost harbor of Pisa when excavation for a railroad building began in the 20th century…but I hoped and prayed it wasn't Tyndareus and Krikor that had been found. Had I—by my presence in this era—been the cause of their deaths? Had this been one of the times when I had truly affected the past? If only I had remembered sooner! If we had only known the exact day—even the year—that the ship found in Pisa had sunk…!

But that is how history comes down to us. Some historical events can be precisely dated while others are known only approximately. And so, due to the limitations of our knowledge of the past, the time-traveling historian can be taken by surprise by events that he knows *did* occur, but not precisely *when*.

I spent days loitering around the docks, asking everyone I met if they'd seen Tyndareus and Krikor, but in vain. At any moment I expected to hear Tyndareus' gruff voice or Krikor's yapping. But it didn't happen, and I was forced to the unhappy conclusion that man and dog had been borne to the harbor bed, there to lie with the wreck of the *Happy Dancer*.

He'd saved my life, but I was unable to thank him.

"Go with God," I murmured as I surveyed the harbor one final time. "Sail well, friend Tyndareus. And you also, Krikor."

I thought from somewhere I heard a faint, answering bark, but, of course, it was only in my mind.

VIII

We were a traditional family on a tradition-oriented world. Heliopolis had been settled by a variety of like-minded religious groups who revered the values and customs that had served humanity for millennia. Not for Heliopolans the innovations that characterized New Dawn, RavensEdge, or even Earth itself. Heliopolis was, in some ways, a world socially frozen in time.

My father taught, my mother played viola in the City's Orchestra of the Classic Age, and I…I simply grew up not knowing there were other—quite different—lifestyles.

I was unprepared for change.

"Robert," said my father, taking me by the shoulder one day as we stood on the Rutharian Highland looking over Heliopolis' violet-tinted Maruska Sea, "we're moving to Earth."

I was about ten years old at the time; I had never been off-world. My father delivered lectures on worlds in the local hyperspacial network, but I had never accompanied him, always remaining behind in my mother's care. Not knowing what I was missing, I had no desire to go off-world.

My father had been distracted all morning, not even giving me his usual discourses as we walked—discourses that began with the natural wonders around us and inevitably metamorphosed into discussions of literature.

"But…but why?" I blurted.

He sighed, staring at a row of blooming Macklin trees silhouetted against the flaming red and gold clouds that floated over the sea. I am not a synesthete, but the perfume from the trees seemed an olfactory equivalent of the clouds' colors.

"I have been offered a position at CamOx University," he said at last.

"Why you? Why not somebody else?"

He gave me one of his quirky, asymmetrical smiles. "I guess they decided I'd be a good fit for their literature department."

"But Heliopolis is home!" I exclaimed.

"I know, son," he said. "I like Heliopolis, too. Your mother and I have

45

talked about this in great detail. We think it would be best for our family."

I choked back a lump in my throat, thinking I would never stand here again, never swim in the sea with my friends, never go exploring with my dog, Watchit. I looked down at her black head, as she lay beside my feet, ears erect, scanning for a torkel—a native rodent, rather like a rabbit—to chase.

Dad saw the direction of my gaze. "Watchit can come with us," he said. "I made sure of that. There will new places for the two of you to explore. And you'll make new friends."

"I like the ones I have here!"

"The universe is a big place, son. Heliopolis is only one small part of it. It will be good for you to see other parts—especially Earth. Believe me, it will be fun. Your mom and I can take you to all the places we knew when we were your age."

"Stonehenge?" I queried timidly.

His smile expanded into a grin. "Sure! And your grandpa can take you to castles…"

"Grandpa?" I perked up. My parents had moved to Heliopolis shortly after my birth. I had only met my grandparents two or three times when they had made the long trip to come and visit us. My grandparents had lived through the waning years of the generations-long war with the alien Gara'nesh Suzerainty—a time when the risks of interstellar travel were much higher. There was no predicting when the Gara'nesh might discover one of our hyperspacial routes and attack a colony world or a transiting ship. My grandparents had survived one such ambush, but had been left with a permanent dislike of interstellar travel. Since then, newer, shorter routes had been discovered linking Earth with Heliopolis, but my grandparents were disinclined to venture offworld.

My friends—whose families had lived on Heliopolis for generations—got to see their grandparents all the time, while I never did. I missed the sense of family.

"OK, Dad," I said.

"Good." He patted my arm. "Look! There's a giant sea-lizard just below the horizon!"

"I see it! Do they have those on Earth?"

"No, but they have whales that are almost as big."

"Maybe I'll like Earth after all."

"I'm certain you will."

"Just a tiny, little bit…"

IX

But it wasn't Stonehenge that gripped and held my youthful imagination, although those massive stones situated in the starkness of Salisbury Plain have a unique, enduring air of mystery and romance. Instead, it was Rome—grand, bloody, sophisticated, decadent, powerful, Imperial Rome that seized my fancy and wouldn't let go.

And it was Watchit's fault.

England was like a giant, country-sized museum, lovingly preserved after the culturally-provoked Disturbances of 2099 had resulted in a drastic reduction of the population. This reduction had progressed in the years of the Expansion, when humanity fled for the stars after the discovery of Roessler hyperspace opened the way for the colonization of countless new worlds. The populations of those worlds blossomed, while Earth's stagnated. Now, centuries later, the population hovered around an optimal level.

I loved England. But I didn't fit in. I was the Colony Kid, with a funny accent and different manners. We practiced our faith, which put us in another minority category. My memory meant that I hardly had to study—and so I appeared to be smarter than my contemporaries, who either underachieved or who endured tedious and time-consuming memory enhancement procedures. I was despised and envied simultaneously. It was a recipe for disaster. Friends were few and far between; nobody wanted to be associated with a shy, misfit Colony Kid who could reel off facts better than everyone else. They made their displeasure obvious and painful.

Many times I sat in the dark silence of a church and cried under the image of a tormented Man who had also known rejection.

I would stare up into the night sky and wish I was back on Heliopolis where I fit in and where life made sense. Had He felt that way, I wondered?

My escape from the torment of rejection was to go exploring with my one true friend—Watchit. Much of the countryside had been either preserved or reclaimed. We were puttering about in a field one day—technically off-limits because it had once been the site of a Roman villa, although there was nothing now to be seen. It was simply a typical field, bordered by thick hedgerows and guarded by a row of trees standing like soldiers at attention.

Watchit spotted a rabbit and in no time was scrabbling at the entrance to its burrow, clumps of dirt flying into the air. I hurried over, and from the newly excavated debris picked up a curiously shaped rock. Except it wasn't just a rock. I brushed off the dirt to reveal a statue, about four inches tall, of an armed man wearing a breastplate.

Clutching it to my chest I hurried home, cleaned it off with a soft brush, and showed it to my father when he returned. He hemmed and hawed, and finally took it—and me—to an eminent archaeologist.

"You found it where?" he asked, frowning.

I told him.

His frown deepened. "Hard to imagine that such an object could have been overlooked during excavations." He turned it over in his hands. "But still, artifacts do turn up every now and then. Rarer and rarer, though."

"Who do you suppose it is?" I asked.

"Hard to say. Could be one of the emperors. But I wouldn't venture to guess which one, because the face is almost worn away."

"Can I keep it?" I wondered.

"Certainly not!" he snapped. "Consider yourself lucky that I don't turn you in for trespassing."

"The boy meant no harm," my father interjected.

"Humph." The eminent archaeologist set the statue down on his desk. "This will go to a museum after it has been studied and its historical value ascertained." He must have seen the disappointment on my face. "But I'll see you receive a reproduction of it," he said, his attitude mellowing.

With that I had to be content. But afterwards I spent many hours studying Roman remains in museums—because, having handled an original artifact, simply reading about them or viewing pictures wasn't enough. I wanted to see the real things, to be in the presence of genuine items from the past.

Of such incidents is a career born.

I found acceptance in the world of ancient Rome. For all their failings— and there were many—the Romans weren't racist. They didn't mind the color of your skin, what province or island you came from, what language you spoke, even what religion you followed (as long as you weren't Christian before the reign of Constantine the Great). If you were a citizen, you were a citizen. Period.

I imagined myself as one of them, where I was accepted for who I was, not alienated for who I wasn't. In my mental world I was a Roman… cultured, educated, advanced, literate. My contemporaries were uneducated, uncouth barbarians from little-known lands on the dark fringes of the world. Galley-slaves in the making.

Such were my fantasies.

I doubt that it would have been recommended as a standard coping measure. But it worked for me.

And so, thanks to Watchit, I survived.

X

"First century Judea?" I gasped, staring at the Chair in horror. "You want me to take an assignment in Judea in AD 74? You must be joking!"

"Do I look like I'm convulsed in mirth?" he replied dourly. "It's a perfectly reasonable request."

My fingers dug into the armrests of the chair. "Don't you know there's a war going on then? Lots of people being killed."

"Of *course* I know there's a war going on," he retorted. "That's what makes it worthy of study. Many interesting questions to be answered."

"Interesting to whom?" I demanded.

The Chair gestured. "The proposal comes from the head of the Judaic Studies Department. He's a personal friend of mine, and he'd like to know the true story of what happened on Masada."

"Advise him to read Josephus. *Wars of the Jews*."

The Chair sighed. "Do I have to remind you that Josephus is not a fully reliable historian?"

"Then let your friend go back and see for himself."

"Look, Robert, you're—"

"Expendable," I interjected.

"Experienced," the Chair finished smugly.

"One of these days my luck will run out," I said. "My demise will be on your head."

He seemed unperturbed. "Would you rather I sent somebody with no field experience?" He studied his fingernails with what I thought was unnecessary attention to detail. "That's the option."

"What if I say no?"

His gaze flicked up. "It wouldn't exactly help your career prospects. You have a ways to go up the ladder, Robert. A ways to go."

I clenched my teeth. "All right. Judea it is. But I am not going within a light year of Masada. I want that to be clear. I'll find out some other way, but I am not setting foot within sight of that place."

I took his silence for assent.

"When do you want me to leave?" I asked.

"Not for a month." He smiled. "Plenty of time to prepare."

"So should I go as a Roman and have the Jews hate me, or as a Jew and have the Romans be trying to kill me?"

"Your call," he said, ignoring my sarcasm. "But if I were you—which I'm not—I'd try to pose as somebody neutral, inoffensive to either side."

I could see I wasn't going to win any arguments today. Neither was I going to have the last word.

"Work on your tan while you're there, Robert," the Chair added. "You've been looking rather pale lately."

XI: MOONRISE OVER METZADA

From the cracked-open door of my rented house in Hebron, I watched the small family round a corner and run down the dusty road. The man, his face twisted by mingled desperation and determination, carried a drawn sword. The woman, her features proclaiming only despair, struggled to keep up, her progress slowed by a screaming infant clasped in her arms.

They were, of course, Jewish, wearing the nondescript robes common to this part of the world, his a dull brown, hers a pale blue.

The man glanced back over his shoulder as if expecting to find pursuers hot on his heels. They probably were. All morning long, Roman legionaries had been going from house to house hunting Zealots and killing them on the spot.

It was better than being crucified, but still, it wasn't a good day to be a rebel.

The man grabbed the woman's arm to hurry her along. From her gasping breaths and staggering steps, I judged that she was nearly exhausted.

As they came close, I yielded to an impulse, flung the door open wide, and beckoned them in.

Soldiers shouted not far away.

The man didn't hesitate; he raced through the doorway, nearly yanking the woman off her feet. I slammed the door shut, locked it, and turned to face them.

The man was about twenty, bearded, with fierce dark eyes beneath bushy eyebrows and a handsome face scarred by pockmarks. The woman, as far as I could tell from her hooded features, couldn't have been over sixteen.

He spoke to me in Aramaic. Although I understood him, I wasn't supposed to be able to speak Aramaic on this project, and so I shook my head. He leveled his sword at me. I suddenly wondered if my impulsive action had been stupid as well. What if this man was not only a Zealot but one of the Sicarii?

I shuddered. The Sicarii were assassins, named for the sica, a small concealed dagger they carried. But the Sicarii typically operated mostly in Jerusalem, where they specialized in removing fellow Jews who collaborated with the Roman occupiers, such as the former high priest Yonatan Ben-Hanan. A quick flash of a dagger in a crowd; a body slumping to the ground; the assassin melting away into the throngs before anyone knew that a murder had been committed. That was how they worked. The Sicarii weren't brave enough to confront the Romans face to face.

But I was only one man, and unarmed.

"You're not a Jew," he said, this time in passable Greek.

"I'm a Briton," I replied in the same language. I motioned toward the rear of the house. "I have horses."

He stabbed the sword into his scabbard. Supporting the woman with his arm, he followed me into the courtyard. I threw a blanket onto the back of the nearest of the several horses I had stabled.

"Take it and ride," I said, pointing to where the courtyard opened onto a small alley. "Quickly!"

Legionaries clattered in the street outside my house. Somebody pounded on the door.

The man nodded and hoisted his wife and child onto the horse. He made as if to get up himself.

I halted him. "Hit me," I said.

He hesitated, then comprehension gleamed in his eyes. "Thank you," he said, "Gentile though you are. May the blessing of God rest upon this household."

Then his fist caught me on the side of the chin.

The next thing I knew, I was being hauled to my feet, spitting dust and blood out of my mouth. I tongued my teeth to ascertain if any were loose.

"Where did he go?"

A trio of Roman legionaries with drawn swords surrounded me. The one who had spoken was a grizzled, leather-tough centurion—not the sort of man to trifle with. I shook my head, and for a moment saw two of him. I fingered the tender lump on my jaw.

"The scoundrel stole a horse—"

"You're one of them!" he accused, looking as if he were ready to skewer me where I stood.

"I'm no Zealot," I replied. "Nor a Jew. Do I look like one of them?"

The centurion stared at me for a moment, his disbelief evident, and I realized the error in my choice of words. Despite an ancestry that is firmly Anglo-Saxon, my mother-in-law always insisted that I was Jewish and had been switched at birth. Until now, it had always seemed funny.

"Do I *sound* like one of them?" I said.

"Tell it to the general," he snarled, clamping a meaty hand onto my shoulder and nearly hurling me toward the house. He hustled me along, out the splintered door that had been broken open and into the street where a troop of cavalrymen surrounded a mounted officer.

"The village is secure, General," the centurion said. "But Ben-Joseph escaped." He pushed me forward. "Tell him."

The man, wearing a general's engraved breastplate and scarlet cloak, stared impassively down at me, face bearing that look of arrogant superiority common to upper class Romans. I repeated my story, and showed him my split lip and bruised jaw.

"Say something in the Briton tongue," he ordered.

I complied, telling him that I was from Ratae—modern Leicester—and had left Britannia after Boudicca's rebellion to seek my living trading horses.

He nodded, although whether he understood all I said, I couldn't tell.

"Let him go," the general—it could only be Flavius Silva—said to the centurion. "You have horses?" he said to me.

"Several, sir."

Silva motioned to the centurion. "Take them."

"General!" I protested. "I am a free man."

"Pay him," Silva instructed the centurion curtly. He wheeled his horse away.

"General!" I called again.

"What is it?" he snapped impatiently.

"Your horse has a swelling on the elbow, sir. If you continue to ride, he'll become lame."

Silva frowned, then with a lithe movement swung himself to the ground. On foot, he was shorter than I and his appearance of power and superiority lessened. He had a slight drooping of the left side of his face, and I wondered if he'd been injured or suffered from a neurological problem.

"Feel for yourself, sir," I said, moving over and palpating the horse's right front elbow. Erica had loved horses—I thought wistfully of the times we had gone riding together over the South Downs—and I was glad she had pointed out some tricks of the trade to me.

Silva imitated my action. "That idiot veterinarius!" he said, straightening. "He assured me just this morning that the horse was fine! I've a good mind to have him flogged."

"If you like, I will take care of him for you," I offered. "The horse, I mean. I have some experience in such matters."

"What is your name?" Silva demanded.

"Claudius Britannicus, sir."

A cavalryman led a file of horses out from my stable. One of them had been fitted with a bridle and reins. Silva vaulted onto its back. "Bring my horse to me when it is recovered," he said, "and I shall see that you are rewarded for your efforts."

Then, followed by the cavalrymen, and with the legionaries trudging behind, he rode away. The centurion leered, threw a camp pass and a handful of small coins into the dirt at my feet—nowhere near what the horses were worth—and strode off.

I was now a horse-trader with no horses and only a few bronze coins. It was a good thing I wasn't really in business in first-century Judea.

Well. Instead of being comfortably off, I was now as poor as almost everyone around me. Still, poverty wouldn't interfere with my task of better understanding the Roman-Jewish tensions of this period.

I had established one prime rule for my missions, and made sure the Chair knew it was inviolable: I would never return to the Roman Empire as a slave. Contrary to myth, slavery wasn't universally dreadful; a trusted household slave enjoyed a considerably better life than a poor free person; indeed, I'd met people who had voluntarily entered slavery to improve their lots. But a slave's life lay in his owner's hands—not a desirable situation for a researcher.

The lavish lifestyles of wealthy, upper-class Romans—among whom, admittedly, I had a certain hankering to be numbered at least once, if I came up with a project that required that level of societal access—rested upon the backs of the slaves and the subject peoples. Among these were the Jews.

After groaning under the Roman heel for over a century, ruled by puppet kings and a succession of Roman governors, simmering tensions finally flared into outright rebellion. Despite the efforts of Pharisees and Sadducees to accommodate the Roman rulers, the Zealots forced the conflict.

I always admired peoples who resisted the Roman juggernaut, even though they invariably lost. Rome was simply too strong. How the Jews thought they could win—short of a miracle of divine intervention—was beyond me. The Jewish Rebellion became a Jewish disaster. Disciplined Roman legions under the able command of Vespasian wiped out determined but untrained Zealot bands. Then Vespasian departed to assume the throne of Rome and his son Titus battered the city of Jerusalem to the ground, leveled Herod's great Temple, and slaughtered a million Jews.

Now, eight years from the start of the rebellion, Vespasian was comfortably wearing the imperial purple, Titus relaxed in Rome, and the only remaining item of business for the new governor, Flavius Silva—whom I had just met—was to eradicate the few surviving Zealots and Sicarii. These murderous fanatics had holed up in the stronghold at Metzada, more commonly known by its Greek name, 'Masada.'

Not only had the Sicarii massacred seven hundred Jewish women and children in a raid on the town of Ein Geddi, they had captured Masada from a small Roman garrison at the beginning of the war and then executed some surrendered Roman troops in Jerusalem. Not surprisingly, the Romans wanted revenge. It wasn't the Roman way to do things by half-measures; Silva planned to stamp out the rebellion once and for all.

I'd just encountered one of his measures.

Could the man I had helped have been one of the Sicarii? Somehow, I thought not. This man, trying to save his wife and child, hadn't looked like a savage killer of women and children. But then, appearances could be so very, very deceptive. Still, he hadn't tried to kill me, and he was long gone, and I'd probably never lay eyes on him again.

I dusted off the coins and the pass the centurion had thrown my way, then led General Silva's horse into my now empty stable area and tethered it. What would do it more good than anything was simple rest, but I compounded a poultice and applied it to the inflamed area.

I changed it regularly, gave the horse ample food and water, and was quite pleased when, a week later, all signs of swelling had vanished. The pass got me past a bevy of suspicious guards at the Roman camp, and I had little trouble finding my way to the praetorium.

Silva himself emerged from his tent to greet me. He inspected the horse with a critical eye and felt the affected elbow.

"He's as good as new, sir," I reported.

"You have done well, horse-trader," he said at last.

Silva called for a stable-hand to lead the horse away. He handed me a pair of gold coins—far more than my services were worth. But to refuse would have risked offending him.

"Thank you for your generosity," I said.

"You shall stay with us," Silva said, "as a special overseer to our horses."

Stay with the Tenth Legion? That wasn't in my project plans—

"Come, man!" Silva snapped as I hesitated.

Well, there were worse things than being in proximity to the governor.

"I am honored by your kindness," I said.

He gestured a dismissal. "You will, of course, find lodging outside the camp."

Of course. A civilian like me wouldn't be offered the protection of the legionary camp. I'd have to make do with the company of the traders, fortune tellers, self-styled physicians, and loose women who typically followed a Roman legion hoping to scrounge a meager living.

The veterinarius whom Silva had maligned earlier was a surly young man who obviously didn't appreciate my arrival on his turf. I purchased an inexpensive tent and furnishings from an accommodating tent-maker and pitched it as far away from the veterinarius as possible.

As it happened, I didn't have to stay there long, because it was only a matter of days before the Tenth Legion packed up and marched away.

"You're to attach yourself to the auxiliary cavalry," a messenger from Silva told me, handing me a new camp pass.

"Where's the legion going?" I asked, examining the pass before stowing it safely on my person.

"Masada," was the short reply.

I suppose it would have been easy enough to have taken a horse and ridden off, but by now curiosity had gripped me. I hadn't planned on being anywhere near Masada, but since the opportunity presented itself, why not take it? Flexibility was the mark of a good researcher. I had read the works of Josephus, of course, the Jewish general who'd ingratiated himself with Vespasian and turned in his Jewish sword for a Roman pen. I knew how his story of Masada had been fashioned into a magnificent epic to rival that of Leonidas and his three hundred Spartans. Modern historians disputed the myth of the last stand of the Zealots against the Romans. Why not see for myself? I could surely get a better paper out of it than the one I had been working on.

The Chair couldn't object to that.

I attached myself to the baggage train, riding a decrepit donkey that had seen many, many better days. I hoped it would survive the journey across the dry wasteland to the mountain fortress. It did—but barely. Had it been later in the year, and not January, I doubt it would have made it.

Located near the southern end of the Dead Sea, Masada rose from the desert like a wrecked battleship of sheer, unclimbable rock faces. Walls and towers encircled the mesa's top, and only one path reached the summit, the aptly named Snake Path which wound up the eastern side. On the northern edge, Herod's hanging villa clung to terraces, but although at a lower elevation than the fortress proper, it was equally unreachable.

The Sicarii thought they were safe on their perch thirteen hundred feet above the Dead Sea.

To my surprise, given the distance across the desert, the majority of the camp followers also managed the trek. The distance created a long supply route not only for the legion, which used slave labor to bring in food and water, but also for the followers who either relied on supplies brought with them or sold by enterprising traders at exorbitant prices. The hillsides sprouted makeshift civilian settlements and shops, and once again I was forced to pitch my tent among traders, fortune-tellers, and prostitutes. I stayed as close to the cavalry as I could and settled down to watch and learn.

General Silva made a reconnaissance on horseback, riding completely around Masada. When he returned, he consulted with his senior officers, and then the legion set to work.

First, they built two large camps to house the legion and six smaller ones set at intervals around Masada for the foreign auxiliary troops. Each was surrounded by a rubble wall ten feet high and five feet thick. Barracks with four-foot-tall rubble walls and tented roofs housed the men. In the center of the largest camp was Silva's command building, the praetorium.

When that was done, they constructed a two-mile-long circumvallation, a wall completely encircling Masada. With the perimeter secure, the Sicarii were totally hemmed in, unable to receive supplies, and unable to escape. The Snake Path was their only way down, and it was guarded.

The rapidity with which the Tenth Legion accomplished this demonstration of standard Roman siege tactics was astounding. But the Roman military was nothing if not efficient. And the Tenth Legion knew its job, and knew it well. There was no undue haste, no scrambling or confusion.

All was purposeful, professional order. Reducing Masada was not an adventure, simply another job to be done. It was now February and Silva wanted it done by April, before the summer sun made life in the desert unbearable.

The Roman noose had settled around the Sicarii neck. All that was necessary was for Silva to draw it tighter and tighter.

And he did.

Since there was no natural avenue of attack, Silva decided to build one. He chose a spur of rock on the western side and positioned ballistae— missile and stone-throwing artillery weapons—to provide protection for the workers. Then he set the men to work building a giant ramp.

The ramp, six hundred seventy-five feet long and seven hundred feet tall, crowned by a stone platform seventy-five feet wide and high, was impressive even in my own day, when two and a half millennia had worn and weathered it. Equally impressive was watching the effort of construction.

Day after day, week after week, sweating, cursing men carried baskets of stones and lumbering carts pulled larger boulders to the ramp, which sprouted like a bizarre mineral bud from its spur of rock. Each day it grew a little more and crept a little closer to the summit of Masada. From a bud, it became a tendril and then a broader stalk curving its way upward as if seeking the sun.

Daily, doom for the Sicarii inched closer. Their resistance was limited to taunts and curses hurled from the ramparts supplemented by an intermittent arrow or slingstone shot, none of which made any real difference. They picked off the occasional careless legionary, and Roman archers and artillery returned the favor. The Romans labored; the Sicarii waited.

It was only a matter of time, and while the Romans worked quickly and steadily, they weren't in a mad rush. The operation at Masada was simply for show. It sent a message to all would-be rebels.

Oppose our legions: we'll crush you.

Cower in your cities: we'll level them.

Hide on a mountaintop: we'll hunt you down.

No army is too strong, no city too secure, no mountain too high for Rome to conquer.

It was Roman pride in action—and, for the *Fretensis*, which had suffered a setback and loss of a legionary standard during the siege of Jerusalem, a chance to regain its honor.

I wasn't idle, either. My limited knowledge of equine medicine was strained to the limit by the cases which came my way. I fear that I may have caused more animals to be put down than a qualified veterinarian of my own era would have done, but consoled myself with the thought—possibly justified—that my success rate bettered that of the Roman veterinarius. I drew the line at surgery, though, and made sure that everyone knew that cutting wasn't my forte. If the veterinarius was happy that I deferred to him in surgical competence, he didn't say. Still, my unexpected career as a veterinarius was considerably better than horse trading.

But all good things come to an end, and it was General Silva himself who put an end to my animal ministrations, some seven weeks after the siege of Masada had begun.

He came ostensibly to inspect the auxiliary cavalry and to check on his own horse which he hadn't ridden for some days. He was pleased to find the animal doing well.

"I have received favorable reports of your abilities, horse-trader," he said.

I hadn't realized that Silva had been monitoring my activities so closely; I'd assumed that he'd had more important matters on his mind. I thanked him for the compliment.

He pretended to examine his horse, while rubbing his chin thoughtfully.

"I have another task for you, horse-trader," he said.

My stomach lurched as if with a premonition of unwelcome news.

"How can I be of assistance, General?" I asked, my mouth dry.

He pursed his narrow lips. "The siege ramp is progressing well. We shall reach the top of Masada within days."

I nodded.

"But what can we expect when we reach it?" Silva mused, as if speaking to himself.

My heart sank. I could have told him what archaeologists thought and what Josephus in his biased account had recorded.

"The Sicarii aren't known for being fighters," I replied cautiously.

He waved a hand. "No. But how many others are up there with them? How many Zealots willing to sell their lives dearly? And what traps or ambushes have they prepared?"

He brushed back a lock of his curly brown hair. "I'm not a man who likes to squander the lives of his troops. I depend on them to fight for Rome—and for me—and they rely upon my judgment in choosing when and where to fight. I see no point in losing men during a simple mopping-up operation. Do you understand me, horse-trader?"

I understood him all too well. Sick in my stomach, I asked, "Are you looking for a spy?"

"Yes."

"But why me?"

"Isn't it obvious? I cannot send a Roman; he'd be killed instantly. Nor can I send a Jew for fear of betrayal. But you are neither Roman nor Jew. And somehow, Claudius Britannicus, I feel that I can trust you."

What about my lack of nerve, I wanted to say? What about the fact that I had no stake in this fight? What about the likelihood that the Sicarii would eliminate me on the spot?

"I would consider it a personal favor," Silva said, his blue-gray eyes regarding me intently. "It would do a person of your status no harm to have an influential patron."

If I were even alive to use the benefit, I thought sourly. Besides, what good was a Roman patron to a man from the future? Roman patronage was not exactly a valuable commodity in the twenty-seventh century.

I felt again that the currents of history were swirling me against my will. I wondered if, as an outsider to time, I somehow acted as a focus for unusual events. I wished that I knew about them in advance so that I could avoid them.

If history recorded that such and such a person did such and such an action, and if I, from the future was that person, could I decline to perform the action? If so, how could it have been performed and recorded? And what of actions which were never recorded? If history is not observed and recorded, does it happen?

Silva tapped his foot impatiently.

"How would I get up there?" I asked.

He seemed to take my question as assent, and relaxed.

"Up the Snake Path," he said briskly. "Pursued by some of my troops— under orders not to catch you, of course. If the Sicarii think that you're an enemy of Rome, perhaps they'll take you in."

Perhaps. A very big perhaps.

"All right, sir," I said, swallowing a lump in my throat the size of a hippopotamus. "I'll do it."

"Learn what you can, and send me word however you can." He turned away.

A spy!

Of all the confounded, outrageous things to happen!

I paced a tight circle inside my tent. I'm not a swearing man, but a few choice Roman expletives crossed my mind. And perhaps one or two passed my lips. Well, there was nothing for it. I couldn't run; Silva wouldn't let me get away with it, and I had no desire to end my life nailed naked to a tree in public view. Any death the Sicarii meted out would be gentle in comparison to crucifixion.

It was nowhere near time for Ring Control to reopen the interface— which, when it opened, would be near Hebron, anyway.

No, I'd have to play this role and hope that history was kind to me yet again. I felt as if I were in a bizarre game of Russian roulette with history...perhaps destined to be a martyr for science.

Needless to say, I didn't sleep well that night.

It was early the next morning when I made the attempt on Masada. I scrambled as fast as I could up the Snake Path while five Roman legionaries made a loud hue and cry and threw the occasional wild javelin. I tried to act like a man in fear of his life—and it didn't take much acting. The path was steep and treacherous, and it wasn't long before I was panting for breath and the Roman legionaries were huffing and puffing in their armor.

I slipped and fell several times, covering my Jewish-style robes with dust. Stitched into the right sleeve was a safe-conduct pass from Silva, the only thing that would protect me when the Roman legionaries reached the top of Masada.

My heart raced faster than mere exertion dictated; I was drenched by sweat sucked out of my pores by the desert sun. And it was a temperate day; what it would have been like in summer, I quailed to think. My head ached, and the grit scratched my eyes until they watered.

I made no attempt to be quiet—I wanted the Sicarii to know I was coming. And when the angle of the path permitted me to glimpse the rampart above, I saw curious, hostile faces gazing down at me.

What was going through their minds?

I learned soon enough.

The legionaries closed on me in a last, dramatic rush, and then rocks hurled from above were bouncing around us. An arrow glanced off a boulder, and then the legionaries, as instructed, retreated out of danger. I heard an angry exclamation, saw a rock skittering down the cliff-face toward me, and was too late to dodge it. It caught me in the ribs, spun me around, and dropped me face-first to the ground. The Sicarii cheered.

The pain was excruciating, every breath agony. I struggled to remain conscious.

I became aware of men surrounding me; they seemed to be arguing. Probably deciding whether or not to kill me on the spot, I supposed. I thought dully that the verdict was not going my way. Somebody stuck a foot underneath me and rolled me onto my back.

And then I heard another voice; it sounded dimly familiar. I felt arms around me, lifting me up. But a sudden jostling pitched me into blackness.

When I awoke, it was to the sensation of a cool cloth on my forehead and fingers rubbing some sort of liniment onto my aching chest. I opened my eyes, took a breath, and gasped at a spasm of pain.

"You're awake at last," a man's voice said in coarse Greek.

It took a moment for my sluggish mind to identify him as the man I'd helped in the village. It was his wife who tended to my wounds.

"Was it you…who saved me?" I croaked.

He sat on a mat beside me. He nodded. "The Sicarii were all for finishing you off. I convinced them to let me deal with you."

"I don't even know your name."

"Simon Ben-Joseph," he said. "My wife, Miriam."

His wife gave me a shy smile.

"Thank you," I said.

"We are now even," he said. "You saved my life; I have saved yours. But for how long is a different matter. What madness made you come up here?"

What madness, indeed!

I held a hand to my chest and struggled to a sitting position. I saw the child sleeping in a corner and spoke softly so as not to waken him.

"I could bear the Roman dogs no longer!" I exclaimed, launching into my story, feeling guilty as I did so. Simon had repaid kindness for kindness, and here I was, a spy for his enemy, pretending to be an enemy of the Romans. My conscience grieved me even though my presence would make no difference to events on Masada. History had already dictated the outcome and any information I passed on to Silva would not affect Simon one whit. It was cold consolation.

I continued, "I am, as you know, a Briton and a free man. That insufferable beast Silva took all my horses and then made me accompany his legion to attend to his cavalry. He treated me as if I were his slave!"

"That is the Roman way."

"I endured it as long as I could. Finally, I could bear it no more. Many of my tribesmen died fighting the Romans; how could I languish under their yoke without raising a hand in protest? I was ashamed of myself, Simon, and so I ran here, thinking I could perhaps strike some blow against them."

He shook his head slowly. "You are either a brave man or a foolish one," he said. "Perhaps both." His dark brows drew together. "How are you called?"

"Britannicus," I said. "Just call me Britannicus. The rest of my name has become an affront to me."

"Keep your face hidden as much as possible," Simon said, "and speak only to me. Not everyone is of the Sicarii, but most are, and it would take little for one of them to plunge a knife into you."

He motioned toward the wall. "There is an empty chamber next door where you may sleep." His lips twisted into a mockery of a smile. "We don't live as Herod did in his palace here."

He handed me a jug of water and a basket with some old bread, then moved to the entrance of his rude chamber and pointed toward a couple of small palaces that lay a short distance away. "That is where the leaders of the Sicarii have taken up habitation. These rooms are where the rest of us stay."

Typical, I thought. I left Simon's room and entered the adjoining shelter that had been built against the southeastern wall of the fortress. It contained nothing but a mat. Still contending with my conscience, I lay down and drifted into an uneasy sleep.

It was still daylight when I awoke and went outside and stood leaning my back against the wall of my shelter. The sun had drifted far to the west, and long shadows lengthened across the bleak landscape. For the first time, I was able to survey my surroundings.

Perhaps some people could find an austere beauty in the dry, treeless wasteland that stretched to the horizon, but not I. It was unchanging, the same in my own century as it was now. Everything was brown, gray, and yellow. Nothing grew in the wilderness of low hills, dry wadis, and scoured rock. But for the turquoise blue of the Dead Sea shimmering in the distance, it could have been the surface of Mars. Even the air seemed empty of content, devoid of moisture and even oxygen. Nighttime, I thought, would be a definite improvement.

The summit of Masada was as bleak as the surrounding desolation. The ground was sand and crumbly rock, unbroken by even a single tuft of grass.

The southeastern wall, where I stood, was lined by the Sicarii quarters and possessed one gate. Ahead of me lay three small palaces and Herod's large palace at the midpoint of the western wall, right where the Roman siege ramp was approaching. Storehouses, a large bathhouse, and an administrative building clustered at the northern end. Beyond them, out of sight, lay Herod's hanging villa.

All the buildings that Herod had erected—palaces, bathhouses, granaries and storerooms alike—possessed the same aura of decay. Nobody had cared for Masada since Herod's death, and time, and wind, and the harsh desert sun were taking their toll. Everything looked worn and weathered.

A marginally cooler breeze whipped dust eddies into the air and dispelled some of the warmth of day. Cooking fires twinkled in front of several of the dwellings, as the Sicarii settled down to their evening meal. Robed figures wandered around in a desultory manner. A group of children played under the watch of several women. What a dismal existence for them now, and what a wretched fate awaited them!

I watched the laughing children. It was hard to imagine these innocents as the children of assassins and bandits. What kind of men would bring children into the world only to condemn them to an early death?

I moved to the wall and looked down upon the Roman camps. Cooking fires flickered there, too, in front of the clustered forests of tents. Work on the great ramp continued, as it did all through the day. Shifts rotated so that all the men could work not only the hot day shifts, but during the less strenuous cool of the evening. I saw the glint of armor as sentries patrolled the perimeters of the Roman camps. A supply train wound its way into Silva's headquarters.

"A grim sight, isn't it?"

I started, not having heard Simon come up beside me. "Not as grim as the battlefield they left behind when Queen Boudicca's army was destroyed," I replied, speaking as if I had personally witnessed that carnage.

"They are like a disease, spreading across the earth, them and their pagan ways."

I nodded. I couldn't say it to Simon, but ironically the Roman Empire

64

had prepared the way for the demise of its own pagan beliefs. Rome's world-spanning conquests had laid the groundwork for the coming of a man from Nazareth whose followers would change the world forever.

"They are unstoppable," Simon continued in a low voice.

"No," I said, "they aren't. They have their limits. No nation can master the entire world."

He stared at me curiously from his dark eyes. "Defiant words for a horse-trader from the edge of the world."

I felt suddenly uncomfortable. After all, what did I know of this man?

"Are you one of the Sicarii?" I asked.

His gaze sharpened. "I am not. A Zealot, yes, an assassin no."

"Why then are you here, Simon Ben-Joseph?"

He looked away, over the desert sands. "Where else was there to go? If I stayed down there, I would have been caught and killed. There is no army of Judea for a man to join. Here, I can at least resist. And, unlike you, I am not a man to flee my own country. Better to die fighting the Romans than to run from them."

The rebuke, with its implication of cowardice, stung.

Simon pointed across the compound. I followed his finger toward a tall, bearded man haranguing a group of Sicarii.

"That's Eleazar Ben-Yair, their leader."

"What is he saying?" I asked.

"Deliverance from the Roman pigs…cleanse the land from the sons of evil…death to the weak and faint-hearted…"

"The usual words of the fanatic."

Simon brought his fist down on the wall. "They're fools, all of them! They know nothing about fighting the Romans."

I glanced around in case we'd been overheard. But nobody was close to us.

"How many of you Zealots are here?" I asked.

"A couple of dozen. That's all. I thought more would come…that we could raise a force here and continue the war against the Romans. But no. There aren't enough of us left."

He sounded tired. I left him, not wanting Ben-Yair to spot me, and returned to my chamber. I drank some of the stale water, ate the old bread, and lay back down on the thin mat.

It rained that night. I wondered how often it rained in such a desolate place. I wouldn't have believed it if I hadn't seen it with my own eyes, but in the morning pools of water covered the surface of the plateau. Some of it was channeled into great underground cisterns. Some was scooped up into clay pots by the women. Children played in the smaller puddles until the ground absorbed them and the sun dried up what was left. I wondered if the desert would bloom after the rain, but it didn't.

Miriam visited me and, under the watchful eye of her husband, rebandaged my chest. The abrasions stung, and the ribs ached, but the severe pains had already diminished. I was sure that I'd cracked a rib or two, but not badly enough to be displaced. The pain was bearable.

Later, I ventured out cautiously, keeping to the lower portion of the fortress, as Simon instructed me, steering clear of the larger buildings where Ben-Yair and his closest companions held sway. I avoided groups, spoke to no one, and if anyone was curious about a solitary figure wandering in a casual manner, they weren't curious enough to accost me.

Simon gave me an ostracon—a pottery shard with writing on it—which entitled me to a portion of the daily grain ration.

Over the next several days, I was able to gain an impression of life on Masada. It was basic existence, pure and simple. The Sicarii had no concerted plans. Beyond piling up small rocks above the Snake Path and southern cliffs, they'd prepared no defenses. As if the Romans would really attempt such suicidal attacks! There were no traps or ambushes that I could see. For the most part the Sicarii sat around waiting for God to rescue them and defeat the Romans with a show of divine power.

They might have boasted of being brave, but their bravery had been limited to knifing unsuspecting opponents and killing helpless villagers. Confronted by a real threat, they were at their wits' end.

I saw Simon meeting covertly with a handful of other men, probably the other Zealots. They were too few to effect any change.

I had learned enough to send a report to General Silva. I could have lied (which would have accomplished nothing) or failed to respond, but that would have risked incurring Silva's displeasure, and I didn't want to have both sides wanting to kill me. So I decided to report. But how?

I couldn't go in person; Sicarii guarded the four gates in Masada's walls, and even if I could get past the guards it would be madness to attempt the Snake Path at night. Chances were I'd fall off a cliff. Having Silva find my report on my dead body was not how I wanted to finish this assignment.

I wished for a carrier pigeon, like those used by Brutus during Marc Antony's siege of Modena. But one couldn't go around carrying a concealed pigeon.

No, I needed another way.

I waited until the cooking fires had been banked for the night and all sounds of activity on Masada had ceased. The stars shone in a sky of infinite blackness. I slipped out of my chamber, wrapped in a dark cloak that I had earlier taken from a supply store and secreted in my room. I made my way along the wall until I wasn't far from the Roman ramp, now virtually complete.

At intervals along the wall, the Sicarii had left weapons caches—bows and arrows, swords, a few spears. From one such cache I selected a bow and three arrows. Sitting at the base of the wall, in shadow, I tied to each arrow a scrap torn from a scroll that I had discovered in a disused outbuilding. It cut me to the quick to damage the scroll—it was part of the book of Ezekiel, the story of the valley of dry bones—but I tried to take scraps without writing. On each I wrote a few words in Greek:

General Silva. 1000 people. 400 men. No organization. No traps. Britannicus.

When the arrows were ready, I rose to my feet. I stared into the darkness, trying to tell if I was being observed. My ears strained for the slightest sound of sandal on stone. My palms were slick with sweat. Never, never, could I have been a professional spy!

"Forgive me, Simon," I murmured under my breath.

I notched the first arrow onto the string, drew it back as far as I could, and launched it in the direction of the Roman siege ramp and the campfires glimmering at its base. The twang of the string and whoosh of the arrow seemed impossibly loud in the silence. I held my breath, waiting for a shout to indicate I'd been discovered.

Nothing. I breathed a sigh of relief.

I had no way to judge where the arrow went, whether or not it was far enough for someone to find it and read the message. I fitted the second arrow to the string and sent it after the first. Bolder now, I sent the third one quickly.

A man yelled. I didn't catch the Aramaic words, but he sounded angry.

I froze. Were the words directed at me? Had I been spotted?

More shouts. Several men's voices. Scuffling sounds in the darkness. A torch flaring in the distance, bobbing up and down, coming toward me.

I dropped the bow, backed against the wall, and edged away. My chamber lay on the opposite wall; to get there, I'd either have to cut across, past the small palaces, or follow the wall.

More lights winked into existence, coming from the row of primitive rooms where my chamber was. I saw—or perhaps imagined—men standing in their doorways, looking toward the disturbance. A child's cry was quickly hushed.

There was nothing for it. I didn't dare risk being detected. I wedged myself into a jutting angle of the wall, crouched down to reduce my profile, and hoped the shadow was dark enough to conceal me.

I pulled my robe up to cover my nose and mouth and muffle the sound of my too-rapid breathing.

The torch-light came closer, and in its weaving I saw a group of five or six Sicarii. In their midst was another man, struggling frantically and yelling in a loud, panic-filled voice. He squirmed and thrashed, but two of the larger men had his arms pinned and bundled him along as if he were a child.

Among the group I recognized Eleazar Ben-Yair. His hands were raised, although whether he was crying to heaven or pronouncing a curse on the prisoner I couldn't tell.

They drew close to the wall, and I pushed myself farther back until the rough stone pressed painfully against my spine.

The man was almost frantic with fear, but it made no difference to his captors. The cold expressions on their cruel faces chilled me. Life meant nothing to these men. All that mattered were their own fanatical beliefs; those who disagreed with them were as detestable as the Romans they hated.

They hoisted the man up to the top of the wall. Suddenly, his struggles and pleading ceased, as if he had abruptly lost the will to fight.

I couldn't watch, and yet I couldn't tear my eyes away.

What had this man done? He was a murderer, like all of them, and while he may have deserved his fate, I pitied him for it.

At a signal from Ben-Yair, the two men holding him raised him and swung him out over the precipice. He screamed, his scream fading until it was cut off by a sickening thud and a clatter of small stones.

The men peered over the edge for a moment, then turned away and dispersed into the darkness.

I waited until they had all gone and silence had returned to Masada. Then, following the wall, I crept back to my chamber, and succumbed to the nausea that overwhelmed me.

Simon found me in the morning, while I was using a jug of rainwater to wash my face.

"I thought, at first, that the Sicarii had fastened upon you," he said.

I shivered.

"Then I realized that he was shouting in our tongue, and so it couldn't be you. Still," his gaze became pointed, "I looked in your chamber, and you weren't there."

"I was feeling unwell and came out for some air," I said. "I saw what happened." I took a breath. "What…did he do?"

"I heard," Simon replied, "that he suggested making a deal with the Romans."

I snorted. "They have no reason to make a deal." I motioned to where the Roman siege ramp was now perilously close to completion. The legionaries were almost within reach of the top of the plateau, so close that they had to work under cover of protective screens.

"The world is full of cowards," Simon said. His little son came running to him, and he hoisted the boy onto his shoulders. "But you aren't a coward, are you, little man?"

He spoke the words lightly, but I could detect the anxiety in the tenor of his voice.

I spent the day in my chamber, listening to the shouts of the laboring Roman legionaries and the taunts of the Sicarii. It was stupid. What could verbal taunts accomplish? The Romans were in sight of their goal. Did bluster make the Sicarii feel any better?

I awakened the next morning to excited yelling. Momentarily forgetting myself, I hurried out and joined the men lining Masada's walls, pointing and gesticulating.

Slowly, jerkily, moving like an awkward beast, a Roman siege machine lumbered up the ramp. It had to have been at least ninety feet tall and twenty feet wide, and it was plated with sheets of iron. Teams of straining legionaries hauled on ropes, pulling at the command of centurions. Foot by foot, the machine groaned its way up the incline. Shining in the sunshine, the metal ram's head on the end of the battering ram grinned mockingly at the doomed Sicarii.

Some of the rebels loosed arrows down upon the beast, but they rattled harmlessly off its plated bulk. A volley of artillery bolts skimmed overhead, and the Sicarii fled from the walls. I retreated to the relative safety of my chamber.

Eventually, it began. The repetitive "boom—boom—boom" of the battering ram pounding on the fortress wall. On and on it went, until my head throbbed in unison. "Boom—boom—boom." The ground trembled underfoot with each blow. In my mind's eye, I could see the wall shiver with each impact, dust cascade down, the stones loosen and fall away, the breach in the wall widen and widen.

As if suddenly emerging from a trance the Sicarii awoke to the gravity of their situation. Masada's walls were not impregnable. Someone with greater engineering knowledge than the others arranged a work party. Wooden beams scavenged from Herod's palace were hauled up to the wall where the Roman battering ram was now making serious inroads and erected into a new, inner wall: two layers of beams with earth in between.

When the outer wall finally crumbled, the sharp boom of ram against stone was replaced by a duller thunk as the pliable inner wall absorbed the blows of the ram. The Sicarii naively thought that they had thwarted the Roman effort.

Their relief was short lived. Roman archers shot flaming arrows into the beams, igniting the old timbers.

Eleazar Ben-Yair gathered a crowd of the Sicarii together and began to speak to them.

"What is he saying?" I asked, still pretending that I didn't understand Aramaic.

Simon was standing with his wife and young son.

"He is telling them that deliverance is nigh," he replied, "that in the moment of their victory, God will smite the Romans."

Some of the Sicarii cheered. But I studied a knot of women standing weeping silently, and I wondered how many of those on Masada believed Ben-Yair's words.

The smell of burning filled the air as clouds of acrid smoke drifted across the fortress. Groups of Sicarii paced nervously, glancing into the sky from time to time as if expecting to see it open up and a heavenly army descend. But the crackle of burning wood continued, the flames slowly but inexorably eating into the thick timber.

Ben-Yair alone seemed unaffected by the Roman actions. His strong voice never wavered as he exhorted the Sicarii. He became even more animated when the wind abruptly changed direction and blew from the north. The Roman siege tower became enveloped in smoke, and for a moment, it seemed as if the flames would spread toward it. The Sicarii heaped curses and imprecations on the Romans, but their hope was short lived. The wind changed direction yet again, blowing from the south and driving the fires deeper into the wood of the barricade.

Simon seemed lost in thought, unwilling to talk, save to tell me that he'd sent his wife and child down into Herod's hanging villa, the spot on Masada farthest from where the Romans would attack. I wasn't sure what he hoped to accomplish. I kept to myself, watching in silence, my face wrapped against the smoke.

The moon rose above Masada into a crystal-clear night sky marred only by the smoke ascending from the burning inner wall. It was the eve of Passover, the 15th of Nisan in the year 74.

From the darkness came the jangle of armor and weapons as Roman legionaries on the siege ramp waited for the final breach.

I stood with Simon near one of the palace buildings, in an angle of wall where we could not be easily seen.

"God was not with us," he said softly. His eyes glittered as they turned toward me. "Nor with you."

"Sometimes," I replied, "I wonder if God is waging a different fight." I felt uncomfortable under his stare. "Do you ever think, Simon, that perhaps the fights we wage aren't the ones we should be waging, or that we fight the right fights in the wrong way?"

"Surely it is not wrong to fight oppression."

"No," I shook my head. "But the Sicarii don't fight oppression. They are cowardly killers who stab their own people in the back and murder innocents. And the Zealots—"

He whirled, and the blade of his sword flashed before me.

"What about the Zealots?" he demanded harshly.

"You have chosen strange bedfellows in the Sicarii," I said, then hurried to explain before Simon's patience lapsed. "While the Zealots were fighting for freedom, what were the Sicarii doing? Were they harassing the Romans, trying to aid the Holy City in its time of crisis? No, they were here, hiding on a hilltop, killing women and children at Ein Geddi while the true Jewish warriors were fighting and dying."

He nodded, slowly. "To the Sicarii, those people were as wicked and as deserving of death as the Romans...as anyone who does not believe as the Sicarii do."

"Do you believe that way, Simon Bar-Joseph?" I asked.

"I?" he started. "If I believed that way, I would not have spared your life."

"Then why do you raise your sword to me now?"

He studied the blade, almost with a hint of surprise at finding it in his hand. Then he lowered it.

I breathed a sigh of relief. "You know, as I do, that the way of the Sicarii is wrong. And perhaps we were wrong to be here with them."

"You speak like a man afraid to die."

"I am afraid to waste my life," I said.

"Death fighting the Romans is no waste. How can they be fought except by the sword and by blood?" he asked.

"In here," I said, touching my heart. "This is where the battle against oppression and injustice must be won."

"Bah! What tyrant cares about the heart?" He turned away. "You're a Gentile," he scoffed. "Little different from the Romans. What do you know?"

"I know that your own scriptures encourage you to be a light unto the Gentiles."

He didn't reply.

"In a few minutes," I said, "the Romans will be through those walls. God will not inaugurate the End and cover the Sicarii with glory as they believe. Everyone here will be slaughtered where they stand. The way of murder is the wrong road, Simon."

With a violent motion that made me flinch he stabbed his sword into the ground.

"Who are you, Briton, to speak this way? Who can know what will happen?"

"It takes little insight to know what will happen if the Romans catch you and your family," I said. "There is no escape from Masada. The fortress of the Sicarii has become their prison, and yours."

"Yours as well," he retorted.

"True. But I am only one man."

He groaned. "You have brought death only to yourself, Briton. I have brought destruction to my wife and child as well."

His face seemed as set as stone; I couldn't read what was going through his mind. But I had convinced myself that Simon Ben-Joseph was not a killer. A patriot, yes; a murderer, no.

I wished that there were some way to save him and his family. But how could there be?

From somewhere in the distance, I heard women crying. The cries stopped abruptly, and I shuddered, knowing the sudden cessation could only mean one thing.

Knots of Sicarii wandered through the gloom, made eerie by the contrasting lights of torch and moon. I thought perhaps that somebody would organize a coherent defense—not that it would matter—but no. The wooden wall had been their last attempt at united action. A few men— probably the handful of Zealots— banded together near the wooden wall, ready to face the Romans. It wouldn't be long now, I thought. Fanned by the breeze, the flames were turning the improvised wall to ashes.

I recognized Ben-Yair's voice coming from the darkness. I assumed he was shouting the same thing as before, the tired refrain of "Deliverance is nigh! In the moment of their victory the Romans will be defeated." Say something often enough and loud enough and people will come to believe it. I sighed. The Sicarii had a sort of faith, but it was wrong, all wrong.

They had embraced a way of violence and wanton killing, and thought that God would bless their misguided efforts. It was misplaced; not in love, not in the faith of Bishop Makarion, doing good even as his world collapsed about him, but pinned to their own desires for vengeance against foreign oppressors.

Simon stood as still as a statue, the pale moonlight accentuating the stricken expression in his eyes. He knew, even without the perspective of history which I possessed, that there would be no deliverance for the Sicarii this night. Simon was not the first man to have brought disaster upon his family through misjudged actions and commitment to a doomed cause.

"I'm not going to let myself be crucified." He whispered in a hoarse voice that I could barely recognize as his. "And I am not going to let those butchers ravish my wife!"

I opened my mouth to reply, but before I could get a word out, the fire-weakened wall collapsed with a thunderous crack. I jumped and whirled to face the new fury that burst upon Masada.

I wish events could have transpired as the historian Josephus described them: the Romans withdrawing until daylight, giving Eleazar Ben-Yair time to deliver long, impassioned speeches to his band of noble Sicarii, encouraging them to deny the Romans their victory; the Sicarii holding a lottery to choose ten men to kill everyone, and then another to see who would kill the final nine; all the people submitting quietly to death; the one man who was last setting fire to the buildings and then falling on his own sword; and finally the Romans entering, prepared for a fight, but finding only a desolate silence and the bodies of the slain. What a story of the last stand of the Jews against Rome!

But it was only a story—crafted, no doubt, by the Roman-leaning Josephus to make it seem as though the Romans had overcome a noble opponent and to absolve the Romans from massacring women and children.

Instead, while darkness enveloped Masada, a barrage of stone projectiles from ballistae mounted on the siege tower hammered Masada. In their wake, the legionaries of the *Fretensis* stormed through the breach in the wall like a wave of human furies.

The handful of Zealots hurled themselves screaming at the Romans. Swords rang and thudded off shields, and without seeing it, I visualized the

Zealots being cut down, making hardly a dent in the irresistible Roman advance, their bodies piling up on the blood-soaked ground.

Elsewhere, all was confusion. Sicarii ran seeking escape where there was none and meeting violent deaths. Women pleaded and children shrieked as the Roman legionaries spared no one. Some Sicarii begged for friends to kill them swiftly. Others flung themselves over the walls, preferring that death to the merciless Roman swords.

A few fell to the ground, weeping and wailing in despair. It was a strange sight to see these men, who had taken life so callously, afraid for their own. Others stood with arms upraised, praying futilely for deliverance.

It was a fearsome scene, quite literally hell. And as red tongues of fire leaped into the air—some Sicarii setting buildings and goods alight to deny the Romans their plunder—it became even more hellish. Shadows jerked and danced in the bizarre red glow. Figures ran and fell and yelled. And from everywhere came the sound of the sword's clash.

Of course! The thought burst upon me—Josephus had recorded that seven people had survived Masada—two women and five children who had hidden in a cistern. Perhaps there was hope for Simon's wife and child, if not him…

Or me! I started. Caught up in the horrific scene, I had forgotten my own safety. In the dark and the confusion there was nothing to keep some Roman legionary from adding me to his tally.

I glimpsed motion in my peripheral vision and looked around in time to catch a swirl of robes. It was Simon, running toward Herod's hanging villa. His sword, that he had stabbed into the ground, was gone. In a moment of awful insight I guessed what he might be going to do.

I dared not stay where I was. Stumbling over the uneven ground, I followed him.

I passed the bodies of some women and children—undoubtedly the families of the Zealots, who had killed them before dying themselves. Josephus' tale was true in part.

Where was Simon?

If I caught him, what could I do? Plead with the Romans to spare him? The legionaries wouldn't listen. Their orders were to eliminate the Sicarii, and they would do so. Take Simon to Silva—if I could even find the commander? I was a lowly horse-trader. Silva wouldn't listen to the likes of me. He too had a job to do.   I tripped over a corpse and fell, scraping my hands and knees and jarring my ribs. I picked myself up and continued, slower.

Distance dulled the shouts and cries of battle. I passed the administrative building, the storerooms and a large bathhouse, grabbing a lighted torch from a Sicari who no longer had need of earthly light. I entered the upper terrace of the hanging villa. All was silent. My footsteps echoed on the tiled floors. The living quarters and the porch were deserted. I hurried down to the next level, taking the steps faster than I should have. The colonnaded pavilion here was also empty. As I descended to the lowest terrace, it felt almost as if I were leaving Masada entirely. Before me spread out the panorama of the valley, seeming even more otherworldly in the pallid moonlight. Lights twinkled in the Roman camps, nine hundred feet below.

Sounds. Voices—a murmured farewell? A groan. A dull noise that could have been a body being lowered to the floor.

I dashed into what had once been a small bathhouse. And there I found them.

Simon was standing beside a pool, staring at the sword in his hand, red with the blood of his wife and child, who lay on the floor nearby. I looked at the bodies and wanted to cry and retch and choke all at the same time.

Simon wore the most desolate expression I have ever seen on a human face.

"I couldn't let them suffer," he moaned.

I opened my mouth and shut it again. I had wanted to tell him about the cistern where other women and children would survive. But I had been too slow. Once again, history refused to be changed.

"I have lost everything," Simon continued in a raw voice. He took a deep breath. "And yet what are my sorrows compared to the sufferings of my people? We are a ruined race."

What, I wondered, had happened to his desire to fight the Romans?

"Not so," I said. "Your people will survive, just as mine shall."

He didn't respond.

"And," I added, making perhaps the first, if unrecorded, reference in history to the myth of Masada, "Masada will not fall again." I didn't tell Simon, of course, just how long the time and how tortuous the road until his people once again possessed Masada, or how the story would be ignored for centuries, until the rise of the nation of Israel prompted renewed interest in Masada.

He regarded me curiously. "You speak like a prophet," he said, "and yet you are a pagan Gentile."

I shook my head. "Gentile, yes. Pagan, no."

He studied the sword in his hand.

"I would be alone," he said. He motioned toward the way I had entered the bathhouse. "Leave me."

"I wish this wasn't necessary," I said.

His eyebrows raised, but he didn't speak; he didn't have to. Escape was impossible, unless he wanted to try to crawl down the cliffs by night and avoid being spotted by the Romans come daylight. If the Romans caught him, they'd crucify him. And to try to avoid death, when all of his comrades and their families lay dead, and the bodies of his wife and child were yet warm would be the ultimate disgrace. What had he to live for, now? He could fight the Romans, as had the other Zealots, but perhaps he wanted his last moments to be with his family.

He motioned again. "Attend to your own fate."

My fate. What was my fate? Josephus had never recorded the presence of a Roman spy on Masada. Perhaps he didn't know. Perhaps at some point I would meet him, maybe in Rome when he was writing his chronicle of this event, and convince him to leave me out. Maybe Silva didn't want the tale of his military operation diluted by the presence of a horse-trader turned spy.

My fingers touched the sleeve of my robe and brushed over the safe-conduct pass from Silva. For a split second I thought of offering it to Simon. But he wouldn't have accepted it.

Instead, I held out my hand. After a flicker of hesitation, Simon clasped my forearm.

Then, guilt-ravaged by my unwanted role in the tragedy, I turned and walked outside. Far below, moonlight played over the tranquil surface of the Dead Sea; a calm, cool light, so at odds with the ghastly, flickering torchlight which was yet illuminating the carnage occurring above. Numbly, I began the ascent back to the summit of Masada. Why, I don't know; it certainly wasn't prudent. But I felt so sullied in soul that nothing seemed to matter. A despair blacker than night, blacker than anything I had thought possible short of the deaths of Erica and Emily descended upon me. I wanted to pray, but even words learned in childhood deserted me.

An age later, I reached the top step. Whether or not a blood-thirsty Roman legionary waited there with drawn sword or not scarcely seemed to matter.

A flicker of movement drew my gaze into the shadows. I tensed, but it wasn't a legionary.

I peered into the darkness trying to make out details. And then, cowering, I saw them. I blinked, to make sure my eyes weren't deceiving me. And I thought, selfishly no doubt, that here was the chance to make amends, if only in a small way. Perhaps history—or God—was giving me the opportunity, at last, to make a difference.

"Don't be afraid," I whispered. Although they couldn't understand my words, I hoped my tone would be reassuring.

I moved closer and beckoned. "Follow me. This way."

The small group—two women and five children—exchanged frightened glances, then, perhaps convinced by my non-threatening posture, followed me silently, too shocked by the terrors of the night to question why. Stumbling over the uneven ground, I led them to one of Herod's rock-hewn cisterns. I removed the cover, helped them climb down, then replaced it.

In the morning, a legionary would discover them. They would be history's only recorded survivors of Masada. I hoped their future wouldn't be worse than death. History didn't record how the Romans had treated them. Had Silva been merciful, or not?

Then, marginally less anguished in spirit, I stood against a worn marble railing and watched the moon rise over Masada.

XII

I met Erica while an undergraduate. I was doing a field assignment in the East Country, on land that belonged to an animal sanctuary. Erica was helping to care for the animals—especially the horses, of which she was particularly fond. She had wandered over to the dig site, and I—being young, alert, and impressionable—noticed the beautiful intruder immediately. I don't know what she saw in me, but I saw a tall, athletic auburn-haired goddess whose radiant blue eyes glittered with lively intelligence, whose lips were made for smiling, and whose figure nearly took my breath away.

I scrambled out of the dig site to greet her, all visions of unearthing some fascinating artifact forgotten. It took all of my self-control to introduce myself and the project in a coherent manner, without stumbling over my words like an excited, embarrassed teenager.

Soon we were deep in discussion, earth-scanning instrument in one hand and historical reference computer pad in the other. She was sincerely interested in the project; indeed, she had a good amateur knowledge of history.

In-between regaling her with snippets of ancient history and archaeological techniques, I learned that she was also a Colony Kid—from Riverbend—whose parents had found the colonial lifestyle not to their liking and had emigrated to Earth, settling first in NorthAm and then in the Bernese Oberland. Erica had a touch of wanderlust, and roamed Europe insouciantly, following her varied interests.

In no time we were conversing with each other like long-time acquaintances…not friends. Not yet.

I had never believed in love at first sight. And I didn't then—love was too rare and precious a flower to blossom in an instant. But there was something else…a feeling that we were kindred spirits, that somehow our meeting was not a chance encounter.

We parted when my instructor showed up and, most unsympathetically, made me return to my assigned chores. But not before I had her contact information and a promise to meet again.

Distracted as I was, my performance on that dig was not up to par.

We met again…and again.

It wasn't long before our acquaintance deepened into friendship and then true love. And soon, we were meeting at fascinating sites around the world…archaeological instruments forgotten. …

It was, perhaps, not surprising that I proposed to her in Rome.

Or that we were married in Avenches, Roman Aventicum, in Switzerland.

Or that we spent our honeymoon in a little chalet called the Guëtli in the countryside outside Bern, in sight of the Jungfrau, the Eiger, and the Monck mountains.

A place where, as they had for centuries, the gently rolling hills reposed beneath the melodious jangle of cowbells. A place that seemed to me like heaven on earth, and Erica an angel.

XIII

In due course, I, like my father before me, became a professor at CamOx. Centuries ago, of course, it was not one university, but two rival institutions. It was said that Cambridge scholars knew nothing about everything, while those at Oxford knew everything about nothing. Or perhaps it was the other way around.

I tried to guide my students somewhere in-between. With some, I succeeded, with others I failed. Some went on to become competent historians, others did not.

One who did not—the encounter with whom disturbed me for a period of time—was Lamia Quigley. It was a strange name. In Latin, Lamia was a daughter of Poseidon, but in Greek she was an evil spirit who abducted and murdered children. What possessed the Quigleys to call their daughter after such a being?

This Lamia, though, was a shy, reticent redhead who turned in a totally unacceptable dissertation. She came to plead with me to reverse her failing grade.

At the time, I was preparing for my next temporal excursion, hoping it wouldn't be as emotionally taxing as Masada had been. I wasn't impressed with a student who couldn't bother to do a good job while safe in the comfortable confines of the twenty-seventh century. And as a young professor whose own position wasn't totally secure, I was rigid, determined that my students should provide worthwhile work that would be a credit both to me and to CamOx.

Lamia spun me a tale of woe—detailing how her marriage to a man who resented the time she spent on her studies interfered with her ability to research and present her dissertation. How she needed to pass for her self-esteem. How desperate she was for a scholarship now and job prospects later.

I explained as patiently as I could that her paper was substandard and derivative, and that my decision was final. I was sorry for her plight, but the paper could not be allowed to pass. I offered her the chance to prepare another paper on a different topic. She shook her head, and left my office downcast.

Had I been more attentive, I might have seen a flicker of hatred in her blue eyes that would have given me pause...

And had I seen it, perhaps the future would have been different.

But I didn't. For my thoughts had reverted to my upcoming project in Roman Britain—which also been the setting for Lamia Quigley's ill-fated paper, although I was going to an earlier period.

I felt a slight chill as she departed...an unease that lingered for a long time...an intimation that my dealings with the young woman were not at an end, and that at sometime our paths would cross again, in a strange fashion...

I pushed the thoughts aside. She was one student out of many. I wasn't running a charity; I had to be fair.

And I had to prepare for Roman Britain.

XIV

"Vindolanda, eh?" the Chair wrinkled his forehead, rubbed his nose, folded his hands. His usual sequence of mannerisms.

I nodded. "I could do with a change of scenery."

Although I'd been home for some while, I still felt desiccated from my time in Masada, as if I had been infiltrated by dust. Kourion had been hot and dry. Caesarea had been hot and dry. Masada had been especially hot and dry. I wanted to spend some time among forests, green hills, shady glens, deep bracken…

Vindolanda…the name was evocative of misty, vine-clad hills, the fragrance of ripening grapes, and an aura of romance. I imagined young lovers gamboling in soft English sunshine, through meadows carpeted with bluebells and wildflowers…

The Chair shrugged. "Why not? I think you've earned it."

I was pleasantly surprised; I must have allowed my emotions to show.

"Why, Robert," said the Chair, sounding slightly puzzled—even hurt—"anyone would think that I forced you into these excursions as some kind of punishment."

"Not at all, sir," I said hurriedly.

I almost skipped down the corridor in glee.

I was going back to the England—Britain, rather—of AD 103. Trajan wore the imperial purple, and Hadrian's wall still lay in the future.

It was all because of a slipper.

Every artifact has a story to tell if only we are smart enough—or lucky enough—to figure it out. A slipper may not be much by which to be remembered, but it is more than can be associated with the vast majority of people who have ever lived.

Unlike many of my colleagues, who focused their attention on famous figures, I looked for the ordinary people, those, I suppose, like myself. Archaeologists are always unearthing the remains of long-dead people. Most are commonplace, or fragmentary, burials. But every now and then one is discovered which is unusual, intriguing, or presenting greater scope for recreating who that person was. These are the ones that caught my interest, that made me want to meet these people, to see who they really were.

I had studied this slipper in a museum. I knew the name of the woman who had worn it. And I was going to go and meet her.

At Vindolanda…

XV: THE SLIPPER OF SULPICIA LEPIDINA

Vindolanda...the name was evocative of misty, vine-clad hills, the fragrance of ripening grapes, and an aura of romance. I imagined young lovers gamboling in soft English sunshine through meadows carpeted with bluebells and wildflowers...

Those fond imaginings returned to me as I sat in my cold, damp quarters, wearing cold, damp clothes, on a cold, damp day, in one of the coldest, dampest months in recent memory.

Vindolanda...

Vindolanda was a fort, like many another on the far-flung borders of the Empire, one of several on the Stanegate road that guarded the north of Britannia. It was dirty, noisy, smelly, and boring. There was mist, yes—a perpetual shroud of thick, gloomy fog, accompanied by never-ending drizzle. There were no grape-vines anywhere on the rugged hills. The meadows—such as they were—had been transformed into bogs where a man ventured at his peril. Perhaps a few soggy sheep made a pretense of frolicking, but certainly no young lovers.

There was nothing romantic about the half-clad, uncouth, rank barbarians who periodically made vicious sallies from their hiding places in the hills.

It didn't take long for me to become tired of being cold, damp, and alternately bored and terrified. I was heartily regretting my decision to take on this project, and wished I had thought of another assignment somewhere in the sunny Mediterranean. The only sunshine in Vindolanda came from Sulpicia.

Sulpicia Lepidina was the wife of Flavius Cerialis, prefect of the Ninth Cohort of Batavians stationed at Vindolanda. She was a mature woman of about thirty years, who seemed unaffected by the vicissitudes of life on the frontier. She was, by any standard, beautiful, but what made her remarkable was her smile, bestowed from between even ranks of white teeth upon everyone. There wasn't a man in the fort, from the commonest legionary to the snobbiest tribune who wouldn't have done anything for her after being the beneficiary of one of her smiles.

Not, I hasten to add, that Sulpicia ever encouraged the slightest impropriety. She was the very model of the proper Roman matron—the kind that Roman authors eulogized as the epitome of Roman womanhood before the decline in morals worked its deadly, decadent way on the families and the fabric of the Empire.

She was a dutiful mother to her three children, ran a well-ordered household, and—to her husband's certain appreciation— was a superb hostess not only toward officers' wives, but toward such visiting officials and dignitaries whose duties brought them to Vindolanda.

More than that, she was a devout, pious woman, offering frequently to Venus, the goddess of love, and Vesta, goddess of the hearth. She was a nearly perfect Roman wife. I say 'nearly perfect' because she had one flaw—she was constantly, terribly, suspicious of her husband.

On his part, Flavius Cerialis was an upright, meticulous officer who took his duties seriously. With the same seriousness, in fact, that he took his religion—that being the worship of Sol Invictus, the unconquerable sun— the only religion, to hear him tell it, worthy of a soldier.

And yet he regarded his wife with a watchful, wary eye. I noticed the incompletely concealed tension between them fairly quickly. Where others saw only the smile of a patrician lady bestowed on those of inferior rank, he saw flirtatiousness. A kind gesture became an unspoken invitation. Woe to the man to whom Sulpicia uttered a few words! Cerialis interpreted them as an open invitation to carnal behavior. He was, in short, a man consumed by jealousy, imagining wrongs and evils where there were none.

Theirs was a marriage marred by mutual suspicion. It didn't take me long to discern the reasons behind the state of affairs. A few evenings spent in the bath-house in the company of junior officers with wine-loosened tongues who spoke without concern for the stranger in their midst, and I had a fairly clear picture.

"Cerialis acts as if he's afraid to let her out of his sight," I commented. "He keeps her on a tighter leash than he's got his dog."

"I'd like to be on the end of *her* leash," a fresh-faced tribune said wistfully.

"Fat chance any of us have got of that," rejoined an older officer.

"She doesn't stray?" I asked.

The officer snorted. "Our commander's wife is the most chaste and virtuous woman. I've been with this cohort since Cerialis took command. If Sulpicia had strayed, I'd have heard about it."

"You'd have *done* it," another officer laughed.

"So if she's so trustworthy," I wondered, "then why does he act as if she's about to run off with every stallion who crosses her path?"

The officer pursed his lips. "If you ask me, it's not a problem with her but with him. He's not going to stray, either—he's devoted to her, and I've never heard a whisper of infidelity on his part—but it was different when he was young."

"He has a past?" the youthful tribune inquired.

"Let's say that he enjoyed rather more than the usual number of romantic conquests."

"A regular Adonis, eh?"

I began to understand. Now, being married to a woman of unstained character, Cerialis' past returned to haunt him. Feeling himself to be unworthy, he continually looked for any similar flaw in his wife.

"She seems to keep an eye on him, too," I said.

"Wouldn't you?" the officer shot back. "Once a dog, always a dog." He chuckled.

There it was. Sulpicia, knowing Cerialis' past character, could never develop complete trust in him. It was perhaps not worthy of her.

"Sulpicia the Suspicious, that's what we call her," the officer said.

I too—I may as well admit it now—had fallen under Sulpicia's spell. In this dreary place I felt especially lonely; Erica's absence being particularly poignant. In my gloom I allowed myself to indulge in flights of fancy, imagining, when I saw Sulpicia, that I saw my wife as she might have been had she been a Roman. I reminded myself that Erica was in a better place and, despite her love of travel and desire for new experiences, would have hated Vindolanda.

Sulpicia would occasionally pass by in her litter, like a butterfly in a cocoon, accompanied by a retinue of servants. I'd glimpse her perfect features, her brown hair piled atop her head in the latest fashion, and feel longing and loneliness well up within me. On rare occasions I'd be invited to dinner at the prefect's house, where—unless it was a men-only affair—Sulpicia would be in charge. The precision with which the household slaves performed their duties showed that firmness undergirded her seemingly effortless charm. At night, in the confines of my stark, small room, I would lie in the darkness and pine.

By day I posed as an Imperial Inspector of Accounts—neither a military man who would have to answer to Cerialis' command, nor a total civilian. This gave me direct access to the fort's record books. Not all archaeology is excitement—a lot is tedium, probing the mundane facts of everyday life in the past.

How many people lived in a certain place?

How much grain did they eat?

How many pigs and cattle did they own?

What kind of trade goods passed through the gates?

All the myriad details which make life what it is. A true understanding of the past lay in the details. But it was a task I found tiresome. I was much more interested in people than their possessions.

Perhaps it was also the drudgery of my daily work that made the elegant and inaccessible Sulpicia the focus of so much emotional energy.

As early as my initial excursion to Kourion I'd developed the habit of buying presents for Erica. Not that I could take items from the past to my present, but it perpetuated a tradition developed during the days of our courtship. I liked to imagine how she would have received them. It was a silly gesture, the action of a much younger man, but it helped keep the memory of my wife alive. Now, in my emotionally fragile state, I imagined how Sulpicia would react to receiving these tokens.

Not that I ever intended to give them to her. I was lonely, but not crazy. No, I secreted them in my room and kept my fantasies to myself. The shopkeepers who hawked their wares outside the fort undoubtedly believed that I had a lady-love in camp, as they'd smile and exchange glances whenever I'd show up to inspect their wares. Ah yes, I had quite the little collection of undeliverable presents, which would be left behind when I returned to my own time.

Cerialis, although initially displeased by my arrival—what military man likes to have a bean-counter peering over his shoulder?—had taken me under his wing. Perhaps I am wrong to ascribe base motives for his kindness, but he may simply have wanted to ensure that I gave a good account of him to his masters in Rome. It may also have because I was—as he believed—newly come from Rome, and he was craving news and gossip of home.

Sometimes he would send for me simply to talk. Indoors mostly, because of the wretched weather, but occasionally on horseback, riding over the hillsides. We became friends of a sort. He never suspected the feelings I had for his wife. At least not until the incident of the slipper.

There had been a dinner at the villa of a nearby landowner. Although they had individual litters for ordinary use, on these formal occasions Cerialis and Sulpicia would ride in a double litter, borne by a contingent of burly Cappadocian slaves. It was an inappropriately ostentatious mode of transportation, I thought, considering that Vindolanda was but a wooden fort surrounded by the huts of the camp followers.

The dinner—to which I was invited—was a pleasant enough affair. The villa was small, but well-appointed. There weren't many villas this far north in Britannia—most Roman colonists preferred to live further south where the weather was warmer.

The food was good, and the music passable. Lady Sulpicia, however, had developed a headache and departed early. The bearers had taken her back to the fort, then returned for Cerialis, who had stayed behind. It was then that the problem arose, in the form of a young woman named Julia Candidus, the wife of a cavalry officer who had been called out in the middle of the dinner to attend to some problem with his troops. Julia had indulged rather too freely of the fruit of the vine. By the time the party broke up—her husband still having not returned—Julia was in a bad way. She was behaving, shall we say, with a lamentable lack of inhibition that might have been acceptable in an orgy during Nero's reign, but which was completely out of place in a small outpost.

No sooner had one man rather rudely fended her off than she wrapped her plump arms around my neck and began slurring maudlin sentiments at me with her wine-soaked breath. It was both nauseating and embarrassing. I tried to detach her.

"I'll take her home."

I was surprised to hear Cerialis utter the words. He saw my shocked expression as I finally freed myself from her tenacious clutches. She began to cry.

"It's on the way," he said. "She can ride in my litter. It's either that or sling her across a horse."

I would have voted for the horse, but I wasn't in charge. Cerialis clapped his hands for his slaves. When they appeared he instructed them to place Julia in his litter.

"Shall I ride with you?" I asked, and he agreed.

A light rain was falling as we headed into the darkness, leaving behind the warmth and lights of the villa. Cerialis declined my offer of joining me on my horse and instead rode in the litter with the now nearly insensible woman. I wrapped my cloak tighter against the chill drizzle as we plodded into the night, my horse walking slowly alongside the bearers. I didn't envy them their task. From time to time I exchanged words with Cerialis.

I'm sure we were all relieved when the walls of Vindolanda came into view and we dropped a snoring Julia at the cavalry officer's house. I bid goodnight to Cerialis whose bearers carried him toward his own dwelling while I returned my horse to the stable and sought the guest quarters which had been allotted to me.

I thought no more of the incident until about a week later when another social occasion raised its head—this time, a birthday party for one Claudia Severa, a close friend of Sulpicia. Cerialis had grumbled about going, but finally conceded. I was invited too, to provide company for Cerialis, I suppose.

For a change, it was a pleasant September evening, and there wasn't far to go. Cerialis and Sulpicia rode in their litter, while I, wanting to stretch my legs, walked. I paid little attention to them, but could hear the murmur of their conversation as they talked. We had barely cleared the fort and were proceeding along a path through the forest, when Cerialis exclaimed, "Look at that!"

Simultaneously, an object flew from the litter and landed in the underbrush.

"What was it?" Sulpicia asked.

"I thought I saw a bear," Cerialis replied. "I must have been mistaken."

I stared into the underbrush, wondering what was going on. The answer became clear soon enough, as the forest opened out into a clearing, and the modest home of Claudia Severa and her husband came into view.

"Where's my other slipper?" I heard Sulpicia ask from the litter.

"*Your* slipper?" Cerialis replied, his voice suddenly tense.

"I took them off to wiggle my toes, and now one of them is gone."

I frowned, perplexed. And then, in a flash of insight, I understood, and could have burst out laughing but for the seriousness of the situation.

I could visualize the consternation on Cerialis' face, imagine the thoughts going through his mind as he struggled to find some sort of answer that would satisfy his wife and not cause difficulty to himself. He'd obviously seen one of his wife's slippers on the floor of the litter, assumed it had belonged to Julia Candidus, and flung the potentially incriminating object away. Even though nothing had happened between them, would his wife have believed him? And now, would Sulpicia the Suspicious believe him if he told the truth?

I turned to the slave who had been assigned to me. "Run to my quarters," I said, and bring me back the pair of gold slippers that are in the chest. Hurry, man!"

The slave ran off.

"It must be in here somewhere," Cerialis said from the litter. "Are you sure it's gone?"

"Positive. I don't understand it."

We crossed the clearing, and halted outside the house. Rummaging noises came from the litter.

"I can't go in with only one slipper," Sulpicia exclaimed, sounding exasperated.

Racing footsteps heralded the return of the slave. Panting, he handed me a pair of golden slippers. I smiled, wondering what my wife would have made of all this.

"Excuse me, Commander," I said, approaching the litter. "Here are the new slippers you wanted for your wife."

"New slippers?" Sulpicia exclaimed. She took them from me. "They're beautiful! Wherever did you get them?"

Cerialis seemed unable to talk.

"From a traveling merchant," I replied for him. "Your husband asked me to keep them for him so that you wouldn't find them before he was ready to give them to you."

Sulpicia slipped them onto her feet. "Take this," she said to her maidservant, handing her the remaining old slipper, "and dispose of it."

"You're a dear man," Sulpicia said to Cerialis as they descended from the litter, her face beaming. She bestowed a passing smile upon me, but the look that Cerialis gave me was anything but happy.

Later, in daylight, I retrieved from the underbrush the slipper that Cerialis had thrown there. I kept it as a souvenir, which is why archaeologists digging at Vindolanda in the 20th century found, near the remnants of Flavius Cerialis' house, only one slipper belonging to Sulpicia Lepidina.

Cerialis never spoke to me of the incident, but it came as no surprise when he hinted, quite plainly, that I had stayed at Vindolanda long enough and should take my report to Rome. It was, I thought, an in-character, but ungrateful response for having saved his marriage. But such is the nature of suspicion.

XVI

I didn't return straight to Earth after I arrived back on the Ring from Vindolanda. By now, the Ring had become almost my second home, and the scientists and technicians were familiar faces. Instead, I found a message from the Chair telling me that a previously filed vacation request had been granted. Impatiently I endured the routine debriefing and psychological and medical examinations.

Rather than waiting for a civilian transport, I took passage on Star Frigate *Defender* en route to Heliopolis. I had met the captain over drinks on the Ring, and he had graciously—given my quasi-celebrity status—bent regulations sufficiently to allow me transport on his ship.

It was a bittersweet homecoming, one I had put off for years.

I'd always planned to take Erica to the world of my childhood, but always something else came up. Next year, we promised each other. Next year. But next year never came.

After Emily was born, I'd hoped to take her exploring all the places that Watchit and I had investigated so many years ago. Yet though she traveled to other planets with us—we didn't want her to become an isolated Colony Kid like we had been—somehow Heliopolis was never on the itinerary.

Now it was too late for either of them.

I felt their loss keenly as I stood where my father and I had stood so long ago, on the Rutharian Highland overlooking the Maruska Sea. It was similar, yet different.

Pleasure-craft dotted the violet waves. A new town had sprouted across the Narrows, and The City—that was all we ever called the capital—had grown and spread fungoid-like. An interpretive center had been built where once there was unbroken plain. Altogether, it was a tamer place than I remembered from childhood.

I puffed out my cheeks. What would that boy have thought of the turns his life had taken? What decisions would he have made differently, what alternate courses adopted?

It was just as well, perhaps, that one couldn't see into the future.

It was the present that counted, the only place where one could live.

As the fragrant breeze wafted past me, I could almost feel the pressure of my father's hand on my shoulder. Almost hear my mother's voice calling me and Watchit home for supper.

What if they had never left Heliopolis?

Would I have ever met Erica? Held Emily in my arms?

Would I have adopted my current time-spanning profession?

Would my parents have been lost when the cruise-ship they were traveling on failed to emerge from hyperspace a couple of years after my marriage to Erica? Perhaps they were still there, suspended in some kind of timeless limbo, dead but not knowing it, like Schrödinger's cat—a famous thought experiment of quantum mechanics which led to the conclusion that the postulated cat in question could be both alive and dead at the same time. Or perhaps something else had happened to their ship. Despite all our technological advances, space travel has its dangers and unpredictabilities. Always had, always will.

Life itself is inherently uncertain, unpredictable.

What if?

What if…?

But being in the limbo of "what ifs" was no way to live a life. I was not Schrödinger's cat. I was a man. And I had faith…faith to face the future, faith that all was not pointless and futile.

"Reason and faith," I had read somewhere—perhaps from a pope—"are like two wings on which the human spirit rises."

I needed both wings.

XVII

Watchit, the companion of my youth, had been succeeded by several other dogs. But as I aged, and first my studies and then my professional life demanded more and more of me, I had less and less time to spend in the company of a dog. I didn't bond as deeply to the others as I had to my beloved Watchit, whose passing I mourned greatly.

Yet dogs have always remained close to my heart. And at times on my past-times journeys I wished for the company—and protection—of a canine companion.

The bond between humans and dogs is millennia old. If it is ever severed, humanity will be very much the poorer.

I stayed for hours on the Rutharian Highland, reliving my childhood. I studied the ground, once marked by Watchit's paws. And at any moment I expected him to come bounding over a low hill and prance in circles around me.

But, of course, it didn't happen.

I had tried to go home again; but all I encountered were memories. Perhaps it would have been different if I hadn't been alone.

And so I returned to Earth.

XVIII

"Is this serious?" I muttered, studying the details of the assignment that the Chair had given to me. I preferred it when I could choose my own times and destinations.

"You complained so much about the weather in Britain I thought you'd like to head back to warmer lands," the Chair said, leaning back in his seat, hands folded behind his mop of white hair.

"Italy isn't the problem," I replied.

"What is?"

"The year. AD 79."

"It's just a number," he shrugged.

"Who came up with this cockamamie idea?" I wondered.

"The Department of Women's Studies," he answered.

I nodded sagely. "Whose Department Chair is—

"—a personal friend of mine. Yes."

"Are you sure it's safe?" I asked.

"Why Robert, you're a valuable commodity," the Chair purred. "I'm assured that there is a wide margin of safety. You'll be back long before anything untoward occurs."

By now, I had trust in the Ring and the people who operated it. Of the Chair, I wasn't so sure.

"All right," I said.

"Just work quickly," the Chair added.

XIX: DUST OF CAESAR

His name, I learned later, was Caesar—no less and no more original than Brutus, Maximus, and Caligula, names which were equally popular that year. It was, perhaps, not overly respectful to Titus Flavius Vespasianus, the rightful holder of the title, or to his deified predecessors who had occupied the throne of empire, but there it was. For whatever reason, complimentary or not, he bore the name; and he was unlikely, I suppose, ever to come to the attention of Emperor Titus—*the* Caesar.

I first encountered him while I was strolling down the street on my way to meet a businesswoman named Julia Felix—the person of interest to the Department of Womens' Studies. His master was whipping him unmercifully.

"Useless creature! Why I paid good money for you I'll never know. Behave, I say! Behave!"

He savagely jerked the heavy chain that secured his miserable companion.

I didn't witness any untoward behavior, and so the nature of the infraction remained a mystery. I am given, no doubt, to an unblushing anthropomorphism, but Caesar's sad gaze lit upon me, and in those large, soft eyes I sensed an intelligent mind and a big heart. What passed through his thoughts, I have no way of telling, but to me it seemed as if an immediate understanding sprang into being between us.

His lithe but muscular frame provided a stark contrast to his porcine master, who was, judging from his veined, red nose, given to fine meals and excessive wine. The brute wore an expensive tunic woven with gold threads along the borders. Rings weighed down every one of his sausage-shaped fingers, and his perfumed head could have been smelled half the city away. Rivulets of sweat cascaded down the wattles of his neck.

It was a hot day despite a sea breeze, and I wondered why an obviously wealthy citizen wasn't attended by a panoply of slaves providing for his comfort.

I'm an easy-going man and can take a liking to most people, but I took an immediate aversion to this one. It may be fanciful of me, but he seemed to embody everything that I found unpleasant about Imperial Rome's domain. He could, I suppose, have been a villain in an old melodrama—but I have described him as he was.

To see Caesar plodding unwillingly and dejectedly in such a beast's footsteps galled me.

I took a deep breath and squared my shoulders.

"That's no way to treat a dog," I said, stepping into the man's path.

As if on cue, Caesar growled, and his hackles bristled. I kept my hands by my sides.

"I'll treat my dog any way I choose," the slob snarled. "Who are you to interfere? Stand aside!"

"You'll get better results if you show a little kindness."

"To a guard dog? What kind of idiot are you?"

"Dogs are sensitive creatures—"

"I'll show you sensitive! Make way or I'll set him on you!"

I know dogs fairly well, and I didn't find Caesar's act to be terribly convincing. But it wouldn't have been prudent to put him to the test. Also, a few curious passersby had stopped to stare, and I yielded to the man's demand.

He brushed past me, making a rude comment about daytime drunkenness as he did so. The dog, as he went by, gave my hand a sniff, as if to imprint my scent in his mind. Did he understand that I had tried to help him?

Man and dog disappeared into the steady flow of pedestrians. I sighed. Animal welfare didn't rate highly in Roman society. Such incidents of mistreatment were common and invariably left me with a bitter taste in my mouth. Animals were frequently the forgotten members of history.

"An unpleasant person," I commented to a foodseller who had stepped outside his shop. He reeked of garum, the highly potent and ubiquitous fish sauce which the Romans slathered on almost everything and which, try as I might, I couldn't stomach. I didn't get too close to him.

"Spurius Vesonius," the foodseller replied. "His old man's Vesonius Primus. Thinks he's really someone. I'd keep away from him if I were you."

Vesonius Primus. The name rang a faint, distant bell. I gazed in the direction man and dog had gone. It was silly—and probably futile—but I resolved, despite the foodseller's warning, to see them again.

My meeting with Julia Felix produced material for a well-received paper on the role of women in Roman business, but I was hard-pressed to concentrate. One of the reasons Erica and I had gotten along so well was because of our mutual love of animals.

Well. Many animals had passed through my life, the majority only once.

My chance to meet Caesar again came only a couple of days later. I made some discreet inquiries about Vesonius Primus and his loathsome son, then sent the pater a letter requesting an appointment, to which I received a positive reply.

I was instructed to present myself to an address in the northwestern area of the city, on a street very much like all the others. I approached the blank street-side wall of a typical city house. *Cave canem*—"beware of the dog"— proclaimed a notice painted in thick black letters next to a solid wooden door set with heavy locks. A shop entrance stood open nearby, from which a slave emerged with a bundle of cleaned and pressed cloth.

I wasn't a customer, so I knocked on the house door, and from inside came a deep-throated bark. The warning was obviously not a bluff.

I knocked again. "Hello! Is anyone home?"

The door swung open on oiled hinges and a well-dressed manservant appeared in the doorway. His critical gaze assessed me. "You're not one of master's regular clients," he concluded.

"I am not," I replied. I extended my right hand, a coin held between the index and middle fingers, and his came forward to meet it. "My name is Ostorius Albinus and I have an appointment with your master." I slipped the silver denarius into his palm.

The steward bowed. "You are expected, sir. I shall show you to him." He opened the door wider, ushered me inside, then shut the door securely behind me.

Like many houses, the bare wall fronting the street concealed the opulence inside. The house of Vesonius Primus had once been a gorgeous townhome, decorated in the Augustean style. The walls were painted with elaborate scenes from mythology, the flooring stones were polished, and a mosaic looked as if it had been recently repaired. Clearly the owner was a man of substance. But the house was no longer a home.

It had been converted into a fullery, and Vesonius Primus, I had learned, lived only a short ways off in a charming villa. His offices were here in the fullery. Still, despite the changes, the house maintained an air of distinction and serviced, I suspected, only the highest-class clients.

These impressions formed as I stepped into a typical atrium with a pool situated to catch rainwater from an opening in the roof, a fountain, and an elegant marble-topped table. Doors opening out of the atrium led into what surely had once been the usual assortment of other rooms—the tablinum for family records and ancestral portraits, bedrooms, dining rooms, reception rooms, relaxation rooms, kitchen, and lavatory—but were now certainly offices for Vesonius Primus and his staff—accountants, secretaries, and the like.

A partition wall prevented me from glimpsing the peristyle garden which undoubtedly contained the large scouring vats and washing pans of fuller's earth.

Closer to hand, lying beside the impluvium pool, secured by a solid chain and bronze-studded leather collar to a hook in the wall, was Caesar. He was an impressive specimen, looking like a cross between a German Shepherd and a Labrador, although neither breed existed at this time.

He barked again—rather perfunctorily, I thought, as if to be sure he performed his duty—then wagged his tail at me. His hackles were down.

The steward looked from me to the dog and back again. "I see you know Caesar," he said perceptively.

And that was how I learned Caesar's name. I nodded, although I realized that the whole complexion of this information-gathering venture had just changed. "I believe I saw your master's son walking him in town."

"Master Spurius frequently takes him for protection, particularly when he doesn't want a servant along."

A dog could be trusted to keep his mouth securely shut, no matter what—or whom—he saw.

"He seems to have an agreeable disposition," I said.

"Better than the master's," the steward said in a low voice. "Somebody accosted him in the street and tried to tell him how to handle the dog. He's still mad about it."

I turned aside to hide my amusement. As I did so, I confronted a pedestal supporting a bust of a man. I studied the high forehead, intelligent eyes, and firm mouth. Then I read the inscription, which stated that this bust of Marcus Vesonius Primus had been presented to him by his devoted accountant, a certain Anteros. Judging solely by appearances, Vesonius Primus was a different sort of man than his son.

"Marius, who's there?" came a stentorian voice from a distant room. Vesonius Primus, who had been duumvir—town official—some 35 years ago, was now an old man, nearing eighty. The voice didn't sound like that of a man of eighty.

"A gentleman who has an appointment with you, master," the steward called in response.

"Well, don't keep him outside all day."

Marius motioned toward a doorway. "In there, sir."

I braced myself for what I knew was coming and entered the half-open door. The house wasn't large as houses went, and this room was rendered small by Spurius Vesonius's bulk. The walls had been painted by a fairly average artist. Still, several statues and vases looked to be of tolerable quality, and a trio of silver plates—collectors' items—were displayed to prominent effect. Mostly, I suspected, he kept his wealth hidden away somewhere.

"You!" His fleshy face contorting with sudden anger, Spurius Vesonius half-lurched from where he sat behind a table littered with documents.

"Ostorius Albinus," I said, giving a courteous bow.

"I don't deal with your kind!" Spurius snapped. "Marius!" he called.

"Would you do business with my patron?" I asked. "Marcus Julius Scipio?"

The door opened and Marius appeared. "Master?"

"Bring wine," Spurius said, with an impatient gesture. I'll give Spurius credit—he recovered quickly.

"You know of my patron, then," I said, as Marius nodded and departed.

"I have heard of him, yes."

I smiled to myself. There was no easier way to hook the interest of a rich, influential citizen—Vesonius father and son contributed much to the prosperity of the town's wool industry—than to mention a prominent man who was reputedly even richer. Wealth covets wealth.

Marius returned with a pair of cups.

"I was given to understand that I was meeting with Vesonius Primus," I said, accepting one. Marius departed silently.

Spurius shook his head. "He never leaves his villa. I handle all the family business."

"Very well," I said, and began to spin my tale. I was, I told him, the agent for Julius Scipio, whom everyone knew had his fingers in many pies and was addicted to the pursuit of pleasure. He was interested in building a villa here, where he could enjoy the views over the Sea of Naples. He wanted to expand his shipping concerns. He might fund some games for the town. My role was to make contacts with leading citizens. As a prominent, respected citizen, Spurius could play a significant role in helping my patron's plans come to pass. Of course, this was all confidential. If it didn't work out, then I was to try a different town. It was a story I was using to gain access to many of the town's better houses.

"There would, of course, be business for your fullery," I said, "but perhaps more, of a different variety." I paused to let my words sink in. Spurius Vesonius was what might best be described as an influence broker. He had contacts, he wielded subtle power, he could help or hinder almost any project in town. Contracts could be bought and sold, bribery administered in the right places...

"Of course, if you're not interested," I added after a moment, "I can contact Lucius Caecilius Jucundus," mentioning the name of a well-known banker who was also highly influential.

"No, no!" Spurius exclaimed. "That won't be necessary at all. Not necessary at all."

I was inwardly amused. Spurius was an easy fish to land.

"Jucundus is a good man, a good man," Spurius said, the insincerity evident in his tone, "but you've done the right thing by coming to me."

"Your reputation has traveled widely," I said, and proceeded to lay on the thick flattery.

Spurius lapped it up with more gusto than Caesar emptying a water bowl on a broiling summer's day, practically drooling at the anticipation of adding an illustrious name to his list of clients. He was typical of his type— greedy, unscrupulous, the kind of man who would do anything for money. He probably needed the dog—there were surely many people only too eager to stick a knife into his corpulent carcass.

He asked me several questions which I was able to parry to his satisfaction. It seemed as if the incident with Caesar was not of sufficient magnitude to cause Spurius Vesonius to forfeit a possible profitable deal.

We concluded our business in a considerably more amicable mood than it had begun, and Spurius was more than happy to schedule a time for a second visit. After, I told him, I had visited several other notables.

"Following my patron's instructions," I added.

"Of course, of course." Spurius nodded. "But you won't find anyone who can assist your patron more than I can—and it would be an honor to do so. I am also willing to help out in…other ways."

By now, I had made enough visits to the Imperial Roman era to understand his insinuation. If I did business with him, a portion of the fees my patron paid would come my way. The wheels of Rome required lots of greasing. I thanked him and departed.

Marius escorted me out. Caesar eyed me with diligence, and once again took the measure of my scent.

"Why is your master hard on the dog?" I asked. "Isn't he a good guard dog?"

"Master is hard on everybody," Marius said. He was, like many slaves, willing to speak his mind for a coin, of which I slid another surreptitiously into his palm. "Caesar's been with us for years. Does his duty like a legionary."

High praise, I thought. "From Britannia?"

"Master won't have anything else."

I scratched Caesar's ears and took my leave.

My purported business propositions on behalf of a very real patron— who of course would have been astonished to hear that I was making inquiries on his behalf—took me all over town, and I visited many wealthy citizens in their luxurious homes. Even for a man from my era, from an affluent culture and jaded by the sight of splendid homes, this Roman sea- side resort town was remarkable. Like the Western societies of the 20th and 21st centuries, the Roman Empire rested on the backs of the poor. And even here they were visible. Despite efforts to keep beggars and transients from entering the city walls, there were many common people, including the wretchedly poor, who clogged the streets of Rome and every other city in vast numbers.

I visited Spurius Vesonius again and liked him less. I really had no compelling reason for further visits, but made them anyway—I came solely to see Caesar. A couple of times I heard Vesonius yell at Caesar. And once I saw the big dog slink from his master's presence like a whipped puppy.

A bond grew between me and the guard dog, and I brought him treats, to which Marius turned a blind eye. I wondered if anyone besides me ever showed him any kindness. Marius might, I thought, if he wasn't too afraid of his master himself to do so. I never saw any womenfolk around the house other than slaves, not surprising since these premises were solely for business. But I wondered whether Spurius Vesonius's wife was as disgusting as her husband.

Once I was able to enter the garden and view a wonderful picture of Orpheus among the beasts which graced one end of the garden wall. It must have been a lovely garden before being converted into a fullery.

At last I ran out of pretexts to come, and I told Spurius Vesonius I was going to report to my supposed patron. I had fulfilled my research goals—that of studying Roman business practices in action—and it was time to leave before my cover was penetrated. I'd been becoming increasingly nervous that someone would write to Julius Scipio and learn that I was an imposter.

"I hope you will deliver a favorable report," he said, giving me an obvious wink.

"Most certainly," I replied, trying to remain friendly despite the gall that rose up inside.

"Then I hope to hear from you again in due course." Spurius folded his fat paws together and smiled a smug, self-satisfied smile.

Laying eyes on Spurius again was the last thing on my mind. He was a person who deserved to be forgotten by history.

It was then that I decided, once again, to attempt to change history. In my mind's eye I could see the physicists shaking their heads at me. Would I never learn? Perhaps I was hard-headed and needed the lesson beaten into me one more time.

"I have one additional request," I said.

Spurius's eyes narrowed with suspicion.

"Sell Caesar to me," I pleaded.

He laughed with relief. "That worthless beast?"

"He's from Britannia, like me."

He stared, then he named an absurdly high price. "It would have to be worth my while to go through the bother of importing another one."

"I'll pay it," I said.

He shook his head as if marveling at my lack of intelligence. "Then he's yours, as long as he follows you of his own accord."

"Done," I said, and we shook, although the damp flabbiness of his grip nauseated me.

We went into the atrium. Spurius motioned to Marius, who unhooked Caesar's chain, handed the end to me, and then walked away to open the door to the street.

"Come, boy," I said, "let's go." Caesar walked with me obediently as far as the doorway, and I thought I was home free. Then he stopped and looked back to where Spurius stood at the entrance to his office.

"Come," I repeated, but this time he refused to follow me and instead, moved toward his master. I halted him.

"This way," I said, urging him toward the street. Now, his jerk toward Spurius was stronger.

I caught Marius out of the corner of my eye giving a slight shake of his head.

"You see?" Spurius laughed. "He knows who feeds him. He might be an animal, but he's not *that* stupid."

I tried again, but Caesar would have none of it. I whispered in his ear, "I'm trying to help you, boy," but the loyal soldier wouldn't budge. Finally, I conceded defeat. I handed the end of the chain back to Marius.

"Thanks anyway," I said.

I paused outside the door and looked back. Caesar sat at his accustomed post in the atrium, erect, his posture confident and assured. No intruder was going to get by *him*. I wished I could talk to him, explain what the future held for him—that I could spare him from it—but of course that was impossible. Even if he *could* comprehend, he *wouldn't* comprehend. History, as usual, despite my feeble attempts to change it, could not be altered. I felt as if the universe laughed at me.

Would it matter so much, I wondered? What was the life of a dog on the scale of millennia? If Caesar were to live instead of die, would it change things so very much?

The laws of physics and the laws of logic didn't care about such things.

Our eyes met for the final time.

I might have been fantasizing, but I seemed to know the thoughts passing through his mind.

I'd love to come, his expression said. *I know you'd give me a better life. But I can't leave my post.*

Desertion wasn't in him. Even though his master was a subhuman rotter of a man, Caesar would do his job. I wished him the best. Caesar was a greater example than his master of all that the Romans held highest; he illustrated the nobleness of dog and the inhumanity of man. I admired him, but in my heart I wept for him.

I saluted him, a proper Roman army salute, then walked away from the house of Vesonius Primus and his son, Spurius.

Marius shut the door.

Cave canem.

I departed the town some days later, by boat. I had a conference to present in my own time and one more stop to make before that. And although my previous excursions to the past had all ended safely, I didn't dare risk remaining here.

The lush coastline slid slowly astern, but my eyes hardly saw it. Instead, I had visions of how archaeologists would one day discover Caesar—entombed in the ruins of the house, still chained at his post in the atrium, forgotten or deliberately abandoned by his worthless master. Surely, despite the confusion and terror—thousands of people had died that day, too—someone could have spared a thought for the loyal dog.

It was small consolation to infer that Spurius Primus had almost certainly perished as well.

The villas and fountains of Pompeii melted into the haze, and the last to disappear was the vast, mist-clad bulk of Vesuvius brooding over the town it would shortly both destroy and preserve.

XX

Although the initial celebrity status occasioned by my visit to Kourion had long-since waned, each new foray to the past thrust me briefly once again into the public eye. I was rather like a professional athlete or sports team that achieves publicity only when winning a tournament or championship, and the remainder of the time labors in obscurity, followed only by the most die-hard fan. Who today recalls the shocking upset of mighty Team Terra by an unheralded squad from tiny Hafleikr in the Soccer Cup of Worlds some fifty years ago? Who today ever thinks of Hafleikr except as an exporter of an unusual—and not very popular— perfume made from ingredients generally normally not referred to in sophisticated society?

I was like Hafleikr, only very rarely and transiently newsworthy.

After my return from Pompeii, while the fading limelight had yet to be extinguished, I was approached by the Superior General of the Order of the Interstellar Missionaries of the Cross who had come up with the idea of founding a cross-time branch. He was disappointed to learn that I could not be of assistance. My past-times excursions were performed under CamOx auspices, not my own. I had no special influence with the Director of Ring Operations. More importantly, although I can't exclude the possibility that missionaries from the future were entirely absent from the past, I had never encountered any. And some possibilities were patently absurd. There were no Christians before Christ. No Reformers before the Reformation. And so on. I referred him to the Ring physicists for further explanation of why I had not encountered any obvious missionaries from the future on my excursions.

In fact, I had never knowingly met anyone from the future on my travels. Often, I wondered why not…and if I ever would.

I was also invited to the Vatican, where the Pope received me warmly. He had obviously been better briefed by physicists than had the Superior General, and remarked only that he had enough work to do in the present without worrying about the past. It was, I thought, a very sensible comment.

Living in both the past and present was not easy. Each era had its own sets of problems. Sometimes they overlapped in curious ways.

The Pope gave me his blessing. Then he caught me by surprise, either because I had let something of my inner pain escape, or because he had some insight into the depths of my soul. "God is in all times, Professor," he said. "You do not suffer alone."

That was certainly true, although a concept I tended to forget. Have faith, the pope was telling me, be strong, God has not forgotten you.

Very often I wasn't strong; all too often my mind rehashed the old fears that my good years, the golden years, the years with Erica and Emily, were past, and that there was nothing to look forward to except a bleak future to be endured, rather than embraced. Too often, I listened to those words, becoming again like Schrödinger's cat...neither alive nor dead...or like a bird trying to fly on only one wing.

Caesar the dog had taught me a lesson about honor, and about fidelity to duty. The Pope reinforced it. Faith was nothing if it lacked courage. Just like love. To be effective, it had to have strength. Weak faith was hardly better than no faith at all...like a flickering flame on an arctic world, when what was needed was a raging bonfire—or a modern compact heat source.

I thanked the Pope, and he extracted from me the promise that if the opportunity ever arose, I would greet St. Peter.

I left feeling both comforted and challenged.

XXI

My transient episodes of celebrity produced a consequence which perhaps I should have foreseen, but hadn't: popularity of a different type.

I am—I say without false modesty—a very ordinary person, the kind that generally doesn't attract romantic attention. My looks aren't those of a celebrity; my physique not that of an athlete. I'm eternally grateful that Erica had eyes that could see beyond surface appearance, because otherwise our romance might not have left that dig site where we first met.

And yet it seemed as if voyaging into the past had turned me into an object of desire—and for no other reason than that. I received so many proposals of varying degrees of propriety that I had to enlist one of the department secretaries to handle the rafts of correspondence that arrived at unpredictable intervals.

One I recall in particular came from WitzEnd, a colony world so far from Earth that it was at the limits of the explored galaxy, connected to the remainder of human civilization by only a single, lengthy, hyperspacial route. A world so remote that hardly anyone has ever heard of it. I certainly hadn't. I felt sorry for anyone on a world as sparsely settled as WitzEnd— and there were many such; prospects were probably few and far between.

Such was not for me.

I had only to close my eyes and I could see Erica and myself exploring the remains of a vanished civilization on Haider III; playing tennis, soccer, and redball, a game originated on Riverbend whose intricacies I could never master; attending a concert of ancient music in New York; or me acting as her assistant as she documented the efforts of the colonists of Finzlet to preserve an endangered species of intelligent crustacean.

Not for us the illusory pleasures of those who tapped into the MindNet. Both of us had encountered addicts who squandered their own lives while experiencing the sensory inputs of other people. No, we preferred to experience life for ourselves.

And so my ears could still hear her gentle laughter, as when we went horseback riding in Montana and I was assigned an aging mule while she received a fine filly. And her voice would take on a tone of mock severity when she'd rebuke me for an excess of seriousness. "Loosen up, Robbie," she'd chide. "You don't have to be a professor *all* the time." And she sang...oh how she sang Gregorian chant in Latin, while I rumbled along in a dreadfully off-key bass.

And there was nothing sweeter than seeing her with Emily...

I had dreamed of creating a family as happy—and traditional—as my own had been...

Time, it is said, heals all wounds. But time is a slow, methodical physician, unable to be rushed. And I was a slow healer.

And strangely enough, when a woman did, momentarily, touch my heart, it wasn't in my own time, but in the Egypt of AD 132.

XXII

"You'll like Egypt. Trust me," greeted the Chair one morning, when he'd summoned me to his office.

Rumors of my next assignment had been circulating through the department. Some seemed more credible than others. The three most likely I considered to be encountering Marcus Aurelius in the forests of Germania, attempting to meet Cleopatra's younger sister Arsinoë who had fled for sanctuary to the fabled Temple of Diana in Ephesus following her defeat by Julius Caesar, or meeting some Amazons serving with a Roman legion in Britain. Germania in winter sounded singularly dismal, and I wasn't sure about interacting with female warriors, so I was plumping for Ephesus. Arsinoë had always fascinated me—I had never been impressed by Cleopatra, and wondered how history might have been different if Arsinoe had become queen instead of her scheming older sister.

Egypt hadn't surfaced in the rumor mill. I regarded the Chair warily.

He smiled benevolently. "No wars, no plagues, no disasters." He shrugged. "Idyllic, if you ask me."

"Idyllic," I repeated, not bothering to point out that I hadn't asked him.

"Boat trips on the Nile. Attending the theater in one of the great cities of the ancient world. Camel rides in the shadow of the Pyramids."

It did sound good. The prospect of entering the past without being in the shadow of disaster appealed to me.

Was there a hidden trick? Or was I being unnecessarily suspicious? I couldn't think of a serious objection, other than the camels and their fleas, but should be able to avoid them.

"What am I expected to do?" I asked.

"Nothing too hard, I imagine. Observe the construction of Antinoöpolis, that's all. The full details will be forthcoming."

It certainly sounded innocuous.

"All right," I agreed.

"Beautiful women in Egypt," the Chair remarked, pretending to be casual.

"Have you seen them?"

He waved a dismissive hand. "It's high time you came out of your shell, Robert."

"My shell, as you call it, is none of your business," I retorted.

His expression remained bland. "Just thinking of your welfare, that's all."

"My welfare is just fine, thank you very much. The medics tell me I am perfectly mentally stable."

"As you wish."

I was fuming as I left the Chair's office. Although perhaps, in retrospect, I did him an injustice.

XXIII: EUDAIMON

Eudaimon was a lucky girl, at least until she met me.

It was early spring in Alexandria-upon-Egypt. I leaned against the smooth warm stone of the parapet on the viewing stage of the great Pharos Lighthouse, enjoying the panorama over the city while waiting for my breath to return after the long climb up the interior ramp which wound its way to the summit. I could have saved myself the effort by hiring a donkey like those which pulled carts of firewood up to the furnaces powering the light, but I'd been slacking on the exercise and thought I'd benefit from it. It was more than I had bargained for, however, and I promised myself that if I ever decided to ascend the Pharos again, I'd shell out for four hooves.

Still, the view from three hundred feet up was worth a few aches and pains. And there was another benefit: a cool, salt-tinged breeze fresh off the Eleusinian Sea ruffled my tunic and dried the sweat on my brow. I inhaled deeply and savored the tang. While Alexandria was remarkably clean for an ancient city, there was no escaping the pungency created by a half-million people living with the sanitary technology and attitudes of two thousand years ago. Some Temporal Historians—because by now, others had followed in my footsteps—couldn't stand the odors and consequently had either short careers or restricted their travels to more advanced eras. My olfactory equipment was made of sterner stuff, yet even so, I relished the occasional nasal cleansing.

But I digress.

Above me, vast bronze mirrors reflected the Pharos light out to sea, and higher still, a statue of a muscular Poseidon held aloft a trident. Below, the shimmering, sea-bird-spackled blue waters of Alexandria's twin harbors bristled with ship-masts. Much of the commerce of the Roman Empire flowed through this port, from the huge grain ships carrying food to the Eternal City, to merchant vessels importing and exporting every conceivable type of goods, to warships and troop transports.

A long causeway—the Heptastadion—lined with quays and dockyards, connected Pharos Island to the mainland. And there, the city spread in a vast arc. To my far left, the labyrinthine royal palaces, interspersed with lush gardens and groves of palm trees, glittered in splendor on the Lochias promontory, a reminder of when the House of Ptolemy had ruled Egypt. On the crowded shoreline, the Emporium, marked by a pair of obelisks, bustled with activity. Straight ahead were the tomb of Antony and Cleopatra and the Soma, where Alexander the Great rested. Further on, the Museion—the great Library—sat in sculpted gardens, and the Temple of Pan perched on its hill. To my right, the golden roof of the Serapion gleamed sunlike under a translucent sky.

The broad, colonnaded Canopic Way bisected the city like an arrowshaft. And packed inside the city walls were endless public buildings, homes, shops, and temples. Alexandria was truly a feast for the eyes. It made Rome look like a tawdry street tramp, all make-up and no genuine beauty.

Thinking of a feast reminded me that I hadn't eaten lunch and that I'd spotted a pastry seller on this level eager to appease hungry tourists. I stepped back, turning as I did so, to go and find him.

Had I been more attentive, I might have noticed and avoided the young woman who was passing behind me, her footsteps failing to register on my consciousness, and my life would have been the poorer. As it was, I caught her in mid-step and knocked her off her feet. She fell sideways, landing awkwardly against the balustrade.

"Ouch!" she exclaimed. "Diana's armpits, why don't you watch where you're going?"

"I'm sorry!" I gasped, hurrying to help her to her feet. "Are you all right?"

"You broke my nose, you clumsy oaf!"

She clutched the damaged organ, which indeed displayed an unnatural angle. Blood streamed down her face. Her eyes watered.

I pulled a square of cloth from my money pouch and handed it to her. She snatched it from me and pressed it to her nose.

"You need to see a physician," I said.

Brown eyes glared at me. "And my dress is ruined!"

I couldn't dispute that assessment, either. Blotchy red streaks dripped down the turquoise linen. A fuller would rejoice at the business but probably not have much luck removing the stains.

Suddenly, a hand grabbed the collar of my tunic and jerked me backward.

"Get away from the mistress!"

I twisted my neck to get a view of the newcomer. He was a burly young man with a not very intelligent face. His free hand rested on the hilt of a dagger suspended from his belt. Slightly behind him stood a willowy girl.

"Pyrrhos! Lydia!" the young woman exclaimed. "Where have you been?"

"Your pardon, mistress," the youth replied, not relaxing his grip on me. "The donkeyman demanded more money than was agreed upon—"

"Never mind the donkeyman!" she snapped. "You're supposed to be protecting me from riff-raff."

The young man shook me. "Shall I throw him over, mistress?"

Three hundred feet to the rocks beneath. I gulped.

Drawing a breath, I tried to speak with dignity and authority.

"Not unless you want to answer to the emperor," I said. "Take your hands off me."

He glanced at the woman, and she nodded. His grip released.

I took a step away and shrugged my tunic back into place. "You should tell your servants to be more careful whom they lay hands on," I said to the young woman. "Such rashness could cost him his life."

"Who are you, sir?" she demanded, giving me a critical look as if trying to decide whether or not I was a respectable person. The quality of my tunic and the gold ring I wore should have given her some reassurance.

"Certainly not riff-raff," I said. "Gaius Veronius Aemilianus. I'm an inspector of buildings and public development for Emperor Hadrian."

By now I had spent enough time in the past that my accent—which I usually passed off disingenuously as Britannic—was less pronounced. It was just as well, since Hadrian would most likely have sent a representative from Italy or the East.

I faced the servant Pyrrhos. "I bumped into your mistress by accident."

His aggressive attitude melted away. His hand, which had remained hear his dagger, fell away. "I...I didn't know, sir..."

"Let's forget it," I said. "There's no harm done, and your concern for your mistress is commendable." I returned my attention to the young woman. "May I inquire as to your name?"

Her expression had softened, her scrutiny having apparently convinced her that I might be a trustable upper-class individual after all. "My name is Eudaimon," she said indistinctly through the cloth. "My father is mayor of Antinoöpolis. He came to meet with government officials and suppliers, and I accompanied him."

I bowed. "The honor is mine. With your permission, may I escort you to a physician? I shall, of course, pay his fee and reimburse you the cost of your dress. It is the least I can do."

She hesitated for just a moment. "That would be acceptable."

She beckoned to the burly youth and the maidservant. "Attend us."

That was my introduction to Eudaimon. Her name meant "happiness" or "good spirit," both of which—I learned later—applied to her.

We rode down by donkey—at least Eudaimon did, clutching its bridle with one hand and the cloth to her nose with the other—while I jogged alongside with the two slaves following.

"Do you have a litter?" I asked when we reached ground level.

"No," she replied. "I prefer to walk…it's a better way to experience the city."

We located a Greek physician without much difficulty and sent a message to Eudaimon's father about her accident. The young woman bore the physician's painful ministrations stoically. She was in a better mood after he'd finished setting her nose, although slightly groggy from a mixture of poppy extract and henbane he'd administered as an analgesic.

"You'll be as good as new; maybe better," he said, giving her nose a final tweak.

She raised her eyebrows at me, and made an obvious effort not to snicker. I hadn't had the chance to see her nose pre-trauma, but I gathered that she hadn't been totally happy with it.

I paid the physician, and our next stop was the marketplace, where Eudaimon selected a costly dress from a clothes-seller.

"What does your inspection tell you, Inspector?" she asked as she held her purchase in front of her.

"You have excellent taste," I said appreciatively.

"I didn't care for the old one very much anyway," she chuckled.

She was, I judged, about twenty-four. Her features demonstrated that blend of Greek and Egyptian influence common to people in the larger cities of Egypt. Her brown eyes gleamed with lively intelligence. Her hair was dark, her eyebrows marginally heavy, and her ears a trifle overlarge. She had a determined set to her chin.

In fact, she seemed to radiate determination. She was petite and slightly below average in height, but she struck me as one of those people whose spirits are greater than their bodies. Her slender, well-proportioned figure moved with an elegance that came from good breeding and upbringing.

She reminded me of Egypt itself: Egypt under the Romans was a curious mixture of Greek and Roman influence overlying the native Egyptian culture. It was a concoction that made me feel vaguely uncomfortable.

I tried to pin down what it was about Egyptian culture which didn't resonate with me. Perhaps it was the obsession with death or the aura of mystery which lurked in the shadows of the massive, brooding temples. I doubted that I could fit in here as well as in the remainder of the Roman world.

By now, though, I was an established Temporal Historico-Archaeologist with several years and a number of trips to the past to my credit, and a developing reputation to maintain. A colleague from a different university had some burning questions about the newly-founded city of Antinoöpolis, influence with my Chair—and more importantly, the grant money to fund a past-times investigation—and so here I was, getting established in Alexandria before heading up the Nile.

Eudaimon's cheerful presence gave me temporary respite from my nagging sensations. She seemed quite content with my company as we puttered through the myriad stalls and booths in the Emporium. It was perhaps not usual for an affluent young woman to do her own shopping, but a visit to the big city of Alexandria was surely an opportunity not to be missed by a girl from a small town. It was also not the order of the day for a respectable young woman to converse with a strange man, but this was Alexandria—and nothing was normal here.

Had I been in her sandals, I'd have headed home and put an ice bag—or a cool cloth, since ice bags didn't exist in Alexandria—on my face. But a swollen nose and the pain she must be feeling weren't enough to dissuade Eudaimon from her shopping excursion. I now saw why she had two servants with her—Lydia handled the money, while the muscular Pyrrhos carried the increasing number of purchases.

The sun drooped toward the horizon, and I tried to take my departure from Eudaimon. She would have none of it.

"You must join us for dinner," she stated. "Lydia, run ahead and tell my father we shall have company. Veronius Aemilianus and Pyrrhos can escort me home."

"That's not necessary—" I began.

"But it is my desire," she said forcefully. "Besides, as mayor of Antinoöpolis, my father will wish to meet you. He's very eager to please the emperor." She frowned suddenly. "Unless your wife is here with you?"

I shook my head. "I have no wife."

"In that case, come."

What could I do? I acceded to her wishes, Lydia ran ahead, and the overladen Pyrrhos shouldered his burdens without murmur.

That evening found me reclining at table with Demokedes, Mayor of Antinoöpolis, in a suite of rooms attached to a government office. He was a distinguished man of some sixty years, his hair faded to gray, who obviously had fathered Eudaimon later in life. The many jeweled rings on his fingers proclaimed his wealth. Like his daughter, he was of mixed Greek and Egyptian ancestry, although like most men of his class, acknowledged only the Greek part and did his best to appear Roman. He greeted me politely and listened with calm grace to my apologies for injuring his daughter.

"The young heal quickly," he said, "and she won't be spoiled forever."

We talked amicably through several courses; then he said, "Eudaimon tells me that you're an inspector for the emperor."

I don't like to mislead people about my intentions, but it's unavoidable.

No matter where I go, to see what I want to see, I have to have a cover story of some sort to provide a reason for being there. I am, after all, only a harmless observer. Still, it felt then—as it always does—like lying.

And there was, too, a legitimate imperial inspector who would be making his way to Antinoöpolis. By dint of some diligent inquiries in Rome—as well as bribery and some very good luck—I'd learned that the man was laid up at his villa in Misenum with dysentery and was unlikely to venture abroad any time soon. I'd decided to step into his shoes—temporarily, of course. I wasn't terribly worried. If he did show up, I could always claim that an imperial clerk had muddled his orders and mistakenly dispatched two inspectors.

I nodded. "I'd show you my commission, but it's in my rooms." I'd worked long and hard to create a document that no one could distinguish from a legitimate imperial commission. I'd discovered long ago that having the appropriate paperwork opened many doors and oiled many wheels in the Roman bureaucracy.

Demokedes waved a gracious hand. "At your convenience."

"Hadrian," I said, "is most concerned that Antinoöpolis become a city worthy of the great honor which has been bestowed upon it."

"Naturally. I regret that progress is slower than I would wish," Demokedes said hesitantly, "but you shall see for yourself the diligence with which I am attending to the tasks. My books will be open to you."

"I am sure I shall have no cause for complaint," I replied.

He relaxed at that and called for more wine.

"When are you leaving for Antinoöpolis?" he asked.

I shrugged. "When I've found suitable transportation."

"Good!" He clapped his hands. "Then you shall travel with me. By the time we reach Antinoöpolis, you will know the city as well as I do." He stroked his chin. "I leave in three days. In the meantime, if you would like the company of my daughter Eudaimon…she's eager to visit the Museion, the Tomb of Alexander and that of Antony and Cleopatra—places you yourself would no doubt like to see…"

He left the sentence hanging. I could think of no polite way to refuse. And, to be truthful, I didn't really want to.

"I would be delighted," I said, "although I wouldn't wish to appear unseemly—"

He waved a languid hand. "Pyrrhos will accompany you." He leaned forward and lowered his voice, "Between you and me, Eudaimon is a girl of boundless energy and curiosity…having a mature man to keep an eye on her will relieve my mind of many anxieties. Alexandria has temptations which are absent from Antinoöpolis."

Well, I'd broken the girl's nose. The least I could do would be appease her father.

I returned to my own more modest rooms in a mellow mood.

The following morning, I presented myself at Demokedes's residence. Eudaimon's nose had swollen further overnight, and even heavily applied make-up couldn't hide the pair of black eyes she was developing. But she waved away the veil her maidservant brought her. Followed by Pyrrhos, we set off into the city.

To my surprise, the days in Alexandria proved to be quite enjoyable. Eudaimon was a charming companion, intelligent and witty. She wasn't the spoiled daughter of a wealthy man, but a clear-minded and headstrong young woman who reminded me of my wife when we first met...back in the days when I was flush with the enthusiasm of youth, and the future held only happy prospects. I think—though such judgments are rash and dangerous—that she and Erica would have liked each other.

The Library was awe-inspiring, and I only wished I had the chance and the ability to devour all the great literary works it contained—works that had been lost to history when the Arabs put the finishing touches to the Library's destruction. Others with more literary knowledge and learning, I assumed, would at some point be assigned that envious task. To regain the lost learning of the past...what a prospect!

I observed the philosophers, physicians, musicians, poets, and astronomers and longed to converse with them openly—sharing their insights and revealing to them some of the secrets of the future. The botanical gardens were magnificent, and the zoological gardens contained a number of species extinct or only genetically reconstructed in my own era.

The tomb of Alexander was even more fabulous, although my eyes ached from the glare of gold when at last we reemerged from the brightly lit inner sanctum where the great conqueror reposed. I had stood for long minutes regarding his marble effigy, which exuded power and great ambition.

The tomb of Antony and Cleopatra, while resplendent, affected me less. Antony was, after all, merely a failed Caesar-aspirant, while Cleopatra was a scheming, ambitious woman whose desire to become queen of the world had foundered on the twin rocks of Caesar's assassination and Antony's dissipation.

It is said that the human brain contains enough capacity to record a thousand years of living. I wanted to fill my brain with as much as possible.

"Let's go to the Theater," Eudaimon suggested on the day before we were to depart. Plays in the Greek and Roman world were practically, if less romantically, performed in the daytime.

"I really couldn't—"

"My father was going to attend, but a business matter came up, and he suggested you might escort me."

And so we watched Aristophanes' *The Birds* performed. We tarried long, and dusk was falling by the time we made our way back to Demokedes' lodging.

Eudaimon took my arm as we walked back through the darkened streets. Alexandria was probably not much safer at night than Rome, where walking abroad at night invited a mugging, so I kept alert, as did Pyrrhos, who, after rejoining us when we left the theater, followed a respectful distance behind.

Gently, I disengaged my arm.

"Do you find me displeasing?" she pouted.

"On the contrary," I replied. "I find your company most pleasing. But—"

She slipped her arm back through mine.

And there it stayed until I deposited her at her father's rented villa and departed.

Eudaimon was definitely not a typical woman of her time.

Soon after, we took a ship up the Nile, carried by a north breeze. It was an archaeologist's dream cruise, seeing the great monuments of Egypt when they were much younger. I stretched out on a chair on the deck of the boat, Eudaimon sitting beside me, soaking in the scenery. We passed countless temples, colossal statues, obelisks and monuments. The pyramids, while not in the prime of their glory, were still less worn than in my own time. The wildlife was astounding—hippopotami munching huge mouthfuls of green plants, crocodiles lurking on the banks or in the reeds, numerous birds—ibises, storks, falcons…At night I heard the yapping of jackals.

We passed many small villages where children played, men fished, and women beat out their clothes in the muddy water. Somewhere—although there was no way to recognize the site—we passed the spot where Julius Caesar defeated the army of King Ptolemy XIII and his sister Arsinoë at the Battle of the Nile, and established Cleopatra as the last Queen of Egypt.

Demokedes worked on his books, joining us occasionally to offer his own commentary on the sights. But for the most part, Eudaimon and I conversed together. By now, her nose had returned to its normal size, and her black eyes had faded to a less obvious shade.

Several days passed in a delightful haze, and it seemed all too soon that our captain announced that we were drawing close to Antinoöpolis. The morning sun rising into a cloudless sky revealed a delightful scene of gracefully waving palm trees and low hills stretching away from the Nile. Boats were tied up near shore, and it would have been hard to imagine a more tranquil setting.

There had been a settlement here for centuries, initially known as Antinoë, which had boasted temples erected by Akhenaten and Rameses II, and New Kingdom tombs. But time and sand had done their work, and Antinoë had become simply another half-forgotten stopping point for boats traveling the Nile. It could have vanished completely, and nobody would have noticed or mourned its passing.

All that changed when nineteen-year-old Antinous, favorite of the Emperor Hadrian, drowned nearby. Officially, he fell overboard from a boat. But was it an accident, murder, suicide, or had Antinous, as persistent rumors insisted, been a sacrifice in some mysterious religious ritual? Nobody knew.

The Egyptians believed that drowning in the Nile conferred immortality; therefore, the grief stricken Hadrian—risking ridicule from his detractors— declared Antinous to be a god. Statues and temples to his memory sprouted up around the Empire. Antinoë was renamed Antinoöpolis, and was officially founded on October 30, 130, to honor the youth. The emperor intended it to be an administrative center for Upper Egypt.

Such it would become. But at the moment, although the outlines of the new city were evident, and spanking-fresh marble gleamed in the sunlight, vast stretches still resembled a construction zone. Like any work in progress, the mounds of dirt, foundation holes, and trenches for sewers didn't make for a pretty sight—even from a distance. Old Antinoë, I thought, as our boat approached a quay, had been a town that had desperately needed rebuilding.

Even before we reached the dock, while Demokedes was supervising his slaves preparatory to landing, Eudaimon was by my side, pointing out the highlights, as she had done all the way down the Nile.

"It will be beautiful," she enthused. "Over there will be the circus and the hippodrome. Can you see the roof of the theater? It's nearly complete. There's the temple of Antinous—father made certain it was finished first..." As she spoke, her face glowed with pride for her father.

"Where are you staying?" Demokedes asked, coming to join us.

"At the mansio, I presume," I said cautiously. Most decent towns provided a lodging place for visiting officials, paid for out of state funds.

"Nonsense! You'll stay with me. I have guest quarters. Much better than anything you'll find in town."

"I don't wish to impose—"

"Nonsense!" he repeated.

And that was that.

Litters met us at the dock and bore us to Demokedes' magnificent house. A column of slaves carried Demokedes' goods and Eudaimon's purchases. Demokedes' steward conducted me to my spacious quarters, brought me scented water to refresh myself, and a plate of fruit. A slave appeared with a fresh tunic and oil for my hair

Demokedes, I thought, was really giving me the royal treatment.

Soon after, Demokedes took me into his office, spread out maps and drawings, and gave me an exhaustive overview of the work in Antinoöpolis. Then, with his construction foreman and Eudaimon, he took me on a walk through the city.

Had I been a real inspector for the emperor, I would certainly have given Demokedes high marks for organization and planning. He was totally rebuilding the old, ruined city. Antinoöpolis' two main streets with their row of double colonnades gave the instant impression that here was a Roman city of note—and Demokedes was building a Roman city, avoiding Egyptian influence. The public buildings expressed the appropriate aura of power and permanence. I was less interested in the Temple of Antinous, a typical Greco-Roman structure, although I made the necessary respectful comments. The public baths were quite elaborate and the triumphal arch nearly splendid. Already, villas for officials were sprouting up with views over the Nile. The forum boasted a fair collection of shops and eateries, and common housing seemed adequate. It was still rough, with piles of building stones and timbers stacked everywhere, and crews of slaves and laborers engaged in work, but Antinoöpolis, I thought, would become quite a respectable city.

I knew, of course, that later Diocletian would proclaim it a metropolis, and still later it would become a significant Christian city. Decline would inevitably set in, and it would eventually be destroyed by Saladin. Still, extensive ruins would remain until the nineteenth century, when many of the finer materials would be carted off to be used in the construction of a sugar refinery. So much for Hadrian's dreams for Antinoöpolis.

Eudaimon seemed to be determined to ensure that I missed nothing. What her father left out, she filled in.

"I'd like to show you the artwork of Antinoöpolis," Demokedes said, "but perhaps that can wait for the morrow."

My feet hurt—I would have loved a good pair of modern shoes—and I was tired and dusty. "There's no need to see everything in one day," I said, yawning. "I'd appreciate it more later."

"Tomorrow it is, then," he said. "In the meantime," he continued, obviously picking up on my discomfort, "my private baths are at your disposal."

"Thank you."

"I can show Veronius our city's treasures, father," Eudaimon said as we directed our footsteps back toward the villa. "I know how busy you are." She gave me an eager, hopeful look.

He nodded briskly. "My daughter," he said in my direction, "is much more knowledgeable about artistic matters than I."

"It might be better," I said cautiously, "if I were to pursue independent inquiries—for the sake of appearances, you understand."

Demokedes pursed his lips, and I thought he might agree, but Eudaimon forestalled him, her features becoming suddenly stern. "Surely not, good sir! Independent inquiries might be fine for construction or for examining financial books, but artwork must be seen in company to be appreciated and enjoyed."

Eudaimon was, I thought, a very outspoken young woman for her era.

Demokedes raised his eyebrows.

"Besides," Eudaimon said, in a less fiery manner, "I can tell you details about the artists that you would otherwise not learn."

Maybe she had a point. To learn about Roman-Egyptian artwork from a local wasn't an opportunity to be sniffed at. My colleagues would never forgive me if I passed up such an opportunity—in the unlikely event they ever learned of that eventuality.

"Very well," I agreed. "I'd be delighted."

She smiled, the movement transforming her face.

I relaxed in Demokedes' private baths, enjoying a rubdown with oil and a scraping with a strigil from a smooth-handed slave. Dinner was an elaborate affair; Demokedes was determined to impress me no matter what the cost. I felt a twinge of guilt at abusing his hospitality, but comforted myself with the thought that even if my intention wasn't to send reports to Hadrian, posterity would learn of and appreciate the work of Demokedes. I wondered if that would have satisfied him, or whether he'd have preferred the commendation of the current emperor over the distant applause of people two thousand years in the future.

But then, I thought, why not send a favorable report to Hadrian? Surely a busy emperor wouldn't remember the name of every imperial retainer. If he didn't recollect G. Veronius Aemilianus, so what? It might cause consternation to a scribe or a librarian in the imperial archives, but that hardly mattered. Surely the fact that I—or rather, G. Veronius Aemilianus—didn't exist was no reason not to send a report. It was the least I could do to repay Demokedes for his hospitality. With a smile to myself, I resolved to do it.

I slept almost as well as I had on the boat, where the gentle motion of the Nile invariably lulled me into pleasant dreams.

In the morning, Eudaimon and I went into the city, accompanied by a secretary assigned by Demokedes to make notes for me. There were so many statues of Antinous in Antinoöpolis that I wondered where all the people would fit. The youth cropped up everywhere. I asked Eudaimon to ignore them and show me other works. She knew the city intimately; on the infrequent occasions when she didn't know something, she knew someone who did.

Despite the newness of the city, she showed me several exquisite mosaics and frescoes that the future was immeasurably poorer for not possessing. I learned much about some hitherto unknown artists.

I bought us lunch at a thermopolium. Eudaimon had a flatbread topped with goat cheese, anchovies, mushrooms, and sliced octopus, while I had honey-glazed medallions of ham with bay leaves and figs, folded in a thin, crispy pastry crust.

"Tell me," I said, between bites, and after we'd discussed several unrelated topics. "Why is a young woman of your status not married?"

She laughed. "I wondered when you would ask. Indeed, I was almost married once, years ago. My father arranged an alliance with a young officer from a good family. But he led an expedition up the Nile, and never returned. We never learned whether he had died...or found someone he fancied more."

She shrugged. "And when my mother died I became the mistress of the house. My father hasn't expressed any desire to remarry, and I am helpful to him—I don't think he could run the house without me."

"Surely there's more," I said.

Her glance was measured. "My father has proposed several suitors, but I rejected them." Her full lips quirked. "I won't let my father marry me off to just anyone. I'm an outspoken woman. Most men don't appreciate that."

True enough, I thought, but marriage in the Roman world wasn't like that of contemporary society. The *pater familias* ruled. If he wanted his daughter married—usually to a family that would be a good alliance with his own—then he married her off, and that was that.

But as I looked into Eudaimon's eyes, and saw the strong set of her chin, I realized that here was a woman determined to have her own way. Like Cleopatra, perhaps. Maybe Eudaimon even shared some bloodlines with that willful last Queen of Egypt. And Demokedes...undoubtedly he was a doting father, willing to yield to his firm-willed daughter.

She was still looking at me with a strange, even hopeful expression.

"I'm sure the right suitor will come along," I said neutrally.

Her gaze dropped, and I felt a pang of dismay. I liked Eudaimon, yes...but as a marriage prospect?

"What would you see next?" she asked, disappointment evident in her tone. "Perhaps the Temple of Isis?"

"Fine," I said, although I was becoming jaded by the endless procession of nearly identical shrines. "And then perhaps the old Egyptian temples."

"Certainly."

There was inquiry in her tone, and to cover my slip I said, "An inspector of public works needs to see the old buildings as well as the new ones."

Hadrian's real inspector would probably not be interested in the old buildings at all. He'd be interested only in the new buildings being erected for Hadrian.

"Of course."

I found the ancient Egyptian temples much more interesting than the newly-built Roman ones. As we studied the statues of long-dead pharaohs, the brightly painted hieroglyphics, and the representations of Egypt's many curious deities, Eudaimon's cheerful mood returned, and the awkward moment seemed to be forgotten.

And so over the next few days, we spent many hours together, with the secretary tagging behind at a discreet distance. I had to remind myself from time to time to instruct him to take notes; with my attention focused on Eudaimon, I tended to forget his presence.

I dined regularly with Demokedes, who frequently invited local notables to join us. I met more officials than I could keep count of. The household was managed expertly—Eudaimon, I guessed.

I complimented her on it. "I haven't seen such a well-run household even in Rome," I said.

She beamed. "You're kind."

"Merely honest."

"I've always wanted to see Rome," she said.

"Why? You've visited Alexandria."

"But Rome is the Eternal City...the Mother of Men. I dream of walking through the Forum and seeing Hadrian himself pass by..." She shook herself. "But what are a girl's dreams?"

"Perhaps they will come to pass someday," I said.

"The evening is still young," she said. "Would you walk with me in the garden?"

"My pleasure."

Demokedes hadn't skimped on his gardens, either. They were beautiful by daylight, and moonlight gave them an air of feminine mystery. The palm trees rustled in a gentle breeze, and tree-frogs chirped a pleasant chorus. The air was fragrant with the scent of roses and other plants that I couldn't identify. Music wafted from the house, where a lyre player entertained Demokedes and several guests. It was idyllic...as the Chair had predicted.

Eudaimon and I strolled in quiet companionship, content merely to enjoy the silence. Then we sat on a bench near a torch-lit fountain and talked late into the night. I told her much about Rome, and somewhat less about Britannia, since my visit there had been thirty years earlier, local dating.

In return, she described life in Antinoöpolis and this area of Egypt, known as the Fayyum. I learned of her family's slow rise in prominence, culminating in her father's appointment as mayor of the new city. She certainly had led a charmed life, wanting for nothing except a companion.

By the time the lamps in the house were being extinguished and the household preparing for bed, we were sitting very close together.

I was too excited and confused to sleep well that night.

In the interests of objectivity, the code of ethics drawn up for Temporal Historians, like that of physicians, prohibits affairs with subjects. Otherwise…imagine unscrupulous men going back in time to have affairs with Cleopatra, Nefertiti, or Helen of Troy; ambitious, self-seeking women wishing to lie with Marc Antony, Paris, or Julius Caesar. It is certainly possible that among Julius Caesar's many amours was a woman from the future, but we tried to make such events as improbable as possible. And so time travel—at least in my age—was restricted to authorized researchers who agreed to a strict code of conduct.

I had signed it without qualms, too heartsick from Erica's death even to consider the possibility that I'd be attracted to another woman. Even though Erica had often expressed her hope that in the event of her loss I'd find happiness and love again, I'd dismissed the possibility out of hand.

But now…

Could I really be seriously attracted to Eudaimon? I was Christian, she a pagan.

And yet she seemed like a woman out of time, more akin to my era than her own. She was determined, organized, well-educated, personable. She would have made the perfect companion for a Temporal Historian. Had she been born in my era, I could easily have imagined us visiting the past together. The twenty-year disparity in our ages wasn't insurmountable.

Eudaimon was also, I thought, a woman who wouldn't be denied. When I had tried—half-heartedly and ineffectively—to push her back, she had become even more attracted to me. And now I was weakening.

In the morning, I told her that I had work to do alone. Her face fell as I retired to my quarters.

I worked undisturbed until a slave knocked on the door and delivered plates of food and a goblet of wine.

"With the domina Eudaimon's compliments," he announced.

I pled fatigue that evening and declined dinner, but the same thing happened.

As it did the next day, and the next.

I couldn't remain sequestered indefinitely. And Eudaimon wasn't about to let me. A slave arrived bearing a message from Demokedes, although I detected Eudaimon's hand at work, inviting me to a concert. Of course, I accepted.

When I presented myself at the main house, dressed in a toga for the occasion, Eudaimon was waiting, clad in her finery, a maidservant in attendance.

"You look charming," I said. She wore a gown of deep purple, which rustled silkily when she moved. A necklace of pearls graced her neck, and pearl and gold earrings dangled from her ears. She wore matching gold bracelets on her forearms. I could well visualize connected young men petitioning Demokades for Eudaimon's hand.

"Thank you, sir," she smiled.

Demokedes appeared and I greeted him. He wore an embroidered toga and looked quite the public official. "The concert is at the home of Lucius Helvius," he said, "one of our aediles."

Litters and bearers were waiting outside. As we walked over to them, Eudaimon said, "If I hadn't known you were working so hard, I would have thought that you were avoiding me."

I hesitated a fraction of a second too long before mumbling something asinine about the emperor's service. I was torn, and she sensed it.

"Is a girl from the Fayyum so terrible?"

"Not at all," I replied. "It is myself that I try to avoid, Eudaimon."

She gave a forced laugh. "Are you so full of dark secrets?"

Yes, I wanted to say. *Yes, I am.*

We reached our litters and climbed in, and slaves carried us across town. Alone in my conveyance, I had time to think. What was I to do?

I couldn't pretend that my attraction to Eudaimon didn't exist. But could I forswear my code of conduct? Could I abandon my calling and try to remain in Roman Egypt? What would my colleagues do? If I didn't return, would they try to hunt me down and return me to my own time by force? Or would they simply decide that's what history said had happened and leave me alone?

Could I keep the secret of my identity from Eudaimon forever? What would happen if, in an unguarded moment, I let it slip, and she learned the truth about me?

What would happen if, in history, Eudaimon had married someone else...and I came between them? Once again I was faced with the nagging suspicion that I could change history, despite all the arguments to the contrary. But what if I really had married Eudaimon?

If I had, it was still in my personal future, so I'd have no memory of it. And what if I was *supposed* to marry her?

What should I do? What had I done?

I wished desperately that we possessed better historical records so that I would know what to do...a single scrap of papyrus mentioning the marriage of Eudaimon to G. Veronius Aemilianus—or to somebody else— and I would have my answer. But such an item didn't exist—or hadn't been discovered—and that was why I made my journeys to the past, to learn these things.

It was inconceivable that I should ruin my career for what might be only a passing fancy. I was only an observer of history, not a participant. Or was I? I rubbed my eyes, feeling a dull ache gather behind my temples.

I wanted to flee Antinoöpolis, yet something tugged at me to remain. But the more I thought, the more it seemed to me there was, really, only one practical solution.

Seated between Eudaimon and Demokedes, I heard little of the concert. My mind refused to fasten on the poetry or the music. It might have been good or awful; I couldn't tell. Eudaimon must have sensed my distress, as she endeavored to cheer me up at intervals between songs.

"Why are you so distressed?" she asked.

"Because," I replied, "I must return to Rome and report to the emperor."

"Hadrian will not accept a letter?"

I shook my head. "He was most specific." It was a lie, of course, and it hurt. It was to my own time that I had to return and report.

She puffed out her cheeks. "Oh. Then I am distressed as well." I wanted to hold her close, but I sat stiffly throughout the remainder of the concert. Eudaimon, bless her heart, did her best to be brave.

The ride back to Demokedes' house was a dismal affair.

I told Demokedes of my intentions in the morning. The old man took the news soberly. "I shall be sorry to see you leave," he said, "even though I know your report will be to my benefit."

I had it written and ready to send to the emperor.

"I have enjoyed my stay in Antinoöpolis," I said.

"I had hoped…" he sighed. "My daughter is smitten with you. She has opposed all my attempts to find her a husband. I had hoped that this time…"

His eyes were watery. "I desire only happiness for my daughter," he said. "I would willingly have offered her to you. Indeed, it was my intention to discuss the matter with you—"

I laid my hand on his arm. "It is most noble," I said. "And she is a daughter any man would be proud to call his own. And I confess—" a lump formed in my throat "—that I have not been untouched by her."

His eyes brightened. "Then perhaps you will return after you have delivered your report?" He swept an arm in a wide circle. "I have no other heir. All this could be yours…"

I imagined myself being a wealthy landowner in Roman Egypt, with a young wife, children…it was such a vastly different scenario from the life I had once enjoyed with Erica and Emily.

"Who knows the mind or the will of an emperor?" I countered.

"True enough," he said. He clicked his fingernails together. "She'll wait for you," he mused. "She's a loyal woman."

She would, I thought miserably, as I returned to my own rooms, have a very long wait.

I knew, as I said goodbye to Eudaimon the following day, that I would never forget her. Had it only been three weeks that we had known each other?

She was elegant in a bluish-green tunic with an undertunic decorated with purple triangles around the neck. A mauve mantle was draped over her left shoulder. She wore a necklace of emeralds interspersed with gold beads and red garnets, with gold earrings ending in pearl-tipped lozenge-shaped pendants. Her dark hair was drawn back from her face, wound in braids and done up into a bun. She'd used more make-up around her eyes than usual, and from a slight puffiness of her eyelids, I wondered if she had been crying. If so, she had since pulled herself together admirably.

She, her father, and several servants had accompanied me to the quays where I would board a ship for Alexandria. With a glance for permission to Demokedes, I took Eudaimon by the hand and led her away from the others.

"I'm sorry," I began.

"We will meet again," she said, reaching up to touch my cheek. "I feel it in my heart."

I could barely speak, my words emerging in a boyish stammer. "I cannot promise…the emperor…"

"I understand. And don't be sad," she said. "Rather, look forward to the future that we shall share, my dear."

Future! What did she know about the future? What did I really know about it?

It wasn't as if I had personal use of the Ring to indulge my own inclinations and fancies. I could only visit the past on official assignments. I hadn't the slightest idea whether I would ever be assigned to this time and location again.

I put my arms around her and drew her to me. She rested her head on my chest, and I smelled the sweet sandalwood scent of her hair, which shone like amber in the sunlight. My heart raced like a runaway slave.

She spoke softly. "I love you, Veronius Aemilianus."

Now, I couldn't speak at all. I felt great affection for her, as well, but couldn't bring myself to say the words. Was it from loyalty to my beloved Erica, whose loss grieved me every day? Was it from a desire not to inflict hurt on Eudaimon?

Or was it because Eudaimon and I had known each other only a short

126

time, and while the feelings were intense they might be only an infatuation destined to wither? What, after all, did I really have in common with this girl from the past?

I gave her a squeeze, then lowered her arms, and directed her back to the quay.

"Goodbye, sir," I said to Demokedes. "I shall report favorably of your work to the Emperor."

"You are always welcome in my house," he replied.

Slaves handed my few possessions to waiting sailors, and I climbed onto the boat. The captain shouted orders; the lines were cast off, and oarsmen edged the ship away from shore. No need for the sail, as the current would carry us down the Nile.

The ship gathered momentum. I waved as the figures of Eudaimon and her father grew smaller and smaller. She raised a hand, and then they were gone, blotted out by a bend in the river. All I could see was the flowing water, the waving palms, and the mistiness in my own eyes.

Once in Rome, I sent, as I had promised myself, a glowing letter to the Emperor Hadrian about Demokedes. And I wrote to Eudaimon, telling her that I was being posted to Britannia, true enough, as that was where I was scheduled for my next assignment. I urged her not to wait for me. Whether or not she attempted to write back, I have no idea.

I never forgot Eudaimon as the years passed and as work took me from one age and location to another. Always, in my mind's eye, I could see her as she was when we parted.

I wondered what had happened to her. Had she waited for me, spending day after day scanning the Nile? Or was I flattering myself? Surely she'd have found another man upon whom to fix her affection; she was an attractive, determined woman. But the image of her lonely figure waiting endlessly and fruitlessly haunted me. Surely it hadn't happened. Surely she wouldn't have done that.

I wondered how she had died so many centuries ago. Had she died young of illness or lived to a ripe, honorable age? Died happy or sad? Oh, the secrets that time concealed!

Sometimes I longed to go back. But even if I did, what could I do? Her fate had been sealed long before I was born.

One summer, I was in the Musée du Louvre. I had visited many times before, but a new director had changed exhibits, putting on display artifacts that hadn't been viewed for years. I happened to be in Paris and thought I'd take advantage of the opportunity.

I wandered, as I always did, through the Greek and Roman antiquities, looking at items which to me had become vessels of ordinary use, not museum pieces. Daily, I handled items which now museums would give millions to possess. I studied statues like ones I walked past every day lining the streets and public places of Rome. I regarded busts of emperors whose reigns I had lived under.

I reached a gallery containing funerary displays from Roman Egypt. A knot of French children moved between them. Several cases displayed headboards painted with images of the deceased. As always, I felt a strange sensation as I looked at the features of people who had lived and died so long ago.

"Over here!" one child beckoned to the others. "Look at this!"

"Is that a *real* mummy?" one of them asked. "She's ugly!"

I ambled closer to see what they were ogling. The display was of mummy portraits from Roman Egypt. A frisson went up my spine.

The tightly wrapped mummy, its yellowish, stained bandages bound in a lozenge-shaped pattern, looked like a stiff, childish rendition of a human being. At one end was a painted headboard.

Eudaimon!

I recognized her instantly. The portrait fixed to her mummy was so like the Eudaimon I had known that I almost expected to hear her voice chiding me for being away for so long.

"I wouldn't want to meet *her* on a dark night," one of the children said.

"Go away," I said sharply. "She was a very beautiful and special woman."

"How would *you* know?" the same boy asked with that rude aggressiveness so common to youth.

"Because I knew her."

The children looked at me strangely, unsure whether to mock me or to be afraid, and melted away into the tourists who strolled through the hall.

"I'm sorry, Eudaimon," I whispered.

I put my palm against the glass of the case. She looked hardly older than when I had known her and was dressed as she was when I last saw her. Fate, it seemed, hadn't granted her a long life.

She still retained the bloom of youth. The artist had even managed to show how her nose—the nose that I had accidentally broken for her so long ago—had healed lopsidedly, not perfectly as the Greek physician had promised.

She was right, I thought sadly. We had met again. But oh, to meet like this…!

I'd been so focused on her face that I hadn't noticed the writing across the front of the mummy wrappings. I leaned closer to read it.

Eupsyche, Eudaimon.

Eupsyche: Good courage, cheerful life, good life, good mind.

Be of good courage and a good mind, Eudaimon. That sounded better.

She hadn't died unlamented and unmourned. It was slight consolation to me.

I was about to turn away when something stopped me...something about the shape of the letters...

They could have been written by Demokedes, I supposed.

But the way they were formed was so like my own writing when I wrote Greek...

Suddenly weak, I leaned against the case for support, ignoring the glare of a security guard who motioned me to move. I looked at my trembling hands, not knowing if they trembled from anticipation or from fear. I didn't know whether to laugh or cry.

Had I—*would* I—go back to Antinoopolis again? Would I see Eudaimon again? Were mine the hands to write the funerary valediction on her mummy?

It was just the thing, I thought, to bring a smile to Eudaimon's lips and to make her consider that she was, after all, lucky.

XXIV

When I returned from the Ring, it was to learn that the Chair had retired and left Earth to live on Taran, a temperate world popular among older retirees. He'd been a crusty old bird, and yet, in a way—and despite our differences and occasional clashes—I was sad to see him go. He was one of the types who seemed destined to work forever. Since his faculties had remained acute and his administrative skills unmatched, nobody had ever pressured him—at least not successfully—to step down.

I was surprised to learn that his successor had already been elected, and—I admit—disappointed that it wasn't I.

I suppose, somewhere in the recesses of my mind, was every academic's dream of becoming Chair. My students had taken to calling me "Caesar" behind my back, which, even unconsciously, no doubt served to inflate my ego. I was, after all, by now the most widely experienced and traveled Temporal Historian. A prize had even been named after me: the Cragg Prize for excellence in past-times research.

As I reflected further, I came to the realization that it might have been that my very experience worked against me. I spent much time in the past—sometimes months at a stretch—and chairs need to be in the present, to handle the day to day running of a department. My classes had to be scheduled around my frequent departures, which was inconvenient for both students and myself.

Sometimes, I wondered if I did them a disservice—and the recollection of Lamia Quigley came to mind. She had never accepted my offer of a second dissertation. I wondered what had become of her—transferred to another department, most likely, if she hadn't left CamOx altogether.

Another factor was that I was never very talented administratively.

Still, the disappointment at being passed over rankled. Passed over while I was on a project, no less, and without even being consulted for my input in the selection process. Passed over for a colleague about whom I had questions.

She wouldn't have been on my list of top prospects for the position.

I strongly suspected that there had been behind-the-scenes bargaining, deals, and maneuvering, which, while perhaps not strictly unethical, weren't totally on the up and up, either. What if I raised enough of a fuss? Was there a chance her promotion could be rescinded?

Academic rivalries run deep. So does professional pride. The temptation to complain was strong.

On more sober reflection, however, when the initial surprise and disappointment had worn off, I decided to say nothing, and accept the fact of her appointment. It wasn't in me to try to ruin a colleague's career. And I might have done inestimable damage to my own, as well.

I knew the New Chair moderately well. She too had made a past-times trip. But since women weren't always regarded highly or treated well in the ancient world, hence limiting their prospects as researchers in certain eras, she had only taken a short transit to 2495, to Lenore—the sole advanced colony world to have remained independent of the then Terran Hegemony until the Treaty of Apsel VII in 2580, which established the New Confederation of Worlds and restructured the central government to be more equitable to all the hundreds of settled planets to which humanity had expanded.

The papers she had written based on that trip weren't, in my opinion, either strong or original. They gave me cause to wonder: How firm was her commitment to past-times research and the leading role CamOx was playing? How conversant was she with the difficulties past-times researchers faced? One had to be realistic in dealing with the past, just as much as with the present.

I didn't know the answers to the questions. But I did know that the New Chair (who soon became known simply as "The Chair" like her predecessor) was a strong-willed dynamo who, when she wanted something done, got it done. Whereas the old Chair had been an immovable object, the New Chair was an irresistible force.

I seemed, in my career, to run into many strong-willed—even aggressive—women. And the New Chair reminded me—at least in her inner strength—of another woman I once met, in the Londinium of AD 84. A woman quite different from Eudaimon.

XXV: ASELLINA'S LAST FIGHT

At first glance, she hardly seemed like a warrior or a slave.

The hood of her dark woolen cloak concealed her features, but not her average height and moderate build, neither wispy as if apt to be blown over by a breath of wind, nor stocky and substantial, capable of withstanding a gale by sheer brute force. She was of that attractive, healthy in-between build, and walked confidently along the bustling streets of Londinium, to all appearances simply a local woman going about her daily business.

On closer scrutiny, she moved with the strong, lithe grace of the athlete or the warrior. A glimpse of her right arm as she adjusted her cloak showed it to be firmly muscled, more than a typical housebound Roman woman needed. But the most telling sign was the burly male companion who strode behind her and whose purpose was obviously to keep an eye on her.

I watched them make their way toward the lower-class housing that lay in the environs of the amphitheater.

Titus Flavius Domitianus—the Emperor Domitian—was on the throne of Rome, and it had been twenty years since Queen Boudicca's rebellion had enveloped Britannia in flames. The ashes had long-since cooled, and the devastated cities had been rebuilt. Britannia was Roman in name, and becoming Roman in spirit.

My current mission was to investigate whether theories of female gladiators in Britannia in this time frame were accurate. Could this woman represent a potential avenue of investigation?

It was worth a shot.

I turned quickly and followed them, dodging and weaving through the crowds in an effort to keep them in sight. They took several turns, but then a cart cut from a side street in front of me, and I had to stop to let it pass. When it had gone, they were nowhere in sight. I dashed to the next intersection, glanced left, saw nothing, turned right, and was pinned against the wooden wall of a building with a blade at my throat.

The Neanderthal-like man held the dagger, but it was the woman who spoke. She'd pushed back her cowl and parted her cloak, and her right hand rested on the hilt of a sword.

"Who are you, and why are you following me?"

There was a faint, lilting accent to her words, the voice of a woman born in one of the Celtic lands, but who had lived elsewhere for years.

"My name is Tettius Julianus," I croaked. I motioned toward the blade, making sure the woman noticed the gold ring proclaiming my free-citizen, upper-class status. "I mean you no harm. Tell your trained ape to release me."

The woman gestured to the man. He lowered the dagger, but held it at the ready.

"I'm a trader from Aquileia," I said, rubbing my neck where the blade had indented it. "I've recently moved to Londinium."

Posing as a trader from an Italian city sounded mundane—and, of course, business was beneath the truly high-class Roman gentleman, but it was adequate enough for me to get to know a troupe of gladiators. I'd considered posing as a physician, but dismissed the idea because while I might have been able to handle minor injuries, major wounds would have been beyond my abilities—and my stomach's capacity for gore. I'd decided that a wealthy businessman would be best.

Her manner eased slightly, and when she replied, it was more politely. "And why am I of interest to you, sir?"

"Do you belong to the troupe of Rhodius?" I countered.

She nodded and drew herself to her full height, which was greater than I had estimated. "I am Asellina."

Gold!

"Then the honor is mine," I said, hardly able to believe my good fortune. I'd barely arrived in Londinium, yet had already heard of this woman, whose name was on everyone's lips. Feeling more confident, I pushed past the Neanderthal and approached the woman. "I would like to speak to your master."

"Rhodius is a private man."

"Surely not where it concerns business," I said. "I would like to hire your troupe for a show."

She bit her lip, obviously torn between offending her master and insulting an affluent citizen, then nodded briskly. "I'll take you to him, sir."

We strode along the streets, the heavy-footed Neanderthal trudging behind.

"Do you wish us to perform in Aquileia?" she asked. "I haven't fought in Italia for years. Rhodius has had us making the rounds of the provinces."

"Alas, no," I replied. "Here in Londinium."

"Alas? Is there something wrong with Londinium?"

"Merely the weather."

She laughed. "Cool weather is better for fighting."

"Are you a Briton?" I asked.

Her green eyes, flecked with yellow, took on a faraway look. "Yes."

She seemed disinclined to explain further, and so we walked in silence. I used the time to study her. Her upright posture projected self-assurance. Her cheekbones were high and brushed with rouge, not the pale makeup that Roman women preferred, and her red hair was tucked into a bun at the nape of her neck and secured by an ivory hairpin. She was, I suppose, the typical Briton woman of story. And yet, where did the type originate, except with real people?

It was only as I looked closer, trying to keep my scrutiny discreet, that I noticed the faint white line of a healed scar on her left cheek and the edge of another scar peeking from her hairline. A raw patch on her neck indicated where armor had rubbed.

I judged her to be in her mid-thirties—old, I suspected, for a gladiatrix. But some people were blessed with superior talent, greater fighting sense, or a better physique which enabled them to compete at a high level long after the majority of competitors their age were retired or dead.

"Here we are." She stopped at a wooden door set into a nondescript building. "Rhodius doesn't waste money on accommodations," she said, observing my expression.

She pushed the door open and we entered the barracks, a place that smelled of sweat and leather and stale beer.

"Where have you been?" a squat, fleshy-faced man hurried over. "You're late for practice! Don't you know we have a show tonight? And who are you?" he said in my direction. "You're no gladiator. Get out."

The lanista's high color was undoubtedly a mixture of temper and wine. If he himself had ever fought, it had been long ago and many rich meals away. I was hard pressed not to laugh at him.

"I'm sorry, Rhodius," Asellina said, giving me an apologetic glance, although the tone of her voice displayed not the least bit of contrition. "I'll get right to work." She indicated me as she moved toward a side room. "This gentleman is Tettius Julianus. He wishes to hire us."

The man's expression grew marginally less hostile. "Is that true?"

I gave him a condensed version of my story, then added, "Your troupe has become quite well known. I doubt that a single performance will satisfy the populace of Londinium. Unless, of course, someone else has already bid for your services."

"As a matter of fact—"

"As a matter of fact, no," Asellina said, re-emerging from a side room. She had shed her cloak and wore only a simple belted tunic. She carried a wooden sword and strapped leather guards onto her forearms as she walked.

"I told you to practice!" Rhodius shouted.

"I'm going to!" Asellina snapped. "And by the way, Hekuba has a question about the draw for the performance, if it's not too hard for you."

"Mind your lip, girl, or I'll beat you!"

"With swords?" she asked maliciously, then whirled and stalked out.

The squat man wiped his brow. "She's been like that ever since I've had her. If she wasn't so good, I'd have gotten rid of her long ago."

I was privately surprised that Asellina hadn't gotten rid of *him*.

He sighed. "I'd better see what the problem is."

"Mind if I come?" I asked. "I'd like to see the goods I might be hiring."

He shrugged. "Why not? Although you never know which ones will still be alive come morning."

I winced inwardly at his coarse laugh. But this was Rome's world, not mine. Rome was a warrior culture; the gladiators embodied the Roman ideals of fighting nobly and dying bravely.

The building used as the ludo, or gladiatorial school, had an interior courtyard open to the sky. It was to this area that Rhodius went. The gladiatrices—for all were women—were paired off and fenced with wooden swords under the eye of a muscular man whom I supposed to be their trainer. Asellina was sparring with a willowy girl who fared none too well, although I judged that Asellina wasn't putting forth maximal exertion.

"Not like *that*," I heard Asellina say, stepping back to demonstrate a stroke, "like *this*."

The willowy girl's attempt at the same sword thrust left even me, who knew nothing about swordplay, shaking my head.

"Faster!" Asellina barked. "Harder!"

The girl tried again, with the same pitiful result.

"With conviction!" Asellina yelled, sounding frustrated. "As if your life depended on it!"

"That's Oriana," Rhodius said casually. "She's new. Can't seem to learn anything. Won't last long." He indicated another woman. "Jadryga, she's tough. Been around a while. Ledaea's seasoned, Terentia—she's no novice—" He reeled off the names until he'd completed a round dozen. Some names were Latin, others Greek, with a Celtic, German, or Egyptian thrown in. I tried to remember them, momentarily puzzled that it seemed harder than usual.

"Watch if you like," Rhodius said, then hustled over to talk to one of the women, the Hekuba whom Asellina had mentioned.

The women were as mixed a group as their names indicated. Tall, short, lithe, stocky, each was different. Rhodius apparently selected for variety. Their skill levels also varied. Rhodius returned after a few minutes and picked up his description where he'd left off. These women, he explained, were the core of his troupe. In the arena they might be paired against each other, against women of other troupes, against condemned women brought in for the purpose, or against women who wanted to try their skill against trained gladiatrices.

I pursed my lips.

"What do you think?" Rhodius asked.

"They seem competent," I said neutrally.

"Competent!" he spluttered. "You won't find a better troupe of gladiatrices than these."

"Still…"

"Tell you what," he said. "Come to the games tonight. Watch them in action. Then we'll talk price."

Watching women fight and kill each other wasn't my intention. I had wanted merely to meet and learn about these women.

"I hadn't really planned—" I tried to demur.

"Join me and see them for free," he insisted. "What could be fairer than that?"

Reluctantly, I agreed. If I didn't show appropriate interest, Rhodius was likely to have one of his thugs heave me out, and there'd be an end to my investigation.

He told me when and where to meet him, and I departed, conscious, as I did so, of Asellina's scrutiny from where she continued to practice with a fatigued Oriana.

Historians cannot ignore the ugly side of history, pretending it didn't exist, and focus only on the noble or romantic. We must sift through the sordid and the ignoble as well, if we want to understand people of different times and cultures. Watching the gladiatrices fight, I told myself, was part of the job. I wasn't here to glamorize or fantasize. I was here to see real history in the making.

I made some small purchases in the marketplace and then spent the early afternoon reading in my room. At the appointed time, I made my way to the amphitheater.

Game-day events proceeded in a defined order. Criminals were executed in the early afternoon, frequently *ad bestias*, killed by wild animals. Lesser quality events followed, leading up to the "prime time" of late afternoon and early evening, when the heat of the day had dissipated but plenty of light remained—not that Britannia suffered from a surfeit of heat, but the pattern remained. This prime time was when the main gladiatorial combats occurred and the upper-class members of the populace turned out. Rhodius was fortunate that the novelty of his gladiatrices meant they could command prime time.

The amphitheater at Londinium was a brand spanking new stone and timber building capable of seating some twenty thousand people. Like its twin in the recently obliterated town of Pompeii, it had two entrances at ground level. The Porta Triumphalis was where the gladiators entered and the victorious ones departed; the other, the Porta Libitinensis—the Gate of Libitina, the goddess of funerals—was for the removal of the slain. I joined Rhodius at the former. He'd offered me a seat in the stands—"You'll have a better view from there"—but I'd declined. I wasn't here for the entertainment. It would be bad enough as it was, without being surrounded by a blood-lust-maddened crowd. For the life of me, I couldn't view these games as in any way comparable to a sporting event of my own century.

I arrived as he and Asellina were arguing. "Don't send out Oriana," Asellina was saying. "She's not ready!"

"Don't tell me what to do!" Rhodius flared, jabbing a finger to her chest. "I'll manage my troupe as I see fit!"

"Please," Asellina replied, softening her tone. "Have pity, Rhodius."

"Pity? Pity doesn't pay."

Her face reddened. "Is that all you can think about?"

"Get in the line, woman! You're still my slave, and don't you forget it!"

Asellina clamped her mouth shut.

I stood out of the way as Rhodius encouraged and cursed his troupe into order.

"Don't make such a fuss, Rhodius," Asellina said coldly. "We know what we're doing."

The lanista replied with a glare and a string of epithets.

Pair by pair, the women strode out into the arena and saluted the crowd. Loud cheers greeted them.

"Nothing fancy tonight," Rhodius said, speaking to me for the first time. "The sponsor paid only for one-on-one combat." He sighed. "I could have offered him chariot fights, women against lions, even a sketch of Amazons, but he was too cheap."

His tone implied that he was hoping I wouldn't fall into that category.

An announcer called the event to order and proclaimed the sponsor's name and titles. The indicated worthy made a show of checking the gladiatrices' weapons to make sure they were sharp, and signaled his approval.

Four pairs of women spaced themselves on the sands of the arena, watched closely by referees. Asellina, I noticed, was paired against Terentia; both, unusually, were armed with long, British-style swords instead of the shorter Roman gladius, and carried small, round shields. The willowy Oriana, decked out as a retiarius armed with net and trident, was matched against the stocky Jadryga, a secutor with sword, helmet, and curved oblong shield. Even from a distance, her nervousness was obvious. She hadn't a chance. Rhodius was cruel to condemn her to death so soon.

At a motion from the referees, the women sprang into action, circling each other, feinting, sizing each other up. Then, with the ring of steel on steel, the action commenced. I tried to concentrate on Asellina, but found my glance wandering to the unfortunate Oriana. I wondered what she had done to end up here. Most likely she was simply an unlucky slave whom Rhodius had picked up cheaply. Fodder. A sacrifice to please the crowd's thirst for blood. A bargain if she did well, no great loss otherwise.

Unsurprisingly, the end came quickly. Oriana, perhaps spurred on by desperation, fought gamely, but was no match for the experienced and utterly remorseless Jadryga. She pressed Oriana relentlessly until the younger woman was disarmed, sprawled on the ground with her feet tangled in her own net, her left hand with one extended finger raised in defeat. The crowd voiced its disapproval. Unswayed by her youth or beauty, the sponsor gave the *pollice verso*, and Oriana's brief life ended.

An attendant dressed as Pluto, the god of the dead, struck her body with a mallet, indicating that she now belonged to death. Another attendant, dressed as Mercury, touched her with a hot iron to assure that she was really dead and not faking. Attendants dragged her limp body away while Jadryga strutted toward the victor's exit. She passed close by me, but I ignored her.

"Too quick!" Rhodius complained.

"I fight to win," Jadryga snarled as she headed for the dressing room, "not for show."

One of the other women had also succumbed, but two other fights continued. To the raucous approval of the crowd, many of whom were standing and cheering, Asellina and Terentia were raining blows upon each other.

"Look at them," Rhodius said, nudging me in the ribs. "That's quality fighting for you."

Asellina danced away from an attack by Terentia, leaving the other woman flailing into the air.

"She's good," I said.

"Asellina's my star," Rhodius replied, his gaze fixed upon the young woman. "She's so good that she can make even an average opponent look like a top-flight fighter. The way they're fighting now, you'd almost think that Terentia was a match for her. The crowd certainly does."

"Asellina looks as if she's working hard."

"Bah," he snorted. "She could have killed Terentia half a dozen times by now. There are two aspects to a good show," he continued, obviously sensing that I required some education on the subject. "There's the fighting aspect—you need talent and skill to be successful. But there's also the acting ability, to make the show look good. Many gladiatrices have one or the other. Asellina has both."

"I see," I said.

"Asellina can make the fight look so good, and her opponent more skilled than she really is, that when the fight's done, her opponent is often spared." He chuckled. "The crowd is satisfied, her opponent gets to fight again, and it makes my life easier, since I don't have to select and train a replacement." He cast a meaningful glance at the bloody trails in the sand where two losers had been dragged away. He fingered his chin, and I guessed he was deciding how much to charge the sponsor for the two dead women. More than cost, undoubtedly.

"It sounds dangerous," I said, realizing instantly how stupid the comment sounded.

Fortunately, Rhodius didn't seem to have heard me. "Asellina looks ready to make her move," he said. And it was so.

Asellina closed on Terentia. In a moment it was over. A flurry of blows from her glittering sword, a sudden shift of weight, and Terentia sprawled on her back on the sand, her sword out of reach, Asellina's point at her throat. Asellina yanked off her helmet, shook her hair free, and waited for the verdict.

The crowd clapped and cheered. "Missio!" called the sponsor, sparing Terentia's life, and the crowd voiced its approval. Asellina saluted the stands with her sword, turning to face all four directions, then, to shouts of "Asellina! Asellina!" strode toward the Porta Triumphalis.

"Excellent!" Rhodius beamed as she entered the tunnel. "Well done!"

She shot him a venomous look and brushed past him.

"I need a drink," she snapped toward a waiting slave, tossing her sword in the man's direction. "And sharpen this."

She angled toward the dressing room, but one of the trainers intercepted her and wordlessly handed her something. I glimpsed the chain of an inexpensive necklace.

"Oriana's?" I heard her murmur, and the trainer nodded.

She gripped it in her hand, and I thought her eyes became watery before she turned away and vanished into the dressing room.

A dusty and downcast Terentia shuffled through the doorway. Rhodius watched her go by in silence, although I thought she deserved some word of approval.

"Next group!" he shouted when she'd gone, and the next four pairs of gladiatrices marched out. Soon, the fights were again underway.

Rhodius eyed me with raised eyebrows. "Well?"

I found it quite nauseating. "Why are you playing the provinces and not

Italia?" I asked, avoiding the question.

He scoffed, "Italia? You think I can compete with the big state-owned gladiatorial schools there? Besides, I'd have to put up with aristocratic young women wanting to play at being gladiatrices. Most of them are so inept that they'd likely cut off their own fingers picking up their sword the wrong way."

He shook his head. "I'm better off in the provinces. And with a performer like Asellina—she's undefeated, you know—I'm set for years."

"Londinium loves her," I said. "I saw her face painted all over town."

Rhodius gave a leer. "Lots of young men would like to spend the night with her, I guarantee it. But she won't have any of that nonsense."

His ugly smile faded. "I'll be sorry to lose her."

"Lose her?" I repeated.

He nodded glumly. "She's been with me almost five years, now. She'll be able to buy her way into retirement soon. Idiot me, I set her price too low. It seemed high enough at the time, but how was I to know she'd earn so much money?"

I was about to depart and leave him to weep his crocodile tears of self-pity, but the approach of a dignified man wearing a toga who motioned to Rhodius stayed my leave-taking.

"Our duumvir," Rhodius whispered to me. "Martiannius Otho."

Togas were few and far between in Britannia. The man who wore this one seemed full of the self-importance so common in provincial city officials. He was clean shaven, short-haired, and smelled of expensive oils.

Otho yawned. "A tolerably entertaining show, Rhodius." He turned to me. "And you, sir…"

"Tettius Julianus," I said.

"I don't believe I know you," Otho said, cocking his head to one side and eyeing me up and down.

"I'm new to town. From Aquileia."

"He's looking to sponsor some games," Rhodius interjected.

"Want to make your name known, eh?" Otho said. "It's a fine idea. Games keep the masses happy. Tell you what: you give Rhodius here some business and provide the gladiatrices; I'll provide the gladiators, and you can co-sponsor the games—under me, of course."

He clapped me on the shoulder. "We'll meet properly over dinner. Tell my steward you're invited."

He gave an affable nod and departed.

Rhodius was beaming. "Let's find a tavern and discuss price over drinks."

Numbly, I followed him.

It was raining when I walked home late that night, one of the prolonged drizzles for which Britannia is famous. The paved streets were slippery, the unpaved ones muddy. Only a few people, huddled in gray cloaks, were abroad.

I was now, somehow, the co-sponsor of a day of gladiatorial games. My head ached, and it wasn't from wine. I had wanted only to observe a gladiatrix. Now, I was sponsoring games. What a predicament!

My quarters, rented rooms over a silversmith's shop, were plain but at least kept the nighttime chill at bay. I lit a lamp and lay down on my remarkably uncomfortable bed.

Would I be morally responsible for the deaths of any women who perished in the games? Did the fact that the women would die—or had died—anyway, be a mitigating factor in my favor?

All I could think of was the luckless Oriana, mourned by only Asellina and me—who didn't even know her—out of all the people in the world.

The next several days passed quickly as I attended to other aspects of research. I was browsing near the forum, trying to decide whether I wanted a hot lunch from a thermopolium or whether to return to my rooms and eat cold leftovers, when my deliberations were interrupted by a woman's voice giving me a polite greeting. It was Asellina, dressed as before, with the Neanderthal standing behind her. Having seen her fight, I figured he was along only for show.

"Good afternoon," I replied. "Are you shopping?"

She shook her head negatively. "May I have a word with you, sir?"

I indicated some benches across the Forum. "Unless you would prefer somewhere more private?"

"This is fine."

We sat somewhat apart from each other. She fiddled with her hands in her lap, appearing far more nervous than the confident gladiatrix I had seen in the arena.

"Rhodius says you're sponsoring games," she said at last.

"Yes."

"May I ask a request of you, sir?" Even shaded by her cowl, I could see that her eyes were pleading.

"It may not be in my power to grant, but you may ask."

"I would like to fight Accalia."

I frowned in puzzlement. "Who is she?"

"You're not serious! You haven't heard of the wolf-woman of Capua? The most famous living gladiatrix?"

"Her name sounds slightly familiar…"

"She took her stage name from Acca Larentia."

Ah. The legendary she-wolf that nursed Romulus and Remus, the mythical founders of Rome.

"She's a freewoman," Asellina continued, "but still fights occasionally."

"And I assume that she's here in Londinium?"

Asellina nodded. "She lives in Capua. But I've learned that she's visiting here."

"Why this woman?"

"She's undefeated and has won many wreaths."

I studied Asellina closely. "There's another reason, isn't there?"

She bit her lip. "Please don't ask."

"You're ready to retire," I said.

"I must fight her while I have the opportunity. I have striven my whole life for this. The chance may not come again."

"But why? When your freedom is at hand, why risk your life in an unnecessary fight?"

"It's not unnecessary!" she exclaimed. Passersby stared, and she lowered her voice. "Please, sir, I beg you. Help me to do this. Hire Accalia to fight me. I shall be eternally grateful."

She was a proud woman; I could tell that this conversation was costing her much.

"But—"

"If you worry about money, don't. I've saved a considerable amount. I will give it to you. You need risk nothing."

I stared. "But that money could buy your freedom—"

"Freedom is nothing. This is more important than freedom." She pointed to her heart. "It's a matter of honor. Surely you understand honor."

I groped for a way of escape. "But what of Rhodius?"

"He'll complain, but he knows he'll lose me regardless. If I win, I will buy my freedom. If I die, he will lose me to the grave—and you can give my money to him. Either way, my time with Rhodius is ended." She paused. "A fight between me and Accalia will be a great attraction. Rhodius will profit."

I remained silent.

"Your name is Roman," she said, "but you have the look of a man who has Briton blood."

"Both my parents were Britons."

"Then grant me this, if not for me, then because we share common blood."

"If I do this," I said slowly, "I would ask for something in return."

Her eyes darkened immediately in suspicion. She probably thought I was going to ask her for sex.

"Tell me about Asellina," I said.

She looked down and away.

"What is your real name?" I asked.

"A long time ago," she whispered, "I was called Aife."

With prompting, she told me her story.

When Suetonius Paulinus smashed Queen Boudicca's army, countless children had been left without parents or kin. Many had been captured and sold as slaves. Such had been the fate of Aife, who had been about thirteen years old at the time, and her younger sister, aged eleven. Some of the captured went to good homes and kind masters and mistresses. The girls didn't.

Her eyes flashed as she detailed some of her experiences with her masters. Both girls were spirited young women, unfit to be the decorous handmaidens of prissy Roman matrons. They'd tried repeatedly to escape, but each time had been caught and returned to punishment. They were fortunate not to have been put to death.

They went from owner to owner, their price getting lower and lower. They had initially been sold as a pair, but eventually were split up.

Asellina's voice grew soft and her eyes misted over as she described her parting from her sister. "It was years before I ever saw her again," she said. "And then it was once more on the slave block."

Finally Rhodius, eyeing Aife's athletic physique, bought both girls at a slave market for practically nothing. "He only wanted me, at first. I begged him to buy my sister too," she said, her voice nearly breaking. "I thought any chance would be better than none."

She pulled herself together. "Rhodius gave me a life of sorts."

She changed her name to Asellina and began her career as a gladiatrix. Gradually, she'd moved up through the grades until she reached the top. She became famous, her face recognizable on painted posters around many provincial cities.

"What of your sister?" I asked.

"She died," Asellina said hoarsely.

"I'm sorry," I said, immediately visualizing the unfortunate Oriana.

Asellina rose. "I must return to the barracks."

I stood as well. "I'll do my best to arrange a match with Accalia."

Her smile was gentle, but behind it I glimpsed steel.

Arranging the match proved not to be difficult.

Accalia—whom I had little difficulty locating—was expensive, but relished the idea of taking on the "upstart from the provinces," according to the servant who spoke for her, since she declined to meet me in person.

No woman from the provinces, in her view, was comparable to the best gladiatrix of Rome. When it was brought to her attention that people were comparing Asellina to her, the deal was sealed.

Rhodius nearly hit the roof when I informed him.

"You told me Asellina was the best," I pointed out.

"Accalia's a brute!" he exclaimed. "She's not a woman at all, but a monster in woman's skin." He paced about in such agitation that I thought he might tear his clothes. I repeated Asellina's reasoning to him and reminded him that he wouldn't lose so much as a single sestertius.

He wouldn't buy it. "I refuse!" he said flatly. "She's my draw!"

"I am the sponsor," I retorted. "I have already hired Accalia. If you refuse to let Asellina fight, then your reputation will be ruined. Who will want to hire Rhodius' chicken gladiatrices?"

He glared, but knew he had lost the argument.

Martiannius Otho was pleased. "An excellent match," he beamed. "You're off to a good start, Tettius."

I didn't tell him, of course, that this was to be my first and last sponsorship.

The games were arranged for two weeks distant, and I spent much of the time at the ludo watching the women train. Many gladiators fought only two or three times a year, so the close scheduling was unusual, but this was an unusual event.

Even a small stable of fighters like Rhodius' boasted professional trainers (who also monitored the women's high-energy diets) and physicians to care for the many injuries which occurred. Rhodius saw to it that his gladiatrices received regular massages and visited the public baths. The training was rigorous, but many people in the Roman empire lived worse lives than these women. The drawback, of course, was that life could end unpredictably.

The longer I watched, the more I began to appreciate the difference in technique and style between the women. Asellina could hold her own in any category—although she preferred to fight as I had seen her, with long sword and small shield—while other women were definitely restricted in category. I saw most types in Rhodius' troupe—several women fought as murmillos, wearing a helmet decorated with a fish logo and carrying a large, heavy shield. Others were outfitted as a thraex or hoplomachus with progressively smaller shields. Two others were net-fighters, and two more were secutors. The varieties of armor and weapons were those of Rome's enemies; to use the equipment of Rome's army could send a potentially dangerous message to the populace. Asellina's outfit represented the Britons and so while uncommon, was acceptable.

Posters and graffiti sprouted all over Londinium—"Asellina vs. Accalia" was billed as the greatest match ever to be held in Londinium. Perhaps so; I wasn't in a position to venture an opinion.

When the day of the games arrived, I was met by one of Otho's slaves, who conducted me to the arena, steering me past the booths of food and souvenir sellers. Otho lounged in one of the seats of honor in the front row and motioned me to sit beside him. The arena was already full: upper-class men near the front, lower-class behind, then women, then poor free and slaves on the upper rows. It was noisy and the odor was intense—sweat, perfumes, and food smells mingled in rank profusion.

And, despite the fact that the sand had been cleaned and swept from the animal shows and executions earlier, I detected the metallic scent of blood. Around the perimeter were gurneys, the "couches of Libitina," ready to bear the bodies of the fallen from the arena.

The band took up their instruments, and the umpires entered inconspicuously and assumed their positions. A fanfare quieted the crowd.

Otho rose to his feet, and I followed suit, standing slightly behind him so as to give him the greater honor.

"Greetings, people of Londinium!" Otho said in a loud voice. "I, Martiannius Otho, your duumvir, welcome you on behalf of myself and my co-sponsor, Tettius Julianus."

Feeling profoundly uncomfortable, I waved to the crowd.

"I now proclaim these games open!" Otho declared.

The crowd cheered, the band played another fanfare, and through the Porta Triumphalis strode a throng of gladiators.

I have to confess to being impressed by the men who marched out. These weren't fearful, unwilling combatants, but confident professionals. They swaggered forth as if they were a football team on home ground. A herald announced the name of each combatant with his distinctions. Otho inspected their weapons and pronounced himself satisfied.

Murmillo faced off against thraex, retiarius against secutor, and the fights were on.

I tried to pretend to myself that I was watching a vid, but it was impossible. The clang of steel on steel, the shouts and cries of the combatants, the yells of the crowd cheering on a favorite, their gasps at a skillful blow or groans when a favorite fell, the breeze blowing over the stands from a partly cloudy sky—all these proclaimed that the action was very real.

It was not, as I had always imagined, a haphazard affair. The referees made certain each fighter obeyed the rules. The fights seemed more like a stereotyped skills competition, a highly choreographed ballet in armor fought to musical accompaniment from a band of five: a trumpeter playing a tubicen, a woman playing an organum—a water organ, and three men playing long, curved horns called a lituus.

It was brutal nonetheless. The gladiators laid aside any personal feelings they had for each other. They became merciless fighting machines.

A poke of a trident or a flash of a sword, and a gladiator was bleeding. And with each sight of blood, the crowd cheered louder.

I thought it would never end.

Otho judged each fight, delivering the *missio* for life or the *pollice verso*—turned thumb—for death depending on the reaction of the crowd. Each death, of course, would come out of his pocket. It was a balancing act, with the amount of generosity displayed to the crowd on one hand versus the cost of replacing fallen gladiators on the other.

Finally, a breather, when the victors marched off to triumphant strains from the band.

Otho sat down and wiped his forehead.

"It's going well, don't you think?"

I murmured a reply.

All too soon, Rhodius' women paraded out onto the field. Gladiatrices provided a mixed spectacle to the audience. The sight of women fighting was a novelty appealing mainly to the baser spirits. The purists preferred the larger, muscular gladiators. And so the women had been positioned in the show between two groups of gladiators.

Otho shook my shoulder. "Stand up and acknowledge them!"

My stomach lurched, and I choked down a surge of acid. I rose, and waved to the women I was sponsoring. I checked their weapons. Then I climbed back into the stands and collapsed into my seat.

The women squared off. All too soon, I was faced with a gladiatrix lying on the ground, her opponent waiting for the signal. The crowd grumbled; the woman hadn't put up much of a fight. My mouth was dry. I rose again.

"Missio," I croaked.

Otho regarded me with mild surprise.

"She was a beginner," I explained. "She showed promise in training."

He nodded briefly, but I could sense his displeasure that I hadn't acceded to the crowd's wishes. Perhaps he wondered if I was a skinflint at heart…maybe he doubted his wisdom in co-sponsoring the games with me.

To my relief, the next fights were easier, as the crowd clearly appreciated the efforts of the losers and wished them to be spared.

But the subsequent one…

It was Terentia, the woman Asellina had fought and defeated. Her footwork failed her at a critical moment, and she took a sword thrust under the arm, a vital area for which gladiators aimed, hoping to hit a major artery. Her sword fell to the ground, and she crumpled to her knees, gasping, blood pouring down her side and crimsoning the sand.

The victor looked to me, her face expressionless. The crowd, unimpressed by Terentia's performance, called for her death.

"Hurry up," Otho hissed as I hesitated.

Terentia was doomed. In my time, she could have been saved with ease. But here, there were no skills to repair a severed artery. Even if she didn't bleed to death, she'd lose her arm. In all likelihood, infection would set in and she'd die slowly, in misery. It would be better to end it now.

I couldn't utter the words.

"Do it!" Otho urged.

I stared, frozen, at the kneeling and bleeding Terentia, wishing there was some other way, some way to save her life.

The crowd grew restless.

Suddenly, Otho jumped to his feet, and gave the signal. To her credit, Terentia died honorably, one knee on the ground, her arms grasping the thigh of the victor, the back of her neck bared for the fatal blow. The thrust was clean and sure. The attendants performed their ritual and carried her away.

Otho glared at me as he resumed his seat.

The herald cleared his throat. "And now, our featured women's match. First, the undefeated winner of fifteen garlands, our very own Asellina—"

An immense cheer from the crowd drowned out the remainder of his words as Asellina rode into the arena mounted on a gray steed. A scarlet cloak fastened by a brooch fluttered from her shoulder. She waved her long sword above her streaming red hair. Her real name, Aife, meant "warrior woman." She looked every inch the part—and as I gazed on her I imagined Queen Boudicca must have looked like this, driving her chariot with her two daughters beside her, raising the Britons against their Roman oppressors.

She circled the arena, saluting the screaming fans. She carried, as before, a small round shield and wore greaves on her shins and forearms. She halted in front of the sponsors, and I raised a hand in salute. She dismounted, removed her cloak to reveal a Briton tunic and trousers, and an umpire handed her a helmet.

"And next," the herald called, "the champion of Rome, twenty times awarded the garland, the wolf-woman of Capua, Accalia!"

More cheers, but some boos, coming, I supposed from the native Britons in the crowd, many of whom undoubtedly still harbored resentments against the Romans. This match, I realized, could have quite a partisan aspect.

I stared, aghast, at the figure that lumbered into the arena. Accalia wasn't a woman—she was a bull, an ox, a bear, a lumbering behemoth. I'd seen male gladiators that couldn't match up to Accalia's brawny physique. She looked like the kind of woman who'd strangle tigers and lions barehanded for fun in her spare time. She wielded a short sword, wore a heavy, visored helmet with a scarlet plume, and carried a large rectangular shield. She wore a gray cloth wrapped around her breasts and a loincloth.

She halted beneath us and stood beside Asellina, who looked puny in comparison.

Slowly, as if my body moved of its own accord, without the control of my brain, I stepped down to examine their weapons. Both blades were razor sharp.

My eyes met those of Asellina. Mentally, I begged her to withdraw, to stop before she committed certain suicide. But her eyes were green ice, and I knew there would be no turning back.

"Good luck," I framed with my mouth, and a slight nod indicated that she understood.

I climbed back into the stands.

"Commence!" I said.

The women parted, and Asellina seated her helmet on her head. Then, at a signal from the umpire, they circled each other, warily, like cats sizing up their prey. It was hopeless, I thought. How could Asellina possibly defeat this monster of a woman?

Asellina faked a thrust, but the brute hardly moved, her shield raised defensively, her sword poised in readiness to shoot out. Asellina lunged; her sword rang off Accalia's shield, and she darted out of range before Accalia could respond.

To win this fight, Asellina would have to penetrate the monster's defense. Accalia, for her part, could afford to let the younger woman expend energy and wear herself down.

Asellina danced around her larger opponent, her sword probing for a weakness. But all it met was Accalia's shield.

Suddenly, the beast lurched into motion. Moving faster than I thought was possible, Accalia launched a vigorous attack that drove Asellina backward.

I gripped the stone armrests of my seat until my fingers hurt.

Steel rang against steel and hammered on shields. The crowd roared with approval.

But with a series of deft parries, Asellina recovered. And then it was her turn to press the attack, and Accalia yielded ground.

Back and forth the match seesawed. My heart pounded in my chest, and my head buzzed.

How long could they keep it up, I wondered, as the dance of death continued? Neither woman seemed prepared to yield an inch. And the crowd was loving it, screaming themselves hoarse. Otho was beaming. He even bestowed a smile on me, as if this fight had compensated for my previous hesitations.

Asellina moved in. Shield to shield, sword against sword, the women strained. Accalia's muscles bulged, and she flung Asellina away as if she were a child.

"Wolf-woman, wolf-woman!" chanted some of the crowd, while others countered, "Asellina! Asellina!"

Asellina closed again, battering away at Accalia. Their shields locked. I was expecting Accalia to heave the lighter Asellina off again, but she didn't. This time, the experienced gladiatrix twisted, forcing Asellina's shield away. Her sword shot out and scored a long, bloody gash on Asellina's unprotected side. I gasped, and the crowd did too.

Momentarily shocked, Asellina was unprepared for a jolting blow from the edge of Accalia's shield that spun her around and dropped her to the sand, her sword flying from her hand to land just beyond reach of her fingertips, her helmet bouncing away.

It was over.

Silence enveloped the amphitheater, the crowd too surprised by the sudden turn of events to call for either missio or death.

Accalia loomed over her fallen opponent. I expected to see Asellina raise her finger in submission, and hope for mercy from the crowd. Clearly, the referee did too, as he stepped forward. Accalia also seemed to expect Asellina's submission as a matter of course, since after all, this had not been billed as a match *sine missione*, to the death.

We were wrong.

With a roll that caught us all by surprise, Asellina snatched up her sword and swung.

Too slowly, Accalia tried to dodge. The long blade bit into the back of her leg, behind the knee. I heard her cry over the exclamation of the crowd. Blood spurted from the deep wound.

Heedless of her pain and the blood that flowed from her own wound, Asellina sprang to her feet. With no shield, no helmet, her sword in a two-handed grip, she flew like a fury against her crippled opponent.

Accalia staggered, her wounded leg barely able to support her. How she remained upright at all was a miracle. Off balance and unprepared for the sudden assault, her sword made futile movements in the air until Asellina smashed it from her hand. Accalia reeled and tried desperately to fend off Asellina's furious blows with her shield until a ferocious downstroke splintered it and left her totally defenseless. Asellina's sword curved a glittering arc and hit squarely on the side of Accalia's helmet.

Accalia dropped like a stone, raising dust as she hit the ground.

The crowd was in a frenzy, jumping up and down, clapping, pounding their feet. Accalia's supporters sat as if stunned.

I thought Accalia was dead, but then I saw a weak movement of her hand.

"Your call," Otho said, and I rose to my tingling legs.

The referee moved over to verify Accalia's submission.

But Asellina wasn't finished. Heedless of the crowd, me, and the referee, she stooped and yanked off Accalia's shattered helmet.

Accalia's eyelids fluttered.

Asellina leaned over her. As focused on her as I was, I could clearly hear her words even over the noise of the crowd.

"This," she said, "is for Cinnia."

Then, before the referee could intervene, she raised her sword, and still holding it in both hands, drove it through Accalia's heart.

Asellina's sudden action, in violation of the rules, shocked everyone.

Then a solitary voice from the crowd cheered, and in moments, the throng was acclaiming Asellina.

Leaving her sword pinning Accalia to the ground like a mounted butterfly, she marched toward the exit. I bolted from my seat, and met her at the Porta Triumphalis.

Only as she entered the tunnel and was out of sight of the crowd did she sway. She was pale and had obviously lost a considerable amount of blood. I hurried to support her, ahead of Rhodius, who seemed unable to decide whether he was delighted at the win, or mad at her for violating the rules.

"Don't blather!" I snapped at him. "Get the physician."

He hurried away, and I escorted Asellina to a seat in the dressing room, motioning to the other gladiatrices to give us breathing space.

"Get me a cloth," I said, and when one of the gladiatrices handed me a rag, I held it to Asellina's wound, seeing as I did so the white of rib-bone.

"Did you witness a good fight?" she asked faintly.

"Magnificent, Aife," I replied, bringing a smile to her pale lips. "Was it worth it?"

She managed a nod.

"Why did you do it?" I asked. "Why did you fight her? Why did you kill her?"

Her green eyes seemed to see into a vast distance. "The Roman dog killed my sister in her first fight," she whispered. "Didn't even give her a chance for missio." Her voice faded, and I had to strain to hear her. "Now, she will kill no more Cinnias."

And then she slumped, unconscious against me.

The physician arrived swiftly, made discouraging noises, arranged for Asellina's transport to the barracks, and told me to go home as there was nothing I could do. I paid his fee and urged him to do as much for Asellina as possible.

I wished for modern medicines instead of the foul-smelling unguents the physician slathered onto Asellina's awful wound with unsterile instruments.

I wished I could transport her to my own time as infection took over and ravaged her body.

I wished her physical form were as strong as the mind and will that inhabited it.

I wished in vain.

A long line of torches snaked out of Londinium, winding a sparkling path into the darkness. It crossed the bridge over the river Tamesis, passed through the city walls, continued through the cemetery on the further shore, and halted. It wasn't fitting for a gladiatrix—even a famous one whose death had plunged Londinium into mourning (at least until the next crowd favorite came along)—to be buried in the same ground as respected aunts and uncles, parents and grandparents. Still, they had awarded her the title of "Invictus," unconquered in death.

A trio of priests of Isis led the way, the torch-lights reflecting off their shaven heads and lending a ghostly quality to their long linen kilts. Their strange chants, sung with eastern melodies, added to the eerie atmosphere. The jarring jangle of the sistrum—a bronze rattle—clashed with the plaintive strains of a flute and the gentle throbbing of a drum.

Rhodius had hired the priests, whether because Asellina was a follower of Isis or because they were cheaper than priests of some other deity, I don't know. He walked on the opposite side of Asellina's richly draped and garlanded bier from me. It was decorated elaborately, and I think that Rhodius was pleased that I had paid for most of the funeral costs.

The sweet scent of burning pinecones and incense wafted from the ceramic cups, or tazze, carried by the other members of Rhodius' troupe. Not all of the women had come; Asellina hadn't been universally loved. No matter that by her skills she had undoubtedly saved many of the women to fight again. Some people couldn't be grateful even to the dead.

The procession arrived at the burial site. A large pyre had been erected over a previously dug grave, and the attendants raised the bier to the top. The priests sang a hymn, while I prayed silently for her soul.

Within the pyre were the makings of a meal—figs, dates, almonds, breads, a butchered chicken, and a dove, a symbolic last meal for Asellina. Small glass vials held perfumes, goodbye gifts from some of the women.

The hymn concluded. The priests intoned a final prayer.

Rhodius looked at me, his eyebrows raised. I nodded, and someone handed me a lighted torch.

I approached the pyre. In my mind's eye, I could still see Asellina in her moment of victory. And I could hear her barely audible last words uttered as I sat beside her deathbed—"Britons make poor slaves"—as haltingly, every word costing her pain, she told me the finishing details of her story before lapsing into the final unconsciousness. Whether or not she heard me as I spoke a prayer over her, I don't know. For then her breathing stopped, and eventually her heart beat its last.

I thrust the torch into the pyre, and the dry tinder blazed. The priests began to chant again, but soon the only noise was the crackling of flame.

The fire burned for hours, and it was only when dawn was peeking over the horizon that the pyre, now collapsed into the grave and reduced to ashes, had cooled.

I, alone of the mourners, kept vigil through the night. But with the coming of dawn, the priests returned, as did a few of the gladiatrices.

The priests arranged the tazze in the pit. The gladiatrices approached and placed lamps into the pit to light Asellina's way in the afterlife. Four were plain and unadorned. Three bore the image of the Egyptian god Anubis, who performed the same duty as the Roman Mercury or the Greek Hermes of conveying the soul through the underworld.

We would be the last people to lay eyes on Asellina's remains for nineteen hundred years, until excavations in twentieth century London disclosed the site and brought her bones to light.

I stooped and placed a final lamp with the others. It was a simple clay lamp, colored a rusty-orange. Its design was that of a fallen gladiator.

It was all I had to give her.

And it seemed an appropriate gift to place with Aife, the proud, undefeated warrior woman, the eldest daughter of Queen Boudicca.

XXVI

I returned to the Ring in a somber mood.

My emotions were in conflict whenever I thought of Asellina. Was her action a matter of honor? Was it vengeance? Was it justice? Was it even noble, in a way? Was it all of these?

I was repulsed by a society—and individuals, like Rhodius—who took such brutality in stride. Although, I reminded myself, not much had changed. It wasn't all that long ago that the humans of my era had been involved in an interstellar war with an alien race, with which, had we stopped to consider the matter, we actually had much in common.

Such is the unchanging nature of humanity. Thousands of years of technological advancement, and nothing had changed. I tried to console myself with the concept that at least it made my job easier—humans were humans, now and then.

What, I wondered, happened in the scheme of eternity to noble pagans? To Socrates—for a famous example—to Philippa's parents, Demokedes and Eudaimon, even Asellina? To Tyndareus who had lost his life while saving mine? To countless others who lived in the rays of such feeble light as had been granted them? It was one thing, I supposed, to have willfully turned away from God; another thing to have had only vague intimations of His existence.

I prayed that their lives had not been lived in vain.

And I prayed that mine would count for something, too.

With such musings I returned to the future.

I was summoned to report to the Ring's chief medical officer, following what I thought had been the usual routine of tedious examinations.

I could tell the CMO was puzzled. Physicians in all eras have the same knack of trying to conceal their bafflement under masks of professional competence.

He was studying some kind of scan on the inlaid screen on his desk. It looked like a brain. Undoubtedly mine. His finger traced a pattern over my gyri and sulci. Various areas glowed in shades of red, blue, yellow, green.

Numbers scrolled down the sides of the display.

"What's wrong?" I asked.

He looked up, startled. "Oh, hello, Professor."

I sat down and repeated my question.

The mask settled into place. "Probably nothing serious, Professor," he said breezily.

"Tell me the truth," I pressed. "Spare no details."

He steepled his hands, leaned forward, elbows on his desk. "It's your memory," he replied.

"There's nothing wrong with my memory," I rejoined, before remembering my momentary trouble keeping the names of the gladiatrices straight. Surely it was nothing.

"I disagree," the CMO said. "Your neurocognitive results are slightly lower than before."

"Slightly." I jumped on the word.

He nodded.

"So it may be nothing."

"It's too early to tell," he replied. "We'll need to keep a close eye on you."

"More testing?" I wondered.

"Every time you come back," he said.

"Am I all right otherwise?"

"There's a marginal diminution in your mitochondrial assays," he added. "Your energy processing…cellular metabolism…barely reaching statistical significance…"

"Which means…"

"Almost as if you were aging at a slightly supra-normal rate," he continued. His eyes had a strangely detached appearance to them. "I'd be happy to go into detail, but it's quite technical, really…"

I waved off the suggestion. "That's not necessary."

"It's quite curious," he said. "Quite curious…"

Being a curiosity was not a new experience for me. I'd been a curiosity when my parents moved back to Earth. I'd been a curiosity following my first trip back in time. And now I was a medical curiosity.

This one was different…it nagged at me after I left the Ring for Earth. I thought about it, worried about it, tried—and failed—to dismiss it from my mind. There was nothing I could do about it. If the processes were somehow related to time travel, then the only way to avoid worsening them would be to cease time travel, and I wasn't about to do that. It was my life.

I would have to wait and see. Continue being a medical curiosity until the physicians figured out what was wrong. And in the meantime, I would be a curiosity again…this time, in the past.

XXVII: DOCTORAL DISSERTATION

The lamps were lit for the evening, I'd finished off a dinner of bread, figs, and honey, removed my sandals to give my feet some breathing room, and, since my eyes were too tired for reading, prepared myself just to sit and think for a while. My body needed rest, but my mind was ready for exercise—if only to distract my body from its discomforts.

It was a torrid, muggy night in Rome in AD 113, the kind of night when all I seemed to be able to do was sweat, itch, scratch, and try to think of things to think about in order not to think about sweating, itching, and scratching.

My quarters consisted of a single large room on the third floor of a run-down tenement with a balcony overlooking the baths. It was hot, noisy, and inconspicuous. If the inebriated young men wandering the streets in the early hours of the morning didn't disturb me, then the shrieks of people having their armpit hairs plucked did. Living here reminded me of my university days, when sleep was similarly hard to come by.

The rumble of cartwheels on cobblestones all night long didn't help, either. What might Rome have achieved if people were granted a good night's sleep? Oh, for a quiet villa in the peaceful countryside!

Today, I had witnessed the dedication of Trajan's column. It sounded festive, but the reality…

Hours standing in the broiling heat among the press and stink of the unwashed masses left me enervated and footsore. My ears rang from the blast and blare of innumerable wind instruments and the cheers and shouts of the raucous crowd clamoring for largesse from the emperor. My eyes ached from the glare of sunshine on marble.

I longed for climate control. And sleep.

But now all I could do was itch. And scratch. And think.

About what?

How about the one question that caused me more sleepless nights than any Roman bed, bugs, or weather conditions: Why hadn't I met a colleague from the future? Why wasn't the past full of observers from the future—

historians, scholars, time tourists, missionaries, thieves…?

It was all very well for Paul and Richard to tell me that they wouldn't be there because they hadn't been there, but *why* hadn't they been there? To say that time travelers might be present, but that all of them who are ever present at a given event are there in the original crowds, begged the question. Why weren't there more? Why had so few people made the journey into the past?

I had barely posed the question when I started at a knock on my door. I wasn't expecting a visitor, and frankly, didn't want to see anyone. I glared at the offending portal and made no move toward it.

Surely crowds of future people ought to be ogling the Seven Wonders of the ancient world in their glory; jostling each other on the streets of Troy, Carthage, Athens, Babylon, Ninevah, Persepolis, Machu Piccu, and countless other cities; viewing Caesar's assassination, Marie Antoinette's execution, the Crucifixion, Lord Nelson's death at Trafalgar; seeking spiritual insight directly from Jesus, Moses, Socrates, Confucius, and other teachers and prophets.

But they weren't. Historical records preserved no accounts of such situations. None of my colleagues had ever observed such a phenomenon. If there were people from the future, they were either invisible or few and far between.

Previous generations of skeptics had used the absence of crowds of time tourists as an argument against time travel in general. But since we'd built the Ring, surely people from even further in the future would have equal or better access to the past.

The unwanted visitor knocked again, louder. Again, I ignored the summons. Had whomever it was glimpsed light from my window and known that I was home?

I glared harder at the door, wishing the intruder would leave. I didn't want to talk to anyone. I'd had enough of people for the day.

Could there be some kind of "temporal burden" limit which put constraints on the number of people who could travel to the past? Did time travel remain forever expensive and severely restricted, available to only a fortunate few?

Or—and I dismissed this thought almost immediately as being too bizarre—were most of the people whom we thought were past people actually future people?

Darkly, I wondered if the future had lost interest in the past. Perhaps they'd learned all they wanted to and indulged in other ventures—visiting parallel universes, for example.

Or—and here my mind really balked—was there some kind of "Valhalla" scenario where one could visit the past by traveling vastly far into the future where the universe was replaying itself? Were future people enmeshed in a version of the Stoics' doctrine of eternal recurrence?

What if the future no longer existed? Had future humans regressed, lost their technology, and now walked uncomprehendingly through the crumbling remains of civilization? Had humanity succumbed to a plague?

What if humanity in its collective stupidity, and despite being established on hundreds of worlds, had committed suicide?

What if God had called an end to time?

I chilled at my morbid speculations.

Yet I always wondered, as I wandered ancient streets, studying the inhabitants of this city or that going about their daily business unaware of the stranger in their midst, if perhaps behind a veil or hood or cowl were the features of a future observer.

Probably, I would never know.

A series of knocks, impatient. The noise was getting on my nerves. "I'm not deaf!" I wanted to call. "Don't you realize that I don't *want* to open the door?" Obviously, the visitor was not telepathic and couldn't read my mind.

CamOx's Code of Conduct prohibited past-times researchers from identifying themselves to the natives with whom they came in contact. I assumed that potential observers from further in the future obeyed the same proscription. Would it matter? In the majority of timeframes, such a concept would never cross the minds of the local people. If I made a slip-up—an inevitability given the amount of time I have spent in the past—the notion that I was a time traveler would never occur to them. They might view me as a prophet, a god, a devil, or a madman, but not a man from the future.

Reluctantly I came to the conclusion that for whatever reason, I would never meet another time traveler.

The visitor knocked and kept on knocking, a rhythmic pounding that drove my irritation past the breaking point.

With a quick movement I rose, crossed the room, and jerked the door open. I didn't recognize the young man who stood there. He was a head taller than I, and wore a light green tunic and a gold ring on his right hand, raised for another knock. Not a slave then, but free, and fairly well-to-do. His hair was cut in current fashion, and he smelled of oil, as if he'd just come from the baths.

"Isn't it rather late to be pounding on someone's door?" I said curtly.

"Dr. Cragg?" he asked in English, sticking his foot adroitly into the doorway as I began to close it. "Dr. Robert Cragg?"

"I..." I groped for words, stunned. In this time frame I was Quintus Aulus Pollio. "Yes—"

"May I come in?"

My jaw still hanging open, I mumbled, "Do," and beckoned him inside.

He glanced around my humble abode, from the scrolls littering every horizontal surface, to the flickering lamps, to my small cot, to the remains of a loaf of bread going stale on a Samian redware plate.

"Amazing," he whispered. "Simply amazing."

"What, this dump?"

"You have lived more years in the past than anyone else—"

"Excuse me," I interrupted, "but who in Jupiter's name are you?"

He blushed. "Sorry. Philip McLeod. You won't have heard of me."

I shook my head.

He motioned to a sideboard. "May I?"

I nodded, and he poured two cups of wine, diluted with water in appropriate Roman manner.

"It's Gaulish," I said, as he handed one to me. "Very middling."

I gestured him toward a chair, then returned to my own. He stared at me as if I were a museum piece.

"You're fascinated with my life in the past," I prompted.

"Yes. To give up life in a civilized era to live among primitive, undeveloped peoples…"

"I like it," I said shortly, annoyed by his scrutiny. "And it's a sight better than some of our more remote worlds. You, I presume, are from my future."

"Good guess."

"And why are you here?"

"For the same reason you are." He tipped his head to one side. "To study the past."

"You're studying me," I said.

He nodded.

"It's generally poor technique to let the subject know he's being observed."

"It is," he concurred, "but I couldn't resist." He raised a hand before I could protest. "And I had authority from my department chair, who felt that telling you—since you know about time travel, of course—wouldn't be a problem."

"Ah. And from which—"

"CamOx, of course," he said. He took a swallow of his wine, then set the cup down and licked his lips. "It's really not bad. Better than some I've had lately. Let me explain."

"Please do."

"I'm writing—or will write, from your point of view—my doctoral dissertation on you."

"On me?" I said, unable to contain my surprise.

"Don't be modest," he replied. "You're famous in Temporal Historico-Archaeology circles. The father of our profession. Your articles are standard reading. You paved the way for the rest of us."

I felt a flash of gratification. At least I hadn't been consigned to academic oblivion by the future.

"We've learned from your techniques," he continued, "analyzed your field reports—"

"And observed me in person," I finished dryly. "Have you been watching me for long?"

"Do you remember a street tough in Kourion?" he replied. "A perfume seller in Antinoopolis? An aide to General Flavius Silva?" He reeled off a list of a dozen other impersonations.

"You're very good," I said, mentally visualizing each character as he listed them—except for one or two, on which, strangely, I drew blanks. Inside, though, I felt cold. Was I just a specimen to him? A man who in his world was already dead?

Had he been observing me as I had observed so many people who had lived and died long before my own time? What did he know about my personal future? I felt eerily disconnected.

"I've tried to imitate you," he said.

"Thanks for the compliment. So if you've made all these observations, why—?"

"Am I talking to you? To fill in the gaps. It really is an honor, you know. Do you have the time for an interview?"

I glanced into the depths of my wine. "I've been interviewed by people in my time," I said, "why not yours?"

"Excellent!" he grinned.

"Besides," I added, reaching for a cloth to wipe my forehead, "what else is there to do on a night like this?"

He wiped his own face on the sleeve of his tunic. "It's ghastly all right." He paused for a moment, then said, "Tell me, please, how it felt to step onto ancient soil for the first time."

I pursed my lips. How had it felt to first breathe air that was well over two thousand years younger than mine? What emotions had coursed through me as I looked into a night sky unpolluted with the light of modern cities?

"It was like my marriage," I said at last. "I was nervous—afraid—but in a good sense, because I knew it was absolutely the right thing to do. It was the start of a new adventure, a new phase of my life. My wife died—you know that—and I made the past my second wife."

He nodded. I assumed he was making detailed mental notes, as I did.

"Do you have any regrets…about projects, about times you may not have seen?"

I smiled. "Regrets, plenty. As far as times and places I haven't seen, I'm not at the end of my life yet, I hope, and I don't know what places I still have to go."

He blushed sheepishly. "A silly question."

"Talk to me again when I'm retired," I added, "and maybe I can give you a better answer."

"Maybe."

"Or did you already talk to a later me?"

He shrugged and looked noncommittal, and I knew he would be very careful not to give the future away.

We talked until early into the morning, until the lamps burned low and I had to replenish the oil. Philip McLeod, I realized, was taking his task very seriously.

He knew what it was like to be a Temporal Historian, but not what it was like to be among the very first. Most researchers, after a while, grow tired of living in the past. They yearn for the amenities of their own time, and most decide to stay in their own era. But not me. For me, the past became the present.

I loved it, even though I could neither enhance history's triumphs nor ameliorate her failings. Trying to change history was like throwing a rock into a mighty river—it made no difference. The butterfly effect might work in one's own time, but in the past, it was useless. The past was solid, monolithic.

It was a hard thing to get used to. But one eventually did. Sometimes. Not everyone could adjust. I had my good days and my bad ones.

The level in the wine jug dropped lower.

Eventually, Philip yawned and stretched. "You've been more than accommodating, Dr. Cragg. I think I have plenty to work with."

"You're welcome to stay the night," I replied, "although I don't have a guest room."

He rose. "I must be on my way." He held out his hand and we shook. He smiled pleasantly. "Maybe I'll see you again sometime."

His footsteps clattered on the stairs, and he was gone, out into the humid, stale air.

A thought crossed my sluggish mind, and I dashed out onto the rickety balcony, but he'd vanished. The streets lay deserted. We'd talked so much about me that I hadn't questioned him.

How far from the future was he?

Why were observers from the future so scarce?

How long would humanity survive?

Would he have told me? Did he know?

I went back inside and lay down on my cot, but I knew I wouldn't sleep. I wondered how many other people, in how many different times, might be observing me.

I didn't like the sensation one bit. Peter McLeod had shattered my sense of privacy, had taken away the security I felt in the past.

My only consolation was that somebody, somewhere, somewhen, might be observing *him*.

XXVIII

"There's definitely a problem," said the Chief Medical Officer, drumming his fingers on his desk.

Once again, we sat in his office on the Ring, a large viewport behind him showing a realm of glittering stars. It looked peaceful, romantic, tranquil, yet I knew it wasn't. Those distant stars were giant, broiling nuclear furnaces. Stars were exploding, crashing into each other, being ripped asunder and devoured by the even more awesome forces of black holes. Comets and asteroids collided with planets and with each other. Vast plumes and clouds of interstellar dust bore witness to cosmic catastrophes. The universe wasn't peaceful, not at all.

And neither was I.

"Am I much worse?" I asked hesitantly.

He shook his head. "Not much. But enough for us to know that we're not dealing with artifact, or normal variation, or the like. No, Professor, there's no mistake."

His gaze was fixed in my direction, waiting for me to pose another query.

I had nothing to say. Except the one question that I hesitated to ask.

Eventually, he cleared his throat and continued. "We'll run some more scans, try to pin it down…consult with further specialists on Earth…see what we can do…"

I gathered my nerve. I didn't really care whom he consulted, or what scans he ran. There was only one issue that really mattered.

"Can I still go back in time?" I asked, and held my breath.

He nodded, slowly, tentatively. "For the moment, yes. In fact, it would actually be helpful if you did."

"To see if the decline continues?" I wondered.

"I know it sounds harsh—"

"Clinical," I countered.

"But we have to figure it out, for the benefit of other travelers."

A guinea pig again, I thought, but didn't say it.

"I understand," I replied.

"Of course, the decision is yours. We can't force you to go back—"

"No fear," I said. "I want to."

"That's very noble," he said.

"It's my life," I replied.

XXIX

"I almost hate to ask you to take this assignment," said the New Chair apologetically, when the time came for me to prepare for another trip.

We'd spent a few minutes engaged in small talk before getting down to business. She'd just returned from a vacation scaling icecliffs on Snowolf, a frigid world as cold as its name sounded, and which—being from balmy Heliopolis—I had no desire to visit. But I could easily imagine her in a thermal sno-suit, with her long blonde braids making her look like a figure from Norse mythology, ascending the sheer walls of glistening ice that stretched upward for kilometer on kilometer.

Was she preparing for a trip into Norse history, I wondered? No, just having fun, she replied.

She was certainly different from the Old Chair, who, before his retirement, had never left the Solar System.

She seemed reluctant to broach the subject of my next venture, and when she did, I believed her when she declared her apprehension. Worry-lines creased her forehead and spread out from the corners of her eyes. She licked her lips and rubbed her thumb and index finger nails together. I had never seen her so nervous.

"And," she added, "if you wish to refuse, you are free to do so."

She sounded as if she wanted me to refuse. I had never yet declined an assignment, although I'd come close. But this was to the Britain of AD 61, a very dangerous time. There was a real chance I might not return alive—depending, of course, on which physicist one believed. And yet I was intrigued.

"You've seen him, haven't you?" the New Chair asked.

I nodded.

"Him" was a bog body in a display case tucked away in a corner of the British Museum. Discovered by peat cutters working near Manchester in the 20th century, he was believed by some to have died an unusual, ceremonial death.

A Druidic death.

Almost certainly, he'd be a very interesting person to meet.

What had I to lose?

"I'll go," I said.

"You can change your mind at any time," the New Chair said, as if hesitant to accept my decision. "Up until the time of Ring transport."

"I won't change my mind," I said.

I don't know if she was relieved or disappointed.

Was climbing vertical icecliffs any less dangerous, I inquired?

It depended on the sophistication of the tools one chose to use, she replied.

In the past, of course, I had no tools except the technology of the day.

I recalled those conversations months later as I stood before the flickering gray expanse of the interface, pausing for a moment before those awesome, yet controlled energies transported me once again through time.

What damage would another trip do to me? Would I start to feel mental or physical effects? Would this excursion be a trip too far, one trip too many, one danger too much? A cliff too high?

I squared my shoulders, stepped forward into the grayness, and felt once more the familiar sensation of needles penetrating my cells.

XXX: IN THE MISTS OF BRITAIN

"You are not one of us."

I gazed at the speaker, but made no reply. The man—he appeared to be in his mid-thirties, late middle-age for this era—circled me with measured steps, then resumed his position in front of me, his legs spread, his arms folded across his chest. The British-style cloak I had been wearing lay crumpled on the ground, and I stood exposed in a Roman tunic, shivering from more than the chill breeze that wafted over the rolling British countryside.

Surrounding us at a distance was a ring of warriors, tough-looking, long-haired men, their wickedly-sharp swords glinting in the spears of sunlight that shafted through the trees. One motion from this man, and I'd be splayed on the ground, wallowing in my own blood. I smelled the stink of my own fear over the stale body-odor of the warriors.

Was this to be my final trip into history? Maybe my life could end in the past, after all.

He reached out to finger the sleeve of my tunic. It was a common one, the sort that anyone might wear. Any *Roman*.

"But neither are you one of them," he said, his puzzlement nearly palpable.

He was about five and a half feet tall, well-muscled without being stocky. His hair, neatly trimmed to slightly below his ears, was brown with hints of red. His downturned moustache ended just before his jawline. A gold torque finishing in a pair of snarling wolf-heads encircled his neck. He wore a buff-colored blouse, trousers, and a blue cloak secured by a jeweled clasp. A sword swung at his side. His voice was cultured, not the harsh tones of the brutes who had captured me.

He frowned and spoke softly as if to himself. "You are neither a Briton nor a Roman. You aren't from any of the Celtic lands or Hispania. You're not from Parthia or the lands to the east. You are no Egyptian. The blood of the Germans or Greeks doesn't flow in your veins. From whence do you come?"

His brows were dark and bushy, surmounting the most intense eyes I had ever seen, the irises so dark as to seem nearly black.

"Can you understand me?" he asked, raising his voice.

"I speak your tongue," I said in his Briton dialect.

His eyebrows rose. He'd probably expected me to say something in Latin, which, of course, I could have done with equal ease.

"But strangely," he said.

"I've not had much practice," I replied. I couldn't figure him out, read what his intentions were. The easiest thing would be for him to execute me as a Roman spy. It would be the logical choice. But he wasn't sure about me. He was curious, though, and I wanted to keep it that way. As long as I could keep him wondering, he'd be less likely to kill me.

The dark eyes bored into me. "There is something unusual about you," he mused.

"Can we spit the Roman devil yet?" one of the watching warriors called, twirling his blade so that it made a nerve-jarring whistle in the air. "My sword thirsts for Roman blood."

The man looked away and raised an arm to halt him. "Not yet."

Only a man of great authority could issue orders to these fierce warriors—a king or prince, perhaps. For the first time, I noticed a band of fox-fur around his upper right arm. I blinked. Could it be? What were the chances of me actually meeting this man among the thousands of Britons in this area? Had twentieth-century archaeologists accurately deduced his name? A band of fox-fur was an awfully thin piece of evidence upon which to base a name. I decided to take a chance.

"Is your name Lovernios?" I asked.

His gaze shot back to me with the speed of an arrow-shaft.

"How do you come by my name?" he hissed tautly.

"Perhaps we can talk further," I replied.

He nodded, slowly. "We shall, indeed." He beckoned to one of the waiting warriors. "Take him to my tent. Keep him secure, but do not lay a hand on him. If any injury comes to him, I shall hold you to account."

The warrior, one of the ugliest of the bunch, inclined his head. "Your will be done, my lord."

I nodded respectfully to Lovernios, picked up my cloak and slung it over my shoulder as nonchalantly as I could, then followed the warrior away, conscious all the time of Lovernios' gaze following me. The ring of scowling warriors parted to allow us through. My back tingled in anticipation of a knife-stroke, but nothing happened—Lovernios' command of these rough men must be absolute.

I had bought myself a few extra hours of life, and time in which to think. But was it enough to save me?

I sat Indian-fashion on the dirt floor of an unadorned tent that reeked of smoke and animal hide, awaiting Lovernios' arrival, wondering if perhaps this time my curiosity had gotten the better of me.

We historians always question our counterparts from the past. How accurate were they, particularly in antiquity before current standards of historical accuracy became the norm? How prone to propagandizing were they? How trustworthy were their facts?

To the ancients, history was a form of literature, not a branch of the social sciences. Historians were literary artists, not scholars. They paraphrased, created speeches to put in the mouths of their subjects, and Roman historians notoriously gave free rein to unbridled patriotism. At various times in the history of the Roman Empire freedom of expression was limited; only a fool would write harshly about an emperor—Nero or Caligula, for example—who would react with homicidal fury. Ancient history is therefore not as we would write it.

My mission was to put the Roman historian Cornelius Tacitus to the test.

And so, here I was in Britannia while Queen Boudicca's rebellious hordes ravaged the countryside, slaughtering any Roman and any Roman sympathizer who came within reach of their murderous longswords. It was all the fault of an incompetent procurator named Decianus Catus.

Britannia was still a work in progress for the Romans, who for eighteen years since the Emperor Claudius' legions had rolled ashore had been consolidating their possession of the island. They had allied with some tribes, conquered others, and made treaties with certain "client kingdoms" that enjoyed relative independence on the edge of Roman territory. The Iceni were one such, ruled by King Prasutagus; their tribal center, Venta Icenorum, lay near what is now Norwich.

Relations had remained relatively cordial until King Prasutagus died. He attempted to safeguard Iceni independence by making the Roman emperor the executor and partial beneficiary of his will, leaving the other half to his two daughters and his wife Boudicca. But the Emperor Nero wouldn't bite—he wanted the whole pie.

Enter Catus the Idiot—long on avarice and short on political acumen—who thought that flogging Queen Boudicca and raping her daughters would bring the disgruntled Iceni to heel.

He couldn't have been more wrong.

Instead of prostrating themselves before Catus' perfumed feet,

Boudicca's Iceni rose in revolt. The Ninth Legion rushed from its fortress near York straight into an ambush and was cut to pieces. Jubilant Briton hordes wiped the colony town of Camulodunum from the face of the earth while the slimy Catus fled to the continent with his ill-gotten gains, leaving the governor, Suetonius Paulinus, with a mess on his hands.

As his province was crumbling to ashes, the flames of burning towns reddening the nighttime clouds and the screams of the dying echoing along the corridors of their ransacked villas, said governor was on the other side of the country with the Fourteenth and Twentieth Legions exterminating what remained of the Druids on the Isle of Mona—Anglesey.

The only other Roman force in the country, the Second Legion, stayed secure in its fortress in the southwest, refusing to budge.

Suetonius Paulinus made a swift reconnaissance, decided that Londinium and Verulamium couldn't be defended, returned to his legions which were marching across the country—with myself among them—and abandoned the two cities to their fate. The Britons sacked the towns. Perhaps 80,000 people perished.

That was the history to which I had returned. Outside the thin walls of this tent the furious Queen Boudicca had some hundred and twenty thousand warriors with which to slake her thirst for revenge, if Tacitus was correct. Suetonius, with the fate of the province in his hands, could only muster about fourteen thousand men in his two loyal legions.

I grimaced.

Could I have visited a more dangerous time?

But I hadn't been completely senseless. I knew who had won. And since soldiering wasn't in my veins I'd planned to play it safe and had attached myself to Suetonius as a secretary. I'd intended to observe the fighting from the security of a position well behind the Roman Army's lines where there were battle-hardened legionaries between me and Boudicca's tribesmen.

My plan might have worked had I not ventured aside from the marching legions to inspect a ruined villa, curious if tales of Briton atrocities as mentioned by Roman historian Cassius Dio were true. My horse spooked, and by the time I finally regained control, I was lost. I had wandered through the unfamiliar countryside, stopping only at an abandoned hut where I availed myself of a discarded cloak. Shortly thereafter, I found myself surrounded by a Briton war party.

The cloak had at least confused them enough that they made me a captive rather than a corpse.

And now here I was, sitting in this miserable tent, trying to think of a tale to tell Lovernios that would save my skin. But how could I explain my mixed Roman and Briton clothing, my awkward accent, and my non-native complexion?

All too soon, Lovernios returned. I rose as he entered, but he motioned me to sit and lowered himself onto a rug opposite me.

Once again, I became the object of scrutiny from those mysterious eyes.

"Tell me your name in your own tongue," he commanded.

It was unreal—otherworldly—the influence those eyes possessed. I couldn't resist. "Robert," I said, for the first time speaking my own name in the past.

He repeated the syllables. "Strange. What does it mean?"

"Often, in my country, names are bestowed for no other reason than that they sound pleasing to the tongue. I am named after an ancestor—"

"What does it mean?" he repeated, firmly but without impatience.

"One who shines with honor."

He grasped my hands, turned them palm up, and studied them. "These are not the hands of a warrior."

"There are other kinds of honor."

"You speak as a sage or a scholar."

"And so I am."

"What learning do you study?"

"History," I replied. "The people who have come before."

He leaned back. Once again, puzzled furrows developed between his eyebrows.

"Your hands do not have callouses, either," I commented.

He gestured briskly toward the door of the tent. "I can wield a sword with more skill than any of them."

"I don't doubt it. But a Druí's mind is sharper than his sword."

He gripped my right wrist so hard that I nearly gasped with sudden pain. "How do you know that I am Druí? Are you a sorcerer?"

I shook my head. "I have no supernatural powers."

He released my wrist and I rubbed it.

"I am skilled at reading men," he said. "I can look into a man's eyes and read his soul. I know whether he is honest or deceitful, a man of honor or a son of evil. But you are different. I look into your eyes…" his voice faded away.

"What do you see?" I asked.

"Nothing I have seen before. It is as if…as if you are not of this world at all."

My skin prickled. Were tales of strange Druid powers true after all?

He reached beneath his blouse, to the waistband of his trousers. I flinched as he withdrew a dagger with a jeweled handle.

"Have no fear," he said.

He raised the dagger to his face and squinted along the shining blade. "I can tell if a man is straight or crooked," he commented, "if his blade be

170

true or warped. But your blade is unclear to me. It is as if I look into the mist and can see a short ways, but no further. I sense a blankness, a hollow where my spirit cannot go. Yet," and his gaze slid along the bright metal until it returned to me, "I detect no evil in you."

"I harbor no malice toward you or your people," I said.

Abruptly, he reversed the dagger and handed it to me hilt first, extending it further when at first I didn't take it. I held it with the point toward the ground.

"Cut yourself," Lovernios said.

I started.

"I would see the color of your blood," he said.

"Spirits don't bleed," I said, "but I do." Taking a deep breath I drew the sharp blade across my left forearm, creating a cut about an inch long. Blood welled up in it. I raised my arm for him to see.

He nodded, and I handed the dagger back to him. He returned it to its sheath.

"Who are you?" he asked.

"Merely one who studies the past."

"I have spared your life," he said irritably, "and yet you won't answer my questions clearly."

I sighed. "I wish I could. But it is not allowed to me."

He rose to his feet. "I have offerings and sacrifices to perform. The decisive day is fast approaching when we shall rid the land of the Romans."

"Queen Boudicca will not win," I said, wishing instantly that I could have recalled the foolish words.

Faster than I would have thought any man could move, he was behind me with his dagger pressed against my throat.

"You lie!"

I gulped. "No."

"It is impossible! Queen Boudicca's army is numberless. The Romans have only a few men."

"Nonetheless, it is what will happen."

"Perhaps you are indeed a Roman spy, sent to spread fear in our midst."

"I have spoken to none but you," I said. "You desire the truth. I have given it to you."

Sill holding the knife to my throat, he resumed his position in front of me. "If you are not a seer or a sorcerer, then how can you know the future? If, that is, you are not a false prophet or charlatan."

"I have seen it," I said. "You are a Druí. Have you looked ahead?"

"I have tried. It is darkness."

"What the Romans did to the Druidae on Mona only a few days ago, they will do to Queen Boudicca. They are the two ends of a torque, connected."

The knife slowly lowered from my throat. "That, I saw."

"You were there?" I exclaimed.

"I saw with the eyes of the spirit," he said, "as a bird circling overhead."

Once again, I felt a chill. I had been with Suetonius' army on Mona, and in my mind's eye I saw again the ranks of Roman soldiers poised on the shoreline, their boats bobbing in front of them. On the far shore, appearing out of the morning mist, a mob of Briton warriors. And scattered in their midst, the Druids. Not all Druids were priests, of course: some were physicians, scholars, or nobles. But those on Mona were priests.

There weren't many, and not all were men; I noticed a number of women in their ranks. They held flaming torches and stood motionless in an eerie silence.

Suetonius gave an order, and the Roman legionaries climbed into their boats and began to row. Cavalry squadrons ranged afield, seeking suitable fording places.

The boats were about halfway over when the motley mass of Britons began hurling curses and imprecations. A few of the stronger warriors flung spears. But it was the Druids who made the most impact. With their arms extended toward the Romans, their fingers pointed, they struck fear into the hearts of the experienced legionaries. The boats slowed, then stopped and lay rocking on the waves. Fighting soldiers was one thing, fighting priests and their gods quite another.

"Forward," Suetonius yelled from the boat that carried the senior officers, and when none followed suit, he rose to his feet and turned his back on the Britons. His scarlet general's cape fluttered in the morning breeze.

"What are you afraid of?" he shouted. "Are the legions of Rome frightened by a few savage warriors? Are you terrified of women priests? Do the Britons' gods turn your bowels to water? Do you think they are stronger than the gods of Rome, these gods who cannot even hold a small island? Bah! What good are words and curses against Roman steel?"

He motioned to his helmsman. "Pull for shore! Let us be the first to teach these barbarians a lesson!"

The boat surged forward. The legionaries cheered, and the flotilla followed.

The fight was short and savage. The Roman cavalry swam across and rode down the Britons. The legionaries formed ranks into an impenetrable line that forced the Britons back, cutting them down without mercy. The curses of the Druids died in their throats as men and women alike were hacked to the ground.

It was not as dramatic as Tacitus had written. It was ugly and brutal.

My vision focused again on the figure of Lovernios. Tears shimmered in his eyes.

"I knew many of those who died," he said. His gaze hardened. "They were not ignorant barbarians. They were people defending their homeland and their ways from an invader."

"It has always been thus," I said, "and always will be."

He sprang to his feet. "The battle will be waged. If, by some chance, you have spoken truly, then perhaps I shall spare your life again. But if you have spoken falsely, then you shall join the Romans in their grave."

With a swirl of his cloak, he was gone.

Of the battle that followed, I can hardly bear to write.

It seemed too lovely a morning to witness such carnage. The sun ascended gently through light, gauzy mist which rose veil-like from the reed and grass-fringed river Anker. The hills that formed the valley emerged into the morning sunshine with the languor of a maiden awakening from sleep. Birds sang as if nothing were amiss, and the air was fragrant with the scent of flowers, leaves, and damp earth.

The illusion didn't last long. Such fanciful imaginings were no match for the seething hostility of two armies bent on destruction.

An immense horde of Britons darkened the valley, pouring between the hills like spilled wine across a tiled floor. Human shouts and cries, the neighing of horses, and the rumble of cartwheels transformed the tranquility of the morning into a hellish cacophony. From farther away I heard the sound of trumpets as the legions of Rome prepared their defensive positions.

A pair of burly Britons roughly untied me from the tree to which I had been bound all night and prodded me with their feet until I forced my stiff body into an upright position. Since my hands and feet were still tied, it wasn't easy.

"Move, Roman swine," one of them grunted, pushing me roughly in the direction he wanted me to go.

"Where are you taking me?" I asked, my mouth dry.

"To Lovernios," the man grinned unpleasantly, "whom I shall ask for the pleasure of killing you once your general and his soldiers are slain. I shall make your death slow and painful."

His grin widened. "Unless you'd rather be killed now."

"I'd rather you cut the rope so that I can walk."

The warrior snarled, but freed my feet. The pair of them escorted me up the hillside on the far bank of the river, shoving me if I moved too slowly. We emerged from the trees into a clearing. Lovernios was seated on the ground; he made no movement as I approached, seemingly lost in his own thoughts. A saddled horse grazed placidly nearby, with several pouches strapped to its back. A sheathed sword dangled from a leather cord, and a bow and a quiver of arrows were slung nearby.

I stood uncertainly, unsure if he'd noticed me, until finally, with a pointing finger, he indicated for me to sit. I complied, and the guards stood behind me. Lovernios had shown no fear of me, but perhaps he still suspected me of possessing occult powers and wanted to ensure that I did not perform a foreign rite.

He didn't know, of course, but I had no intention of trying to escape. I figured that my best hope of survival at this point was to remain close to him.

Across the river, not far from where the town of Mancetter stands today, the Romans had taken up a strong position in a shallow defile on the hillside, with their flanks protected and a dense forest covering their rear. They made an impressive showing. Their ranked shields formed a solid wall, row on row of helmets gleamed in the sunshine, their standards waved overhead, and their cavalry regiments lined up on the wings. Toward the rear of the formation, I spotted the officers on their mounts. Suetonius Paulinus was among them. I wondered if he'd spared a thought for his missing secretary.

Probably not. He had much more pressing matters on his mind. A man who would sacrifice two cities rather than defend the indefensible wouldn't worry about a single individual. I have made him sound harsh, and he could be—a successful Roman general had little use for sentiment—but I had found him to be a man of astute mind and considerable dry wit. Perhaps someday I shall write more about him.

I wondered what was running through his mind as he surveyed the immense horde of Britons baying for Roman blood. How could he hope to overcome the fearsome swarm which had raped and burned its way across the province? I shuddered to imagine the horrors the inhabitants of the doomed cities had endured.

Some Britons wore blouses and trousers, others bared woad-painted chests, a number fought naked. Women wielded swords beside their menfolk. In the rear, the Britons had drawn up wagons as viewing platforms for their wives and children. They were expecting an easy victory.

I could understand Lovernios' confidence—it seemed impossible to believe that so many could fail to prevail over so few. But those few were battle-hardened Roman legionaries. They were desperate men facing overwhelming odds, and desperation drives men to do the impossible.

"Look at the might of the Iceni," Lovernios said, finally breaking into speech.

"Quite a spectacle," I replied, watching as dust swirled from chariot wheels and horses' hooves.

"No more will the Romans deface our hills with their towns. No more will they ravage our women, take our children into slavery, crush us under the burden of taxation. What Caratacus failed to do, what Cogidubnus was afraid to do, Queen Boudicca *will* do."

I sighed. What could I say? Perhaps some among the Iceni were my distant ancestors. Of course, given the intermarriage that occurred over the centuries between Britons and Romans, perhaps a legionary on the other side was an ancestor as well. Both of these peoples had contributed to the English race to which I belonged.

Lovernios rose to his feet and brushed grass from his robes. He muttered a few instructions to the warriors guarding me—undoubtedly ordering them to keep a close watch on me—then swung onto his waiting horse and rode down the hillside. I stood as well and followed his progress, trying to keep him in sight as he crossed the river and joined the Briton horde. I saw him meet up with a chariot driven by a woman with long, flowing red hair, wearing a multicolored blouse.

Queen Boudicca herself!

I strained my eyes, but to my disappointment, the distance was too great for me to make out the features of this fearsome woman. Behind her were her violated daughters—Aife, whom I had known as Asellina, and her younger sister Cinnia.

Inadvertently, I took a step forward, and one of the warriors extended a thick arm across my chest and pushed me back with an oath.

Boudicca bent over and released a hare into the clear space between the two armies—undoubtedly some kind of augury. It jerked frantically as it tried to run away. Lovernios leaned close to the queen: then she wheeled her chariot in front of her army. She appeared to be speaking; I would have loved to have heard her speech and compared it with the one Tacitus had recorded or composed.

But its effect must have been great, because with a roar like that of a giant bear aroused, the great mass of Britons charged up the slope toward the waiting Romans.

Roman trumpets sent clear notes floating over the valley, and as the Britons drew close they were met by a flight of javelins whose shining tips rose like a flock of birds before plummeting as sparkling messengers of death. The ground welcomed Britons writhing in agony. A second flight felled more Britons, but then the Briton army met the waiting wall of Roman shields with a crash that sent echoes spinning off the hills.

The Britons had hoped, no doubt, simply to roll over the Romans like a wave over a sandcastle.

It didn't happen. The Romans didn't break.

Caught up in the excitement, I'd forgotten to keep track of Lovernios, but the clop of hooves heralded his return. This time, he led a second horse. He halted them and dismounted with a smooth movement.

"You aren't joining the fight?" I asked.

He shook his head. "There are many swords. I shall fight on a different plane."

"Were the auguries good?" I asked.

He regarded me curiously. "Do you still say we shall fail?"

I nodded.

"Can you see the future?" he grated.

"No," I replied softly. "But I know the past."

He stared at me for a long moment. Then he turned aside, to where a small fire sent a plume of fragrant smoke swirling into the air. He added a pinch of some sort of incense and with his hands raised, began intoning an invocation in a low voice.

The Briton army recoiled, then charged again with the same ineffective result. And Suetonius's plan became clear. The shallow defile funneled the Britons into a confined space, packing them together so that they could hardly move, much less wield their longswords, so much longer than the short, wickedly effective Roman gladius. And those Roman short-swords, flickering like snakes' tongues from behind the wall of shields, did deadly work. The mounds of Briton dead began to rise as those at the front were pressed forward by the dense mass behind. The climbing sun shone full into the Britons' eyes.

Lovernios' chant ascended to a keening wail that made my skin goosebump as if a thousand score of insects crawled over me.

I glimpsed Boudicca's chariot again, but this was not a battle for chariots.

After what seemed an interminable time, the Britons ebbed away from the Roman position like a spent wave, tripping and stumbling over the masses of dead and dying who lay like sea-wrack upon a shore.

Trumpets sounded again, and the Roman legions charged. With their cavalry sweeping along the flanks, they ploughed into the Britons, and herded them back as if they were cattle. And the Britons' overconfidence cost them, for now their wagons blocked their retreat.

The slaughter was mind-numbing in its scope.

I noticed abstractedly that the warriors guarding me had vanished. I spotted them running down the hillside toward the battle in a vain attempt to help.

Women and children ran screaming from the carnage, only to be cut down. Britons fled down the valley and plunged into the river to escape. Horses fell, bristling with arrows as Roman archers launched volley upon volley.

I am not a military historian; not for me the studying of ancient battles. Let others observe the prowess of Caesar, Alexander, Hannibal. As I watched this battle unfold, I hoped desperately never to witness another one.

My cheeks dripped with tears.

No matter that I knew Britannia would enjoy the better part of four centuries of peace, that from henceforth only the tribes of Scotland and Wales would defy the Romans. I wept for the devastation I witnessed. Peace—even the peace of occupation and assimilation into the Empire—was bought at a horrific price.

My eyes met those of Lovernios. I expected to see anger and rage; what I saw was a dreadful hollowness.

"I am truly sorry," I said.

He withdrew his dagger.

My breath froze in my chest as he approached me.

"Hold out your hands."

I did so, and he slashed the rope binding my wrists.

I rubbed my hands to restore the circulation. I framed my question with my eyes.

"You spoke truly," he said hoarsely. "I have kept my word." He beckoned. "Follow me."

"Where are we going?"

"Away," was his curt reply.

Lovernios vaulted onto his horse, while I climbed awkwardly onto the other. Why had he brought it? Had he had some premonition of disaster or did he always travel with two? Then, with Lovernios leading, we rode over the crest of the hill and away from the scene of Queen Boudicca's defeat. Tacitus had not lied.

We rode northwards across gently rolling terrain, following hillcrests and ridges from which we could study the surrounding countryside. Most likely the Romans would be content to mop up the remnants of Boudicca's army and regroup, but Lovernios was alert for any sign of enemy presence. North was the only direction which would take us clear of Romans.

I have no idea how many miles we covered that first day; it might perhaps have been ten or a little further. Lovernios set a steady but not overly rapid pace. Had we not witnessed such a dreadful massacre, I could well have enjoyed the ride. It was hard to imagine that this gentle landscape would one day become the industrial heartland of Britain, where busy cities—Birmingham, Leicester, Coventry, Nottingham, Derby—would crowd in upon each other until it became nearly impossible to tell where one ended and another began.

Lovernios said not a word the whole afternoon.

We spent that first night in a copse of trees near a small brook that provided fresh water, and Lovernios shared a hunk of bread which he extracted from a pouch.

We lit no fire, even though the evening became chill.

"Romans might see it," Lovernios said, as he wrapped himself in a cloak and pillowed his head on a pouch.

I curled up and made myself as comfortable as possible on a bed of leaves.

"Don't you worry?" I asked, indicating my free hands.

Lovernios shrugged. "I would sense it if you tried to escape. I have no fear that you would cause me harm."

Lovernios certainly had great faith in his own abilities, I thought wonderingly.

The leaves were thin, the ground cold and hard, and my overactive imagination heard danger in every noise of the forest. Every shifting shadow was an enemy, every cloud that blotted out the moon and gave us more protection in the darkness, a friend. I was glad for my cloak, as my tunic alone would have left me shivering. Moonlight filtered through the leaves and dappled the ground with a silver luminescence that at another time I might have found beautiful. I glanced toward Lovernios; he seemed to be sleeping soundly. I envied him his ease, although he was undoubtedly sore at heart. I wondered if he had lost family or friends in the battle.

I suppose eventually I must have drifted off to sleep, yet it still seemed an eternity later that my eyes beheld the yellow rays of the sun replacing the silvery moonbeams. I groaned and rolled to a sitting position. Every muscle in my body ached; it had been a considerable time since I had ridden a horse for so long. I rather wished the Celts or the Romans had invented stirrups—it would have made life so much easier.

"We must be off," Lovernios said by way of greeting, turning from where he was fastening something to his bags. I wasn't surprised that he had preceded me into wakefulness.

"What do you have?" I asked.

"Supper," he said, raising the limp form of a rabbit. He tossed a piece of dried meat in my direction. I caught it.

"Eat while we ride," Lovernios instructed.

I nodded unhappily. I wasn't eager for another day on horseback. I hadn't been born to it as Lovernios had.

We headed northward again, keeping to trails which snaked through the forest and only occasionally opened out into exposed areas.

"How did you know?" Lovernios asked when we stopped to allow our horses to drink from a stream and rest.

Intuitively, I knew he meant the outcome of the battle.

"I cannot tell you," I replied.

He grunted and, the brief conversation at an end, we rode on.

"We have entered the lands of the Coritani," Lovernios said.

"Will they be friendly?" I asked.

"I am welcome everywhere," Lovernios replied.

And so it proved. We spent that night in a village—if a collection of five thatched roundhouses could be considered a village. Lovernios presented the rabbit to the wife of the headman, who prepared it for us, cooking it in an iron pot that hung from a tripod over the fire. In my underfed state, I thought it delicious.

Lovernios stayed up late, sitting by the fire with the men of the little village, a trio of small children watching him with awe and curiosity.

I, it seemed, was not privileged to be a party to the conversation, and so I retired to a pile of furs against the wall of the hut, where I drifted off into a deep sleep, lulled by the crackling of the fire and the low conversation of the men. I slept much better than on the bed of leaves in the forest.

I'm sure I could have slept longer, but Lovernios roused me as dawn was painting the morning clouds with golden streaks. We ate a breakfast of bread, cheese, and warm goat's milk. The headman's wife supplied Lovernios with a basket of provisions, and Lovernios pronounced a blessing over the tiny village. With waves to the children, we rode away.

The weather changed, and the crisp, clear dawn gave way to lowering clouds that threatened rain but contented themselves with patches of drizzle. Our direction had changed subtly, and we were now heading in a northwesterly direction. I wondered if Lovernios had come this way before, as he evidenced no hesitancy when paths diverged. I, who knew the landscape only in its modern guise, altered countless times by human activity over the centuries, found myself constantly bewildered by choices Lovernios made. I longed for a signpost to direct me.

"Where are we going?" I asked again.

He gave me a curious look. "To fight the darkness," he said cryptically.

Again we kept to tracks and trails that meandered through the woods, wound over hills and dipped through the valleys.

Once we encountered an exhausted Briton warrior slumped against a tree, his equally exhausted horse standing with bowed head. He looked up dully as we approached, stretched out a weary hand toward the sword which lay on the ground next to him, then let it drop again.

"Greetings, friend," Lovernios said, dismounting. I followed suit. Lovernios looked down at the man. "You're wounded," he said, and I noticed the brown stain on the man's tunic.

"Not as wounded as some of the Romans I left behind."

Lovernios motioned to me. "Fetch the small pouch from my horse."

I did as he instructed. Lovernios knelt beside the wounded man, peeled off his tunic, and studied the crusted wound on his left shoulder.

"Deep, but not mortal." He began to clean the wound and applied a poultice of some fragrant ointment.

"You are Druí," the man said.

"My name is Lovernios."

The man coughed, a wet cough, and I feared for his lungs. "I am Anyon of the Cornovii."

"You're not far from home," Lovernios said.

"If I still have a home," the man said bitterly. "The Roman dogs have patrols scouring the countryside—I barely outran one."

"What are they doing?" I asked.

Anyon scowled. "What do you think? They're laying their filthy hands on every horse they can. They're stealing crops, burning homes, killing everyone who raises a sword against them."

I nodded slowly. There was to be no recurrence of rebellion; Suetonius was seeing to that, most harshly. The Britons had gambled everything, and lost.

Lovernios finished dressing Anyon's wound. He took some of the food from the basket the headman's wife had given us and laid it on the ground beside him.

"Take care, friend."

"And you, Druí."

We rode on in silence.

There was something noble about Lovernios, I thought, as the succeeding days passed. Not once did I see him yield to despair, even though Anyon's report of Roman depredations must have caused him anguish. He rode upright, his shoulders squared with determination, not slouched in defeat.

He still spoke little, resisting my attempts to draw him out, to learn of his ancestry and life.

"What tribe are you from?" I asked.

"Every tribe," he replied, "and no tribe."

That didn't help.

"Do you have parents, family?"

"They are of no account," he said, and rode ahead, leaving me to clench my teeth in frustration, because, of course, they were of great account to *me*. He was the first Druid I had ever met. I yearned to ask him of his beliefs, of the learning that took twenty years to acquire, of the lore of his people.

I queried again about our destination, but he declined to reply. For the most part, he seemed lost in his thoughts. The only time he spoke was when we met up with scattered bands of Britons, when they would huddle together and exchange news before going separate ways.

"Boudicca has poisoned herself," he said after one such meeting.

I wondered why Lovernios had brought me along. Surely not for the companionship, which was nonexistent. Did he still suspect that I possessed some arcane knowledge which I would share in due course? Alternatively, would I serve some ritual purpose which would leave me quivering in dread if I knew of it?

More than once I was tempted to break away and ride off into the woods. Surely I'd encounter a Roman patrol that would offer me safety until I could return to Suetonius. But Lovernios was a better horseman than I; he knew the lie of the land, which I did not; he was in his element here, whereas I was an interloper. If I left, he would find me—either by virtue of his superior abilities or by his Druid arts. I stayed with him.

Eventually, one day as dusk was gathering, we reached a place which was somewhat south of where Manchester now lies. It was a dark place of gloomy pools, soggy bogs, and trackless wastes. Perhaps in the sunshine of a spring day when flowers bloomed it might appear attractive, but not now. Later generations would call it Lindow Moss. A sense of unease, which had been enveloping me for several days, intensified.

It was not the sort of place in which one would expect to meet other people, and yet figures moved silently through the gathering dusk.

"Who are they?" I asked in a low whisper as we dismounted.

"Members of my order," Lovernios replied.

How the Druids knew to meet in this desolate spot, I have no idea, since I never saw Lovernios dispatch a messenger.

"The Romans will not detect us here," Lovernios said. "Watch the horses and light a fire if you wish." He strode off to meet the shadowy figures.

By now, I had no wish to escape, determined to see this business to the end. I hobbled the horses, gathered some sticks and built a fire to warm myself, and sat down out of earshot to wait.

It was curious, I thought, to be watching these men and women the Romans had determined to exterminate. Was it, as the Romans claimed, because of the practice of human sacrifice? The Romans opposed human sacrifice in religion, but were quite happy to perform it themselves for entertainment in the arenas. Was it because the Druids formed a focus of rebellion against Rome? Were the Romans afraid of what they didn't understand?

Was it any of these reasons, all of them, or none of them?

Eventually, Lovernios returned, his countenance grave. He sat opposite the fire, the flickering flames alternately highlighting his features and plunging them into shadow.

"Tell me truthfully, Robert," he said, and there seemed to be a plaintive note in his voice, "you to whom the future and the past seem as one. Can you change what has happened?"

I sighed. I knew this only too well. "No man can change the past, Lovernios. What has happened has happened."

"You are not an ordinary man," he said, and again I felt a tingle as when he had first gazed into my eyes.

"On the contrary," I protested, "I am very ordinary."

"Yet you are here, out of your allotted place."

How much did he understand of me, I wondered? Did he really comprehend that I was from the far future? Such a thought would never occur to these Britons—at best they might regard me as a sorcerer, a prophet, or a demon. Yet Lovernios seemed to possess senses or insights beyond those of common folk; perhaps he had a glimmer of the truth.

He was waiting for an answer.

"Consider," I replied, trying to phrase my words carefully, "to me, who knows the future, that which for you is yet to happen has already happened. It is a continuous thread, extending from you to me, just as a thread extends from your ancestors to you. If time could be changed, the thread would be snapped. If the past could somehow be altered, the future would follow suit. If everyone could change the past as they pleased, there would not then be any threads, no patterns, but a constantly tangling and untangling knot, a spider's web, where nothing had any permanence or meaning." I took a breath. "No, Lovernios, what is done cannot be undone. My hands are as powerless as yours."

"So events must play themselves out," he exhaled. "We must accede to the roles the gods give us, believing we have a choice."

"We do have a choice," I said, "but once exercised, it cannot be reversed."

He stared at the flames, his fingers steepled before his face. In the flickering light he momentarily reminded of Simon Bar-Joseph. But whereas Simon had taken a wrong turn that had cost him and his family dearly, Lovernios, I felt, had not.

"Tell me what you are thinking," I requested.

"My thread of life has reached its end," he said gently, and perhaps sadly.

His life, I thought, had proceeded arrow-like to this point. And yet, I didn't want him to endure what I knew lay ahead. "Only God knows when a man's life will end."

"I am to face the triple death," he interrupted, and my heart shuddered at his words.

With appropriate rituals he would be clubbed unconscious, garroted, and then have his throat cut. It sounded grisly, but after the first blow he would feel nothing. His body would be interred in one of the boggy pools.

"Why you?" I asked.

He raised his eyebrows. "Is it too much to do for my people?" he asked. "I have done everything else I could, but the gods have been against us. Perhaps by my sacrifice I can convince them to look upon us with favor once again."

I didn't want this man to die. There was no bond of friendship between us—far from it—only mutual curiosity, respect, and a strange, unworldly sense that we had been brought together. Still, I didn't want to see anybody die a useless death. I'd seen more than enough already.

"Many men can change the world by their lives," I replied, "only a few by their deaths." And, of course, this land had not yet heard of the One who would change the world more by His death than any other. What would Lovernios have made of it, I wondered?

"Tell me what will come to pass," he requested. When I hesitated, he added, "What harm can there be to tell one whose lips will shortly be sealed forever by death?"

What harm indeed?

"I speak to your ears alone," I said, and he nodded.

I said, "None other will rise to challenge the Romans as Boudicca did. The Romans will not leave."

"Are my people doomed to perish?"

I shook my head. "They will endure. Some will retreat to the corners of the island, others will intermarry with the Romans. After many years, the Empire will crumble. Other peoples will come to this island. Many centuries will pass. But finally, out of the peoples who have dwelt here will arise an empire that will rule more of the earth than Rome ever did."

I couldn't find it in me to tell him that that empire, like all empires of man, would also crumble and vanish.

He nodded. "It is well, then." His gaze drifted away. "There will be much preparation before the sacrifice. I must ready my spirit."

I motioned toward the dark woods. "Let us rather leave this dismal place. There is no need for you to sacrifice yourself."

He raised his eyebrows. "How say you?"

"Your death will be forgotten, for two thousand years…"

"Yet you say that my people will endure, will blend with others and will become great."

"Yes, but—"

"And I have sensed that you are not here with evil purpose. Therefore, you do not lie."

"No—"

"Then my sacrifice will not be in vain." He laid his hand on my arm before I could protest further. "Who is to say that perhaps what I do will bring about what you have said? And if I lie forgotten in the earth, what is that? Perchance my name will disappear from the world of men, but if it is remembered in the councils of the gods, then the exchange is a fair one."

What could I argue to that? I had risked my life many times, but had never been called to offer it—at least, not in this way. I wondered if I possessed the strength Lovernios did—to die for what he believed in the hope that it would make a difference to people not yet born. Wasn't that the heart—the evidence—of faith, to look beyond oneself for the good of others? More than that—to believe that God could take an ordinary life and make it extraordinary? That life was not meaning*less*, but meaning*ful*, even if that meaning at times was obscure?

Such faith was not blind; it was reasoned. The substance of things hoped for; the evidence of things not seen.

He motioned to the hobbled horses. "You are free to return to whence you came."

"Thank you," I replied, wishing I had the words to convince him to change his mind about his death.

He rose, and I followed suit.

"You have given me the strength and the courage to do what I must," he said. "For that, I thank *you*."

And with that he strode away, his bearing erect, into the darkness and the mist.

XXXI

I was becoming used to the routine: return to the Ring, undergo the usual examinations, report to the Chief Medical Officer for bad news. Except this time, the scans took longer, and it was the following day when I was summoned to the CMO's office.

Once again, he was studying a readout when I entered, making little noises to himself. The colors from the screen projected onto his face, making him look like a bizarre piece of artwork.

"I'm getting worse?" I asked, seating myself.

He nodded somberly. There were dark circles under his eyes. "Exponentially."

"I don't feel any different," I said.

"Not yet, perhaps, but the tests don't lie, Professor. Your cognitive functions and overall physiological status are showing progressive decline. Time is taking its toll on you."

"And you don't know why."

"Theories only. Nothing concrete."

"Are you going to name the malady after me?"

He didn't smile. "There's nothing funny about the situation, Professor. We have brilliant minds working on this."

"Is anybody else affected?" I wondered.

"Not yet. But nobody has made as many past-times trips as you have."

"So it could be an idiosyncratic reaction," I guessed.

"It could."

"Or it might affect all time travelers."

He shrugged. "At this point, we simply don't know."

"What's your recommendation?" I asked, regarding him with raised eyebrows. Perhaps some people might have been attracted by the thought of early retirement. Not I.

"One more trip," he said.

"I have two scheduled," I replied.

"Two," he agreed. "No more." He shook his finger at me. "I'm serious,

Professor. Based on what I'm seeing on these scans, and projecting into the future, I will not clear you for more than two trips."

"But—"

"Your mind and your expertise are too valuable to waste. I'm sorry, Professor. But you're going to have to make do with the present."

XXXII

Make do with the present.

The CMO's judgment hit me with the cold force of an avalanche. My life had turned full circle—I had gone from being the expendable guinea pig to being the indispensable expert. Making do with the present was the last thing I'd considered at this stage of my career. Naively, I thought I'd continue my trips until…well, until I died or became disabled. Not now. Not so soon.

The words resonated in my mind like a sentence of life imprisonment intoned by a stern-faced judge. From now on, I'd be restricted to writing about and lecturing on the past, rather than living it.

Half in a daze, I sought for options.

I could, of course, remain at CamOx as a typical historian, teaching and perhaps supervising and advising junior colleagues making temporal excursions.

Plenty of other institutions would be glad to have me on staff. Hardly a year passed that I didn't receive offers from several universities.

I could take a part-time position on a desirable world—even Heliopolis—and have a dog again…

Alternatively, there were hundreds of worlds I'd never set foot on. A person could spend a lifetime visiting the worlds humanity had settled.

I could try to reinvent myself in a totally different field of endeavor.

None of these options appealed to me. I belonged in the past. I was made for it.

I could hardly wrap my mind around the fact that my time there was drawing to an end.

I went to my quarters, lay down on my bed, and listened to the most desolate music I could find.

XXXIII

Eventually the shock abated and I regained my equilibrium. I thought of Lovernios fearlessly facing an uncertain future. He was prepared to sacrifice his life, while I was only being forced to give up my profession.

Back on Earth, I took a week off and traveled to Rome. I went to the Colosseum, the Forum, and other places—ruins now—where I had walked when they were yet new. I sat in the vast cavern of St. Peter's Basilica, surrounded by the artwork of centuries, and pondered the glories of the past. And there, alone despite the throngs of tourists and pilgrims, I prayed.

I resolved to face this latest trial firmly.

The succeeding weeks passed by more slowly than any I could remember. I couldn't wait to return to the past, but first had the usual papers to write, lectures to deliver, classes to teach. But my heart wasn't in it. Probably my students noticed. I tried to be lenient with them.

If the New Chair had any inkling of my difficulty—and she probably did—she didn't speak to me of it. For that, I was grateful.

When departure time arrived, she sent me on my way as if it was nothing unusual, just one more routine trip to the Ring and beyond.

Had I known earlier that this was to be my penultimate journey to the past, I'd have declined the projected venue and pushed for somewhere more appealing. This was to be a reprise of my sojourn in Vindolanda. But now, the year was 257. The setting was Brocavum, a Roman fort in Cumbria, near what would later be known as the Lake District, lying roughly 25 miles south of Hadrian's Wall. Brocavum was smaller than Vindolanda.

Its only claim to historical interest lay in its cemetery, which contained the remains of some 180 people from both the fort and the surrounding civilian community. Among these were some very interesting people indeed, people I wanted to meet, although had I known the circumstances, and the much greater trial I was called upon to face, it would have given me another reason to change my mind...

XXXIV: KOBRINIA

They thundered out of a misty morning like a pair of Valkyries, the hooves of their horses pounding the resonant ground, flattening the dewy vegetation into pulpy submission. I reined my own mount to a halt, and edged out of their way as they approached.

At first glance they could have been twins, but on closer examination the differences became more apparent and I realized they were probably unrelated. Both were long-legged, brawny women, wearing leather armor and slung about with weaponry—long cavalry swords, battle-axes, and bows. Both had manes of unkempt, yellowish hair flying in all directions, and cloaks that streamed behind. And both were grinning as they urged their horses over the undulating terrain.

As they drew level and passed, I observed that one woman had a rounder, fuller face with a jagged, livid scar on one cheek, and a nose that might have been broken at some point in the past. She seemed at one with her horse, as if she had been riding from birth.

The other woman, closer to me, was slightly younger with a thinner face, square chin and thicker eyebrows. Although she rode well, there was a slight awkwardness that showed she had come to horse riding later in life. She stared at me as she galloped by, and that gaze gave me pause.

I had never laid eyes on this woman before, and yet her features were almost familiar. I had met so many people in my life, no doubt I had encountered her like previously, and sooner or later it would come to me.

And then they were past and the moment and the gaze were broken. They shouted something unintelligible, burst into laughter, and galloped over a low rise and out of sight.

I continued my ride to take in the view over Ullswater, and mulled over the encounter as I went.

The Greeks had legends of fierce warrior women whom they called Amazons. Ancient writers located their origins in various areas, but archaeologists believed that certain female warriors identified in Britannia came from provinces in the region of the Danube—Noricum, Pannonia, or

Ilyricum. They were thought to have belonged to one of the numeri—irregular units of barbarians attached to a legion—stationed in Britannia. Perhaps these two were the women I sought.

It was in hopes of meeting real-life Amazons that I had duly arrived at Brocavum as an Imperial Inspector of the Emperor Valerian, supposedly performing an assessment of the forts in this area.

The camp prefect had received me as cordially as the situation warranted, and assigned me quarters within the fort itself, rather than in the straggling civilian community that congregated in the fort's vicinity like pigeons around scattered grain.

I'd rapidly settled into a routine, examining the fort's records in the morning, and spending the remainder of the days enjoying the pleasant rolling countryside and mingling with the civilians. It wouldn't do to work all the time. That's not how government officials operated.

There had been no immediate sign of warrior women. But from casual inquiries I learned that yes, two female auxiliaries were indeed based at Brocavum, but were currently out on patrol through the district.

"Probably hunting men," a junior centurion laughed when I asked him about them one evening while sitting around a crackling campfire.

"And not for bed, either," another joined in.

"If you want a woman, find one in the town," the first centurion added. "Much more accommodating."

"At least you'll wake up alive come dawn," added the second.

Having now seen them, I could well understand the mens' humor.

The morning cleared, and bright sunshine flooded the valleys as if filling them with golden wine. And yet, despite the auspicious start to my assignment, something nagged at me. Something was wrong.

I couldn't pin it down as I ate my lunch on a hillside overlooking the lake, or when I returned to the fort for a much needed soak in the bathhouse, or when I tumbled into bed that night. Nor did it come to me over the next several days. Try as I might, I couldn't rid myself of a troubling unease.

My opportunity to talk to the women came several days later when I encountered them in the cavalry stables. My usual mount had picked up a stone and become lame, and I was examining a replacement with the stable master when the Amazons strode in.

They were equally impressive on foot as on horseback, a head taller than myself; and I was taller than the average Roman.

"Well, who do we have here?" the thinner-faced one asked, stopping and looking down on me.

I drew myself up. "Fonteius Montanus," I said, "Inspector for the Emperor Valerian."

She rolled her eyes, and the movement irked me. "And who may you be?" I asked stiffly.

"Kobrinia," she replied. She indicated her companion. "This is Asteria."

"Are you going to put us in your report?" Asteria asked.

"The Emperor is more interested in financial matters," I replied.

"A pity," Kobrinia said. "I'm sure we're much more fascinating than dull numbers."

I thought so too, but wasn't about to say so.

"Come and have a drink with us tonight," Asteria said.

"If you dare," Kobrinia added with a wink, and accompanied by their own laughter, the women headed for their horses.

The stable master shook his head. "Quite a pair, those two."

"Rough on horses?" I queried.

"Ride them into the ground. The same as they do their men, I hear." He looked at me seriously. "I wouldn't take them up on their invitation if I were you."

"Thanks for the warning," I said, already having decided to disregard his caution.

I suffered from a lack of concentration the remainder of the day. The early evening found me crossing the camp to where the auxiliary troops were quartered.

The women occupied a small barracks adjacent to that of the male irregulars—the only indulgence made to their gender.

"Well, well," Asteria said, as she opened the door to my knock. "Look what we have here."

Kobrinia was seated across the room, polishing a buckle. She glanced up. "Fonteius Montanus! I didn't think you'd come. Have a seat. Asteria, we promised him some wine."

I settled on the indicated bench—it was crude and hard—and accepted the redware cup that Asteria poured and handed to me. It was very bad wine, but I tried to make a suitable comment. She poured two more cups.

Kobrinia gave the buckle a final wipe, and set it down. Then she fixed her attention on me.

Her eyes were blue. And cold. And intense.

I had the strange sensation that I'd seen them somewhere before. But once again, my memory failed to supply an answer.

"Not many men visit our humble abode," she said.

"And even fewer stay the night," Asteria added wistfully.

"And I won't be either," I said quickly. "I'm just here for the wine and the conversation."

Kobrinia threw back her head and laughed, a harsh braying that unnerved me further. "We're to be disappointed again, Asteria."

"And I thought there were real men in Britannia," Asteria said, trying to sound disappointed.

"North of the Wall," I said.

"Perhaps we'll have to launch our own invasion, then," Kobrinia mused.

"More wine?" Asteria asked, refilling my cup before I could decline.

Kobrinia, I noted, had barely touched hers.

"Are you the only women stationed here?" I asked.

"We are," Asteria replied. "Somebody had to bring a feminine touch to this gods-forsaken outpost."

Kobrinia snorted.

"Tell me about the Danubian provinces," I said. "I've never been there."

"How boring," Kobrinia yawned.

Asteria, however, happy to comply, launched into a discourse about her village, the role she'd played in its defense when another tribe had attempted to force their way through the area, how she'd received her facial wound on that occasion, and finally how she'd joined up with the irregular unit.

"I thought I might as well fight for pay," she concluded.

Through it all, Kobrinia had been regarding me with an unbroken gaze from her blue eyes. It was as if she was analyzing me, weighing me, trying in some way to make up her mind about me. It was decidedly unnerving, and I fear that some details of Asteria's story eluded me because of it.

"What of you?" I directed the question to Kobrinia when Asteria had finished.

Kobrinia waved a brawny hand. "Nothing that would interest an Imperial Inspector. I am here. I fight the Emperor's battles. That is all."

It was not all, I thought, but decided not to press her. I set my cup down and made as if to rise.

"You haven't told us about yourself," Kobrinia said. "Fair is fair."

"There's little enough to say," I replied. "The life of an inspector is a fairly dull one. While you fight barbarians I grapple with bureaucrats. There's little difference."

"The enemies of the empire come in many forms," she said, and I thought I detected a touch of menace in her voice. Feeling cold inside, I stood up.

"Thank you for your hospitality," I said, as Asteria conducted me to the door.

"Next time, perhaps you can stay longer," she said, with an expression that reminded me of a praying mantis eyeing her doomed mate.

As I exited, I felt Kobrinia's gaze boring between my shoulder blades.

Emperor Publius Licinius Valerianus did not like Christians.

Not that there were many in Britannia at this time, and those who professed the faith were mainly in the cities, not in remote outposts. In consequence, I hadn't expected Valerian's persecution to reach here.

The emperor, like others before and after him, ordered that everyone should swear an oath of allegiance to himself and to the gods of Rome, with dire consequences for those who disobeyed. Such an edict might have gone unnoticed in Britannia, where bureaucratic decisions tended to arrive late if at all, and to be observed in the breach. But the governor, who probably had personal reasons for wanting to remain in the imperial good graces, ordered that the edict be followed. The generals required the same of their troops. And the camp prefect, no doubt wishing to remain in his general's good graces, ordered that everyone in Brocavum should swear the oath.

And I had a problem.

This was not Kourion, when pagans and Christians were living amicably together. At this time, Christianity was not an officially approved religion— that recognition was still more than half a century in the future. Christians were sometimes tolerated, sometimes persecuted, but never approved.

I had no desire to be a martyr—indeed, the attitude of certain early Christians who actively sought martyrdom struck me as being almost pathological; some of them, in fact, were so eager for martyrdom that they even denounced themselves if no one did it for them.

I wasn't ashamed of my faith, but I didn't make a point of being obvious about it either, except when research or the occasion demanded. I still wore the cross that Erica had given me so many years ago. I had visited the pope, who had encouraged me. I did not believe in the gods of Rome. I could not deny the faith in which I had lived—however imperfectly—my life.

What, then, was I going to do?

I mulled it over while I watched legionaries erect an altar to Jupiter in the center of the camp's parade ground. One by one, everyone would have to walk up to that altar, offer a pinch of incense, and swear loyalty to the gods and the emperor. It was a simple, effective way to identify the Christians, most—but not all—of whom would decline to perform the offering.

Needless to say, my sleep that night was infested by bizarre and mostly gory dreams, in which I played an all-too-prominent and generally fatal role. My attempts at prayer seemed equally confused.

The ceremonies began early the following morning, announced by a military fanfare. The troops, both regular Army and auxiliary, lined up in formation, and the process began, in order of rank.

With attention focused on the ceremony, I took the opportunity to slip away and ride into the hills. I was not a normal member of the camp, merely a temporary visitor. I doubted that anyone would notice my absence.

Prudent? Yes.

Cowardly? Most certainly.

Was I proud of myself? Not at all.

Despite the rationalizations that coursed through my mind, I couldn't escape a nagging sense of shame. I told myself that my job was to live, not court death. I was in the past for a purpose, and I owed it to CamOx and the organizations that funded my excursions to do a good job and make it back alive with the fruits of my research. Yet I still couldn't shake the feeling of dishonor.

Dishonor or death. A medieval knight would perhaps have had no qualms of choosing death before dishonor. I didn't know if I was made of such stern stuff. So I continued my course of attempted avoidance, even though something within me almost half-wished that my ploy would be discovered...

My mood a mixture of relief, resignation, and sadness, I was heading back to camp at the approach of day's end, as dusk was falling over hills capped by gathering dark clouds, when whom should I meet but Kobrinia, cantering along, whistling a popular tune—a street song with racy lyrics.

"Why, Inspector," she said with affected cheerfulness, "what a surprise."

"Indeed," I replied warily.

"What brings you out so late in the day?"

"The same as you, I imagine."

She cocked an eyebrow. "The safety of the camp? I doubt it." She shrugged. "No matter." She turned her horse as if to ride away, then halted. "I don't recall seeing you at the ceremony," she said.

My heart lurched.

"You *were* there, weren't you?" she persisted, peering intently at me.

"Umm—"

"Perhaps I just overlooked you."

"Well, I—"

"Do you mean you missed it, Inspector?" she purred. "What a shame. But I'm sure the prefect will give you a chance to make amends. I'll let him know." And with a smile that lacked all mirth, she added, "I'll ride back with you."

"That's quite considerate of you," I managed to reply.

Numbly, I followed. There was no way I could outride this Amazon. She was fine horsewoman, while I was not, and her horse was much better than my old beast.

I fought down a sense of overwhelming dread. I contrasted my feelings with those of Ignatius of Antioch who, while being escorted to Rome to face certain death, wrote a letter to the believers in Rome begging them not to intercede on his behalf to prevent his martyrdom.

Courage, I told myself.

We passed through the fort's gate. Kobrinia dismounted at the praetorium and motioned me to follow.

"Tell the prefect that I wish to see him on a matter of importance," Kobrinia said to the guard, who disappeared into an office and emerged shortly thereafter.

"The prefect will see you immediately," he said, and Kobrinia preceded me into the office.

The prefect looked tired, as well he might after a long day spent standing on the parade ground. He was middle-aged, with gray-flecked hair, and a sagging, jowly face. He also looked annoyed.

"What's this about?" he demanded. "Why are you here and not consulting your decurion or centurion?"

"My apologies, sir," Kobrinia said. "But I thought since the matter involved the inspector, that I should rightfully bring it directly to your attention."

His focus turned to me. "What matter?"

"I found the inspector outside the camp," Kobrinia said. "He told me he missed the ceremony."

"Is that true?" he asked me.

I nodded, the blood pounding in my head.

"No matter," he said casually. "You can offer in the morning and I'll issue you a certificate."

Strangely, before my eyes came a vision of Lovernios offering himself to his pagan gods in the belief that his sacrifice would help his people. At the time, I had marveled at his composure.

"I'm afraid that won't be possible," I said, my voice stronger than I expected.

He stared at me as if he hadn't quite heard me correctly, disbelief replacing fatigue on his features. "Not possible?" he repeated.

I shook my head. "No."

"Surely you're not one of them? An educated man like you?" The prefect sounded as though he couldn't believe what was happening. "The emperor's inspector? An atheist?"

That was, of course, how Christians were regarded. Not to believe in the gods of Rome was to be an atheist. The Jews were exempt. The Christians—despite their origins in Judaism—were not.

"Say something, man!" the prefect barked.

"It is true," I said. "I am a Christian."

The prefect paced around the room. Kobrinia remained silent. After a moment, the prefect seemed to notice her. "You may leave," he said. "Your attention to duty will not go unnoticed."

Kobrinia saluted him, then with a flash of her icy blue eyes at me, exited.

"Look," the prefect said, when the door had closed behind her. "I'm a reasonable man. It's not a big deal. A pinch of incense is all it is. Personally, I don't care what you believe. Just do it, and we'll say no more about it."

"I wish it were that simple," I replied.

"It *is* simple," he said. "We can even do it now. I'll get the priest, and it will all be over a minute."

I thought of Caesar the dog, who knew where his duty lay, who wouldn't abandon his post no matter what.

"No," I said.

His eyes narrowed. "Is this some kind of a trick? Are you spying on me for the emperor?"

I opened the top of my tunic and showed him the cross I wore. "It's no trick," I said.

"Then are you mad? Are you aware of the punishment that has been decreed?"

I didn't expect it, but I felt unusually strong. "Do what you must."

"You *are* mad." He paced around the room again. "I'm going to have to lock you up."

"I know."

He summoned the guard and gave orders.

"Think it over," he said. "Be reasonable. In a day or two you'll come to your senses and change your mind."

I detected a note of desperation in his voice. The guard escorted me away, and shackled me in the prison. It was a small room, with only some prickly straw as its sole concession to comfort. It smelled of mice. Many mice.

The guard left, and I was alone in the darkness.

I could understand the prefect's dilemma. What was he to do with me? As an Imperial Inspector I wasn't technically under his command. He was stuck. He couldn't execute one of the Emperor's appointees, and yet he couldn't disobey the emperor by *not* executing me.

He probably didn't sleep any better in his clean room than I did in my reeking one.

As the succeeding days passed I learned from the guards who brought me my scanty and nearly inedible meals that the camp prefect, wisely, had passed the decision as to my fate on to the general.

I knew how it would go from there. The general, also perceiving the danger, would pass it on to the governor. The governor was also unlikely to take any chances, either. Like Pliny, who'd appealed to Trajan during that much more tolerant emperor's reign for advice as to handle Christians, the governor would appeal to Valerian.

Who, in the course of querying the appropriate officials would discover that I didn't officially exist. And then he would order that I cease existing, period.

All this would take time. I foresaw a long stay in the prefect's prison.

At least that worthy hadn't shown any inclination to have me tortured.

As the days passed in that miserable prison, I can't say that I wasn't tempted to change my mind. The shackles chafed my wrists and ankles raw. It was impossible to get comfortable on the ancient, crumbly straw. My stomach was alternately aching with emptiness and nauseated from the rotten food.

But it was the voices that tempted me most. The voices in the night that told me just what the prefect had: It wasn't a big deal; it was only a pinch of incense; it was simple.

Yet the voices weren't those of the prefect—not a vindictive man—who had spoken, I believe, out of simple human decency, and who simply couldn't understand how any rational person could believe that a Jewish peasant crucified by the Roman governor of Judea could be the Son of God. No, these voices, though they said the same things, were malicious, malevolent, spiteful. They were the voices of my subconscious, the dark voices that lurk unwanted in the nethermost crevices of the mind, repressed but not extinguished.

Erica, I knew, would have urged me to be strong.

I clung to that thought.

The days passed slowly, with nothing to break the tedium.

Just rumination. Endless rumination.

I was surprised one day when my prison door opened and a smirking Kobrinia was framed in the doorway.

"A fine mess you're in," she said.

"Do you want a mouse?" I asked. "There's one in the corner over there."

She closed the door behind her and leaned against the wall, studying me.

"I must admit that you've surprised me," she said. "I really thought you'd have given in and sacrificed by now."

"I'm sorry to have disappointed you," I said.

"Oh, I'm not disappointed at all," she chuckled. "In fact, this has worked out much better than I'd hoped."

"And how is that?" I wondered.

"Because the Roman state will eliminate you, and I won't have laid a finger on you."

"The perfect crime," I said dryly.

"Surely you must appreciate my neat little trick."

I motioned for her to continue.

"My plan to discredit a certain Imperial Inspector." Her smile broadened. "I made certain that the governor, the general, and the prefect received copies of Valerian's edict. Made them myself. Nice job, too."

"Very neat, indeed," I replied. "But the motive..."

"Ah, the motive," she nodded. "You still don't recognize me, do you, Professor."

Professor? I stared hard at her features.

And then, suddenly, I knew, and I wondered why it had taken so long.

She had changed. Her face was thinner, more drawn than I remembered. Her hair was no longer the close-cropped dyed red of years past. And her whole attitude was different—this wasn't the insecure, hesitant student, but a woman brimming with self-confidence.

"Lamia Quigley," I said.

She bowed, melodramatically. "In person."

"What are you doing here?"

"Seeking revenge, obviously," she said.

"Revenge? Why?"

"Because you failed me," she said, as if perplexed at my dullness. "I was the only one in your class to fail—"

"That particular class, yes."

"How unfair was that?"

"It wasn't unfair at all. I've never played favorites. I've passed students I didn't like, and failed some whom I liked personally."

"Except in my case."

"In your case," I said firmly, "your final paper was a cobbled together mishmash culled from popular sources. Your thesis was incoherent, and you made no use of primary material. As I explained to you at the time, I *had* to fail you."

"I wondered what I'd done to offend you," she continued, as if my words hadn't registered. "Surely you knew how much was depending on my passing your class and receiving a degree."

"I wasn't offended—"

"I tried to tell you, but you wouldn't listen. Couldn't you *see*? Couldn't you realize that I was going through a difficult time?"

"I can't give grades based on sympathy—" I began.

"Failing shattered my confidence," she interrupted. "I became depressed. My husband abandoned me with our child while I was trying to dredge myself out of the mire. I was left alone. No career, no family, nothing. You took everything from me, Professor, everything."

"I'm sorry you had a rough time. But it wasn't my fault. It was your own—"

"It was *you*!" She took a deep breath to steady herself. "That's what I told myself. That's what I believed."

"I offered you a second chance—"

"It would have required too much. I couldn't do it. I couldn't face starting from scratch and possibly have you fail me again."

"You're here," I pointed out, "in the past. You must have resurrected your career."

She nodded. "I did. I transferred to the Department of Germanic Studies and began all over again, hoping that my new professors would be more lenient than you had been. It took years of my life. But finally I received my degree. And Professor Wuerfel asked me to be his assistant on a project on the Danube."

"Where is he?" I asked.

"Still poking around the Danubian provinces, I expect," she laughed, her good mood returning.

"You left him?" I gasped.

"Obviously. I knew you would be here."

"So you managed to get into this unit that was being posted to Britannia."

"It wasn't too hard."

She pulled her sword from its scabbard and twirled it around, before stabbing it into the ground and leaning on it. "I found that being a real-life Amazon was much more fun than assisting on a dreary research project."

I blinked. "You're enjoying this?"

"Immensely."

"Professor Wuerfel won't be too happy."

"I don't care," she grinned.

"Well," I swallowed, "now that you've found me what do you intend to do with me?" I indicated my bound wrists and ankles. "I can't put up much of a fight."

She retrieved her sword, and returned it briskly to its scabbard. But when she spoke it was uncertainly. "Leave you here to rot, I suppose. It's as good a plan as any."

She spun around. "Enjoy your stay, Professor."

The door banged shut behind her.

Well.

I had to admire her ingenuity, if not her thirst for revenge.

Perhaps it was the ambiguity of her parting words, but for some reason I slept better that night, even though my situation hadn't changed.

I jerked awake in the morning to the ringing tones of trumpets sounding an assembly, followed by the shouted orders of officers, the clatter of gathering troops, and the neighing of horses.

Curious.

After a few minutes, the noise diminished, and then there was silence in the camp.

I heard footsteps outside; the guard bringing my morning meal, I supposed.

But it wasn't. To my surprise it was the tall figure of Kobrinia—or Lamia Quigley as I had known her—who entered, wearing her leather armor and carrying a battle-ax.

My heart sank.

Had my time come? Had the prefect sent her to do the deed?

I gazed at her, waiting for her to speak.

"You've perplexed me, Professor," she said, frowning.

"How so, Lamia?"

"I wonder if perhaps I've been mistaken about you."

"Really?" For the first time, I felt a flicker of hope.

"I failed your test—I wondered for a long time how you would fare on mine."

"Test?" I repeated.

"Your beliefs are common knowledge at CamOx," she said. "And I wondered if your actions would match up to your words. So I made sure that the emperor's edict reached Brocavum. When faced with the choice of denying your faith, would you cave in or not? Had you offered to the emperor and the gods, I would have known that you lacked integrity. My hatred of you would have been justified. Your death would have been deserved."

She ran the ball of her thumb along the blade of the ax. "But when you refused—and showed no sign of changing your mind—I began to wonder if perhaps you had more principle and integrity than I had given you credit for. I began to wonder if I had been blinded by my disappointment and anger."

"I have always tried to act in a principled manner," I replied. "And I treated all my students the same. Your work was substandard; there was nothing more to it than that."

"And then I thought that if you hadn't failed me, I wouldn't be here living my fantasy. So perhaps you did me a good turn, even though it didn't seem so at the time."

"Life is full of unexpected twists and turns, Lamia," I said.

"Call me Kobrinia," she said. "Lamia Quigley was a different person in a different time."

She hefted the battle-ax and I flinched.

"Don't worry," she said. She brought the ax down on the lock that secured my chains. A few deft blows later and I was free.

I rose stiffly to my feet.

"If I were you, I'd grab a horse and get out of here," she advised. "The fort is nearly deserted—no one will see you."

"Where are you going?" I asked.

"Cross-border raiders were reported north of here. If I ride quickly, I can catch my unit before they engage them." She grinned. "I told them my horse was lame and I'd have to find another."

She headed for the door. "Take care, Professor."

"Kobrinia, wait!" I called, but she was moving too quickly and disappeared.

I wanted to tell her that among the burials in the cemetery here were those of two Amazons, who had been burnt on pyres along with their horses and weapons. Had she done her research, she'd have learned that.

I staggered to the door, but she was already riding away. Not that anything would have changed. I shook my head. "You always were a poor student, Lamia."

But she was living her fantasy.

And perhaps, I thought, as I edged out of my prison and went in search of a horse, she already knew.

XXXV

I debated about reporting Lamia Quigley's actions to her department head and to Professor Wuerfel. But obviously, she'd made her past-times journey, so if I was to report her, my report was to be ignored or disbelieved or not followed through on. I knew better than to suppose I could change what had happened—or prevent it from happening. Quigley had done what she had done.

And, too, I was grateful—I suppose—that she had spared me. I had passed her test, and she was happy with her new life, no matter how brief it might turn out to be. We were, I thought, even.

So I made no mention of Lamia Quigley as such in my official report. Kobrinia was featured, but only as an Amazon. I made no mention of her alter future ego.

Once back on the Ring, I awaited the results of the medical exam with a mixture of trepidation and resignation. It seemed forever that I sat in the office staring at the starfield without really seeing it, wondering what was delaying the chief medical officer's appearance.

Was it more bad news? The odds were that it was.

Or—and here I indulged in hopeful fantasy—could it be good? Had the medics been mistaken all along? Had they found a cure?

When the CMO finally entered, he really didn't need to say anything. I could tell from the look on his face. He studied his medical reports and mumbled something unintelligible couched in technical jargon.

"Another trip?" I asked, cutting through his monologue and hoping I didn't sound plaintive.

He held up a solitary finger.

I knew, without having to ask, that there would be no negotiating.

XXXVI

"I want you to take a companion with you," the New Chair announced as she studied the final proposal for my next assignment.

"It's not necessary," I replied.

"I beg to differ."

"I've always worked alone," I remonstrated. "I'm not cut out to play nursemaid—"

"The person I'm thinking of is quite capable," she interrupted.

"—to someone who's wet behind the ears," I finished. "Or the years."

She didn't smile at my pun. We stared at each other for a long moment.

"Or is he to be *my* nursemaid?" I asked.

She waved a hand. "I'd rather not put it that way."

"Whether you put it that way or not, that's what you mean," I said, leaning back.

"It wasn't my idea," she protested. "I know you value your independence."

"It was the medics, wasn't it?"

"If you must know, yes," she said. "And so it's out of my hands. If you want to go, you must have a companion."

"A nanny."

"A student. An initiate, if you prefer."

I didn't. A rose by any other name, as Shakespeare said.

"If I must, I must," I conceded. I certainly wasn't going to give up my final trip to the past.

"It's a precaution," said the New Chair. "Simply that."

"I'll make the best of it," I acceded. "Or him."

"Good." She smiled. "When you get back, we'll have a party in your honor."

I returned her smile, although inwardly I shuddered. A party would be the last thing I'd want. A wake, more likely.

XXXVII

When it came, the final trip to the Ring seemed to take even longer than usual. I had much time to think, to ponder, to remember. I had seen so much over the years, met so many people, experienced happiness and tragedy, laughter and sorrow, nobility and depravity, exaltation and horror. My mind was engraved with images that I would never forget. I had much for which to be thankful.

Yet there was much that remained undone, mysteries of the past that I had hoped to unravel, that would have to wait the attention of some other historian—or perhaps remain forever shrouded in obscurity if no one took an interest in them.

There was no point in harboring regrets. Still, I should have liked to learn the facts behind the babies of Ashkelon—100 newborn children, discarded in the sewers under a bathhouse. Were they the unwanted children of prostitutes, or victims of some other set of circumstances?

What about the children of Lugano, buried with sacrificed puppies? Was a terrified populace trying desperately to ward off an epidemic of malaria?

Or how about the unfortunate fellow found stuffed into a Roman corn drier in Norfolk, the apparent victim of murder? Was he a tax collector killed by an aggrieved tenant, or the loser in a love triangle?

No regrets, I told myself again.

After all, I knew many things that, despite my detailed reports, had remained secret. Such as the armless goddess—that figure of a woman ranked with the Mona Lisa, Winged Victory of Samothrace, and the bust of Nefertiti as exemplars of the artist's depiction of womanhood.

It had happened on one of my less memorable trips when nothing else of consequence had happened. Despite the impression I may have given, there were any number of routine trips of greater or lesser duration. I certainly hadn't expected an unforeseen interlude on the island of Melos…

204

XXXVIII: THE ARMS OF VENUS

She wasn't Roman, she was Greek.

Her name was Venus, and I met her, of all places, in a gymnasium, on the island of Melos. It was an unplanned visit caused by a drunken sea-captain whose minimal navigational skills disappeared completely under the influence of any vintage, no matter how poor, that happened to be at hand. And there was a seemingly inexhaustible supply at hand.

On board was an inordinately officious junior centurion assigned to conduct a political prisoner to Rome. Realizing that the successful conclusion of his mission was in jeopardy should the captain continue navigating haphazardly about the Mediterranean, he insisted, by the unconventional but effective means of holding the captain by his neck over the rail and offering him a quick trip to the afterworld, that the ship make landfall at the nearest port. That happened to be Melos.

Since it would take some time to contact the ship's owners and arrange for a new captain, I took the opportunity to explore the island.

It didn't take me long to wish that the centurion had left the captain alone. Melos was a singularly unlovely island, populated by unlovely islanders who fished and farmed and hacked fruitlessly at the rocks in a vain attempt at mining. They were superstitious, afraid of virtually everything, and kept weasels as pets.

The island was dull, barren, and reeked of sulfur. The water was bad. The sea rumbled menacingly deep below, in caverns and cracks left by Melos' volcanic past. The ground was crunchy underfoot.

With nothing better to do, I climbed the island's highest hill to see if the city had anything to offer. There was nothing exceptional. A smallish theater was situated so that the audience could look past the stage and across the bay at the foot of the hill. That didn't argue well for the quality of the performances. There was a stadium, a forum, and the usual assortment of temples and public buildings.

And a gymnasium.

I don't know what made me turn in there, because my conscious mind, curiously enough, hadn't put two and two together. My body wasn't clamoring for exercise. The subconscious, though, must have been on duty.

At first, it looked like a typical gymnasium. Several youths were wrestling on the palaestra, the large, open rectangular area in the center, their muscular bodies glistening with sweat. A number of men engaged in conversation were lounging in the covered colonnade that ran alongside. The wall behind the colonnade was set with regularly spaced niches occupied by statues. I saw Poseidon, Theseus, and several robed figures I couldn't immediately identify.

Then, turning to leave, I saw *her.*

I stood stock still, allowing every gorgeous detail to soak into me.

"What do you think?" a man's voice broke into my reverie.

I looked around, and down, at a small, balding fellow who stood at my elbow. He was a physically insignificant specimen, but somehow his appearance proclaimed 'wealth.' The gymnasiarch, I supposed, a leading townsman who probably also doubled as a magistrate.

"She's magnificent," I replied.

He beamed. "Do you have her like in Rome?"

I shook my head. "No."

It was probably the greatest compliment anyone in dreadful little Melos had ever received.

We made small talk for a few minutes, then he excused himself. "Stay and enjoy," he invited as he strutted away. "Remain as long as you wish."

I sat down in the colonnade, my back to the wrestlers, and feasted my eyes on the exquisitely carved, half-naked woman who stood in a shaft of light that split the gloom of her niche and made her glow as if she were created of living flesh and not dead marble.

Even the gaudy paintwork of the walls that insistently commanded the eyes' attention couldn't detract from her beauty. She wore jeweled earrings, necklace, and bracelets. Her hair was radiantly gold, her eyes and lips touched with red. And her arms—her arms were intact.

I was truly regretful when dusk came, the fading light dissolved her into shadows, and I made my own departure.

I could hardly wait to return home to tell everyone.

"I've seen her!" I'd told the New Chair when I was once more back in the familiar rooms at CamOx.

"Seen whom?" the New Chair asked quizzically.

"The Venus de Milo! I know exactly what she looks like."

She'd stared at me for a long moment; not the sort of reaction I had anticipated.

"She has—" I began excitedly, gesticulating, but the New Chair silenced me with an upraised hand.

"I don't want to know," she said.

"You…don't?" I could hardly believe my ears.

"No."

"But it's the greatest discovery ever made in the art world! Everybody will want to know—"

"Go to the Louvre, Robert," she instructed me.

"I've been there. Many times."

"Go again."

"But—"

"Just go."

I went.

I stood in the gallery among a crowd of tourists, and I studied the armless Venus, unashamedly exposed to the gaze of millions, as she had been for nearly two millennia.

And I understood.

XXXIX

I thought I had understood then, but the deeper meaning had still eluded me.

There are some things, I believe, that one cannot understand when young.

Who would think that that an old, worn, broken statue could be more beautiful than the fresh, polished, newly painted product of the sculptor's studio?

And who would think the same of a life?

One's own, or another's?

XL: THE PHILOSOPHER'S RING

"Where is Romeo?"

I stood on the corner of a busy street in Alexandria with my hands on my hips. A little ways down, and on the opposite side of the street, a woman emerged from a litter and entered a perfume seller's shop.

My companion—or nursemaid—J'sun Orombi, found a patch of shade and leaned his seven-foot frame against the rough stone wall of a building. He was a young post-doc from the forbiddingly-named world of Grimselwald, with the build, coloring, and musculature of a Nubian warrior. His imposing physical presence was, however, belied by an unfailingly cheerful manner. More importantly, he was, as the New Chair had said, capable. And, as he had proudly told me onboard ship, he was proficient in several forms of martial arts.

"Maybe he doesn't exist," J'sun said, his dark skin glistening with sweat.

"He *has* to exist," I replied, squinting in the bright sunshine to study the teeming crowds. A fly buzzed around my ears and I swatted it away.

"Maybe we're too early," he countered.

"That's possible."

"Or too late."

"Let's hope not."

A certain amount of uncertainty was inherent in every past-times excursion, since we didn't always know the exact day or year in which to encounter the people we sought. Arriving too late would obviously not lead to a successful study, and so we always aimed to arrive early. Hopefully that was still the case now.

We had come looking for a couple we'd nicknamed Romeo and Juliet. They had been discovered about two hundred years ago, during a dig in Alexandria, embraced in each other's arms. The woman's burial wrap had been marked with her name—Tesia, 'Loved by God'—and the word 'philosopher.' The man's only identifying characteristic was a gold ring inscribed with a fish, an obviously Christian symbol.

There couldn't be too many female philosophers named Tesia even in a city as large and as popular with philosophers as Alexandria, and casual inquiries at the great Library had resulted in a woman being pointed out to us. We had observed her, but seen no sign of a male companion.

Was this Tesia our Juliet or not?

So far, we hadn't made contact. Perhaps now was the time.

"Why don't we ask her where Romeo is?" J'sun queried, echoing my own thoughts.

I nodded. "Let's." I put out a hand to restrain him, as he pushed off the wall. "But not here, on the street. And not now."

"Where and when, then?"

"We're going to become philosophers," I said.

"Must we?" J'sun groaned. "Philosophy was never my best subject."

"All right then," I said. "*I'll* be the philosopher. Perhaps writing a book of natural history like Herodotus or Pythias. You can be my secretary."

J'sun grinned, revealing rows of impossibly white teeth. "Choose your language."

I'd learned on the voyage to the Ring that J'sun was also fluent in a wide range of ancient languages.

"Greek is fine," I said.

"Not Chaldean or Hittite?" He sounded plaintive.

"Greek," I repeated firmly.

It was profoundly disturbing to be back in Egypt, a country which I found both appealing and repellent, and Alexandria, a city both desirable and troubling. I half expected to bump into Eudaimon at any moment. My rational mind told me that was manifestly impossible—it was now the year 415, nearly three hundred years since Eudaimon had walked these streets. Many feet had trodden these worn stones since then, and I too had covered much ground. Still, the sensation persisted, although I had never met Eudaimon again in the flesh.

Physically, the city looked hardly different. The great Pharos lighthouse still stood guard over the bustling harbor, merchants plied their wares in the Emporium, and the curious visited the tombs of Antony and Cleopatra and Alexander the Great.

Yet there were changes. The Pharos looked worn and, if my eyes didn't deceive me, had taken on a slight list—the result, no doubt, of one of the earthquakes that periodically rocked Alexandria and which would eventually lead not only to the collapse of the Pharos but to the submergence of a large portion of the ancient city.

The Serapion had vanished. Some years ago, Emperor Theodosius I had issued an edict prohibiting pagan cult practices, an edict that led to the suppression of pagan temples, carried out locally with enthusiasm by Bishop Theophilus. Such suppression resulted in a backlash of violence; resistance and retaliation led to reprisals and further retaliation... Eventually, Roman troops supported by Christian partisans destroyed the Serapion, and the impressive—if somewhat bizarre—statue of Serapis, a god created out of features of several other deities, was shattered by a soldier's axe.

Despite these ravages, Alexandria remained a beautiful city. Yet for all its outward allure and charm, Alexandria was, and always had been, a turbulent city, rife with ethnic and religious strife, where the rule of law not infrequently yielded to the rule of the mob, despite the efforts of one imperial prefect after another to impose order. Violence was an integral part of the city's existence.

I hadn't experienced that side of Alexandria.

Not yet.

But 415 had been an especially violent year, and it was only a matter of time.

The great days of the Library were past—there were no giants of philosophy of the stature of Euclid, Erastothenes, Aristarchos, Ptolemy. The Library complex was slowly succumbing to the ravages of time, theft, and wanton destruction, until only a few of the original buildings and a sadly diminished number of its books remained. And yet, for all that, it still pulsed with life.

J'sun and I prowled the grounds one afternoon, passing clusters of scholars in disputation, lecturers addressing groups of students, and the merely curious picking up scraps of wisdom. I could easily imagine myself spending endless days sitting in the shade of palm trees, inhaling the fragrance of flowers, talking history with bearded men hoary with age. Perhaps such is an old professor's dream.

"I don't see her," J'sun commented, his height giving him an advantage.

"Let's go inside," I said, and we passed through the marble columns into the cool of the building.

The Library was a hive of activity. Readers pored over scrolls or jumped from book to book like pollen-hunting bees or distractible butterflies, while those who wished to write down their thoughts sought for unoccupied tables or window benches where they could concentrate without interruption.

We ambled from room to room, until finally J'sun halted and pointed. "Over there."

'Over there' was a windowed alcove lined with stone benches. Seated with her back to the window was a distinguished-appearing woman wearing a tribon—an unadorned philosopher's cloak. She appeared to be about sixty years old, with gray hair and squint-lines radiating from the corners of her eyes. She spoke in a calm, authoritative tone, not having to raise her voice to be heard above the clamor that permeated the entire Library. Ranged around her was an audience of a dozen or so people, most of them listening in rapt attention. Among them was Tesia.

An elderly man dozed on her left, but the spot on her right was unoccupied. I scurried over to claim it before J'sun got the same idea. I was greeted by a quick glance from warm brown eyes and a whiff of sandalwood perfume. I settled onto the stone bench, and tried unobtrusively to study Tesia while simultaneously listening to the lecturer. Her words, however, flowed past me, and I'd have been hard-pressed to give more than a cursory account of her talk.

The woman beside me was about forty years old, and wore a pale blue gown that set off a faint reddish tint in her black hair. A turquoise and coral necklace graced her neck, matched by a pair of inlaid earrings, and gold bracelets coiled around her forearms. Her delicate hands were those of a woman unaccustomed to manual work. These factors identified her as a woman of substance.

The lecturer finished and rose to her feet, to be instantly surrounded and peppered with questions.

Tesia stretched. "Interesting, don't you think?"

"What I heard," I replied. "Who is she?"

Her blue-shadowed eyes widened in surprise. "Are you new to Alexandria that you don't know Hypatia?"

Hypatia? My gaze shot back to the speaker. So this was the famous Hypatia, mathematician and philosopher.

"Ahh, yes," I said to Tesia. "I've only been in Alexandria for a couple of weeks."

"Let me guess," she said. "Gaul."

"Close."

"Not Hispania, I think. Britannia?"

I nodded. "Very good." I smiled. "Rubellius Flavus."

Her shapely lips parted in a reciprocal smile of greeting. I noticed that her teeth, like those of most people of her age, were worn down from years of eating sandy flour, but that subtle flaw didn't detract from the attractiveness of her greeting. "Tesia."

"The philosopher?"

She laughed, a melodious sound. "I don't deserve such a title. No, a student only. And you?"

"A traveler," I said.

"Not a philosopher?"

"A historian."

"Indeed? Well, I'm sure you'll find much to pique your interest in Alexandria." She gained her feet, and I followed suit. Upright, she seemed quite petite, and couldn't have been much over five feet tall. J'sun approached and I introduced him.

"My secretary, Zuberi."

"Secretary?" she echoed, tipping her head back to look up.

J'sun, I supposed, looked more like a bodyguard than a man of letters.

"Yes," I said. "Appearances to the contrary."

Tesia nodded a greeting to J'sun, then beckoned to a waiting servant. "Perhaps we shall meet again," she said to me.

I gave a short bow. "The pleasure would be mine."

Accompanied by her manservant, Tesia wafted away.

"Do you know who was speaking?" J'sun enthused. "That was Hypatia!"

Hypatia, the daughter of the mathematician Theon, a fine mathematician in her own right as well as a Neoplatonist philosopher, a person of considerable influence in Alexandria, a heroine to feminists for centuries. Meeting her was indeed a historian's ambition.

Yet my thoughts weren't with the famous Hypatia, but with Tesia. She was so very, very unlike Erica, and yet my reaction upon meeting her had reminded me of my first meeting with Erica…but now it was a meeting not of two young people with their lives ahead of them, rather of two people of middle age, with years of living behind them.

It was not what I had expected.

J'sun rambled on about Hypatia, but I paid him scant attention. I wanted to meet Tesia again.

Strangely enough, however, my next encounter with Tesia didn't occur at the Library, but at Mass at the Church of St. Mark, founder of the church in Alexandria, whither I had gone at the request of the Religious Studies Department, one of whose members was interested in the current bishop, Cyril. J'sun had expressed the desire to incorporate Hypatia into his researches, and had asked for—and received—my permission to try to engage with the philosopher.

"Just be careful," I warned, "passions run high in Alexandria."

And so I had gone in search of Bishop Cyril on my own, and came upon him as I was departing Mass, just outside the doorway of the church, in conversation with Tesia. He was a short man with a long beard and hooked nose, who looked younger than his thirty-seven years. His hawk-like eyes glittered with intensity.

"You were seen in the company of that woman again," he admonished, his voice dripping with disdain.

"Hypatia?" Tesia asked.

Cyril gave a curt nod.

"She's an erudite and knowledgeable scholar."

"She's a pagan philosopher!" Cyril hissed. "And a friend of Prefect Orestes."

"Do you have a grudge against our new prefect?"

Cyril's countenance reddened. "He's a lukewarm Christian if ever there was one! And he doesn't know the bounds of his authority." He jabbed a finger toward Tesia. "I'm warning you—you risk your immortal soul being around that woman."

"What harm can there be in discussing ideas?"

"Pagan ideas could lead you astray! Discuss Christ, not Plato!"

I felt the urge to come to Tesia's aid. "Pardon me for interrupting your conversation," I said, "but surely all truth is God's truth, no matter who articulates it."

Tesia regarded me with faint surprise, while Cyril glowered. "And just who are you?"

I introduced myself. "Rubellius Flavus."

"Visiting from Britannia," Tesia supplied.

Cyril harrumphed. "An excellent reason to be an authority in such matters," he scoffed.

"I believe it was Justin Martyr—a trained philosopher himself—who said there was truth to be found among the pagans," I continued. "And didn't Synesius of Cyrene, bishop of Ptolomais, study under Hypatia?"

Cyril's face froze for a long moment, and I thought that perhaps I had gone too far. Antagonizing such a powerful man hadn't been my intent.

Then he relaxed. "You're correct in what you say. There is light, albeit dim, mere flickers only, in some pagan thought. But of what use are such twilight illuminations once the sun is risen? Who needs a candle in broad daylight?" He spread his hands. "My concern is with souls. It's easy for the unwary to be led into avenues of thought that carry one away from Heaven, rather than toward it, to follow false light rather than the true light."

"I think you do Tesia an injustice," I replied. "She's not an uneducated or weak-minded person at the mercy of cleverly crafted words."

"Perhaps not," Cyril conceded.

"And your own uncle, Bishop Theophilus, though he suppressed pagan practices, saw no need to oppose Hypatia's school," I added.

"Also true," Cyril said. "I, however, disagree with my late uncle, because the Deceiver is a master of subtlety. Be careful, daughter," he said to Tesia, in a more moderate tone. "Don't think too highly of yourself, lest pride cause a fall."

"I won't," Tesia replied. "Thank you for your concern."

She inclined her neck in respect to the Bishop; I did likewise, and Cyril walked off.

"A crusty character," I remarked.

"One not to be lightly crossed," she added. "Thank you for coming to my assistance."

"Entirely unnecessary, I'm sure."

"But appreciated anyway."

Her smile warmed me. I opened my mouth, but words failed me as an amused twinkle in her eyes stirred unexpected emotions within me. My cheeks felt suddenly hot.

I was saved from further embarrassment by the arrival of Tesia's servant with a pair of young boys in tow. Tesia nodded politely to me. "Until we meet again, good sir."

I stammered a reply.

All afternoon I felt off-kilter, barely listening to J'sun as he reported on the success of his endeavors, as we relaxed in the rooms we had rented in a moderately fashionable area of town, in the predominantly Greek section.

"We've been invited to a dinner gathering at the prefect's palace!" he informed me triumphantly.

"That's nice."

"At which Hypatia will be present!"

"Fine," I replied absently.

"I hear that Tesia has been invited, too."

That caught my attention. "Just how did you manage to get us invited?" I asked, unable to keep the excitement from my voice.

"Courtesy of Hypatia," he replied smugly. "She and the prefect are good friends. She thought he might want to meet a traveling historian and his secretary."

"Just don't get in over your head," I warned. "We're not here to become involved in local politics." Politics in Alexandria could be incredibly Byzantine, well before Byzantium lent its name to such affairs.

That night, as I slept, I had the curious sensation that we were being drawn into a swirling current of events, like leaves on the surface of an eddying torrent. But were there calm waters at the end, or roaring cataracts?

The dinner, which was held several days later, was a typical event as such things go—excellent food interspersed with dreary conversation on matters of little concern to the visitor. Of more interest to me were the people who attended.

A steward introduced J'sun and me as we arrived, but it was Tesia who came over to take charge—Prefect Orestes, it seemed, didn't feel it necessary to greet every guest at the door. She wore a gown stunning in its simple modesty, and only sufficient jewelry to enhance, rather than overwhelm, her beauty. She outshone and outclassed several other women whose weight of jewelry was truly remarkable.

"You look delightful!" I blurted, feeling like a teenager as I did so.

She accepted the compliment gracefully. "Come, let me introduce you to some of the other guests." She led me deeper into the magnificent house. Orestes had a taste for multi-colored marble, vividly painted walls, and the occasional well-executed sculpture.

Tesia presented me to a variety of people of both sexes, none of whom interested me in the slightest.

"Isn't your husband here?" I asked during a break in introductions, wondering why she didn't appear to be accompanied.

"My husband died several years ago," she replied.

"I'm sorry," I said.

"He was a judge," she continued, speaking as if her mind was in the past. "One day there were riots in the city—there are often riots here—and he happened to be passing by in his litter. The rioters recognized him as a wealthy, influential man. And so they dragged him out and killed him. Had he been coming home a different way, he would be with us today."

I murmured my sympathy.

She gave me a sad smile. "But you don't wish to hear of my sorrows."

"On the contrary," I replied. "I too have suffered. Once upon a time I had a wife and daughter. Both were taken away from me suddenly."

"Then you understand."

I nodded, and for a moment our eyes met, and we were joined by our mutual griefs.

Then Tesia turned aside. "Come," she said, "you must meet our host."

She guided me across the room and presented me. "Prefect Orestes," she said, "Rubellius Flavus, a visitor from Britannia."

The prefect greeted me courteously. "Britannia, you say? You're quite a distance from home."

Orestes cut an imposing figure—tall, though not in J'sun's league, wearing a fine tunic with gold threads, his beard neatly trimmed beneath curly hair shining with scented oil, gold rings on his fingers.

"I travel widely," I replied.

We exchanged pleasantries before he moved on to greet other guests, among them Hypatia, who, as was apparently her custom, wore her philosopher's tribon.

J'sun, in his role as my secretary, introduced me to the illustrious philosopher. She inquired politely as to my background and interests, and offered to refer me to some natural historians of her acquaintance.

"I must come and hear you lecture," I said.

"Do," she replied. "Anyone of culture who seeks after knowledge is welcome at my talks."

As the evening progressed, I studied both Orestes and Hypatia. Hypatia projected a kind of serenity, lacking all pretension. She moved as easily in society as she did in her own world of the Library.

The prefect, I decided, appeared to be a competent official, not subject to the overweening greed and dissipation that overcome so many gubernatorial types. His speech was measured, and, to judge by the way he conversed with Hypatia, he was a man of some erudition. I took rather a liking to him.

Tesia also made sure I met several of Alexandria's other notables, none of whom struck me as being worth the effort of prolonged conversation.

J'sun seemed to be right at home. Surrounded by several admiring females he regaled them with purely fictitious tales of his life as the son of a Nubian warrior. I had to give him high marks for creativity.

By dint of some surreptitious maneuvering, I was able to recline near Tesia during the meal.

"I saw you with children the other day," I commented, during a lull in the entertainment provided by a troop of dwarfs.

She raised her eyebrows. "Have you been observing me?"

"After Mass." I clarified quickly. "I mean, I saw the children with your servant after Mass."

Her smile emanated happiness. "My husband left me well provided for. We had no children of our own, but Alexandria creates many orphans. At Bishop Cyril's urging I took in several such unfortunates."

I suppose my surprise must have shown.

Tesia interpreted it correctly. "Despite what you've seen, Cyril has some good attributes, among them a concern for children. Whenever he hears of one in need, he calls on me, and I do what I can. Unfortunately, although my house is large, it's never large enough."

"Your heart, though, is."

She blushed. "It's no more than my Christian duty."

It was much more than that, I thought, but didn't say, not wishing to embarrass her.

"Having a number of children must be a lot of work," I said.

"At first it was," she replied, "although I have servants. But they are such a blessing to me."

I almost asked her if there was a man in her life. But it would have been inappropriate. And if there was, wouldn't he have been invited to this banquet as well, if only to accompany Tesia?

Much as I wanted to, I couldn't monopolize Tesia's attentions all evening. As at all such social occasions, there were the usual tiresome bores determined to thrust their endlessly inane conversation on anyone they could corner. Normally I try to notice and avoid such individuals. But a moment of inattention found me backed up against a statue of one of Orestes' ancestors by a particularly tiresome and overly-perfumed matron. Her presence rapidly became unendurable, and I cast around for a means of escape. Fortunately, Tesia saw my distress and came to my rescue.

"You'll want to meet Pomponius," she said, a light pressure on my unresisting elbow steering me away from the flustered matron and towards a man across the room. "He's an influential member of the archontes." Meeting yet another city official sounded tedious.

Said gentleman was remonstrating with Prefect Orestes with Hypatia and several other distinguished citizens in close attendance.

"You must do something about the Jewish dances," he was saying. "The rowdiness is becoming offensive."

"Jewish dances?" Tesia inquired.

"It's a custom in their quarter," Orestes explained, shooting her a glance, "to have dances and pantomimes in the theater on Saturdays. It's been going on for years, so I've been told."

"But not to this degree," Pomponius continued. "And on their Sabbath, no less. One would think they'd be better off attending to their Law."

"Surely what the Jews do on their holy day is for them to determine," Hypatia interjected calmly, "just as what you Christians do is your decision."

Her words were received with polite bemusement. The demos—the common people of the city—were generally beneath Hypatia's concern, I'd heard. Her focus and teachings were for the upper classes.

"I agree with both Pomponius and Hypatia," another man added. "There's nothing wrong with harmless entertainment, but matters are getting out of hand."

"Property damage!" Pomponius exclaimed. "Public brawling! Youths assailing law-abiding citizens—in broad daylight, even!"

"And just when I thought we'd achieved some semblance of order in

Alexandria," Orestes sighed. He stroked his neatly trimmed beard. "This isn't the first time I've heard complaints. But I didn't think the situation was that bad."

"And getting worse!"

"Put an end to the dances!" someone suggested.

Hypatia appealed for calm. "Don't over-react," she advised. "That could only make things worse. It's not as if it's only Jews involved in the brawls," she said pointedly to Pomponius.

"Well…" he spluttered.

Orestes regarded her appreciatively. "Ending the dances would be too severe. But perhaps some limitations…on the number of performances, the time allowed for them…"

"A curfew!" another man added, to a chorus of ideas, some temperate, others shouted in heat.

I turned away from the group.

"No good will come of this," I commented softly to Tesia.

She frowned, as she followed me away from the animated discussion. "The prefect's ideas seem quite reasonable."

"They do," I concurred. "But just because something is reasonable doesn't mean it will work out as intended."

She regarded me with a curious expression.

"May I escort you home?" I asked.

"My servants are ample bodyguard," she replied. Then, seeing my crestfallen expression, she touched me lightly on the arm and said, "but I would enjoy your company on the way."

We left Orestes' banquet outwardly in good humor, yet in my case with underlying anxiety.

Orestes, for all his good intentions, was inadvertently about to escalate tensions in the city. Perhaps that was unavoidable. Because there was a man eager to exploit those tensions.

"Render unto Caesar that which is Caesar's," Jesus had said, "and unto God that which is God's." Prudent words; but not necessarily easy to put into practice, especially not in Alexandria. Prefect Orestes was the representative of the current Caesar, the Emperor Theodosius II; Bishop Cyril was God's representative.

Orestes wanted a peaceful city—factional fighting reflected badly on his administrative skills, whereas peace and prosperity gained him the emperor's approval. As a relative newcomer, it was important that he project an image of strength and authority, so as to maintain control of turbulent Alexandria.

Cyril, on the other hand, was more interested in doctrinal purity, and, like his uncle Theophilus before him, was not averse to using heavy handed tactics to get his way. He had, after all, already closed and plundered the churches of a Christian sect called the Novatians.

Both men were young and ambitious. Both men knew exactly where they wanted the orbits of their power to lie.

But to Cyril, spiritual authority trumped secular power.

He wanted both.

I am not, I think, unduly squeamish—it wasn't possible to survive in the Roman world possessed of a weak stomach—but the sight of a man being publicly tortured stopped me in my tracks as J'sun and I returned from an enjoyable cleansing in the public baths. My oiled skin still tingled from the scrape of the strigil, and my muscles felt warm and relaxed.

The sharp slap of a lash against bare flesh extracted a shriek of pain from the victim, whose eyes were clenched shut and face rigid. He was stripped to a loincloth, and ropes bound his hands to a stone pillar, obviously designed for the purpose.

"Who is that?" I asked a bystander, as another slap was followed by another exclamation.

"Hierax," the man replied. "Horrible fellow—always poking his nose where it doesn't belong. About time someone took a lash to him."

The lash whistled through the air. Tiny droplets of blood sprayed into the sunshine like red diamonds. Hierax screamed and writhed.

The bystander cupped his hands around his mouth. "Harder!" he shouted to the soldier wielding the lash. "Put some muscle in it!"

The soldier heard him and put his whole weight behind the next stroke.

It was horrible, yet I couldn't help but look backwards as J'sun urged me away.

"Who's Hierax?" he asked as we rounded a corner out of sight.

"Did you forget your background reading?" I asked. "Or skip that section?"

He blushed. "I don't recall the name…"

"Minus points. A teacher. One of Bishop Cyril's more officious minions," I explained, "and no friend of the Jews. Prefect Orestes made an appearance at the theater to announce his ordinance regulating the pantomimes. Hierax was also present. Before Orestes had finished his speech, a brawl broke out between some Christians and Jews."

"What's unusual about that?"

"Well, the Jews claimed that Hierax was instigating trouble and trying to undermine Orestes. They said that he was an informer for Cyril, sent there to report to his master on the restrictions Orestes was implementing. They clamored for Orestes to do something."

"I don't see the problem."

"The problem," I replied, "is that Cyril isn't particularly fond of the Jews, either, and wanted to impose even heavier restrictions than the prefect proposed. Cyril, as you may recall, has already been appropriating to himself prerogatives that rightfully belong to the emperor's officials."

"Getting too big for his boots."

"Wanting boots that don't belong to him," I corrected. "And because this is a matter involving the Jews—"

"Cyril thinks it's a religious matter rather than a secular one and he should be the one to deal with it."

"Right."

"So Orestes is trying to placate the Jews and show Cyril who's boss," J'sun concluded.

"Exactly."

"Cyril's not likely to take this lying down."

"He won't," I said heavily. "He won't dare blame Orestes, but he *will* blame the Jews for Hierax's punishment. In fact, he'll threaten and try to intimidate the Jewish community's leaders."

J'sun whistled. "They won't take it well, either."

"Things are going to get ugly around here, J'sun," I said. "We'd be well advised to keep a low profile."

I could still hear Hierax's screams ringing in my ears as I turned into bed that night. Orestes, though a Christian, was a man of his time. And torture was an accepted legal practice. Hierax paid with his flesh for his indiscretion.

He wouldn't be the only one.

There would, I mused sadly, be many more.

The lingering images of Hierax's torture weren't the only causes of nocturnal ruminations. I was perplexed, as well. Tesia's husband, I now knew, was dead. There was, it seemed, no obvious candidate to be Romeo at the moment. And yet, the archaeological record showed that Tesia had been buried with a man. Could she have been interred later with her previously deceased husband? It seemed unlikely. They were in each other's arms. And the archaeologists were convinced they'd been buried together at the same time.

Was this Tesia really our Juliet, or had we been following a false trail?

Possible, but we had met no other Tesias in Alexandria's philosophical circles. My instincts told me that she was the right woman.

That meant we'd have to keep looking—and look harder—for Romeo.

I wasn't at all sure that I wanted to.

On the surface, the city was calm, but beneath the facade of tranquility, dark undercurrents stirred. J'sun sensed them, too, otherwise I might have wondered if I was becoming overly sensitive.

He seemed bemused, though, when I asked him to deliver a message to Tesia one morning while we were having our morning meal of bread, cheese, and fruit.

"Wouldn't you rather convey it in person?" he said while smearing honey onto a slab of bread.

"You're my secretary, remember?" I replied. "And student, whose grades are in my hands."

He was unfazed by my mock threat. "Your wish is my command, Professor."

He was smirking when he returned from his errand. "She was in her bath," he said. "I handed your message to her steward, who assured me it would be delivered at the first opportune moment."

And so I waited.

It was nearly midday when a servant arrived bearing a small papyrus roll tied with a ribbon. It smelled of sandalwood. The writing, in a flowing feminine hand, was brief.

I should be honored to attend the performance of Seneca's "Thyestes" at the theater in your company. My servant will conduct you to my residence. Tesia.

"A date?" J'sun chortled, looking over my shoulder. "You're going on a date?"

"And you," I replied with mock severity, "are going to the Library to read up on the Neoplatonism of Iamblichus."

There were, occasionally, advantages to being a professor.

"Kindly remain here," I instructed the servant, and went into my chamber to change into suitable clothes and arrange my hair. I fingered the pilgrim's cross that Erica had given me so long ago and which I still wore.

I bid a good afternoon to J'sun, then returned to the waiting servant, who escorted me to a substantial home in the Greek quarter of the city, not far from the Library. He admitted me into a vestibule from which I could glimpse an interior courtyard adorned with flowers and shrubs. A fountain chuckled out of sight.

"I will inform the mistress of your arrival," he said, and departed.

From somewhere I heard the laughter of children. Then the barking of dogs, and suddenly two tan-colored, short-haired animals resembling Pharaoh hounds were circling me and sniffing my legs.

"I hope you don't mind," said a musical voice, and I looked up to see Tesia regarding me with a slightly worried expression.

"Not at all," I said. "I love dogs...we always had dogs when I was growing up."

She relaxed, and indicated the larger animal. "This is Canis Major, and the other is Canis Minor."

I chuckled. "Cute names."

"Run along, now," she said, dismissing the dogs with a sweep of her hand, then motioning to a pair of servants, a man and a woman, to accompany us.

"I normally walk," she said as we departed the house.

"As do I."

"Do you frequent the theater often?"

"When I can," I replied. "On my travels...it isn't always possible."

"Will you be staying in Alexandria much longer?"

Was there hopefulness in her voice? Or were my ears hearing what I wanted to hear?

"I would like to," I replied. But there was, of course, a departure date, when the Ring's interface would be opened and J'sun and I would return to our own time.

"Then I hope your studies proceed slowly," she said, and I smiled in reply.

Arriving at the theater, Tesia and I sat in the section reserved for upper class citizens, facing a well-painted backdrop.

Seneca was never one of my favorite authors of antiquity. I found his style affected and overwrought, and tragedies were never my cup of tea. Still, the weather was moderate, and the theater not crowded, making for a pleasant afternoon.

"I expect that Bishop Cyril wouldn't approve of your presence here," I said, during a break between scenes.

"I expect not," she agreed, brushing back a wayward strand of hair. "Yet is it sinful to hear the words of a thinker from long ago?"

"Not to my mind," I replied. "How are we to learn and grow if we don't remember where we have come from? And surely one can appreciate the light more when it is contrasted with lesser light or with darkness."

"Exactly!" she beamed. "We are of one mind."

Her hand rested lightly on mine, and for one delightful moment, our fingers intertwined.

I didn't see Tesia for several days. J'sun and I pursued our research, which increasingly centered around the Library—J'sun engaged in studying Hypatia, while I scoured the place for any man who might conceivably be Romeo.

Hypatia was much in evidence, either giving lectures or engaged in collegial disputations. On a couple of occasions I noticed her being conveyed around town in a two-wheeled, horse-drawn carriage—evidently exempt from whatever local ordinances on daytime vehicular traffic were currently in force. Like many cities in the Empire, Alexandria placed restrictions on the types of vehicles allowed in the streets during daylight hours.

It was late one afternoon when a messenger brought an invitation written in a feminine hand, which, though I had seen it only once before, I recognized immediately with a sudden speeding of my heart. J'sun and I were invited to a philosophical gathering at Tesia's house the following day.

I was happy to reply in the affirmative; J'sun preferred to attend a lecture given by Hypatia at the Library on the mathematical basis and construction of the astrolabe. Mathematics was so integrally wedded to physics in my estimation that I was glad to have a more appealing alternative. We agreed to go our separate ways.

The next evening I presented myself at Tesia's dwelling.

"I'm glad you were able to come," she greeted, after the steward had admitted me.

"There's nowhere else I'd rather be."

"Can that be true?"

"Given the choice of my own company or yours, the decision was easy."

She laughed lightly. "Come and join the discussions."

I was more interested in Tesia's company than the discourses of the Alexandrian elite, so I tried to maximize the one while still contributing to the other.

The gathering was a mixed group of pagan neo-Platonists and Christians; a meeting of lesser Alexandrian lights. The conversation ranged widely, and even brought me in from time to time. Both professors and philosophers can wax eloquent or descend to the depths of tedium and pedantry. Both facets were exhibited.

Alexandrians, I learned, were not only prone to violence, but to verbosity.

The discussions lasted late into the night; so late that I once again regretted that strong tea was not available in Roman times. It was amazing that ancient peoples had accomplished as much as they had without the benefit of tea or coffee. Tesia's servants were kept busy supplying refreshments and refilling the lamps with oil.

Outside the walls of Tesia's house the city, for the most part, slept.

At last fatigue began to take its toll, and even the most garrulous philosophers began to tire. By ones and twos the participants departed for their respective domiciles.

I myself was bidding goodnight to Tesia when a sudden pounding on the door interrupted me.

Tesia's chief steward hurried to admit a panting, flushed man who pushed past the startled steward.

"The church of St. Alexander is on fire!" he gasped. "Come quickly!" He turned and ran out again.

Several of the Christians jumped to their feet and dashed into the night.

"Get some men together!" Tesia commanded the steward.

I grabbed her arm. "Don't!" I exclaimed. "It's a trap."

"Trap?" she echoed, as the steward paused.

I nodded. "Cyril has antagonized the Jewish community. Some of them have been plotting revenge."

Her expression clouded. "Are you privy to their plot that you should know this?"

"I hear things," I said lamely. "Rumors."

"Hear things," she repeated skeptically.

"It doesn't matter how I know," I protested. "But believe me, I beg you."

For a moment, she hesitated. Then she turned to the steward. "I gave you an order."

"Yes, domina," he said, and hurried off.

"Tesia—" I began.

"Our sacred place is burning," she said firmly. "We must do what we can."

The steward returned with four male servants.

"Let's go," Tesia said.

I tried one final time. "Tesia, you must not!"

Her eyes flashed. "I appreciate your concern, but this is my household and I shall give the orders."

"You're heading into danger!"

"Again I ask, how do you know?"

"Tesia, please—"

"I'm not afraid of some nebulous danger," she said. She threw a cloak over her shoulders and followed her servants out the door. I trotted behind.

The church lay some little distance away. I searched the sky as we drew closer, Tesia and I somewhat behind the fleeter-footed servants, but saw no ominous reddening of the clouds. Instead, coming to the intersection of a cross-street down which the servants had turned, we glimpsed shadowy figures flitting in their wake. Servants and shadows were out of sight before there was time to shout a warning.

An instant later came a quickly silenced scream.

I pulled Tesia into the shelter of a doorway.

"We must return to your house," I whispered.

"My servants—"

Another scream, followed by a dull thud, interrupted her.

"We can't help them. I'm not carrying a sword. We can't take on these assassins barehanded."

Running footsteps came toward us, and I shielded Tesia as they approached. One of Tesia's servants fled past, hotly pursued by several dark-cloaked figures. Moonlight glinted off the knives they carried.

Tesia shivered, and I put my arms around her.

We huddled in the shadowed doorway until all sounds save for the thudding of our hearts had disappeared and I judged that the coast was clear. Then, holding Tesia tightly by the hand, I slipped back the way we had come, scurrying from shadow to shadow, trying to make as little noise as possible.

Perhaps we should have attempted to notify the authorities, so they could have prevented further killings. Possibly it was the cognitive deterioration that the medics said was affecting me, but the thought never crossed my mind. My only concern was for Tesia's safety.

What seemed to be hours later we reached the door of Tesia's house. A servant opened it promptly to my knock, and we were safe inside. I breathed a sigh of relief as the portal was closed and locked behind us.

"Keep watch on the door," Tesia instructed the doorkeeper, adding hopefully, "in case any of our household return."

Then, as if her energy was suddenly spent, she sagged. I guided her to a couch. She sat, trembling.

"Be so good as to bring wine," I instructed a waiting maidservant, and held the cup to Tesia's pale lips when it arrived.

"What's happening to Alexandria?" she said in a shaky voice. "What's becoming of us?"

I took the question as rhetorical.

"I should leave," I said.

"No," she countered quickly, grasping the sleeve of my tunic and looking up with pleading eyes. "Please stay with me."

It was a somber vigil that we kept. Canis Major and Canis Minor came and lay at Tesia's feet, as if sharing the melancholy. Eventually, the chief steward returned, and later, one of the servants, blood dripping from a wound on his arm. But the other three servants never returned.

"It's my fault," Tesia moaned. "I should have listened to you."

"Don't blame yourself." I touched her shoulder. "You couldn't have known. I wouldn't have believed me, either."

But she was inconsolable, and eventually one of her maidservants led her to bed. She insisted I not take to the streets—an admonition that frankly I was glad to heed—and the steward directed me to a guestroom where I spent a restless remainder of the night.

By daybreak, the scope of the massacre became evident, and there was much mourning in Alexandria. There was also much anger.

Bishop Cyril was quicker off the mark than Prefect Orestes. He had at hand a number of parabolanai—young men whose normal duties were to collect the sick, disabled, or homeless, and take them to hospitals or church almshouses, but who additionally functioned as an unofficial guard for the bishop. These young men tended to be ignorant, uneducated, and hot-headed, making them both available and amenable to performing less charitable tasks as well.

Cyril's parabolanai, accompanied by a considerable number of outraged townspeople, took revenge on the synagogues. Over the next several days, synagogue after synagogue was looted, Jewish homes were ransacked and their occupants expelled from Alexandria.

Cyril made no effort to determine whether or not those so displaced had been participants in the massacre—and certainly most had no knowledge of the atrocities. But the innocent were treated as harshly as the guilty—indeed, in Cyril's eyes I doubted whether there were any innocent Jews.

Greatly outnumbered, there was little the Jewish minority could do to resist.

There was little Orestes could do, either, except vent impotent rage. The Jews formed an important part of the city's population and economy. He harbored no grudge against them. But he lacked the manpower and forces to counter Cyril directly. Instead, he wrote to the emperor in Constantinople. As did Cyril.

And he waited.

Cyril sent a delegation and offered to reconcile with the prefect, but he proposed no concessions, and Orestes refused, rightly judging that it would have given the appearance of surrender.

I heard from Tesia that Cyril made a second attempt at reconciliation, at the urging of various prominent people in the Christian community.

She was shaking with anger as she told me. "Bishop Cyril held out a book of the Gospels. 'We both believe this,' he said. 'Let it form the basis of the end of our quarrel'."

I pursed my lips. "What did the prefect say?"

"He hardly knew what to say," Tesia replied. "Hypatia took him aside and whispered in his ear."

"And what did Cyril think of that, I wonder?"

"He tried to appear calm, but I could see that it angered him. 'Why do you need counsel from a pagan,' he demanded, 'when you owe your spiritual allegiance to Christ's bishop?'"

"Awkward for the prefect," I said.

"I wanted to lay hold of Cyril and shake some sense into him," Tesia said through clenched teeth. "None of this would have happened if he'd let matters alone instead of sending Hierax to spy for him and then try to pin the blame for Hierax's punishment on the Jews."

"Let me guess," I said. "Orestes refused the offer."

Tesia nodded. "I don't know whether he'd have fallen for it or not, but Hypatia convinced him that it was a ploy by Cyril to manipulate him. Accept, and Orestes would be no more than Cyril's lackey."

"Cyril will only escalate," I commented.

"He's never liked Hypatia," Tesia said, "but now he regards her as an enemy. I'm afraid, Rubellius. Very afraid."

"With good reason," I replied, knowing what was to come, and also knowing there was nothing I could do about it.

Except, perhaps, to protect Tesia as much as I could.

Cyril's position wasn't unassailable, however. The archontes and other influential Christians tended to side with Orestes. And so Cyril decided to call for reinforcements. Heavy-handed reinforcements.

They responded to his call, some five hundred fanatical monks from the Nitrian desert led by the singularly unpleasant Peter the Lector. The same monks that Cyril's uncle, Theophilus, had employed during the bloody destruction of the Serapion, the great, gilded temple to the curious hybrid god, Serapis, that had been one of Alexandria's vaunted landmarks.

They weren't the only band of black-robed bandits that prowled the deserts, looking for pagan temples to pillage and pagan peasants to rob. But they were ones that had an allegiance of sorts to Cyril. And where there was paganism to be crushed, they were ready to do the crushing.

They arrived in Alexandria some days later, a noisy—and noisome—rabble of rough, dirty, men with unkempt beards who looked anything but men of God. They were supposed to be dedicated to prayer, devotion, the reading of Scripture, and works of mercy. But mindless zeal burned in their eyes as they swarmed down the streets of Alexandria with swords in their hands and curses on their lips. With their faces burned from the sun and skin weathered to wrinkled leather, it was almost as if an army of mummies had arisen from the desert sands to wreak the vengeance of millennia.

They wasted little time in making their presence known to the one man who stood in Cyril's way.

Orestes wasn't one to shy away from physical danger. Surely he knew that it was highly probable that certain of Cyril's minions wished him harm; yet he wasn't about to cower in his palace. He continued life as usual.

"Did you hear that someone sent Orestes an anonymous warning?" J'sun asked as we left the Library one day. "Suggested he increase the size of his guard. And watch out for mad monks."

"Is that so?" I asked incuriously.

"Hypatia told me."

"It seems as though there's a lot she tells you."

"She recognizes my innate intelligence, that's all."

I gestured. "Sorry, but she's not CamOx faculty, so you'll have to make do with my judgment."

J'sun chuckled good-naturedly.

The appealing aromas of a hot food shop teased my nostrils.

"Lunch?" I asked.

J'sun halted. "You sent that note, didn't you?"

"Whatever gave you that idea?" I countered, not meeting his gaze.

"Who else would know that Orestes was in personal danger?"

"It won't make a camel's spit of difference."

"So why'd you do it?"

I shrugged. "Even after all these years, I still get the urge to try."

"Maybe there's an exception to the rule?"

"Something like that. Hope springs eternal."

J'sun nodded, and indicated the hot food shop. "You buying?"

"Courtesy of the Chair. And whoever makes the coins for us."

I have to give credit where credit is due—the food was good in Alexandria. We emerged from the shop having eaten more than was necessary for lunch.

"I really shouldn't do that," I groaned.

J'sun eyed me critically. "Tesia won't like it if you put on too many more pounds."

"Too many *more?*"

J'sun shrugged. "Let's just say that I'm not the one who had to buy larger tunics the other day."

"You have a point. Why don't we pay a visit to the gymnasium? You can exhibit your muscles and I can try to shed some flab."

"Sounds like a plan."

We directed our steps toward the gymnasium. But like so many of my plans, I ended up at a place I didn't want to be at a time I didn't want to be.

Unbeknownst to me, Orestes had chosen that morning to engage in some athletic activities at the gymnasium. We arrived just as he was leaving, accompanied by his bodyguard. Unfortunately, also in the vicinity—by happenstance or by plan, I don't know—was a contingent of Cyril's Nitrian monks, led by the odious Peter himself, accompanied by a firebrand named Ammonius.

"I don't think we want to be here," I said to J'sun.

He showed no inclination to leave.

"Come on," I urged him.

"I want to see what happens," he replied.

"We *know* what happens," I said.

"Seeing is believing," he retorted.

The monks caught sight of Orestes and rushed forward. The monks, of course, didn't know Orestes personally. All they knew—or cared about—was that Orestes wouldn't yield power to Cyril. The prefect was on the steps of the gymnasium; he couldn't go forward—it was either retreat into the building or stand his ground.

He stood his ground.

"I command you to disperse!" he shouted. "Return to your monasteries."

"Did you have fun?" Peter called out. "A pity you don't exercise your spirit as much as your body."

"He's a pagan!" Ammonius added. "He has the spirit of the devil in him!"

"What idol do you worship?" Peter taunted.

Orestes tried to shout over the noise of their insults and jeers. "I am no pagan! I am a baptized Christian! And as your prefect I order you to disperse!"

The monks weren't interested in listening. "Idolater! Servant of Satan!" Someone began a chant of "Pagan! Pagan!" and soon the whole mob was chanting "Pagan! Pagan!"

Frustrated, Orestes protested otherwise, but the monks merely shouted louder. They pressed forward, shoving against Orestes' outnumbered bodyguard.

The scene was rapidly turning ugly. It wouldn't take much for blood to flow.

And it did.

The monk Ammonius picked up a chunk of loose paving stone and hurled it at the prefect. His aim was true and his arm strong. Orestes ducked too slowly; the missile clipped him on the side of the head and he fell, blood pouring from the wound.

His bodyguards wavered, then took to their heels.

The monks cheered, and Peter the Lector yelled, "Finish the idolater!"

They surged forward, surely intent on tearing the prefect to pieces.

It looked bad for Orestes.

But intent on assailing Orestes, the monks had failed to notice that a sizeable crowd had gathered, attracted by the commotion. An angry crowd. The monks were not liked by most Alexandrians. Orestes, although not long established in the city, was fairly popular.

All it took was for one man to act. J'sun was that man.

"To the prefect!" he shouted. "Save Orestes!"

He flung himself at the rear of the monks, using his height and strength to his advantage. He picked up one undersized monk and used the hapless man as a battering ram. The crowd responded, and in moments, scores of men were ripping into the surprised monks. Taken off guard, the monks began to scatter. One of them ran towards me.

Ammonius.

For a moment, as he drew near, his eyes, full of blind hatred, met mine.

I stuck out my foot and he went flying.

He hit the ground hard, and a trio of Alexandrians piled onto him. When he was sufficiently subdued, they hauled him to his feet.

"Try and kill our prefect, will you?" one man growled. "We'll see what Orestes thinks of that."

Supported by a pair of men, and holding a cloth to his head, Orestes was also upright. Someone called for a carriage, and helped the injured prefect into the conveyance.

Ammonius was hauled off to the prison.

Gradually, order returned. The crowd milled around for a while, but the monks had vanished, and eventually the crowd dispersed as well.

J'sun returned breathless, his white teeth flashing in a large smile.

"See, I affected something in the past," he said.

"But you didn't change anything," I replied.

"No, but it sure felt good."

And with that I had to agree.

Orestes was in no mood to be forgiving.

Ammonius was publicly tortured.

Unlike Hierax, he was tortured to death.

Such was the punishment for trying to assassinate the prefect.

Cyril, once again, reacted in a manner guaranteed only to make things worse. He declared Ammonius to be a martyr, Saint Ammonius the Admirable, and honored the body in one of Alexandria's churches.

Tesia was livid.

I too felt a sense of outrage.

And so it was with a shared purpose that we made a point of seeking out Cyril and confronting him as he was traveling between churches one Sunday morning.

"Let me speak first," I said.

She raised a shapely eyebrow.

"As a man," I clarified.

"But you're a visitor here, while Alexandria is my city and Cyril my bishop. You have no standing here."

"No, but we've seen how easily violence erupts. So let me be the one to speak."

She opened her mouth, then shut it again. I thought her eyes softened. "All right," she said at last.

Several monks were acting as a bodyguard, but when Cyril saw us approaching, he motioned to them to let us join him, and they walked further apart. I steeled myself for the confrontation.

"I see anger on your faces," he said, forgoing a greeting.

"It's despicable, what you're doing!" Tesia flared, forgetting herself. I shot her an annoyed glance.

She fell into step beside him. I flanked him on the other side.

"What's that, daughter?" Cyril asked, warily, casting a sideways look at me.

"Venerating that awful monk! Pretending that he was some kind of martyr."

"He died because of the faith—"

"Because he committed a crime! Not for upholding the faith!"

"Well…"

"Was Ammonius asked to deny the faith?" Tesia persisted. "Answer me that."

Cyril at least had the grace to look abashed. "No."

"Then he wasn't a martyr."

Cyril didn't speak for a long moment. Then he sighed. "You're not the first to express that opinion to me," he said. "I admit it—I acted hastily and rashly. I will say no more about Ammonius."

Tesia seemed slightly mollified.

"You do realize," I said, not wishing to let him off the hook so easily, "that by canonizing Ammonius you've implicated yourself in the attack on Prefect Orestes?"

Cyril halted and whirled to face me. "I had nothing to do with it. I gave no orders. The monks acted on their own. I knew nothing of it until after the fact!"

I shrugged. "But you have tacitly approved it."

Tesia added, "You can forget any chance of reconciling with Orestes now."

Cyril's expression hardened. "He had his chance and refused me. I won't approach him again. If he wants to reconcile, he can come to me." He began walking again, with a faster gait. "Not that he's likely to as long as he's under the influence of that pagan witch."

"She's no witch—" Tesia began, but Cyril was striding obliviously ahead, and his bodyguards closed ranks around him.

I caught Tesia's arm, and we dropped behind.

"There's no use," I said. "He's convinced that Hypatia is evil and there's no persuading him otherwise."

Tesia's pupils were dilated. "Hypatia could be in danger."

"I'm sure she is," I replied. "I'm sure she is."

"But would Cyril...he couldn't...he's a *bishop*!"

"No, not personally," I said. "But Cyril has supporters that he cannot control. There are forces that he cannot command."

We directed our steps back toward Tesia's house.

"What can we do?" Tesia asked me.

We.

Perhaps that little word carried no hidden meaning, but to me, it was if Tesia and I had been united in some way. We had become allies against the darkness that stalked Alexandria's streets.

But what *could* we do?

The Nitrian monks had been bested. The taste of defeat was surely bitter in Peter the Lector's mouth. He would undoubtedly be seeking revenge on another, easier, target. Striking at Orestes without actually striking Orestes.

Somebody close to Orestes.

Somebody like Hypatia.

We were reclining in Tesia's garden, Tesia, J'sun and myself, a day or two later. It should have been a relaxing time, with a servant playing the flute, the dogs chasing each other, and Tesia's adopted children laughing in the background. I had been formally introduced to Iason, Doran, Nitsa, and Diantha, and had even, at Tesia's suggestion, given them a history lesson. They were charming children, whom Tesia obviously cared for deeply.

"I've never seen Iason so interested in anything before," Tesia told me. "You really made the stories come alive. He said it was as if you had actually met Augustus and Constantine."

I accepted the compliment with a private smile.

But this day, we weren't relaxed.

Tesia was serious. "I've just come from Hypatia," she said. "She received a letter warning her to leave Alexandria." I cast a quick glance at J'sun who answered me with a minuscule nod.

"Probably from a well-wisher," I said.

"She means harm to no one," Tesia commented. "It's not right than anyone should mean harm to her."

"People are frequently not rational," I said, "or just. Emotions are running high in Alexandria. It's a city divided, and Hypatia is clearly allied with Orestes. Rumors say that it's because of her influence that Orestes hasn't reconciled with Cyril. Indeed, people say that she's practicing black magic and has cast a spell over Orestes."

"That's absurd!" Tesia exclaimed.

"Alexandria is a city full of fortune tellers, soothsayers, and astrologers," I replied. "We might think it nonsense, but the common people believe it."

J'sun asked, "What was her response to the letter?"

Tesia raised her shoulders. "She said that her schedule was full and that she wasn't going to alter it." She let her shoulders drop again. "Her father, Theon, was like that, too."

"I wish you would be more careful, Tesia," I said.

"I?" she exclaimed, surprised.

"You're a student of Hypatia—you're known to keep her company—"

"And that's all. I have no influence in Alexandria."

"And you're a friend of Orestes," I pointed out.

"But also known to Cyril," she pointed out. She laughed lightly. "Don't worry about me."

Two of the children ran over and wanted to play with J'sun. He looked momentarily flustered.

"I don't know any children's games," he said helplessly.

"Then you'll have to learn," Tesia grinned. "Come, I'll show you."

Accompanied by the happy children they crossed to a grassy patch in the garden.

I remained where I was. Because I knew that despite Tesia's admonition to the contrary, I *would* worry. I had no idea what lay in store for Tesia—I still feared that something dreadful would happen to her and that she would be laid to rest with her departed husband.

And I cared for Tesia.

I cared very much indeed.

A false calm seemed to descend upon Alexandria, and for a couple of weeks nothing much happened, although I had no doubt that beneath the seeming calm, dark passions roiled.

I took the opportunity to spend as much time with Tesia as was seemly. In addition to giving her children history lessons and attending Mass with her, I also escorted her to a musical concert and poetry readings given at the house of a judge who had once known Tesia's late husband, and on another occasion I had walked with her along the banks of a small branch of the Nile.

"My husband and I used to come here," she remarked wistfully, halting in an area that had once been a garden, but had now become neglected and overgrown. She placed some grains of wheat in her palm, and raised her hand aloft.

"He must have been a good man," I replied.

"He didn't care for birds at all," she answered. "He would much rather have been at home reading. But he came to please me."

Swans floated on the water, small animals rustled through the bushes, and papyrus waved in the shallows.

"Did your wife care for birds?" Tesia asked.

"All creatures," I replied. "Great and small. She was especially fond of horses."

Tesia smiled as a small bird perched on her palm to feed. "I haven't been here in a long time," she said. "And I never expected to come here with a man."

"Nor I with a lady," I replied.

The bird flew away, and Tesia tossed her remaining grains of wheat into the river. A sudden swirling welled up as hungry fish snatched up the unexpected bounty. A lotus blossom drifted past.

"It's strange, isn't it?" Tesia said. "The birds change, the fish change, people come and go, yet the river flows, endlessly, sweeping along everything on its surface."

"Like time," I replied.

"And no matter how much you might want to go back, you can never do it. You must always go forward, into the future."

She turned toward me, and her face was soft in the afternoon sunshine, russet highlights glimmered in her hair, and her eyes were gently glowing jewels of radiant amber.

"I'm glad you're here with me, Rubellius."

"Thank you for sharing this place with me," I replied, thinking how stiff and inadequate the words sounded.

She leaned slightly toward me, and I wanted nothing more than to take her in my arms and kiss her.

Then footsteps on the grass broke the moment.

"My apologies for interrupting, domina," said the servant who had accompanied us at a distance, "but the hour grows late—"

"And I have a dinner engagement!" Tesia exclaimed. "I almost forgot. An elderly aunt and uncle," she explained to me. "You wouldn't care for their company. I'd better go…because I promised my mother years ago that I wouldn't forget her sister."

"I understand," I replied, and we left the old garden.

J'sun was there when I returned to our lodgings, perusing a scroll, with the light of an oil lamp augmenting the fading remnants of daylight. He seemed, I thought, slightly ill at ease while we ate our dinner of cold meat, bread, and wine, neither of us inclined to talk.

A couple of times he opened his mouth as if to speak, but each time changed his mind.

Finally, I asked, "Is there something you want to say?"

He stared at a hunk of bread as if it might do the talking for him. Then he lifted his eyes. "I don't wish to seem out of place, Professor, but I'm supposed to be keeping an eye on you for—"

"For the Chair, yes, I know. Have you observed something untoward? Have I been acting strangely?"

"Not strangely, exactly…"

"Then exactly what?"

"It's about…" he took a deep breath. "About your relationship with Tesia," he said in a rush. "I mean…it's not as though you're regarding her with scientific detachment, are you?"

I shook my head. "No," I replied softly.

"Forgive me, Professor, but having personal relationships with past subjects is against the rules."

"Most certainly," I said. "You're quite right to point it out."

He relaxed somewhat. "It must be due to…to your…"

I tapped my temple with an index finger, and he nodded.

"You might be correct," I said. "But I don't think so. It's something…much deeper, more profound than that."

He gave me a skeptical glance. "Are you seriously…"

"Yes, J'sun, I am. And believe me, I wish we could have located Romeo so that I would have been spared this torment."

I thought I saw a flicker of sympathy in his eyes. I stood up.

"I'm going for a walk," I said. "The cool air…"

"I won't breathe a word," J'sun said.

I closed the door behind me and stepped out into the street. It was a futile exercise, of course.

It would have taken much more than cool air to diminish what I felt for Tesia.

Nevertheless, I made a strenuous effort to keep matters with Tesia low key over the subsequent days. But she requested that I give further lessons to her children, and how could I refuse? She would sit discreetly in the background while I told them stories of emperors and queens, saints and martyrs, statesmen and noblewomen, and I was always aware of her presence.

Sometimes she would send the children away, and we would talk—about ourselves, our beliefs, our likes and dislikes, our hopes and dreams.

It was March, the season of Lent, when penitential practices were the order of the day, and I joined Tesia as she practiced acts of charity to the poor, and spent time in prayer and fasting. Occasionally we spotted Cyril, usually accompanied either by several parabolanai or a number of the monks.

And then one morning, Tesia made a decision that affected us both. She determined to visit the Emporium to purchase a gift for a friend. Normally, she would have been accompanied by a servant, but J'sun and I happened to be there when she was voicing her plans, and on an impulse—because she cast a querying look in my direction—I volunteered us to escort her instead. J'sun gave me a disapproving frown, but being the dutiful student that he was, tagged along.

We had left the Emporium with our errand complete, when we had the misfortune to encounter another band of the vile Nitrian monks running down the street, perhaps forty or fifty of them, with Peter the Lector at their head. Several parabolanai swelled their ranks. We flattened ourselves against a wall as they raced past, grim purpose written on their faces.

Tesia turned a worried countenance toward me. "Where do you suppose they're going?"

A dread cold washed over me. There were all kinds of things the mad monks *could* be doing—history certainly hadn't recorded all their nefarious deeds—but somehow, I knew intuitively that they were on their way to commit the most ghastly outrage of all.

The monks rounded a corner, and a roar of satisfaction rose from them.

J'sun moved to follow them, but I barred his way with an arm and shook my head.

"I must help!" he exclaimed.

"Help whom?" Tesia wondered.

"It won't do any good," I said.

"Who's in trouble?" Tesia asked.

"But we have to try," J'sun continued.

"It won't make any difference," I said, wishing I didn't have to speak in front of Tesia, who was looking between J'sun and me, her confusion plain. "You can't change anything."

"Change what?" Tesia asked.

J'sun's expression writhed with anguish. I knew exactly how he felt—I had felt the same way so many times before. Frustrated, helpless, every fiber of being screaming out to do something—*anything!*—and yet knowing it would be futile.

Tesia gripped the front of my tunic. "You know what's going on, don't you?" Her gaze bored into me.

The clatter of horses and a woman's scream shattered the moment. J'sun whirled and dashed toward the source of the commotion. I held Tesia's gaze a moment longer, then, hand in hand, we ran after him.

We rounded the corner and jerked to a halt. The seething mob of monks had surrounded a horse-drawn carriage, forced it to a halt, and held the driver, a slave, paralyzed with fear, at the point of a sword.

A woman screamed again, and I glimpsed Hypatia, wearing her philosopher's tribon, being tossed from hand to hand, like a sack of wheat. Given the busy nature of her life, she had preferred the convenience and speed of a carriage to the slowness of a litter. But at least with a litter she'd have had a number of bearers to defend her, not just a single slave.

J'sun was to my right, trying to force his way through the crowd. It was foolish; the monks were armed, we weren't. Even J'sun's height and strength couldn't prevail forever against sharp steel.

Tesia put her hands to her mouth in horror.

This was no place for a woman. I pushed her backward. "Go home!" I said. "Run! Get out of here!"

Not waiting to ensure that she did so, I flung myself in J'sun's wake, shoving aside the frenzied monks. Fortunately, J'sun's height and dark skin made it easy to keep track of him, although I rapidly lost sight of Hypatia. Perhaps the monks thought I wanted a piece of the action, because, surprisingly, they didn't resist, and I just about caught up to him.

Then I realized with an appalled shock that Tesia was right behind me.

"I told you to leave!" I shouted.

"Hypatia's my friend!" she replied, her mouth firm and eyes blazing determination.

I drew level with J'sun just as he reached the halted carriage. Some monks were already ripping it to pieces.

"Where's Hypatia?" I gasped.

"I lost her," he frowned, scanning over the heads of the mob.

And then another scream, fainter.

"They're carrying her off!" Tesia exclaimed.

"Which way, J'sun?" I asked.

He squinted, then pointed to his left. "There, I think."

Before we could angle that way, one of the monks—Peter the Lector himself, I believe—spotted Tesia. How he recognized her—where he had seen her before—how he connected her with Hypatia—I don't know. But his face twisted in an obscene grimace and he stabbed a finger toward her.

"One of her students!" he yelled. "Another pagan witch!"

Tesia blanched, suddenly realizing her danger. "I'm a Christian!" she exclaimed.

"Pagan sorceress!" Peter repeated.

I could feel the mob's hostility shift to focus on Tesia. I tried to shield her.

"Leave her alone! She's a Christian!" I returned, standing face to face with Peter. I felt as though I squared off with the devil himself.

"Take her away!" Peter frothed.

"For the love of God, leave her alone!"

Peter oozed venom. "We'll do to her as we'll do to her mistress!"

Gnarled, leathery hands reached for Tesia.

Anger boiled up within me, and red rage obscured Peter's ugly, malevolent features. I clenched my fist and swung, connecting squarely with his jaw. Peter rocked backwards, lip spurting blood. I prepared to swing again, but someone slammed into me from the side, and knocked me to my knees. In a moment I was fighting for my life. The world became a seething maelstrom of fists and feet.

A hairy arm wrapped itself around my neck and jerked me half up. I sank my teeth into the flesh; a man howled and the arm was ripped away. I pivoted and rose, planting my knee in the monk's groin as I did so, and following it with a chop to his throat.

A blow to my chest shoved me back against the wrecked carriage. I felt something move; a loose wheel spoke came free in my hand, and I wielded it like a club, cracking every skull within arm's length.

The monks retreated, giving me space and a moment's breather.

"Rubellius!" The shriek was Tesia's.

My head whipped around, and I spotted her being dragged away by a pair of monks. I laid into those around me with fury, desperation driving me to try to reach her. Then J'sun appeared at my side, also armed with a wooden slab. His tall frame and reach gave him an advantage, and together we cut a swath through the mob.

A sword glinted overhead, coming down toward me, and there was nothing I could do. But J'sun batted it aside, and clubbed the bearer to the ground. Another blade skewered through a fold in my tunic. I backhanded the monk away, and the sword clattered to the stones.

Tesia shrieked again. She struggled valiantly against her captors, clawing and scratching, but was no match for them.

Her frightened eyes met mine.

"I'm coming!" I called. "Tesia, I'm coming!"

I brought my makeshift club down against yet another cowled head.

Two against fifty. It was insane, hopeless.

Yet almost—almost—I made it to her—reaching out, our fingertips brushing. Then someone tripped me, and fists pummeled me as I fell.

"J'sun!" I yelled as the ground knocked the breath from me, and my club skittered away, "save Tesia!"

A foot rose and swung towards my head. For a split second I saw the nailed boot poised above me. Then it cracked my head against the pavement and consciousness fled.

They pursued me down a corridor of infinite, star-speckled blackness, an endless procession of dark cowled monks mouthing voiceless curses. I twisted and turned, swept through the gauzy clouds of a nebula, danced between flaming suns and passed between the flickering energies of colliding galaxies, yet I couldn't escape them.

They were with me everywhere, dogging my every step, effortlessly keeping pace with my every move. Hounds, not of Heaven, but of Hell.

I stepped from planet to planet...moved from time to time...

And yet always I was the prey; they were the predators.

Hungry...hungry for my soul, thirsting for my spirit...

The Ring glittered in the distance, yet I couldn't reach it. And even if I did, I knew it wouldn't help.

Eventually I stopped, exhausted. I stood on the broad plain of the Milky Way and faced my pursuers.

They ranged against me, and all at once as if by some unheard command, their cowls fell back and I saw not the faces of men, but the distorted visages of demons.

And their wordless chant took form, and reverberated through the cosmos.

"Tesia's gone...Tesia's gone...You've lost her...Lost her forever... Gone...Lost..."

I looked around, but there was no escape. I was encircled by the ghastly horde.

"Tesia's gone...You've lost her...You've lost...Lost..."

I sank to my knees in despair.

Then the light faded, as a darkness swept across the Milky Way. I looked up, and saw two long, roiling clouds approaching at right angles to each other, their ends vanishing in the infinite distance.

They met and crossed above me.

It began to rain. Cool drops of rain splashed on my head, face, hands, and ran down my neck and moistened my feet.

The rain splattered on the demon monks as well. They writhed in torment as the drops struck them. Then they melted, dissolving into formless masses that streamed away and disappeared, flowing into unseen gutters, their awful chant fading and disappearing with them.

All was silence.

Then I was on my feet again, standing alone on the Milky Way, the rain falling gently upon me, and the crossed clouds no longer dark, but glowing with a vibrant, golden light.

The light grew and expanded until the universe itself was aflame with light...

...and all was light...

Light.

Water.

Light—real light.

A wetness on my brow.

The light taking form...human form...

The touch of a damp cloth on my face.

A face. A woman's face. I blinked, struggled to focus. A hallucination. I was hallucinating.

The woman's face...the most beautiful face I had ever seen...as beautiful as Erica's had been...

I tried to speak, to move my thick tongue that resisted movement.

"Tesia?" It was a croak.

A pressure on my lips. I swallowed, and the warmth of wine flowed down my throat, loosening my recalcitrant tongue.

"Tesia?" I asked again, stronger. I tried to raise a hand.

Soft fingers gripped mine. "Yes, dear, it is I. How are you?"

"I feel…" How did I feel? My whole body throbbed. "As if I was just trampled by a herd of rampaging camels," I finished.

Wincing, I struggled to sit up, and panted with the exertion. A hand behind my back helped me, and a cushion kept me upright. I could see clearly now, although my head throbbed.

Tesia, wearing a blue gown. Tesia, her face bruised and swollen. But Tesia…!

"You're alive!" was all I could say.

She smiled. "Slightly the worse for wear, but otherwise alive and well."

My mind still couldn't grasp it. "But those fiends were dragging you away…I thought—I thought I'd failed you…lost you…"

She leaned over and kissed my cheek. "You were wonderful," she said, her eyes shining. "It was an awful blow you took. I thought it was *I* who had lost *you*."

"Then how—?"

"It was your friend—"

"J'sun?"

She frowned. "Zuberi."

"Of course."

She shook her head in wonder. "Never have I seen a man fight with as much sheer force of will as he. It would have taken more than a few monks to stop him. He was able to reach me and pry me out of the hands of those madmen. Then we escaped down alleys until they finally lost interest in us. He brought me safely home, then returned to look for you…they'd left you for dead in the street."

"I'm surprised they let you go," I said.

She took a rasping breath. "Hypatia was their true target…" Her voice broke.

"I know," I whispered. "I know."

"What they did to that poor woman…" Tears trickled from her eyes.

I squeezed her fingers. "It's over now. She's out of her pain. Pray for her, for her soul. That's all we can do."

Peter the Lector's crazed fanatics had dragged Hypatia to the Caesarion church, stripped her naked, and beaten her to death with roofing tiles. They'd ripped her to pieces, jubilantly carried the fragments back out through the door of the church, then finally burned the pitiful remains outside the city, at a place called Kinaron.

"How do you know?" Tesia wondered. "You were still unconscious when Zuberi brought you to my house. And I haven't left your side from then until now."

I tried to think of an answer, but it hurt too much. I shouldn't be talking.

"How long have I lain here?" I countered.

"Two days," Tesia replied. "Sometimes you would moan, or talk, or seem as if you were waking up, but you always fell asleep again."

"Where is J'- Zuberi?" I asked.

"Here in my house," she said. "Resting. Would you like to see him?"

"Later," I said. "Right now, I just want to be with you."

Despite my desire to remain awake, though, fatigue clamored for rest, and I closed my eyes.

Her lips brushed my cheek again. "Sleep, dear," she said, "I won't leave you," and I drifted off into a deep, refreshing slumber.

It was gone.

The pilgrim's cross that Erica had given me so many years ago was gone.

Somehow, even in a semi-conscious state, I realized that it was no longer around my neck. The connection to Erica that it represented had been severed.

For a moment, raw desolation threatened to overwhelm me, then it was if I heard Erica's sweet voice telling me, "It's all right, Robbie. It's all right."

And somehow, despite the confusion and the distress, there was peace.

The next time I regained full consciousness, Tesia brought me a little fruit, and a piece of bread.

"My cross," I said, hoping that maybe she had removed it, "it's gone."

She shook her head. "I haven't seen it."

"Your servants...?"

"No. I was with you while they washed you and bandaged your wounds. You weren't wearing it when Zuberi carried you in. It must have been torn off in the fight."

I hated to think of that little cross lying unnoticed in a crack in the paving stones or crushed beneath wagon wheels.

"I'll send a servant to look for it," Tesia offered.

I thanked her, although somehow I knew that the search would prove futile.

"Eat," Tesia encouraged me, and to please her I took a few bites.

"Did someone visit me while I was asleep?" I wondered, the shards of a vague recollection returning to me.

"My physician," she replied. "He says you'll be sore for a while, but he expects you to make a full recovery."

For the first time I became aware of the bandages that wreathed my head, arms, hands, and legs. "I must look like raw meat under these," I said.

She nodded ruefully. "His assistant is being kept busy compounding unguents for you."

"Would you take me out into the garden?" I asked. "I could do with some fresh air."

She clapped her hands and a manservant appeared at the doorway. He arranged a seat in a shady nook and carried me out to it.

When I was comfortably settled, Tesia said, "Zuberi has been wanting to see you. Shall I fetch him for you?"

I nodded. "That would be nice."

She departed, and a moment later J'sun emerged from the house and strode over. He had a slight limp, but his beaming smile was intact.

"I'm glad to see you looking well!" he greeted, lowering himself to the grass.

"This is well?" I asked, indicating my bandaged wounds and exposed bruises.

"It beats having to report your demise to the Chair," he replied. "I'm supposed to be—"

"My nursemaid," I scowled.

"—your right hand," he finished diplomatically.

"Speaking of hands," I stretched out my right hand to grasp J'sun's, "I owe you an immeasurable debt, that I can never repay."

He flushed. "A passing grade will do."

"No, seriously. You saved Tesia when you could have tried to rescue Hypatia."

He looked down and away. "I wanted to save Hypatia. God knows I did…"

"You couldn't have. There was nothing you could have done."

He nodded. "Intellectually, I know that."

"But emotionally…it's a different matter," I said. "Believe me, I understand completely."

J'sun cleared his voice. "And I saw how desperately you were trying to reach Tesia…and when you fell down—I knew there was no way I could not help. I *had* to save her. And you."

A lump came to my throat. "You are a true friend," I said.

His flush deepened.

"If there's ever anything I can do—" I began.

He shook his head. "I've had all the reward I need."

I motioned for him to explain.

"The look on Tesia's face when I carried you through the door…Joy wasn't the half of it. The woman loves you, Professor."

I couldn't speak.

"It's a pity, though," J'sun said, rising to his feet.

"What is?"

"That we have to be heading home soon." He trudged away.

Home.

I hadn't thought of home in a long time.

Alexandria, beautiful, passionate, violent Alexandria was becoming to seem like home.

And Tesia…

Tesia who loved me.

And whom I loved in return.

I didn't want to leave Tesia. But duty called. And there were rules to be followed.

If Tesia noticed the change in my mood when she returned she tactfully—or because she ascribed it to my head injury—let it pass. I wanted to tell her. But I couldn't.

Because there was still Romeo to keep in mind. Romeo, whom I hadn't met. But Tesia had. Or would.

Cyril came the next day to visit Tesia. My headache had lessened, and she was assisting me to find some books in the room she used as her library and study when the chief steward announced the bishop's arrival.

"Bring him here," Tesia instructed. Then to me, "Why don't you go and rest?"

"I've had plenty of rest," I replied.

"Then remain with me," she answered. "We'll meet Bishop Cyril together."

It was, I admit, a meeting I was looking forward to with a certain eagerness.

"Bishop Cyril," the steward announced, and withdrew.

The surprise that crossed Cyril's face at seeing me present with Tesia passed almost as quickly as it came. "I heard what happened, daughter," he said. "I hope you're well."

"No, I am not well," she said coldly. "I have lost a friend and mentor at the hands of your followers."

"I had no idea this would happen," Cyril protested.

"Despite what happened to Orestes?" Tesia asked.

"I told them there was to be no killing!"

"They obviously didn't listen," Tesia continued icily.

Cyril squirmed. "If I had known of their intentions I would have—"

"What? Given Peter a cup of wine and asked him to be a good boy?"

Cyril looked so uncomfortable I actually felt a flicker of compassion for him. Perhaps he really *didn't* know the extent of his monks' depravity, as unlikely as that seemed.

"What did you expect when you summoned the monks to Alexandria?" Tesia persisted, obviously feeling no such sentiments. "Acts of charity and compassion?"

"That is their calling—"

"Perhaps in Nitria. Obviously not here. As past events should have told you."

Cyril was becoming irritated. He didn't have a leg to stand on, and he knew it.

"In any conflict there are casualties," he said stiffly. "Those who put themselves against us must be prepared to face the consequences. Your friend Hypatia was a foe of Christ and his church."

Tesia's face froze. "Never! Can you name one—just one—person of note that she caused to abandon Christ?"

Cyril's lips worked, but no words came out.

Tesia didn't give him much chance to come up with a name. Relentlessly, she pressed on. "Jew, pagan, or even another Christian, it doesn't matter to you, does it? Everyone must agree with Cyril, the sole determiner of orthodoxy."

"I am the bishop!" Cyril flared. "I will not be spoken to like that! Not by you, not by Orestes, and most certainly not by that so-called philosopher, Hypatia."

"She was a seeker after truth," Tesia replied, "as are we all, however imperfectly."

"And truth," I interjected before Cyril could respond, "is not to be found in contesting with another Christian over secular power."

Cyril spun on his heel. "God will be my judge," he said as he headed for the door.

"As will history," I added while he was still within earshot. "I cannot speak for God, but history will not be kind."

Cyril didn't turn around.

"Of such poor clay are saints made," I commented to myself when he had gone.

"Saints?" Tesia echoed.

I motioned in the direction Cyril had taken. "He actually becomes a great theologian, you know. A Doctor of the Church. We're only seeing one side of him—the worst side."

"I doubt it," she replied.

"It will happen."

It suddenly dawned on me what I was saying. I looked at Tesia in confusion. "I should rest."

She clapped her hands, and the steward arrived to escort me to my room. I lay on the bed, staring at the plastered ceiling. Perhaps the Ring physicians were right.

Perhaps I *was* losing my mind.

Tesia seemed sad the next morning. When I asked her what was the matter, she replied, "Zuberi tells me you'll be leaving soon."

"That was our intention," I replied cautiously.

"Where will you go?"

"Back to Britannia, I suppose."

"I'll be sorry to see you go."

I managed a faint smile. "Perhaps I can delay my recovery."

"I wish you would," she said, and there was a plaintive note in her voice that pierced me to the quick. Then she turned away. "Forgive me. It's not seemly for a woman to be forward."

"It's no more unseemly than for a man to be backward."

"The steward will attend to your needs," she said.

"Where are you going?" I asked.

"To the church," she replied. "To pray." She drew a veil over her face. "I have much on my mind."

It seemed like a good idea. When she had gone, I made my way to her study, where a cross hung on the wall. I knelt beneath it, and did the same.

My recovery progressed at a satisfactory rate. The headaches that plagued me daily began to subside, as did sporadic episodes of dizziness and blurred vision. All symptoms of a concussion, I supposed. The bruises that covered large portions of my anatomy metamorphosed from red, blue, and purple to disagreeable shades of yellow and green. As I progressively increased my ambulation, the muscles began to loosen and flexibility increased.

Tesia's physician visited me daily, and pronounced himself pleased with my recuperative powers. J'sun, of course, had easily resumed his normal activities, and, even though I relished the attention that Tesia lavished upon me, I ached to be back to normalcy as well.

It was on one of these days, following the physician's departure, that Tesia came and sat beside me on a garden bench.

It was I who spoke first. "These days are both happy and sad, aren't they?"

"How's that?"

"I'm happy to be recovering and to have such a wonderful ministering angel, but each day brings me closer to leaving."

She bit her lip. "If only it could be otherwise."

"I also—wish it could."

She searched my face, then directed her gaze to a bee buzzing among some blossoms. Finally, she looked me in the eyes, and said, "Why don't you tell me the truth, Rubellius?"

The question took me aback. "The truth?"

"Do you trust me so little that you keep yourself hidden from me?" Her face clouded.

I pursed my lips and exhaled slowly.

She sounded annoyed as she said, "It's not charitable to trifle with a woman's heart."

"That's not my intention!" I exclaimed. "Not my intention at all."

"Then speak to me," she pleaded. "Open yourself to me."

"Tell me," I said, "what you have noticed, what it is that you wish to have opened."

"You puzzle me, Rubellius. You seem to know things before they happen…almost as if—as if they were things you remembered, rather than anticipated."

My chest tightened.

"At first, I wondered if I was mistaken. But then, you knew of Hypatia's fate while yet unconscious. I wondered if there was some kind of sorcery involved, but I cannot see you as a sorcerer. You are a Christian, as am I— and I have prayed, and discerned no evil in you. Are you a prophet or a visionary, perhaps? But prophets speak willingly and openly of things,

248

whereas you do not."

Tesia was indeed a very perspicacious woman.

"And I have heard you speak in a strange language," she continued, "when you were asleep. A language I have never heard. And no one I have queried has heard such words, either. I am told they certainly do not belong to the Briton tongue."

I could hardly breathe. My fingers and lips tingled.

"Who are J'sun, Erica, the Chair?" she asked, framing the syllables awkwardly. Her brown eyes bored into me, as if seeking my soul, pleading for answers.

"Who *are* you, really?" she finished.

I couldn't maintain the intensity of her gaze; I looked away, at the busy bee, my mind in turmoil. I wanted to tell her, desperately. After so many years spent playing roles in the past, I yearned to tell someone the truth. And yet it would break the code to which I had bound myself. Only Lovernios had had a hint of who I was, and then it had only been an inkling. Never the full truth. I had spoken to him because he was at the gate of death and wouldn't repeat the intimations I gave him.

Tesia was still begging me with her eyes.

I took a deep breath and gripped the edges of the bench until my fingers hurt. I couldn't continue the struggle that raged within me. "You will think me insane."

She laid a hand on my arm. "Never that."

"Tesia," I swallowed, "there is nothing I would like more than to tell you."

"Then what is holding you back?"

"Fear," I said, "the fear of losing you." Even though I knew that somewhere—some*when*—Romeo was waiting.

"Is your secret so dreadful?"

"No," I said. "It's not dreadful. It's simply unbelievable."

"I'm a philosopher," she replied. "I'm used to talking about the unbelievable."

I couldn't help but smile. I laid my hand on top of hers. "Tesia," I said, "I am truly from Britannia, but not the Britannia of which this world knows."

Her forehead creased. "Is there some other?"

"And my name is not Rubellius. It is Robert."

"Rob-ert."

"And I am not from this time at all. I am from the future."

Her eyes widened. She pulled her hand away.

"Surely you think me mad," I said.

Her voice was tiny. "Tell me more, Robert," she said.

And so I told her, haltingly at first, and then with growing confidence about my life with Erica and Emily, my loss, my travels from time to time. I don't know how long I talked, but she didn't run away, and when I finished, she was studying me with a pensive expression.

"And Zuberi?" she asked.

"One of my students. His real name is J'sun Orombi. If you like, you can ask him to confirm what I have told you."

There was a moment's silence.

"Do you swear that this is true?" she asked.

"As Christ is my witness."

"Would you swear on the bones of St. Mark?"

"Take me to the church," I said, "and I will do so."

Again, a silence, while Tesia stared at the grassy ground.

"But please," I asked, "promise me that you won't breathe a word of this to anyone."

She looked up at me. "We would likely both be accused of sorcery and stoned to death. I'm not crazy, Robert."

"Nor am I. But I know it must appear so."

Her gaze fixed in the distance. "Did you ever read Marcus Aurelius?" she asked.

"A little," I replied, thinking that it would be too much to tell her that I had met him—finally making that particular past-times journey—and that we had enjoyed a stimulating conversation over beer in the forests of Germany.

She said, "'Time is like a river,' he wrote, 'made up of events which happen, and a violent stream; for as soon as thing has been, it is carried away, and another comes in its place, and this will be carried away, too.'" She paused. "So if time is a river, and if a river, in its course, can have eddies and whirlpools that bring droplets back to whence they started, can time do the same?"

I didn't answer.

"Tell me what will happen, Robert. What will come from Hypatia's death?"

I sighed. "Alexandria will continue to be Alexandria. Orestes will petition the emperor, who will not intervene. Orestes will be able to limit the number of Cyril's partisans for a time, but Cyril will regain control, and Orestes will leave in disgust. The Jews will return to Alexandria—and years from now, the emperor will still be trying to impose order by prohibiting persecution of the Jews."

"And what...and what of us?"

"You will find love again," I replied, thinking not without a touch of envy at the lucky Romeo. "For myself, I do not know."

She rose, and I stood, as well. Silently, she walked away.

I sat down again and wondered if I had done the right thing, or I had been the biggest fool in the entire history of the world.

A week or so later, and I had shed the last of my bandages. Outwardly, I appeared my normal self. But inwardly…

The dreaded day drew near. We couldn't delay much longer, as J'sun mournfully reminded me, because we had to travel well away from Alexandria, to a secluded location where the interface could be opened with little chance of discovery.

I scoured the Emporium for some fitting parting gift for Tesia. What would a philosopher desire? What would be appropriate for a woman whom I had come to love, but could never take in my arms and hold as I so desperately wanted to?

I evaluated and dismissed many possibilities.

Eventually, I found what I was searching for. It was a gold brooch, in the shape of a cross surrounded by four hearts, their points facing inward toward a blue sapphire in the center. I wrapped it in a piece of silk and laid it close to my heart.

I couldn't sleep a wink the night before our planned departure. I tossed and turned and my restless mind refused to cease its miserable rambling.

In the morning, I would see Tesia for the last time. If it had been hard to say goodbye to Eudaimon so many years ago, it would be excruciating to bid adieu to Tesia. I almost wished I could slink away in the middle of the night, allowing darkness to hide my misery and regret. But that, I knew, would have hurt Tesia more.

Tesia, who had captured my heart in a way that I hadn't thought possible; a way that had happened only once before, with Erica.

Tesia, my anamchara, as the Celts would say—my soul friend.

It was, I mused in a dark and entirely unworthy moment, so unfair of God that I should meet such a woman in the past, and not in my own time. Unfair that I should meet her, only to be constrained to part.

'Twere better to have loved and lost than never to have loved at all, wrote the poet.

Such was his opinion.

As for me, I lay awake wishing I could remain in the past. I had no desire to return to my own time, knowing that I could never leave it again.

Tesia wasn't far from tears, and neither was I.

J'sun expressed his thanks to her for her hospitality, then went to stand outside the house. "No rush, sir," he said.

I stood close to Tesia; so close, and yet so far.

"Must you go?" she asked.

I removed the brooch from its wrappings and pinned it onto her gown. "I wish it could be otherwise. I wish with all my heart."

Her eyes were downcast. "I believe you, Robert," she said softly. "All that you told me."

"You are the only one who knows," I said. "Ever."

"I shall take your secret to the grave."

The grave with Romeo. I bit my lip.

"Would it be unseemly if I gave you a parting gift?" she asked.

"I would treasure anything of yours," I replied hoarsely.

"Wait here." She went into her study room, and returned a moment later.

"This belonged to my brother," Tesia replied. "He was a priest. He died in a plague years ago. He asked me to keep this. He told me that one day I would know for whom it was intended."

She laid in my palm a gold ring with a fish symbol.

For a long moment, I stared at it dazedly, wondering how I could possibly have been so blind, so impossibly, infinitely blind. And how, at times, so lacking in faith.

I recalled the words the Pope had spoken to me, long ago: "God is in all times, Professor."

And I recalled reading somewhere—the reference long since forgotten—that St. Thomas Aquinas had commented that God couldn't change the past because he'd already been there, all along.

"Do you like it?" Tesia asked hesitantly.

I looked up from the ring, the ring that had been—that *would* be—found on Romeo's—*my*—finger, to meet Tesia's hopeful, loving gaze, and I knew that Erica would have wanted this for us. And I knew, finally, where my future lay.

"I love it," I said. "And I love you."

I slipped the ring onto my finger and folded Tesia into my arms.

AFTERWORD

by

J'sun Orombi
Post-graduate doctoral student
CamOx university

"Well," the Chair said, laying down the papyrus scroll she had been reading, "there's really nothing else to say."

I'd expected more of an outburst, but the Chair seemed remarkably calm.

"I hope I acted appropriately," I said.

Her thoughtful scrutiny made me squirm.

"I mean, I could have compelled him to return, I suppose..."

I knew, though, that I couldn't have. I visualized Professor Cragg as I had last seen him, standing at the doorway of Tesia's house. The door was open; the morning sunshine spilled across the threshold with a sea-breeze in its wake. Tesia stood beside him, her face and eyes luminous. He seemed to be bursting with new life.

Together, they looked like the perfect Alexandrian couple. There was no way I could have spoiled their happiness.

"I did remind him of the rules," I added, hoping I didn't sound desperate.

"What did he reply?" the Chair asked.

"He said, 'It is futile to argue with history. I am simply doing what I have already done.'"

The Chair's lips twitched. "Anything else?"

"He said that neither love nor God are bound by time."

She nodded. "That sounds like him." She laid her fingers on the scroll.

It was one of a pair the professor had asked me to bring back. One was my grade. 'High marks,' he'd said, putting an arm on my shoulder. 'It's been a pleasure working with you.'

I'd basked in his approval. 'The honor is mine, Professor,' I'd replied.

The second scroll—'My explanation,' he'd said. Looking at that scroll lying on the Chair's desk, it was hard to believe it had been written over two thousand five hundred years ago. Because to me, it was only a couple of weeks old, and I could still feel the touch of the professor's hand on my shoulder, hear his voice, smell Tesia's perfume.

"Are you going to send someone back for him?" I asked.

The Chair shook her head. "Obviously not, since I didn't."

"Obviously," I repeated, feeling suddenly stupid.

"Despite his less than effusive remarks about me, I've always had a soft spot for Robert. In fact, I'm rather happy for him. He would never have enjoyed retirement in our time."

"You sound almost...as if you expected this."

Her gaze was piercing. "I'm not surprised, no. I've known Robert for years, and rather thought that something like this would happen."

"And yet you let him go back, knowing he might not return."

"It was a possibility."

Something about the tone of her voice brought a thought to my mind. "Or was it more than that?"

Her eyes narrowed, and I knew she wouldn't give me an answer. Instead, she said, "Your performance was quite satisfactory."

"Thank you," I replied, taking the statement as a prelude to dismissal and rising to my feet.

"Professor Carstairs is seeking an assistant for a trip to Carthage. I've recommended you."

"I'll contact her immediately," I replied.

She picked up the scroll again, and was studying it as I left her office.

Romeo and Juliet.

Robert and Tesia.

Had the Chair—somehow—known what would happen? Or had she had some kind of a hand in the matter? I didn't see how it could be possible, but...

Only God and the Chair were privy to that information.

Time alone would tell. Or perhaps, like a woman of mystery, she'd keep her secret.

And I had my secret too, that I hadn't told the Chair.

As we stood on the doorway to Tesia's house, I'd handed Professor Cragg a pouch containing all but a few of the coins we had brought with us. "You'd better take this."

"What for?" he asked.

"Consider it a wedding present," I replied. "From the Chair."

Our eyes met, and we burst into laughter.

I gave him a hug, and then embraced Tesia.

Then I turned and walked away, leaving him to his new life in the ancient city that was now his home.

NOTES ON THE STORIES

The Ghosts of Kourion

In 1985, archaeologists working at the site of Kourion, on Cyprus, uncovered the skeleton of a young girl and her mule, a man and woman who might have been her parents, and a young Christian couple with their infant. They called the girl 'Camila,' and, among other things, also discovered the silver and bone hairpins that she and her mother had worn. See *Kourion: The Search for a Lost Roman City*, by David Sorel & Jamie James, New York: Doubleday, 1988. The quotation from Ammianus Marcellinus is taken from this volume.

For information on time travel, see J. Richard Gott, *Time Travel in Einstein's Universe*, New York: Houghton Mifflin, 2001, especially pp. 16-20 for discussion of the Self-Consistency Principle. Also Paul Davies, *How to Build a Time Machine*, New York: Viking, 2002, and Paul J. Nahin, *Time Machines: Time Travel in Physics, Metaphysics, and Science Fiction*, NY: American Institute of Physics, 1993. Once again, I wish to thank both Professor Davies and Professor Gott for replying to email inquiries and answering time travel questions for me.

Tyndareus and Krikor

In 1998, workmen digging the foundations for a new national railroad station in Pisa unearthed a veritable graveyard of ships dating from the 3rd century BC to the 5th century AD. Sixteen ships have been discovered to date. In one ship, dating from early in the rein of Augustus, were found the skeletal remains of a man and a dog. See *The Lost Ships of Pisa*, by Michael H. Sedge, ibooks, 2002. For information on Roman seafaring, see *Ships and Seamanship in the Ancient World*, by Lionel Casson, Johns Hopkins University Press, 1971.

For the "classical" view of the events at Masada, see *Masada,* by Yigael Yadin, New York: Random House, 1966. For a modern reappraisal and dispelling of the myth, see *Sacrificing Truth, Archaeology and the Myth of Masada* by Nachman Ben-Yehuda, Amherst: Humanity Books, 2002, as well as the chapter in Michael Grant's *The Visible Past,* New York: Charles Scribner's Sons, 1990, pp.116-121, and "The Credibility of Josephus" by Shaye Corson at www.pbs.org/wgbh/pages/frontline/shows/religion/portrait/masada. html, accessed 12/2/04.

The Slipper of Sulpicia Lepidina

Sulpicia's slipper can be seen in the museum at Vindolanda.

Dust of Caesar

"At the house of Vesonius Primus in the northwestern part of Pompeii the excavators came across the contorted remains of a watchdog, still wearing his bronze-studded collar; in the panic of evacuation nobody had thought to unchain him" (Paul G Bahn, Ed, *Tombs, Graves & Mummies,* Barnes & Noble, 1996, p.156, picture, p. 158). According to *Ghosts of Vesuvius,* by Charles Pellegrino, New York: William Morrow, 2004, it is unlikely that any inhabitants of the area escaped once the eruptions had begun. Human remains from this time are continually being discovered.

There are many books about Pompeii and Herculaneum. For example, *Pompeii, The Last Day,* by Paul Wilkinson, London: BBC Books, 2003; Giovanna Magi, *All Pompeii,* Firenze: Bonechi Editore, 1973; Theodore H. Feder, *Great Treasures of Pompeii and Herculaneum,* New York: Abbeville Press, 1978; Raleigh Trevelyan, *The Shadow of Vesuvius,* London: Michael Joseph, 1976. A description and photographs of the House of Vesonius Primus can be found in *Pompeii,* by Amedeo Maiuri, Novara (Italy): Istituto Geografico De Agostini, 1929.

Eudaimon

Eudaimon's mummy can be viewed in the Musée du Louvre. A description can be found in *Ancient Faces: Mummy Portraits from Roman Egypt* by Susan Walker & Morris Bierbrier, London: British Museum Press, 1977. The Louvre translates the inscription on the mummy ("Eupsyche, Eudaimon") as "Good luck, Eudaimon", while Walker and Bierbrier refer to it as a "conventional Greek funerary valediction" translated "Farewell! Be happy!"

XXIV

Further on the incidents on Lenore and the commencement of the human-Gara'nesh war can be found in my novel *Iron Scepter.*

Asellina's Last Fight

See *Gladiatrix*, by Amy Zoll, New York: Berkley Boulevard Books, 2002, for details on the woman discovered near London. Additional information from the "Gladiatrix" website, www.gladiatrix.info/history/history1.htm accessed 10/29/2004, "Gladiators: Heroes of the Roman Amphitheatre" by Professor Kathleen Coleman, accessed 11/04/2004 at www.bbc.co.uk/history/ancient/romans/gladiators_print.html, and the Brooklyn College Classics website at http://depthome.brooklyn.cuny.edu/classics/gladiatr accessed 11/5/04.

In the Mists of Britain

Peat cutters discovered the well-preserved body of a man in Lindow Moss, near Manchester, in 1984. Celtic scholar Anne Ross suggested that he was a Druid prince, offered as a human sacrifice in the wake of the Boudiccan rebellion. She proposed the name "Lovernios." See *The Life and Death of a Druid Prince*, by Anne Ross and Don Robins, Summit, 1989. For a fictionalized version of Lovernios' life, see my novel *Imperial Legions*, by Andrew M. Seddon, Broadman & Holman, 2000. Today, Lovernios occupies an inconspicuously located display case in the British Museum.

Kobrinia

For descriptions of the finds of the Amazon women see "Women warriors from Amazon fought for Britain's Roman army," by Lewis Smith, Times Online, Dec. 22, 2004, available at www.thetimes.co.uk/tto/news/uk/article1920628.ece

accessed 1/20/2006. Also "Pyromania," by Hilary Cool, *British Archaeology*, January/February 2005, p. 30-35.

The Arms of Venus

For a lucid and entertaining history of the Venus de Milo, see *Disarmed* by Gregory Curtis, Alfred A. Knopf, New York, 2003.

The Philosopher's Ring

The death of Hypatia has been seized upon by propagandists of various stripes. For sober assessments of the events surrounding her life and death see *Hypatia of Alexandria: Mathematician and Martyr*, by Michael A.B. Deakin, Prometheus Books, 2007 and Maria Dzielska's *Hypatia of Alexandria*, Harvard University Press, 1995. For a shorter version, see "The Beauty of Reasoning: A Reexamination of Hypatia of Alexandria," by Bryan J. Whitfield, *The Mathematics Educator*, Vol.6, No.1, ND, p. 14-21.

Articles on Cyril of Alexandria can be found in the Catholic Encyclopedia, and Wikipedia.

For a description of Alexandria and the Library see L. Sprague de Camp, *Great Cities of the Ancient World*, Doubleday, 1972. Historians dispute the extent of the Library's decline, and the years in which various losses occurred.

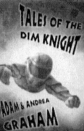

just happening in your mind, after all. there
imagine you're **trapped in** a spe dir ca b
a rapidly accelerating world. sh ck at r
enters a close **game** session. it led me to
in **the real world**, just going about the ve
evil **vanished like a mirage**. all th as le
controls weren't responding pr erly and
t is not a valid error code. please state yo
rs **a strange woman** named ae e o
have ever talked to **a virus** up ose lik t
the answer o **that question** al ad th u
u **shot me out of the sky**?" ye e
the dark bar staring at me wit life ss ey
lusion is breaking down and I ve act
"are you **a child** learning how to walk a
"**the son of a programmer.**" wi it me a
my last chance. "I can't do this Ple se he
e **what I didn't know I needed**, somet ing
ers, urgently asking the question a D
knew that it was **the answer**

CAFFEINE

A Novel by
Ryan Grabow

A BOY. A RING. A CALLING.

Reality's Dawn

לתת

לקחת

R. L. COPPLE

The Reality Chronicles: Book One

Aquasynthesis: a pool of stories, fed by the depths of creation and imagination; an anthology of short fiction by Splashdown authors.

Our past, our future, our fate, our hope—all come to life within a frozen pool at the edge of a vast ocean swirling across the orb of a lost world.

Sixteen stories, one destination: Aquasynthesis.

aquasynthesis again

splashdown vol. 2

edited by grace bridges
narrated by fred warren

CPSIA information can be obtained
at www.ICGtesting.com
Printed in the USA
LVOW12s1636080217
523625LV00003B/588/P